R.D. BRADY

THE BELIAL GUARD

R.D. BRADY

THE
BELIAL
GUARD

vinci
BOOKS

By R.D. Brady

The Belial Series

The Belial Stone
The Belial Library
The Belial Ring
The Belial Recruit
The Belial Children
The Belial Origins
The Belial Search
The Belial Guard
The Belial Warrior
The Belial Plan
The Belial Witches
The Belial War
The Belial Fall
The Belial Sacrifice

Vinci Books

vinci-books.com

Published by Vinci Books Ltd in 2025

1

Copyright © R.D. Brady 2016

The author has asserted their moral right to be identified as the author of this work in accordance with the Copyright, Designs and Patents Act 1988. This work is a work of fiction. Names, characters, places and incidents are the product of the author's imagination or are used fictitiously. Any resemblance to actual persons, living or dead, places and incidents is entirely coincidental.
All rights reserved. No part of this publication may be copied, reproduced, distributed, stored in any retrieval system, or transmitted in any form or by any means, including photocopying, recording, or other electronic or mechanical methods, nor used as a source for any form of machine learning including AI datasets, without the prior written permission of the publisher.
The publisher and the author have made every effort to obtain permissions for any third party material used in this book and to comply with copyright law. Any queries in this respect should be brought to the attention of the publisher and any omissions will be corrected in future editions.
A CIP catalogue record for this book is available from the British Library.
Paperback ISBN: 9781036702458

Chapter One

DELANEY MCPHEARSON SAT STARING at the ceiling of her temporary bedroom at the Chandler School for Children. It was late, and she was tired, but she couldn't seem to get herself to sleep. She rolled over and pulled a pillow to her chest. Her long auburn hair got stuck under her shoulder and she yanked it out impatiently. She blew out a breath, frustration rolling through her, knowing sleep was not going to show up any time soon.

Not that her sleep had been all that restful lately anyway. When she did manage to fall asleep, her subconscious went to work dredging up all her doubts and fears. Had they really stopped the Companion Killers from committing the ritual? Had the Companion Killers been the ones who had gone after the Fallen as well? Was there any way Laney could have known the teenagers were going to investigate Cleo's background and get themselves thrown in the middle of everything?

Her gaze wandered over the small room. About half her wardrobe now hung in the closet. Her toiletries littered the top of the dresser. Even some of her favorite books had made it over here. She'd been spending more and more nights here since they'd returned from Hawaii. She'd told Jake she wanted to be nearby in case Lou needed her.

"Lou" was Lou Thomas, a sixteen-year-old nephilim and one of the reasons the Companion Killers had been stopped. But Lou had paid a heavy price for her actions. She'd been tortured, and she was now struggling to get her life back to normal.

Lou wasn't the only reason Laney was bunking at the school regularly, though, and both Laney and Jake knew it. Something changed between them after he got hurt trying to stop Cain, and ever since, they had been avoiding the conversation they needed to have.

Laney stared up at the ceiling, wishing Agent Matt Clark of the SIA would call with some Fallen incident she needed to address. But those incidents had dropped off sharply after the Companion Killers had been stopped.

But have they really been stopped? That same question had been repeating itself in Laney's mind for the last two months. With the aid of Honu Keiki, she and Jen had stopped the Companion Killers from sacrificing Lou along with the leopards. *But since the Companion Killers were killed in Lou's place, doesn't that mean the sacrifice was completed?* Death had still happened—just with different victims. *So did we stop the sacrifice? Or did we help it come about?*

Laney sighed. Even if the ritual was completed, it wasn't important, not really. The ritual was just an old superstition. The Companion Killers believed the deaths would herald the dawning of a new age in the world. *Just an ancient belief,* Laney assured herself, even though she knew that all the other ancient legends—Cain, the ring of Solomon, Lilith, Atlantis, Mu—had turned out to be true.

In fact, a lot of things were true that Laney would once have never believed possible—like Honu Keiki.

Honu Keiki was a cult that lived on the island of Malama in Hawaii, and was made up of the descendants of the ancient civilization of Lemuria—the mother of all civilizations. The cult had helped Laney in her pursuit of the Companion Killers, and yet...

There was something about the group that Laney didn't trust. It wasn't just that they were secretive, although they were. Laney suspected the members of Honu Keiki, or at least the priestess, knew much more about the deaths of the Fallen and their intimates than they were revealing. After all, the Companion Killers were all former members of Honu Keiki.

Cleo stepped onto the bed and curled up next to Laney, resting her head on Laney's chest. Cleo was a black Javan leopard whose coat was dotted with even darker black spots. Her coloring made her rare, and her size made her even more so—she was almost double the size of a normal leopard. Standing, she was almost four and a half feet tall at the shoulders. And that was not her most remarkable trait.

Thanks to the teenagers' ill-planned investigation, they had finally learned why Cleo was so different from other cats: she was actually part human. Her leopard DNA had been combined with a Fallen's DNA, with human growth hormone being thrown into the mix. The result was a large cat with human intelligence and some Fallen abilities. Which, in a strange way, wasn't as surprising as it should have been. On more than one occasion Laney had observed the humanness in her behaviors—like right now. Cleo looked at her with complete understanding and a desire to ease Laney's pain.

Laney ran a hand through the cat's dark pelt. "I'm okay, girl."

Cleo's stared into her eyes. *Sad.*

"Maybe a little. But I suppose that's just part of life."

Cleo sat straight up, her head turning toward the door.

"What is it?" Laney asked her heart beginning to pound.

Lou's scream cut through the night air.

Laney scrambled out from beneath the blankets even though she knew there was no imminent danger. The danger had passed months before. But the screaming remained.

Laney opened the door, and she and Cleo charged down the hall.

Jen Witt, her dark hair pulled into a ponytail, stood in sweats next to a closed door, her hand hovering above the doorknob. She turned to Laney, tears in her brown eyes. "I don't know what to do for her."

On the other side of the door, the sounds of Lou's sobs could be heard clearly.

"I do." Laney opened the door. "Go on, Cleo."

Cleo padded over to the bed, then climbed up and curled up next to Lou. Lou raised an arm and threw it over the big cat. "Oh, Cleo."

Laney and Jen stood in the doorway as Lou's sobs quieted. In a few minutes, the girl was back asleep, her arm still wrapped around Cleo.

Cleo looked over at Laney. *Stay.*

Okay.

Laney pulled Jen back and closed the door. Jen slumped to the floor, her arms around her knees, looking devastated.

Jen had been the one who had found Lou and brought her to the Chandler home in the first place. But Lou wasn't simply another case for Jen; Lou had become her little sister. And everything Lou was going through, Jen was going through right along with her.

Lou was going through a lot.

She had been saved from the Companion Killers, but a part of her had died that day. Her innocence. Her enthusiasm. And now she seemed to be slipping away from them. For the first month after the incident, she had refused to leave the school. She'd barely even left her room.

They had tried everything they could think of to bring her back to her old self. They'd even discussed the possibility of hospitalizing her. But Lou's response when they had mentioned that idea was so violent it had terrified them. Still, at least after that she began to eat more, and she agreed to speak to Henry, which she'd been doing for the last few weeks. Henry had experienced much the same treatment at the hands of Sebastian Flourent, so he knew what she was going through.

And Henry had made a little headway. During the day anyway, Lou seemed to be doing better. But every once in a while at night, the nightmares would return. At those times, Cleo was the only one who could make her feel safe.

Laney blamed herself for all of it. She had known the kids were looking into Cleo's background—she should have known they'd try something like going off and checking out the lab in New Mexico. But she'd been in the middle of the Companion Killers' killing spree, and she just wasn't paying attention. She didn't notice when they left; no one did.

Laney sank down onto the floor next to Jen.

"It's not right," Jen said. "She shouldn't have to deal with any of this."

"No. She shouldn't. None of you should."

Jen looked up, her eyes narrowed. "What do you mean, none of *us* should?"

Laney sighed. Since they'd returned from Hawaii, she'd given her life and its direction a lot of thought. She was the ring bearer, destined to fight the Fallen back. There was no changing that, and if she was being honest, she didn't really want to change that. She wanted to help. She just didn't want anyone else risking their lives in the same way. And while there was a lot still up in the air, there was one thing she knew with crystal clear certainty: they couldn't continue this way.

"It can wait until morning," Laney said.

Jen shook her head. "No. You've decided something. What is it?"

"Jen, it's late—"

"Spill it."

Laney had known Jen for years, since long before she knew she was the ring bearer and Jen was a nephilim. That friendship had only been strengthened by the trials they had endured. And one thing they both had in common was their stubbornness. Laney knew Jen would not let up until she had an answer.

She sighed, looking at her friend. Jen's normally sharp eyes looked tired, and her sweats were wrinkled. Laney was sure she looked about the same. One of the best things that had come from her destiny was this incredible family of friends. But the down side was that when one of them hurt, they all hurt. And since all of this had begun, there had been too much hurt.

Laney began quietly. "Ever since my destiny found me, all of us have been in mortal danger at multiple times— even the kids. We can't let that happen anymore."

"I agree, but we already decided the kids aren't allowed to be part of anything Fallen related—"

"I'm not just talking about them. I'm talking about you, Yoni, your brother, Henry, even Jake. We can't all put our lives on hold while we handle the Fallen. We need to live our lives."

"What does that mean?"

Laney took a deep breath. "What that means is that the next time, and *every* time a Fallen incident occurs, we're not all going to drop everything to go running. *I* need to go—there's no getting around that. But you guys don't. You need—"

"No, we need to help you."

"Yes. But not all of you. And not every time." Laney nodded toward Lou's door. "We have more important things to focus on. We can't let the Fallen be our whole lives. It's not fair to us, or to the people we care about, and honestly, it allows the Fallen to win in a way, because they determine our lives."

Jen stared at Laney for a long moment. "But you're not part of that. They still get to determine *your* life."

Laney held up the chain with the ring of Solomon on it. She always wore it around her neck. "No, that was determined a long time ago. And you know what? I'm okay with that. I've come to peace with that. This is my life. I can't step away from it, but the rest of you can. And I want you to."

"Laney..."

Laney took Jen's hand. "I love you, Jen. And Henry loves you, and Lou loves you. Be a part of their lives. Help me when you can. But don't put your life on hold for the Fallen. They don't deserve that."

"What about your life?"

Laney looked into Jen's eyes, and gave her a small smile. "I'm the ring bearer. It's time I fully accepted that. Which means letting go of a lot of hopes."

Jen shook her head. "Laney—"

"I'm not sad. I'll find my peace. And part of it is knowing that you all are living your lives. Besides, I'm not saying you're all out. Just that we need to be more selective in how we go about fighting this."

"You're sure?"

"Yes. This is the right course of action." And for once, Laney had no doubts.

"On one condition," Jen said.

"What?" Laney asked warily.

"Noriko. If anything comes up involving her, if she needs help, I need to be included. That's not negotiable."

Laney understood. Noriko was a young woman from Honu Keiki who was part of the team that had saved Lou, and Jen felt indebted to the girl.

"If anything comes up involving Honu Keiki," Laney said, "I'll let you know. But they've been quiet."

"And we stopped the ritual, right?" Jen locked her gaze on Laney.

Laney felt uneasy, but she forced herself not to squirm under Jen's gaze. "Absolutely."

Chapter Two

MALAMA ISLAND, HAWAII

BLUEPRINTS COVERED the table of the priestess's dining area. She pointed to one spot on the plans with a perfectly manicured red fingernail. "And these are my rooms?"

Her architect, Elan, bobbed his bald head. "Yes, priestess. They are exactly as you ordered."

Her eyes scanned the facility. It was huge—over thirty thousand square feet. *And it has all come about because of me.* She smiled. "And you finished two months ahead of schedule."

Elan's cheeks grew red. "Yes, priestess. All to finish your vision."

The priestess ran a finger along his sleeve. "Well done."

He trembled, and the priestess struggled not to smile. Men were so easy to manipulate. She waved her hand. "Now leave me."

Elan's mouth fell open in disappointment, then he nodded. "Yes, of course."

The priestess's gaze returned to the plans. "What do you think?" she asked after the door closed behind Elan.

Vanessa, the priestess's head of security, stepped away from the wall where she had been watching. "He's right. They are perfect."

"Yes, they are." But one doubt about the venture entered the priestess's mind. "What's the news on the ring bearer?"

"She knows nothing. She spends most of her time in Baltimore at that school." Vanessa grimaced. "She occasionally leaves for SIA missions, but not often."

"Has she dug any deeper into the Companion Killers?"

"No, not after the initial investigation."

"So she still believes the ritual was averted?"

"As far as we know, yes."

The ring bearer's involvement with the Companion Killers had been a wake-up call. The priestess had had to move quickly to save all her hard work. She had underestimated the woman's tenacity and the skill of her team. That had been a mistake. But all had ended well. The ritual had been completed, and the ring bearer was now beholden to them. After all, they had saved those abominations for her.

The priestess had heard the tales of the ring bearer long ago, but had never believed they were true—until she was forced to. And if all the rumors about the ring bearer's abilities were equally true, that placed the priestess in danger.

She shoved the thoughts from her mind. The ring bearer was irrelevant. She didn't know what they were up to. In fact, she viewed them as allies.

"Do you have any orders?" Vanessa asked.

The priestess smiled. "We're moving up the schedule. I'm tired of waiting."

Chapter Three

LANEY AND JEN sat outside Lou's door for another hour before they went back to bed. Cleo stayed with Lou through the night, and Lou did not have another nightmare. It seemed that whenever Cleo stayed with her, Lou slept better than ever.

At breakfast, Jen and Laney decided it was time to force Lou back into the world. Since the Companion Killers, Lou had stayed close to home. But Cleo had insisted there were some individuals who wanted to see Lou, and Jen and Laney agreed today was the day to make that happen. Besides, Laney knew that if there was anything that would bring the sparkle back into Lou's eyes, it would be this visit.

Now Jen drove toward the leopard preserve that Henry had had created for the leopards from the GenDynamic labs. It had taken two months to get the cats back to Maryland—the red tape had been enormous—but ultimately Henry and his team of lawyers had prevailed. The cats had been in the preserve for two weeks now.

For the first week, Laney saw to them personally, with

Cleo at her side. She needed to make sure they weren't a danger to anyone. But last week, she allowed vets in to check on them, and some researchers as well, to observe. Laney had no doubts about the cats' ability to be around humans. Each cat had its own personality, of course, but all shared Cleo's affinity for humans. And Laney knew for a fact that they all had a particular affinity for Lou, Rolly, and Danny.

The preserve was a ninety-acre estate halfway between the Chandler School and headquarters that had been out of use for years. The old house on the estate was modified to serve as the shelter for the animals, and the cats were given free run of the place. Near the middle of the property was a tall research hide, thirty feet off the ground, for the researchers and vets.

The whole area was enclosed with a fifteen-foot electrical fence, and a secondary fence had also been erected to keep any would-be neighbors from getting too near the electrified one. At the front gate was a guard hut that was staffed twenty-four seven.

Laney glanced over her shoulder from the passenger seat as Jen drove. Lou was in the back seat, staring out the window. Her normally bright smile was missing, her skin was paler than normal, and even her dark curls seemed to have lost their spring. She was always like this the day after a nightmare.

"We're almost there," Laney said softly.

Lou looked at her as if she had just woken up. "What?"

"We're almost there."

"Oh. Okay." Lou looked back out the window.

Siting next to Lou, Rolly Escabi took Lou's hand. His mocha skin was a little paler as well, but Laney knew that was due to his concern for Lou. Rolly had been through a lot out in New Mexico too, but he was more worried about Lou than himself.

His pale green eyes stared back at Laney, and in them she could see his fear for his friend. Rolly wanted to help Lou perhaps more than anyone. In fact, Jen had found him sleeping on the floor next to Lou's bed most nights the first few weeks they were back. Like Laney, he blamed himself for Lou's condition. It was actually Rolly who had been grabbed by the Companion Killers, but Lou had saved him —and in the process, had been captured herself.

Jen pulled up to the guardhouse. The guard recognized them and opened the outer gate. Jen pulled forward. The gate closed behind them, and then the second gate opened.

Jen pulled forward slowly. "Where are they?"

"Probably at the house," Laney said. She closed her eyes and focused on the pack. One by one she found them all. "They're at the house," she said with more confidence this time. "They know we're coming."

Jen wound her way down the half-mile gravel drive to the house. When Henry bought the property, the trees and bushes along the road had pretty much taken over the drive, but he had had them hacked back. Even now, it looked like keeping them at bay would be a full-time job.

Jen pulled to a stop at the white hydrangea bushes that lined the front porch. The house was an old purple farmhouse with four bedrooms. Henry had wanted to paint it, but Laney said she liked the purple and yellow shutters. It was definitely unusual, which Laney thought fit the occupants.

Henry had retrofitted the inside to meet the cats' needs. Bedding had been placed, as well as water fountains specially designed for the cats. The guards brought in food twice a day. Out beyond the house was a large fenced enclosure that the cats could be placed in when someone needed to be on the grounds.

Cleo stepped out of the house and walked down the porch steps. Yoni had dropped her off this morning. Laney got out, as did Jen, but Lou and Rolly stayed in the car. Cleo rubbed against Jen, then Laney.

"Hey, girl," Laney said, leaning down to run a hand through the cat's pelt.

The rest of the pack appeared one by one from the house, lining up along the long porch. There were twenty-five of them, and they were an incredible sight. All were black Javan leopards, except for two, the youngest members of the pride. One of the young cubs was all white, with the most incredible blue eyes—Laney had named her Snow—and the other cub, Tiger, was yellow with green eyes. Both color combinations were unheard of for leopards; Laney was pretty sure they occurred as a result of the human DNA in their system.

The leopards had been created by Anthony Ruggio. These twenty-five cats represented the two generations created after Cleo's pack. Like Cleo, it was believed these cats had Fallen blood mixed with their own blood, and that a special procedure had been conducted to replace the cells in their brain with human brain cells. The same procedure had been done with lab mice, but the difference was that the mice were killed right after those experiments.

The cats were initially bred primarily to offer a hunting challenge to a Fallen named Amar Patel. But once he was killed—by Laney—Dr. Ruggio decided to sell the cats to the highest bidder.

At least, that was the plan—until Lou, Danny and Rolly found them.

And as much as Laney hated that the kids were going

through a tough time now, she also knew that, without those kids, they would never have found and rescued these cats. With everything going on with the Fallen, researching Cleo's past had taken a back seat. The kids were the only reason these cats were still alive.

Rolly opened his door, stepped out, and cast a nervous glance at the cats. "Is it okay?"

Laney looked at the cats, reading their moods and their thoughts. *My God.* She stumbled back and smiled, trying to hold her tears back. "Yes. It's okay."

Rolly ducked his head back inside the car, and after a few seconds Lou's door opened.

She stepped out, looking at the cats. "They're beautiful," she said softly, tears swimming in her eyes. Lou always seemed to be on the verge of tears lately.

Lou stepped away from the car, and Cleo walked up to her. Lou ran a hand through her pelt with a smile. Rolly walked around the car to stand at Lou's side, and Cleo rubbed against his belly as well. "Hey, girl," Rolly said.

Then, as if on cue, the cats began to walk slowly down the porch stairs.

Jen looked from the cats to Laney. "Uh, Laney? What's going on?"

Laney linked her arm with Jen's. "Just watch."

The cats walked over to Lou and Rolly. They arranged themselves in a semicircle in front of them, then all stood perfectly still.

"Laney?" Rolly called nervously.

"It's okay. I promise."

Cleo stepped forward so that she was just in front of the rest of the cats. Then, as one, they all bent their front legs and lowered their heads.

Laney recognized the show of respect, and felt a catch

at the back at her throat. "They know what you two risked to help them," she said. "They're showing you their respect, their loyalty. They're saying thank you. And that you will always be a member of their pack."

The cats rose. Cleo walked to Lou and rubbed her head against Lou's chest. Then Snow bolted forward and jumped up to lick Lou's face. Tiger did the same to Rolly.

Lou fell down, and laughter burst from her even as tears streamed down her cheeks. Snow buried her head in Lou's chest, purring loudly. Lou smiled and buried her face in the cub's pelt.

"It's going to be all right," Jen said.

And for the first time since everything had happened to Lou, Laney believed it just might be.

Chapter Four

MALAMA ISLAND, HAWAII

THE MORNING MEDITATION was wrapping up. Aaliyah breathed deep, searching for the calm that had been eluding her for weeks.

It still eluded her.

So she went through the motions of breathing in, holding her breath, and breathing out while her mind scrambled to figure out what the priestess was up to. Ever since the incident with the Companion Killers, the priestess had been conducting more and more business behind closed doors.

The priestess had also started having Noriko come to the temple once a week for instruction—and just the thought of Noriko near the priestess made Aaliyah feel ill. But she didn't know what to do. She wanted to reach out to Delaney McPhearson, but she couldn't expect the woman to jump at her every whim. She was the ring bearer—surely she was busy. And what if she didn't see what Aaliyah saw in the priestess? No. Until she had more, Aaliyah couldn't reach out to her. She needed to find some proof first.

The gong rang out, signaling the end of the meditation. Aaliyah opened her eyes. The two hundred people surrounding her smiled and spoke quietly with one another while gathering their mats. Aaliyah watched them all, wishing she could go back to a time when she, too, believed fully in their way of life and the righteousness of the priestess's guidance.

Honu Keiki were the direct descendants of the people of Mu, the world's first civilization. They had lived their lives according to the tenets of their ancestors—as one with nature and with one another. Greed, competition—these things were not a part of their lifestyles, and never had been. And anyone who could not live by the tenets of the Honu Keiki was encouraged to find another path.

At least, that's how things used to be. Everything changed when the priestess took over.

The gong sounded two more times, and everyone stopped what they were doing to look with curiosity toward the platform at the front of the meditation square.

Vanessa, the head of the Guard, stood there. Strong, tall, her dark hair pulled tightly back from her face, she scanned the crowd, looking for any threat. Next to her stood the priestess, looking beneficent in comparison. She was wrapped in white robes, golden bracelets encircling her arms. Her dark hair was pulled loosely back to give everyone a clear view of her face and her darkly rimmed eyes. Standing with the sun hitting her just right, she looked like a goddess of old brought to life.

Aaliyah knew her appearance was deceptive.

The priestess, formerly known as Xia, had been the head of Honu Keiki for fourteen years. Before that, Honu Keiki had received guidance only sparingly from their priestess and from the Naacal, the High Council of six priests, of which Aaliyah was one. Their roles had been to provide beneficent guidance rather than to rule. But this priestess had changed all that, further cementing her role as ruler with each day that passed. Now she made decisions without even consulting the Naacal, never mind the people. And the changes had been so gradual in coming that most of the members hadn't even realized what had occurred. For a long time, Aaliyah didn't really notice the changes either.

But the last few months had made everything crystal clear in Aaliyah's eyes. The priestess had staged a successful coup of Honu Keiki, wresting control from the people and consolidating it in her own hands. And despite the fact that the priestess had sent the Guard to help the ring bearer defeat the Companion Killers, Aaliyah believed the priestess had been working with the Companion Killers in some way. She just didn't know how.

Or why.

Now, Aaliyah waited with trepidation to hear what new change the priestess had planned for them.

A light tap on her shoulder caused her to turn. She looked up at Kai, her best friend, whose deep brown eyes reflected her concern. She and Kai were the longest surviving members of the Naacal, but their friendship extended beyond even those two decades. Even with the gray hair beginning to appear above Kai's ears, and the wrinkles that grew deeper when he smiled, Aaliyah still saw the strong young vibrant man she had always known and secretly loved.

He slipped his hand into hers as the priestess began to speak.

"Good morning." The priestess extended her arms in greeting.

A rush of good wishes were shouted back at her.

The priestess smiled, and Aaliyah's stomach curdled. "I know there have been some concerns surrounding the events of the last few months. That there have been rumors about violence committed by our members. I am here to assure you that the violence that was perpetuated was not committed by our people, the true Honu Keiki. It was committed by those in the outside world. We did, however, aid in bringing an end to that violence."

And right there was a perfect example of why the priestess shouldn't be trusted. The Companion Killers were former members of Honu Keiki, but few knew that, and the priestess apparently didn't think the rest of her people deserved to know the truth.

The priestess's voice took on a somber tone. "Much was asked of our Guard who participated in this mission, and they acted with bravery and honor."

A burst of applause erupted from the crowd. Aaliyah and Kai did not join in.

The priestess raised her hands, and the people quieted. "You have also probably heard the rumors that the ring bearer was involved in those activities. Sadly, that is also true. She has been called into duty. We fought on her side and prevailed, but as you know, her arrival signals that the world is moving into a dangerous phase."

A murmur ran through the crowd. In the lore of Honu Keiki, the appearance of the ring bearer always heralded the beginning of a time of strife and turmoil.

"But I have good news for you today," the priestess continued. "We are about to embark on a new and exciting journey together. I have foreseen what is coming and have found a way to keep us sheltered from the human storm. Now more than ever, we must stand united and trust the path laid out in front of us. We will move past this dark time and return to our way of life. *The* way of life."

The priestess scanned the crowd. For a second her gaze caught Aaliyah's—and Aaliyah could swear it hardened just a little. "Our way of life is the true way. We will let no one destroy it." The priestess stared into Aaliyah's eyes, and Aaliyah's pulse raced. "No one."

Then the priestess lifted her eyes to the rest of the crowd, a smile gracing her face. Aaliyah felt lightheaded.

"For now, though, be assured that plans are in the works, and in the next few weeks you will be made aware of them. You may find that some of the things asked of you will be difficult. But have faith that in the end, all will be as it should be. Be peaceful. Be well."

Applause followed the priestess off the platform. People turned to one another with excited chatter about what the priestess had meant by all of that. But Kai and Aaliyah just turned and made their way out of the crowd, not a word spoken between them.

Kai stepped into a small copse of palm trees, pulling Aaliyah in with him. "Do you have any idea what she's talking about?"

"No."

It made no sense. Honu Keiki was already isolated from the world. They lived on the island of Malama, off the coast of Maui. They had very little contact with anyone who was not a member. In fact, most members of the group had never even *spoken* with anyone outside of Honu Keiki, never mind actually leaving the island. And that isolation—chosen deliberately, in order to keep them from being corrupted—had kept them safe. It had kept them from being pulled away from their oneness with nature, from being distracted from the rightness of their path. Honu

Keiki were the direct descendants of the Children of the Law of One. And their goal in life was simple: to live a good life.

But the priestess, she cared little for that. And now she had plans for them. And that didn't just worry Aaliyah; it terrified her.

Aaliyah shook her head, remembering the priestess's eyes boring into her own.

"What harm is she talking about?" Kai asked. "And how is she going to protect us from it?"

"I don't know. But I think, for all our sakes, we need to find out. And soon."

Chapter Five

DAVOS, SWITZERLAND

ELISABETA ROCCORIO LAY on a chaise lounge in the ten thousand square foot chalet that dated to 1764. Through the wall-to-wall windows of her bedroom, she had a perfect view of the Swiss Alps. Her part of the valley was isolated from all other chalets and skiers, so the snow fell undisturbed on the long valley, without a single sign of human life. Up above, the sun poked through the clouds, and the snow sparkled where the light touched it.

It was a beautiful scene, and Elisabeta was sick to death of it. She'd seen nothing but this idyllic winter wonderland for the last half year. The chalet was comfortable, she supposed—it was styled from the baroque period, with lots of bulbous dressers, ancient mirrors, and ornate, heavy drapes reaching from floor to ceiling in all forty-two rooms —but Elisabeta was not impressed. After all, her family home in Italy had sixty rooms and none of this horrible weather.

Besides, she was Samyaza, the leader of the Fallen. Over her incarnations she had spent time in much more sumptuous surroundings. She had been a pharaoh in Egypt where her every whim was met, a tsar in Russia, an emperor in China. In comparison, a lonely chalet in Switzerland just didn't cut it. If this was the modern idea of luxury, then people in this era had no idea what they were missing.

In today's world, people often spoke about the power the government held over their lives, and Elisabeta struggled not to laugh out loud. These people didn't know what real power was. They had no idea. As tsar, she had people brought in to fight to the death for scraps of food simply for entertainment. She'd had people boiled alive as punishment for tiny transgressions in ancient Rome.

And those were only two examples. She had thousands of incidents stored in her memories. And in most cases, the displays of violence had nothing to do with anger, or retribution, or justice. She had done them simply because she could.

Now *that* was power.

And she had every intention of getting that kind of power back in this current lifetime. *I just have to get one small obstacle out of my way.*

She turned her gaze away from her portrait-inspiring view. At least the self-imposed isolation had been fruitful. Her philanthropic endeavors had increased, her businesses had expanded—as had her bank account—and she had made successful inroads into multiple governments. Not to mention all the plans she had laid for her future endeavors.

And now she was on the cusp of her greatest accomplishment, one that would make the rest pale in comparison.

With a smile, she reached over and pressed the intercom. "Bring me some champagne."

She pushed off the lounge and walked to the cold glass

overlooking the grounds. A friend had lent her the home; she'd claimed she was making some life changes and needed a secluded spot for quiet and reflection. And no one had been able to find her—not even the ring bearer, although Elisabeta had no doubt the woman was moving heaven and earth trying to track her down. Elisabeta's resources far outshone those of the ring bearer or even her brother, and she had no intention of being found until she chose to step out into the spotlight.

A soft knock sounded at the door. "Enter," Elisabeta said without turning.

The maid was reflected in the glass window. She wore a black dress with a starched white apron. She pushed the cart into the room. "Ma'am? Would you like me to pour you a glass?"

"Yes. Then leave it on the side table."

The woman removed the champagne bottle from the ice bucket, poured a glass, and left it next to the settee before leaving.

Elisabeta spared the outside one last look before returning to the chaise lounge. After a quick glance at the clock, she pulled out her phone and dialed.

The call was answered quickly by one of her most competent lieutenants, Raol. "Yes, Samyaza."

"You have arrived?"

"Yes, Samyaza, just a short while ago."

"And you are ready?"

"Yes, my liege. I am just waiting for your go-ahead."

"Well, you have it. As soon as an opportunity presents itself, I expect you to take it. Contact me when it is done."

"Yes, Samyaza."

Elisabeta disconnected the call without replying and settled back into the lounge. Placing the phone on the side table, she picked up the champagne glass. With a smile, she lifted it up. "To you, Delaney McPhearson. May you get everything you so richly deserve."

She took a swallow, enjoying the feel of the bubbles coating her throat. Then with a satisfied sigh, she wrapped her hand around the glass and curled it into her chest.

Let it begin.

Chapter Six

THE TRIP to the preserve yesterday had left Laney feeling optimistic about life. The cats' show of respect had been so touching. Lou and Rolly had spent hours with them. And Lou had smiled more in those few hours than she had in the last two months.

And even though Laney was still plagued by questions about Honu Keiki and the Fallen, life had become a little quieter. There was a routine. And like she'd told Jen, she'd accepted who she was and what her role was. One side effect of that acceptance was that she'd learned to appreciate the little things—like this peaceful trip to the coffee shop.

Laney sipped some of the foam off the top of her drink with a smile and a sigh. *Heaven.* Climbing back into her Jeep, she mentally ran over her plan for the afternoon.

First up was a meeting with a senator's aide who seemed to be supportive of their work. Laney was pretty sure there was an incident somewhere in the senator's past that made him more open to what they were doing.

It was nice to think that they might get some support rather than resistance from the Senate. It was not long ago that they had been facing hearings on Capitol Hill. Thankfully those had been put on hold after Laney saved most of the members of the Senate committees from getting blown up. The senators must have recognized that it would be more than a little ungrateful to turn around and interrogate the hero who had just saved your life. Still, Laney knew their forbearance wouldn't last much longer.

After the meeting with the aide, Laney was heading over to the school to finish up the paperwork that never seemed to end. Finally, she hoped to have a little time with the teenagers before she headed to the preserve to see the cats.

All in all, not a bad day.

Laney looked over her shoulder as she reversed out of the spot. Cleo was in the back seat, but she had a blanket draped over her, as Laney didn't want anyone glancing in the car and freaking out at the sight of a giant leopard in downtown Baltimore. Laney unwrapped the biscotti she'd picked up at the coffee shop and handed it back to Cleo as she headed down the road. The cat leaned forward and took the treat gently from Laney's hand with her teeth, then settled back down.

Laney headed toward the Francis Scott Key Bridge. Traffic was pretty light, for which Laney was thankful.

As they pulled onto the bridge, a minivan was beside them, with a little girl of no more than three strapped in a car seat in the back. Cleo pressed her face against the window to get a look, and the little girl's eyes went large. Cleo loved watching kids in other cars.

Laney laughed. "Cleo, get down before you cause an accident."

Up ahead, a bright yellow school bus lumbered over the

bridge. They'd pass it in another minute or so. "Don't even think about it," Laney warned.

With a grumble, Cleo lowered herself back down again.

"I promise, when we get to the school you can play with some of the kids."

Cleo grunted.

Laney shook her head. Learning Cleo was part human had explained a great deal about the cat's behavior and her needs—mainly her need for socialization. She didn't just *want* to interact with both people and her panther pack, she *needed* to.

A loud bang sounded from ahead of them. The bus wobbled and then veered across two lanes of traffic toward the side of the bridge. Cars swerved out of the way, but one sedan didn't move quickly enough, and it bounced off the back of the bus.

Laney could see bits and pieces of rubber flying off the bus's rear left tire. *It must have blown.*

The bus's brakes squealed as the driver tried to bring the bus under control, but the rubber from the rear wheel was entirely gone now, leaving just the rim, and the bus kept swerving toward the bridge's low railing.

Oh, God. It's going to go over. Laney slammed on her brakes, and the cars behind her did the same.

Laney was out the door and running, not even sure what she was going to do. She yanked her ring off the chain around her neck and placed it on her finger just as the bus slammed into the railing. There was a screech of metal as the bus scraped against the railing, and then one of the bridge's support cables snapped, whipping back toward Laney. She dove out of the way as it flew over her.

The supports held, but Laney heard the squeal of brakes behind her. She turned. A propane truck was trying to stop to avoid the stopped cars ahead of it, but it was moving too fast, and slammed into the rearmost car. A small fire burst out of the back of the truck.

"No, no, no." Laney's head whipped back to the bus, which continued its assault on the edge of the bridge.

Then the railing broke away.

"No!"

Laney called on the wind to shove the bus back. The bus was halfway off the bridge, the nose pointing down off the side, the back lifted into the air, six feet up, wheels still turning. Laney struggled to create enough wind to keep it from tumbling, and at the same time she sent a smaller wind to the tanker fire. Sweat broke out on her brow.

"Get the kids out of the bus!" Laney yelled at the first two people she saw: a construction worker and a woman in workout gear. A guy in a suit jumped out of his car and ran for the bus as well.

The three of them ran to the back of the bus and yelled for the kids to open the emergency door. The door shook and flew open. Kids leaned out. Laney's heart skipped a beat. They all looked so young.

The adults held out their arms and told the kids to jump down. A girl in a pink shirt took charge, arranging the other kids and helping them out. One by one the kids jumped out of the bus, the girl in pink going last.

"Are they all out?" Laney shouted when no one else appeared.

The construction worker shook his head. "No. The driver's still in there. The kids say he's not moving."

An ache had formed in Laney's shoulders. Every muscle in Laney's body was taut and she was dripping in sweat. She couldn't hold the bus much longer.

"Cleo!" she yelled.

Cleo burst from the open door of Laney's Jeep and sprinted for the bus.

Some of the kids screamed as Cleo pounded toward them. The adults pulled the kids back and placed themselves protectively in front of them. Cleo ignored them all. With one graceful leap, she flew over the people and landed in the bus's open rear doorway.

Come on, Cleo, Laney urged, struggling against the wind. She'd never held a sustained wind like this before.

The woman and the man in the business suit hustled the children away to the other side of the highway, behind the divider. The construction worker just stared at the back door of the bus, his mouth hanging open. Laney stared at the door as well, praying for Cleo to hurry up. Gravity was tugging the bus toward the water.

Please, Cleo, she begged, tears springing to her eyes.

Cleo appeared in the doorway, holding the bus driver in her mouth by the collar of his shirt. Beneath her, the construction worker's eyes were huge.

"Help her!" Laney yelled through gritted teeth.

The man moved forward and stood under the back door. Cleo set the driver down on the edge of the doorway, nudged him over the side into the construction worker's raised arms, then vaulted over both of them.

Able to release the bus at last, Laney dropped to her knees and sucked in a huge breath, spots dancing before her eyes as the bus plunged off the bridge to a chorus of screams from the kids.

Cleo walked over to Laney and nudged her shoulder. Laney put an arm around her, but her legs were too shaky for her to stand. "I'm okay, girl. Just need a minute."

The construction worker had laid the driver on the road

and was doing chest compressions. Poor man must have had a heart attack.

Cleo let out a roar, and Laney's head jerked upright.

The fire had reappeared at the back of the tanker, and dark smoke wafted from it. With a whoosh, the tanker exploded. A wall of fire and shrapnel raced toward Laney, Cleo, the kids, and everyone who had stopped to help.

Without a thought, Laney threw her hands up. Using every last ounce of her energy, she created a rush of wind that blew the flames and shrapnel out over the water.

Then she collapsed to the ground and slipped into unconsciousness.

Chapter Seven

HENRY STARED at the bridge below. "A car accident," he mumbled angrily. "She said it was a car accident."

Fire trucks, police cars, and ambulances were spread across the bridge, their lights spinning. Part of the bridge railing was torn away, and the burned-out ruin of a tanker lay a hundred feet away. And for some reason, about two dozen school kids were huddled over to one side of the bridge.

Henry gestured for the chopper pilot to land. Wind buffeted the small craft, and Henry sucked in a breath.

Laney had called him about fifteen minutes ago and told him she'd been in a car accident on the bridge. She'd asked him to hurry because she needed to get Cleo out of there. But it wasn't her words that had made him get in the chopper and fly right here. It was her voice—weak, shaky.

The chopper set down on a clear section of the road, and when Henry stepped out, he felt the people's stares. He knew they were looking not only because of his dramatic entrance, but also because of his height. At seven foot two, he attracted attention no matter what—doubly so when landing a helicopter on a bridge in the middle of what looked like a movie disaster scene.

An officer walked up to Henry. "Sir, you're going to have to—"

Henry held up his SIA badge. "Federal agent. Delaney McPhearson?"

The officer gestured at one of the ambulances.

"Thanks." Henry strode past him without waiting for permission.

The officer hustled after him. "Sir, you can't just—"

"Where's her cat?" Henry asked.

The officer was jogging to keep up with Henry's long stride. "In her car. It was locked in when I got on scene. Someone said the cat waited until the woman regained consciousness and then turned and sprinted for the car."

Henry nodded. *Good thinking, Cleo.* "She still there?"

"Yeah, it's contained, but we've got a call in to Animal Control—"

"That won't be necessary. I'll take it from here."

Henry quickened his pace, and the officer had to either stop or literally sprint to keep up. Apparently he decided saving some dignity was a little more important than preventing a federal agent from entering the scene, because he dropped back.

"Damnedest thing I've ever seen," a construction worker was saying to a cop as Henry passed. "All the flames, the pieces of the truck—they just changed direction."

Henry smiled. *My little sister's been busy.*

Laney was sitting on the back of an ambulance, a blanket over her shoulders. She looked up when Henry was still two hundred yards away, and Henry knew her abilities had warned her of his approach. It was one of the side effects of being the ring bearer—she received an electrical tingle whenever a Fallen or nephilim was near.

She gave him a wan smile. "Hey."

Henry raised an eyebrow and gestured to the chaos surrounding them. "Hey? That's the best greeting you can come up with?"

"Sorry. How was your morning?"

Henry laughed, taking a seat next to her and throwing an arm around her shoulder. "Probably not as exciting as yours. You've only given me the condensed version—how about the longer version now?"

Laney sighed. As she recounted the accident and her reaction to it, Henry watched her in awe. She had no idea how amazing she was. Not once had she stopped to worry about her own safety, only about protecting others. And yet he knew if he used the word "hero," she'd deny it.

"I'm going to need your help getting Cleo out of here," Laney said.

"That won't be a problem. Your car's unharmed, and it's not actually a crime scene, only an accident. Did you give your statement yet?"

"Yeah, although I had to be a little creative."

"Creative?"

"Basically to anyone watching, I was just standing in the middle of the bridge with my hands out. I didn't actually *do* anything."

"So what did you tell them?"

"I was frozen in fear, not sure what to do." She grimaced. "And it all became too much, so I fainted."

Henry snorted. "And apparently they don't know you, so they bought it. What did you say about Cleo?"

"That she's well trained and not a harm to anyone." Laney pushed herself off the back of the ambulance and dropped the blanket inside. "But I'd like to get her out of here before they ask anything more."

Henry gestured to the news choppers circling above and the journalists who had been roped into one section of the bridge. "What about them? Did they see anything?"

"I don't think so. There was a chopper overhead during some of it. I doubt it was focused on me, but I can't guarantee it didn't get a shot of Cleo. To be honest, I don't even know if it was a news chopper."

Henry frowned. "Okay. I'll have the SIA spin department get to work on that. We'll get an announcement together with all of Cleo's paperwork."

Laney took his arm and leaned into him as they started across the bridge toward her car. "Good, because the last thing we need is attention."

Henry patted her arm. "I'm sure it'll be fine."

But as they headed to Laney's Jeep, he noticed more than one person looking not at him, but at Laney. A few of the kids were even pointing. Laney's actions might not have gone as unnoticed as she thought.

Chapter Eight

VENICE, ITALY

THE LIGHTS from behind the camera had grown increasingly hot, but Elisabeta Roccorio sat across from Emmanuel Rialdo with a smile on her face. With a muted pink blouse, a pale gray skirt, her dark brown hair pulled back into a bun, and limited makeup, Elisabeta thought she gave the impression of a very stylish nun. The irony of the idea had made her smile when she'd looked in the mirror this morning.

Emmanuel, forty-five with dark hair and eyes, was lead journalist for *The World Today*. He was a preening peacock, but a well-liked one, and he was part of a very carefully crafted public campaign that Elisabeta had set in motion months ago.

Emmanuel gave Elisabeta his serious look—no hint of smile, his brows drawn close together but not close enough to wrinkle his skin. "The school you have created in Afghanistan has brought a lot of hope within that community, but also a lot of turmoil," he said. "Why did you choose that region of the world to build a school, especially with all the danger that surrounds it?"

Elisabeta leaned forward, keeping her mouth turned down, her eyes filled with concern. "That is exactly the reason why. Women in Afghanistan have been thrown back into the Stone Age. They are forbidden from learning. They are married off as early as ten. They have no say in the way their society is run. Education is the key to changing that."

"It's not just for girls that you are doing this, though, is it?"

Elisabeta shook her head. "The state of all education in Afghanistan is horrible. Childhood in Afghanistan is itself a nightmare-inducing situation. Did you know that children in Afghanistan have one of the highest risks of death in the world? There are fourteen thousand schools in Afghanistan, but a full half of them do not even have buildings. Children, both boys and girls, study either out in the open or in tents. We can do better for them than that."

"That's horrible."

Elisabeta nodded, careful to keep her face downcast. "It gets worse. More than half of all marriages are *child* marriages. A young girl is married to a man, most of the time a man old enough to be her father or even grandfather. Education is the key to help turn that around. Educating women, but also men on what the world has to offer them. It is ignorance that keeps people in the dark. Education brings them into the light."

Emmanuel nodded. "This is only one of a dozen schools you have funded in multiple parts of the world. You are known for your philanthropic endeavors. Why this particular approach?"

Elisabeta clasped her handkerchief in her hand and let out a breath. "My mother. She was from a small village."

She pictured her mother—*that cow*. She'd slept her way into money. "She had no prospects, no family backing to achieve anything. Yet, through education, she was able to make something of herself. I have never forgotten her story, and I want that to be the story of thousands of little girls."

"And thanks to you, I'm sure it will be. Elisabeta Roccorio, thank you for agreeing to speak with me."

"Thank you for taking the time to focus on an issue that is so very important not just to me, but to the rest of the world."

"And cut," the director called from behind the camera.

Emmanuel took Elisabeta's hand and kissed it. "That was wonderful. I believe you just may be the first person declared a saint while still alive."

Elisabeta smiled as a production assistant came over and removed her microphone. "You're too kind. We all do our part."

She stood, and Emmanuel did as well. "And thank you for letting us shoot in your home," he said. "It's beautiful. We should be out of your hair in about thirty minutes."

"No rush. My staff set out lunch for your people in the kitchen. Please make sure everyone gets something to eat, would you? I'm afraid I have business to attend."

"Of course. And thank you again."

Elisabeta inclined her head and graced him with a smile. As she walked out of the room, she was careful to turn and smile at each member of the production crew as well. But when she entered the hall leading to her office, the fake smile dropped from her face. She rolled her neck. *God, that was tedious.*

As she opened the door to her office, Hakeem stood up from behind her desk and bowed. Hakeem had the dark looks of his Spanish mother and Indian father. He was tall, strong, and only passable in bed. "Samyaza," he said.

Samyaza grunted. Hakeem was a good, loyal soldier, completely devoted to her. But he wasn't Gerard. She had found Gerard when he was only sixteen, his powers just developing. She had shown him what he was capable of, shown him a world he had only dreamed of. They had traveled the world together, and she had been his first—in all ways. He had been loyal, and a constant presence. The one she could rely on.

And then Victoria took him away from her, with one placement of her hands. *If the old woman weren't dead already...* Elisabeta paused, realizing she wasn't. Victoria would have been re-born by now. *Perhaps that bears a little looking into.*

Hakeem stepped away from her desk, and Elisabeta sat. "Raol called while you were being interviewed," Hakeem said.

"Good news?"

"He sounded... good."

Elisabeta rolled her eyes. Another reason she missed Gerard: he could tell from a pause in conversation all that the speaker was trying to keep hidden. Hakeem could barely tell when they said it aloud.

She waved him out of the room. "Leave me."

Hakeem bowed and left, closing the door behind him. Elisabeta pulled her cell from the desktop and dialed Raol.

"Samyaza?"

"Was it a success?" she asked.

She could hear the pride behind his words. "Yes. It went perfectly."

Elisabeta settled back in her chair. Strategizing was as natural to her as breathing, and this plan held for her more satisfaction than any she could remember. "And you caught it on tape?"

"Yes. What's my next step?"

Elisabeta spun her chair so she was looking out at the canals. She had missed this place. Ever since China, she had been in hiding. Finally she was done with that, and everything was as it was supposed to be.

"Has it made the news yet?" she asked.

"Just an afternoon broadcast. The news chopper was in the area, as you wanted."

"Excellent. Was the ring bearer featured?"

"Not particularly, but her leopard was mentioned."

A good start. "Make copies of your recording and then get me the original."

"Yes, Samyaza." He paused. "Might I ask what you are planning?"

Elisabeta smiled, contentment rolling through her. "I am planning on making sure Delaney McPhearson gets her fifteen minutes of fame."

Chapter Nine

SCREAMS RANG out through Aaliyah's home. She sat straight up in bed, clutching her blankets to her chest, her heart pounding. She recognized the voice behind the screams.

Noriko.

The screams cut off abruptly, but the silence terrified Aaliyah even more. Stumbling from bed, she banged her knee before finding the light switch. She ran down the short hallway to Noriko's room and opened the door.

The light from the hall cast shadows across the room. Noriko's bed was empty, but a whimper drew Aaliyah's eyes to the corner by the window. Noriko sat there, her knees curled into her chest, tears streaming down her cheeks.

"Noriko!" In a flash, Aaliyah was kneeling by her side. Her hands ran over Noriko's arms and legs, searching her for an injury. "Are you all right?"

Noriko sat silent, her body shaking as if she was freezing.

Aaliyah grabbed Noriko's arm and looked straight into her eyes. "Noriko, what is it? You're scaring me."

Noriko just stared straight ahead.

"Noriko."

Finally, Noriko focused on Aaliyah. "Mama?"

The old endearment tugged at Aaliyah's heart. Noriko hadn't called her that since she was a child. In Honu, the priestess had forbidden the endearment. But at home, away from prying eyes, Aaliyah had loved hearing the word in Noriko's little voice.

Aaliyah ran a hand over Noriko's head, pushing the hair out of her eyes. "It's me. I'm here. I'm always here."

Noriko leaned into her. "It was so real."

Aaliyah sat down next to her, wrapping an arm around her shoulders. "What was so real?"

"The dream."

A shudder ran through Noriko, and Aaliyah hugged her tight. But a sense of foreboding fell over her. It *could* be just a dream—but Noriko was no normal girl. She had two abilities that set her apart: she could understand animals, and she had visions of the future. In their history, many of the members of Honu Keiki had developed abilities such as these. But Noriko was unique in having more than one.

"Are you sure it was only a dream?" Aaliyah asked quietly.

Noriko turned toward her. "It had to be. It was too horrible."

"Tell me about it."

"It—" Noriko took a breath. "The priestess was there. She was standing on high, the world at her feet. I was next to her, along with most of Honu Keiki. But you weren't there. You were under her—with the rest of the world."

Aaliyah rubbed Noriko's arm. "That's not so bad."

Noriko shook her head, her eyes troubled. "That's not all. It began to burn. They were all burning."

"Who was burning?"

Noriko's horror-stricken expression pulled at Aaliyah's heart. "Everyone. The world."

Chapter Ten

THEY WERE ALL BURNING. Noriko's words remained lodged in Aaliyah's mind even as she comforted Noriko, helped her into bed, and held her hand while she eased back into sleep.

There was no sleep for Aaliyah. She stayed up, watching the night sky turn into a brilliant pink. And with the coming of the dawn, she knew she had to do something. Ever since the priestess's announcement, she and Kai had been trying to learn what the priestess was up to, but carefully, without drawing attention. Noriko's dream had changed all that. Because as much as Aaliyah wanted to write the dream off as the product of an overworked imagination, she knew Noriko too well for that. Noriko did not entertain visions of violence; her dreams were peaceful. Which meant this was no dream—it was a vision. And Aaliyah could no longer wait and hope they found out what the priestess was up to.

She had to be bold.

Now the sun shone down on her as she made her way to the temple. The juniper berries were in bloom, and the fragrance drifted on the light wind. She smiled at the people she passed, but it was growing increasingly difficult to pretend that everything was all right. Her home had become something foreign to her. Part of her wanted nothing more than to take Kai, Noriko, and Oasu and just leave.

But another part of her knew she could not abandon Honu Keiki to the priestess. And now, with Noriko's vision, she knew the stakes were even higher. If Noriko was right, the whole world could pay for whatever the priestess was up to. It might sound crazy, but she knew the priestess was connected to the Companion Killers, and they had had a global reach. So was it really insane to believe that whatever the priestess planned had global ramifications?

There was only one thing Aaliyah could do: she needed to find out what the priestess was up to, and stop her. Once the priestess was handled, Honu Keiki would be safe once more, and then she wouldn't have to think about leaving. There was no other course of action that would allow her to live with herself.

But doubts still plagued her as she walked. They pounded away at her, reducing her resolve.

Enough, she shouted at herself. *This must be done, for the good of all of us.*

She had already searched the temple as well as she could, even though she knew the priestess would not trust whatever her plan was to somewhere it could easily be found. Which meant any plans could only be in one place.

As she made her way down the path toward the priestess's home, she went over her cover story again: that the priestess had asked her to bring her the bracelets from the first Council to her home for safekeeping. The priestess was always collecting bits and pieces of jewelry from everyone, so the rationalization should not raise too much attention.

Aaliyah clutched the linen bag with the bracelets, sweat developing on her palms. *Calm down*, she warned herself. She took a few deep breaths, and her heart rate slowed some.

Ahead she saw the priestess's home. It sat away from the rest of the homes on its own patch of land, overlooking the lagoon. There had once been ten other homes nearby, but the priestess had had them demolished when she took over, explaining that their presence interrupted her concentration. Now her home stood alone at one of the highest points, overlooking all of Malama Island. It was three times the size of any other home on the island—two stories tall, with the rooftop deck effectively serving as a third floor.

Aaliyah walked up the seashell-lined front path to the front door and knocked before she lost her nerve. She waited, but there was no sound from inside. She knocked again. Still no one answered. Heart pounding, she pushed the door open. Although the priestess's home was much more sumptuous than anyone else's, it did share one attribute with all the other homes on Malama: no locks.

"Hello?" she called into the encased front foyer, her voice echoing off the Carrera marble.

No one answered. She walked in slowly, her heart nearly pounding out of her chest. She cleared her throat and called louder. "Hello?"

Still no response. The house was silent.

Go, a voice urged.

She stepped into the living room and stopped short. It was beautiful. Deep white couches flanked a fireplace that was covered in white and gray cultured stone. A white fur rug was cast between the two couches. A wall of windows overlooked the lagoon. Aaliyah was dumbstruck; anger overcame her awe. *How much did this cost?*

Clutching her bag, she walked through the room into the attached kitchen. It, too, was stunning: contemporary, sleek, not a thing out of place. Stowing her anger, Aaliyah opened a few drawers, but nothing jumped out at her—just normal kitchen supplies.

Aware of the time ticking by, she made her way into the dining room. A long mahogany table with ten chairs stood in the middle of the room, with an enormous crystal chandelier above it. Aaliyah ignored the opulent furniture, zeroing in on the papers neatly lined up at one end of the table.

She picked through them with a frown. They were reports on purchases: bedding, seeds. Her eyes bulged at a fifty-thousand-dollar invoice for an air-conditioning unit. There was even a purchase order for a large plane. The more she saw, the more confused she became. What on earth was all this for?

Next to the papers was a long cardboard tube. Aaliyah popped off the lid, pulled out the papers inside, and unrolled them on the table.

They were schematics for a giant facility. There were areas for bedrooms, kitchens, exercise areas, farming areas. At the bottom right of one of the blueprints she found a location: Perth, Australia.

She looked back at the stacks of purchase orders, and she knew what the priestess had in mind.

Oh, Holy Mother.

Chapter Eleven

AALIYAH HURRIED to Kai's home. She couldn't believe this was happening, even though she had seen the plans with her own eyes.

With relief, she saw Kai's house ahead. All the houses on Malama—apart from the priestess's—were similar in design: one story with a small porch in front or a lanai out back. Some had steps and some didn't, depending on the terrain. All were done in light colors to combat the heat.

She knocked on the door before opening it. "Kai?"

"In the kitchen," he yelled.

Aaliyah walked down the hall to the kitchen, where she found Kai and his son, Oasu, sitting at the table finishing up breakfast. "Oh, Oasu, hi."

Oasu had Kai's dark hair and eyes, but otherwise he looked nothing like him. His face was more narrow, and he was lean, not muscular like Kai. There was little reason for the two men to look alike, since they were not biological father and son. Like many on Honu Keiki, Oasu's parents had relinquished him to be raised by someone else.

Among the Honu Keiki, there was an old tradition of relinquishing one's children to another, in the belief that a child would be better raised by teachers. But prior to the current priestess, only a few parents still followed that old practice—and even then, it was always the parents' choice. The priestess, however, had taken away that choice. She had decreed that children were not allowed to be raised by their biological parents. This had led to the exit of dozens of members over the years, as they could not bear the thought of being separated from their children. And those that had stayed, and had had their children taken from them, had been heartbroken.

Oasu stood and placed a kiss on Aaliyah's cheek. "Good morning, Aaliyah."

Aaliyah patted his arm. "It's good to see you. I don't see you much these days."

"I've been stationed at the other side of the island and doing extra shifts. Speaking of which, I need to get ready."

He started to clear his dishes, but Kai waved him away. "I'll get it. Go on."

Oasu smiled before disappearing down the hallway toward his bedroom.

Kai picked up Oasu's plate and cup, and Aaliyah joined him at the sink. She spoke quietly. "I've found out what the priestess has planned."

Kai turned to her. "What? How?"

"I snuck into her home."

Kai's eyes grew wide. "Aaliyah, how could you? If you had been caught—"

She pictured Noriko's terrified face last night. "I had to do it. And I wasn't caught. And now I know. Oh, Kai."

Kai glanced toward the hallway where Oasu had disappeared, then wiped his hands on a dishtowel. "Let's take a walk outside."

Aaliyah followed him out of the house. Neither spoke until they were a hundred yards away.

"What is it?" Kai asked.

"We're being moved."

Kai's brow furrowed. "Moved? Where? Why?"

"I don't know the answer to any of those questions. All I do know is that we're going to be evacuated starting next week."

"I don't understand. This is our home. In our entire history we've never—"

"Kai!"

At the sound of Vanessa's yell, Kai and Aaliyah spun to find her standing a short way down the path, four of the Guard behind her. Aaliyah couldn't help but notice that all of them were armed, their hands on their guns.

"What is the meaning of this?" Kai demanded.

Vanessa smiled. "You are being exiled for failure to follow the rules of Honu Keiki."

Aaliyah felt cold. "What? That's insane. He's a member of the Naacal. How dare—"

"We have proof that Kai helped Hanake leave the island to join up with his child and the mother of his child." Vanessa's gaze slid to Aaliyah. "Although we have yet to determine *how* he knew where they were."

A shout drew their attention. Oasu was running down the path toward them. "What's going on?" he asked as he drew up to them, placing himself in front of both Kai and Aaliyah.

"Your father has broken the law. He is to be exiled," Vanessa said.

Oasu shook his head. "No. That's crazy. He would never—"

Vanessa's voice was cold. "Step out of the way, Oasu, or you will also be exiled."

Kai placed his hand on Oasu's shoulder. "Son, it's all right. It will be all right."

Oasu's look was incredulous. "*How* will it be all right?"

Vanessa ignored the question and addressed Kai. "Due to your service in the High Council, the priestess has deigned to allow you to pack a few things before you leave. You have one hour. These guards will accompany you."

Oasu pulled Aaliyah out of the way as the four guards formed a tight square around Kai and headed for the house. Kai was forced to go with them or be swept along.

Without another word, Vanessa turned back the way she came.

As Aaliyah watched her go, she was amazed at the feeling of hate that stole over her. She pictured the priestess's penetrating gaze at the assembly, and she realized something. The exile of Kai was being done as a warning—but not a warning to the entire community. *It's a warning specifically for me. But then, why not just exile me, instead of Kai?*

Oasu took her arm and led her to follow Kai and the guards. She could see the worry on his face. "What's going on, Aaliyah?" he whispered.

She shook her head, unable to speak. Kai was being exiled. She would never see him again unless she left, too.

How can this be happening?

Chapter Twelve

LANEY RAN THROUGH THE PRESERVE, Cleo at her side. She'd just spoken with Matt, who had assured her they had the Fallen incidents under control. There were still Fallen incidents, of course—there always were—but they were small scale and back under the radar. The showboating had all but disappeared.

Laney still wasn't sure what all the high-profile incidents had been about in the first place, and Matt didn't have any theories, either. There were a few websites dedicated to the incidents, but they didn't seem to get much traction. Their claims of "enhanced human beings" were sneered at by the mainstream media the same way they laughed off sightings of Bigfoot and UFOs. Even the hubbub about the bridge incident had quieted down. There'd been a few media inquiries, but Henry had had the Chandler Group's public relations arm handle that. Laney had avoided almost any publicity.

And now, things were, well, back to normal.

And that really worried her. Because "normal" was not

a word she'd use to describe her life the last few years. In fact, for the last year she'd been run ragged going from one crisis to another. She knew she should just enjoy this period of relative calm, but in the back of her mind, she was waiting for the other shoe to drop.

A noise behind her made her turn, and she saw Lou sprinting up the hill, with Snow, Tiger, and six of the other cats at her sides. Laney smiled at the image. Lou's dark hair blew behind her as her long stride ate up the ground. She looked free and fierce. She looked like a warrior.

She looked like her old self.

Catching sight of Laney, Lou changed direction and sprinted toward her. Laney had asked Lou to join her on her run at the preserve today. Laney liked to run here every day if she could manage it. They had all started off running together—Laney, Lou, and the seven cats—but then Lou, with her enhanced abilities, had decided to really give the cats a *run*. Only Cleo had chosen to stay with Laney.

Lou's breath now came out in pants. Laney smiled, and Lou returned it. Neither of them said anything for a few minutes, each seemingly content to stare at the undisturbed land in front of them.

Finally, Laney turned to Lou. "How are you doing?"

Lou looked at Laney, then away. "Okay. Better."

On the car ride over, Laney had sensed that Lou wanted to ask her something, but so far all their conversations had been kept light and easy. "Anything you want to talk about?" she asked carefully.

Lou was quiet for a moment, and Laney let the quiet stretch out. "Do you ever—" Lou stopped.

"Ever what?"

Lou shrugged. "I don't know—get fixated on something and not be able to let it go?"

Laney watched the struggle on Lou's face. This girl had already dealt with so much in her young life. If she were any other teenage girl, her "fixation" would be boys or clothes or something else normal teenage girls worried about. But Lou was no normal teenage girl.

"Yeah," Laney said. "After Rocky died, I couldn't stop playing it over and over in my head. If I had made her run away, gotten her away—if I had moved right instead of left. If I had seen the ambush before—" Laney shook her head and sighed. "I still wake up some nights thinking about what I could have done differently."

Lou took in a shuddering breath. "So you've never gotten past it."

Laney paused, trying to figure out how exactly to convey what she felt about Rocky's death. "No. Rocky, Drew—I don't think I'll ever be okay with them being gone. But I've accepted that they are. And I've also accepted that, as much as I *wish* I could have done things differently, things played out the way they did, and I can't change that. All I *can* do is try to make sure it doesn't happen to anyone else I care about. Which is why—" Laney bit off her words. Now wasn't the time to lecture Lou about not getting involved in Fallen activities.

"Which is why you want us to stay away from Fallen activities," Lou said quietly. "How do you do it? You face them, and others who are just as evil, over and over again. Aren't you ever scared?"

Laney thought back to the bridge. She remembered what it felt like when her grasp on the bus was slipping while Cleo and the bus driver were still inside. "I'm always scared," she said.

Surprise flashed across Lou's face. "Then how do you do it? I mean, I had one incident and I'm just—"

"Hey," Laney said. "It wasn't just one incident. What you did was amazing, was brave, was reckless all rolled into one. These cats wouldn't be here without you. You saved them. And you paid a price. Whenever we risk ourselves, we pay a price."

"What about you?" Lou asked softly.

Laney looked away, pictures of Drew, Rocky, Ralph and Victoria flashing through her mind. "I've paid a different kind of price. I'm haunted by what's happened as well. And the fear? At times, it's almost paralyzing."

"So how do you make yourself move?"

Laney wrapped an arm around Lou's shoulder. "Because I'm more scared of what will happen if I *don't* act—a world where the Fallen can run around unchecked. I can't let that happen. There are too many good people who would get hurt. And that's what makes me move forward when part of my brain is telling me the best idea is to run away."

Lou's voice was barely above a whisper. "I don't know if I can do that."

Gently, Laney turned Lou until she was facing her. "And you don't have to. Lou, being a teenager is tough enough. Having to deal with the Fallen? I can't imagine that at your age. I became the ring bearer at the right time—when I was old enough to deal with it. And still, at times it's overwhelming. But *you* shouldn't have to deal with any of this. In fact, I forbid you from dealing with any of this. Any Fallen issues, we adults will take care of."

"But I—"

"You need to enjoy your life. Henry, Jen, Jake, ,me—we were all teenagers once. We got to do the stupid teenage things. You need to do the same. The stupid stuff you should be doing now should be the kind of thing that maybe gets you grounded, *not* takes your life. The Fallen are not your problem. In a few years, if you want to help, you can—but for now, you're benched."

Lou looked away. "That feels like hiding."

"No. Your job is to enjoy your life so that later, if you do join the fight, you know exactly what you're fighting *for*."

Lou leaned into Laney. "Thanks."

Laney kissed her on the forehead. "Just be a kid, Lou. You'll be an adult soon enough."

Chapter Thirteen

DO NOT CRY, Aaliyah reminded herself. But every time she looked over at Kai, she felt the catch at the back of her throat.

"This isn't fair," Noriko said, tears on her cheeks.

Kai pulled her in for a hug, but his eyes stayed on Aaliyah. "Perhaps. But it is how it is."

The four guards waited outside. Noriko had come running into the house only minutes ago. Oasu looked completely devastated as he stood against the back wall, his shoulders slumped, his eyes wild. As a member of the Guard, it was his responsibility to protect the members of Honu Keiki and carry out the demands of the priestess. But today, Aaliyah knew he couldn't believe what he was being asked to do.

"It must be a mistake," Oasu said. "Maybe I could speak with—"

"No," Kai said swiftly, then softened his tone. "It is done. And the truth is, I did help Hanake escape to find his family. I am not ashamed of that act."

Noriko looked to Aaliyah. "There must be something we can do."

They did not have traditional families on Malama, but Kai had been the most important male figure in Noriko's life. Aaliyah hated this loss for her.

Aaliyah shook her head. "There is nothing. I wish there was."

Kai looked from Noriko to Oasu. "Will you two wait for me outside? I'd like to speak to Aaliyah alone for a moment."

Noriko hugged Kai tight, then wiped her cheeks. "I'll be right outside."

Oasu's voice was full of regret. "You only have a few minutes."

"We'll be right there," Kai assured him.

Oasu hesitated, looking like the little boy Aaliyah remembered so well. "I hate this."

"I know, son. Go on. I'll be right there."

Oasu gave him an abrupt nod and hurried from the room, but Aaliyah caught the glint of tears in his eyes. Aaliyah watched the doorway even after he left.

"Will you not look at me?" Kai asked.

She shook her head, feeling the weight of her tears at the back of her eyes. "No."

She felt him walk up behind her, and she took a trembling breath. He gently turned her to face him, tipping her chin up. "Aaliyah."

Her name on his lips sounded like a caress. A tear slipped down her cheek.

"Protect yourself," Kai said, staring into her eyes. "The priestess will be focused on you now."

She held his hand to her face. "I know."

He leaned down and kissed her gently on the lips. She

trembled at the feel of him. He broke away too soon, leaning his forehead against hers. "We have wasted too much time not saying what we feel. And now there is no time left. I love you, Aaliyah. You are the reason my heart beats. And you are the smile in the back of my mind."

A shudder ran through her, but she couldn't find the words to tell him what he meant to her. There was just too much to say. So she settled for simple. "I love you too."

His arms tightened around her. "Be careful."

She leaned her head on his chest. "I will."

With a final embrace, he strode from the room. Aaliyah wrapped her arms around herself, feeling his absence. The banishments had been increasing in the last year—almost as if the priestess needed to whittle their group down to a specific number. And with a shock she realized: that was exactly what she was doing. The priestess was making their number more manageable for the move.

Aaliyah sank down onto the bed, overwhelmed at how her world was spinning out of control. *How did we get here? And how can I stop this on my own?*

Chapter Fourteen

LANEY WALKED from her cottage to the main house on the Chandler estate, her conversation with Lou still on her mind.

As she headed up the circular grand staircase that led to Henry's office, she couldn't help but wonder at what a difference a few months had made. The cats were settled, relatively speaking, and they were each going to be as smart as Cleo. Cleo was their leader, they all looked to her, for now anyway.

And most importantly, Lou was coming along, some of her sparkle returning. Laney knew she was forever changed by what had happened, but she did seem better. There was no denying that. Part of the reason was the cats, but another part was that she had been given the time and space to heal away from the machinations of the Fallen—which just reinforced Laney's conviction that the kids should not be allowed anywhere near these incidents.

The door to Henry's office was open, and Jake and

Henry's laughter drifted down the hall. After a tense half year, they were all heading back to where they needed to be. As Laney entered the office, she smiled at the sight of Jake—but the butterflies that normally accompanied the sight of him were decidedly muted. She loved Jake—she always would. But something had changed between them in the last year.

He was a warrior, and he needed to protect those he loved. But Laney was a warrior too, and she couldn't be protected from the dangers of this world. Not when it was her destiny to fight them. And that was the giant chasm that stretched between them.

After everything they had been through, she supposed it was inevitable. Still, neither of them was ready to cut the cord quite yet. So by mutual silent agreement, they kept everything light and easy—which wasn't hard. And Laney had noticed that creating a little more distance between them had actually served to make Jake less stressed—which was really all she wanted.

Jake and Henry both turned to Laney, bright smiles on their faces. Laney sighed. Yup—she could get used to all this good will.

"Good run?" Jake asked as Laney sat on the couch next to him.

"Yes. The cats are really growing, and they all adore Lou. I think they may be helping her more than anything." She looked quickly at Henry. "After you, of course."

Henry chuckled. "I have no problem taking a back seat to the pack. Whatever helps Lou, I'm all for."

Laney looked at her brother, amazed at how well he handled everything. Henry's experience at the hands of Flourent out in Red Canyon had unfortunately made him one of the only people to truly understand what Lou had experienced. She had been tortured—there was simply no other word for it—and Henry knew what that felt like. Yet he still ran the Chandler Group, even if he'd handed off a lot of the day-to-day tasks, and he balanced his responsibilities to the company, to Danny, and to his destiny with a grace that Laney could only hope for.

It was also Henry and his responsibilities that had helped solidify her new approach to her own destiny. She had been thinking of her Fallen experiences as if they were something she had to get through and *then* she could have a life. But that wasn't right: these experiences *were* her life. And she needed to get on with it. It was the people around her who needed to get back to living more ordinary lives.

She glanced at Jake. *Even him.*

Over the last few months, she had come to realize that if Jake was to have a life, it couldn't be with her. And she was pretty sure he had come to the same understanding, despite how much they cared for one another. He couldn't handle her being the ring bearer. He wanted to protect her and keep her safe—that's just the type of man he was. But her job was to *face* danger, not stay protected from it. And as much as it hurt to admit it, that meant she and Jake couldn't be together. Not like they had been.

Laney shoved all those thoughts aside. Her boys were smiling, and that's what she would appreciate at this moment.

"All right," she asked, "so what's going on? What are we chatting about today? The school?"

Henry's smile dimmed a little. "I'm afraid not. There are developments on two fronts you need to be aware of." He nodded to Jake.

"Elisabeta has left hiding," Jake said.

Laney looked at him in surprise. They had been looking for Elisabeta since China, but had been unable to find any trace of her. Elisabeta had disappeared from view after Victoria's death, and Laney had let herself hope that maybe, just maybe, she would stay away. *Apparently I'm not that lucky.*

They all knew that Elisabeta had to be behind the recent spate of public Fallen incidents, though for the life of her, Laney couldn't figure out why. And then there were the Fallen murders. They had ended after the Companion Killers incident, but Laney had never fully believed the Companion Killers had been responsible for killing the Fallen. After all, the former members of Honu Keiki weren't even trained in combat—there was no way they could take down a Fallen. No, Elisabeta had to be behind that too. But again, why?

"Where is she?" Laney asked.

"Globetrotting," Jake replied. "She's done some interviews in various countries and she's been seen at three charity events over the last week. One in Milan, one in London, and one in Geneva."

"Charity?"

"Yes," Henry said. "Her charitable foundations have all seen an influx of cash in the last year, and their charitable activity has increased across the globe."

"What kind of activity?" Laney asked.

"The digging of wells in Africa, schools in Afghanistan, cancer research, malaria tents... you name it, she seems to be part of it. She was even part of President Jimmy Carter's effort to eliminate the guinea worm."

Laney frowned. "Is all this charity a cover for something?"

"I don't think so," Jake replied. "I sent some operatives to go to a handful of the sites and verify that they were doing what they said they were doing. And believe it or not, everything is on the up and up. In fact, Elisabeta is believed to be one of the top contenders for the Forbes 400 Lifetime Achievement Award for Philanthropy."

Laney looked between Jake and Henry. "But why? Where's the angle? How do the Fallen fit into this?"

Henry shrugged. "We don't know, but I doubt she's turned over a new leaf. Maybe it's just a smoke screen so if anything negative about her ever comes out, people will have a hard time believing it of someone with this history of good works."

"I'm not so sure about that," Laney said. "People always seem willing to see a person's bad side."

Jake frowned.

"What is it?" Laney asked.

"Elisabeta has increased all this activity in the last few months."

"You mean since everything happened with Honu Keiki," Laney said.

Jake nodded. "Yeah. And I just have a feeling like something is on the horizon. Something we need to be ready for."

Laney felt the same way. She had felt that way ever since they had rescued the cats and Lou. That there was a big part of the story she just couldn't see. And she still felt blind. "Any inkling what that might be?"

"Not yet," Henry said, "but I have people digging. Sooner or later, she'll show her hand."

Laney knew he was right, but she wasn't sure whether to hope for *sooner* or *later*. "So, you guys said there were two developments."

"The second one involves Honu Keiki," Henry said.

"Have you heard something from them?" Laney asked. Although the group was secretive, Aaliyah, the woman Laney had spoken with, had been forthcoming, and Laney had liked her. Laney had tried to reach her a few times since then, but unsuccessfully, and that had caused her some concern. She'd left messages asking Aaliyah to call, but so far, there had been only silence.

"No," Henry said. "But I knew you were concerned, so I had some of our people look into them a little more deeply. And it seems they've made some purchases for an off-island site that doesn't really fit with what we know about the group."

Off the island? Laney frowned. Honu Keiki members rarely left the island. One of the tenets of the group was that they stayed away from the rest of the world so as not to be corrupted. Phone calls, computer usage, even TV viewing were severely restricted for that reason. "That's strange, all right. But what exactly are they up to that has you so concerned?"

Henry handed her a few papers. "We've learned that they've purchased large swaths of land around Perth, Australia."

Perth sat on the western coast of the Australian continent, and many of its suburbs were strewn along sandy beaches. It was only one of five areas in the world with a Mediterranean climate—hot summers and warm winters, with only a few periods of high humidity. If the priestess was thinking of a retirement spot, it was a good choice.

Laney flipped through the papers. "These purchases were made by Lotus Corp. Is that them?"

Henry nodded. "It's a shell company. It traces back to Honu Keiki, but it took some digging."

The last sheet of paper was a map of Australia, with the land purchases highlighted. Laney's eyebrows shot up. "That's a lot of land."

"Over seven hundred acres," Henry said. "But what's more worrisome is that they've been building." He pulled his tablet off the coffee table and flipped it around for Laney and Jake to see. "This is a satellite feed of the land they've purchased."

Laney leaned forward. "Are those bulldozers?"

"Yes. The purchases began over three years ago. After they acquired each piece, they ousted the original tenants and razed whatever structures were in place."

"How come we didn't find this when we were researching them before?" Jake asked.

"The Lotus Corp was hidden under a string of other businesses. It's a huge knot to unravel. And it took our people a while."

Unsaid was that Danny hadn't been the one doing the search. If he had been, they probably would have discovered it sooner. But he, too, was being kept out of any dangerous undertakings. He was still working for the Chandler Group, but Henry made sure none of his projects touched on any Fallen-related activities—and right now, they weren't sure whether or not that included Honu Keiki.

Laney took the tablet and expanded the picture. "It looks like they've built one building here." She pointed to the screen.

"Zoom in on it," Henry said.

Laney did. It was a brick building, only one story, with one door and no windows. And it looked to be only about twenty feet square.

"That's awfully small for so much land," Jake said.

"Unless…" Henry cocked an eyebrow at Laney.

Laney realized what Henry was suggesting. *It can't be.* She looked up, knowing an expression of surprise was splashed across her face.

Henry's voice was grave. "They're building a bomb shelter."

Chapter Fifteen

NORIKO SAT on the couch with her head on Aaliyah's shoulder. Aaliyah held her close. They had been sitting together for an hour, neither quite ready to let the other go —and neither truly able to believe that Kai was gone.

Finally, Noriko straightened and wiped away the tears on her cheeks. "What do we do now?"

Aaliyah pushed a stray hair back from Noriko's forehead. "We continue doing what is best for our people. It is what Kai would want us to do."

Tears sprang back into Noriko's eyes. "What will *he* do? He'll be all alone."

Aaliyah took a shuddering breath, trying to hold back her own tears. The idea of Kai on his own broke her heart.

"Maybe he'll seek out the ring bearer," Noriko said.

Aaliyah's head jerked up. "The ring bearer? What makes you say that?"

"I—I was coming to tell you. I was with the priestess when she received a note that the ring bearer had been trying to reach you."

Alarm flashed through Aaliyah. "Does the priestess know you saw the note?"

Noriko shook her head. "No. I'm sure she doesn't."

Aaliyah put her hand to her chest, her heart racing. "Good, good."

"I got the impression this wasn't the first time she had tried to reach you."

Aaliyah felt a spring of hope bloom inside her. The ring bearer hadn't abandoned her. She took Noriko's hand. "Do not tell anyone about this. It must remain between us."

Noriko nodded. "What are you going to do?"

Aaliyah had a phone; Kai had picked it up for her on his last trip to the mainland. But she wasn't ready to speak with Laney yet. Right now, she didn't have any solid information to give her—just her own fears and speculations. She needed more. And when she had it, *then* she would lay it all out for the ring bearer—and pray there was something she could do to help them.

Chapter Sixteen

LANEY STARED at the screen in disbelief. "It looks almost identical to Dom's bomb shelter."

Henry nodded. "We don't know for sure that's what it is, and of course no one from Honu Keiki will confirm or deny it. But their activity supports the idea. We've found purchases for the Lotus Corporation that range from basic bedding to seeds to building material to canned goods and water filtration systems. They also have entrances at other locations on their land."

"I don't understand. You think, what—they're survivalists? Waiting for the end of days?" Laney asked. She hadn't gotten that impression from Aaliyah at all, and the few reports generated on the group didn't suggest anything along those lines either. Of course, they did have a ritual in their past called "the ritual of the end and the beginning," so it wasn't out of the question.

"I don't know," Henry said. "But I'm concerned. Australia *is* in the Pacific, though—there has to be a Mu connection, right?"

A few months back, they had learned that Atlantis hadn't been the world's first civilization, but rather Lemuria was—the mother of all subsequent civilizations. The ancient archipelago had stretched across the Pacific from the coast of Chile to Easter Island, and remnants of the civilization could still be found all along the ring of fire. But precious little was known about it. Even Edgar Cayce had spoken very little about the ancient group. When pressed about their absence in his life readings, he'd explained that unlike the Atlanteans, the Lemurians had very little karmic debt to work off and therefore were not reincarnated as often. But what they did know was that the group's philosophy was the same as that of the Children of the Law of One: anti-materialism, anti-war, and anti-cruelty.

Jake shook his head. "I've never heard of a link between Australia and Lemuria though."

"Well, there's nothing in the official history of course. And even with the unofficial history, there's not a clear link." Laney paused. "But the Australian aborigines—there might be something there. The Aborigines actually have one of the longest consistent histories of any group in existence today. They showed up on the shores of Australia a minimum of forty thousand years ago. There was at one point eight hundred thousand of them, and they settled in the coastal areas."

"Until Captain James Cook and the Royal Navy showed up," Jake said.

Laney nodded.

At Henry's confused look, Jake explained. "Cook claimed the eastern coast of Australia in the name of King George III. And he claimed the land was *terra nullius*. It was recommended as a great location for a penal colony."

Henry frowned. "Wait, *terra nullius*? Empty land? I thought there were Aborigines."

"There were," Jake said. "Like Laney said, eight hundred thousand of them. In fact, when the first ships approached the shores in 1788 with their immigrants, they were shocked at the line of natives watching them from the shoreline and angrily gesturing at them.

"Over time, one hundred sixty thousand prisoners from Great Britain were transported to the east coast of Australia. That migration ended in 1852, but by then other people had heard of Australia's vast land. And gold was found in Australia in the 1850s, which attracted even more people. In fact, at one point one third of the world's gold came from Australia."

"I never knew that," Laney said.

"But I've never heard of a Mu link," Jake said. "Of course, when I learned about Australia's early history, I wasn't exactly looking for one."

Laney shook her head. "Like I said, there's not a clear-cut link. But the description of how the Aborigines lived aligns closely with what we've heard about Lemurians. They lived in communion with nature. They took no more from the land than what they needed. In fact, they didn't even have homes. They wandered. They could work for only a few hours a day and survive very well. It was paradise. And they considered it their duty to protect both the land and the animals."

"I'm guessing that all changed when the British arrived," Henry said.

Jake nodded. "The British overfished, reduced the kangaroo population dramatically, cleared land, polluted water, and brought disease."

Henry sat back. "Prior to that, the Aborigines must have

been geographically protected from the diseases that affected the rest of the world."

"They were," Jake said. "They had no immunity to European diseases. Within a year of the British people's arrival, half the natives in the Sydney basin were dead. And the British view of the Aborigines was akin to the early Americans' view of African slaves: they saw them as an inferior race, little more than animals, and they could be killed without repercussion."

"That's horrible, although not really surprising for that time in history," Henry said.

Laney knew Henry was right. History was full of man's inhumanity to man. And modern day wasn't always much better. ISIL took slaves in the Middle East in their march to the creation of a caliphate. The situation in Syria was a humanitarian nightmare. Even at home in the United States there were heartbreaking cases of child abuse that made you question how people could be so cruel. Back in upstate New York, Laney recalled one particularly cruel case where a young man had actually placed a newborn in a microwave and turned it on. *What is wrong with us?*

"But why is Honu Keiki building there?" Jake asked.

Henry shrugged. "With an operation of this size, they're obviously preparing for something. They think something's coming."

"Is anybody living at their Australia compound now?" Laney asked.

"No. But they just finished construction a few days ago. The question is, are they just being paranoid? Or…"

Laney finished the thought for him. "Or do they know something we don't?"

Chapter Seventeen

AS LANEY HEADED down to her cottage, Henry's discovery twisted and turned through her mind. The idea of the Honu Keiki creating an underground structure on a separate continent had her more than a little worried. She knew that most of the Honu Keiki had lived on the island of Malama for their entire lives, without once setting foot on any other land. So why would they create a separate structure almost six thousand miles away? What was their plan?

As soon as she was inside her cottage, she pulled open her laptop and placed a call to Honu Keiki. Her call was picked up by the same technician who had responded to all her other attempts to reach Aaliyah.

"Hi, Keon," she said. "How are you?"

The man on the other side of the screen gave her a smile. "Hello, Dr. McPhearson. I'm well. How are you?"

"Good. Can I speak with Aaliyah?"

"I'm afraid she's not available. But there is someone

who would like to speak with you. If you'll hold for a moment?"

Laney wondered who would be interested in speaking with her. "Of course."

Keon disappeared, leaving Laney a view of his empty chair.

While she waited, Laney pulled out the map of Honu Keiki's holdings in Perth. It really was extensive. Henry had had a structural engineer plot out how big an installation he thought it was. From the location of the three blast doors, they knew it was at least a half-acre in size. They didn't know if that was tunnels or living space or what, but either way it was big. *What are you up to?*

On screen, a woman sat down in Keon's chair. Her dark hair was pulled back severely and her eyes were penetrating. She inclined her head. "Dr. McPhearson."

"Vanessa. Hi." Vanessa was the head of security for Honu Keiki and not exactly a fan of Laney's. In fact, Laney was pretty sure the woman was physically incapable of smiling—or even being polite. "I was looking for Aaliyah."

"So we have heard. Dr. McPhearson, while the priestess appreciates your interest in our community, she would prefer if you waited until *you* were contacted. These constant phone calls are disruptive."

"Constant? I've called three times in the last month. That's hardly—"

"Good day, Dr. McPhearson."

Vanessa disconnected the call. The screen froze on a shot of her reaching forward.

Laney stared at the screen in frustration. *Goddamn it.* She still couldn't reach Aaliyah, and she was worried. Why couldn't she speak with her?

The door opened behind her, and Jen walked in.

"Hey," Laney said. "I didn't know you were coming by today."

"Well, I was taking Lou to see Dom, and thought I'd stop over."

"Lou? Really?"

Jen grinned. "Yup. I swear, those cats are now my favorite living beings on the planet."

"Well, I'd say that calls for a celebration."

Jen raised an eyebrow. "What do you have in mind?"

"Ice cream." Laney stood up. "Let's go see what's in the fridge."

Jen laughed. "It's not alcohol, but I'll take it. What have you got?"

Laney opened the freezer. "Let's see... Rocky Road or mint chocolate chip."

"I'll take both." Jen pulled two bowls from the cabinet. She placed them on the island and then went still.

Laney frowned. "Jen?"

Jen didn't move and didn't say a word. Laney put the ice cream on the counter and went to Jen's side. Jen was staring at Laney's computer screen, where Vanessa was frozen in place.

Laney placed her hand on Jen's arm. "Jen?"

Jen nudged her chin toward the computer screen. "Who is that?"

Laney looked between Jen and the screen. "Her name's Vanessa. She's the head of security for Honu Keiki. Why? Do you know her?"

Jen nodded her head slowly.

"Jen?"

Jen tore her gaze from the screen. "I think she's my mom."

Chapter Eighteen

AALIYAH WAS on the other side of the island, looking for some peace. People had already been moved off the island, the worry was palpable, and Aaliyah had simply not been able to be around it. Her own emotions were too raw. She still couldn't believe Kai was gone, and she was having trouble figuring out why she was still here. She had needed some time to get her head together.

But when Noriko tracked her down to let her know that the priestess had called a meeting of the High Council, she shoved those thoughts aside and hurried back to the temple.

Now she was late. *Of course, I would have been on time if the priestess hadn't waited to announce the meeting at the last minute.*

She hastened up the steps. The two guards on duty opened the doors for her, and she nodded her thanks as she passed. She started to head toward the Council room, then made a quick detour to the bathroom, where she splashed water on her face and looked at herself in the mirror.

Stay calm and without emotion. You can't help anyone if they see your anger.

She took a few calming breaths, then nodded at her reflection.

Now I'm ready.

She headed to the bathroom door and started to pull it open when she heard voices coming down the hall. She wasn't sure why, but she pushed the door closed, leaving just a crack to allow her to hear.

The voices belonged to two of the Guard.

"—begin in two days."

"It's going to be a monster. I don't know how we'll get it all done."

"We'll get it done because the priestess has instructed us to get it done."

"And once Project Jerusalem is complete, the world will be a changed place."

"Do you think it will succeed?"

"I have no doubt."

They reached the end of the hall and turned, and their voices became inaudible.

Aaliyah leaned against the door. *Project Jerusalem? What is that?* She'd never heard the name associated with the move, but it had to be that, though, didn't it?

She had no time to think about it now. She was already late. She pulled open the door, hustled down the hall, turned the corner—and ran smack into a guard.

Two arms reached out to steady her. "Aaliyah?"

Aaliyah looked up into Oasu's concerned face. "Oasu. Sorry. I'm late for the Council meeting."

"It just started." He released her and stepped out of her way.

"Thank you." She walked past him, then stopped and looked back. "Have you ever heard of something called Project Jerusalem?"

He frowned. "No. But I could ask—"

"No, no. It's nothing. In fact, I'm sure I misheard. It's been a difficult few days."

Oasu nodded, his eyes reflecting her own sadness. "I know. I miss him too."

She nodded and squeezed his arm, then turned away without another word. After all, what was there to say?

Chapter Nineteen

BALTIMORE, MARYLAND

JEN'S MOM had disappeared when Jen was seven. Jen had come home from school one day, and her mom had simply been gone. No note, no disturbance, just an empty apartment. Jen had spent the next few days getting herself to school and not telling anyone.

But finally a neighbor had noticed and the authorities were contacted. Jen landed in foster care before running away at age ten and spending some time on the streets. When she was caught again, she lucked out and got placed with the Witts, who had gone on to adopt her. Jen had never looked back.

But Laney knew her mother's disappearance still nagged at her. And although Jen had never said it explicitly, Laney knew her friend had believed her mother was dead.

Now Laney looked at Vanessa's frozen image. There were similarities. Both had dark hair, dark eyes, and a yellow tint to their skin. "But I thought you were part Korean," Laney said.

"I thought so too. That's what my mom always said."

"Then it can't be her."

"I don't know, it's just—she looks just like her."

"It's been over twenty years. Are you sure?"

"No." Jen studied the image. "But they look so much alike."

Laney led Jen over to the island. "What do you remember about your mom?"

"Not much. I mean, she was, I don't know, serious, I guess. Hugs were in short supply. In fact, I can't say I remember ever being hugged. But she took care of me—food, shelter, clothes."

Laney didn't think Jen realized just how telling that statement was. When it came to kids, it wasn't just food, shelter, and clothing that mattered. Love played a big role too.

"What was her name?"

"Vanessa. Vanessa Rutledge."

The first name was the same, but that could mean—Oh, hell, who was she kidding? Jen didn't wander down imaginary roads of what if. If Jen thought Vanessa was her mother, then she was probably right.

"But isn't this too much of a coincidence?" Jen said. "I mean, we come across a secretive cult which just happens to have my biological mother as a member?"

Laney watched the struggle play across Jen's face. Jen kept her emotions under wraps at almost all times, but she was clearly having trouble doing that right now. Jen hadn't spoken much about her early life, but Laney knew it had been hard, even before she went into the foster system.

Laney glanced back at the screen, where Vanessa's face was still frozen. She could see the resemblance—the dark hair, the strong cheekbones, the strength.

She put her arm around Jen, pulling her into her side.

"No, I don't think it's too much of a coincidence. Our lives... they seem to have been plotted out in advance. You and I met before we knew who either of us was. Drew sent me that paper and it led to all of the rest. For us, there are no coincidences. There are patterns and trails to follow. I've followed mine." She nodded at the screen. "And I think now it's your turn to decide if you want to follow yours."

Jen took a shaky breath. "She just left me, Laney. For the longest time, I thought..." She went quiet.

"That she had no choice. She was forced to leave."

Jen nodded. "But she didn't. She's alive and well. And she never came back for me. She never checked up on me."

"You don't know that. Maybe—"

Jen turned, her eyes filled with pain. "You know what it was like for me after she left. How could anyone submit someone they loved to that kind of life?"

All Laney could think about was Abe Hanley, the Alexandria bookstore owner and member of the Companion Killers, talking about his quiet childhood on Malama Island. Vanessa had apparently returned to that, but had done so without her daughter.

"There has to be a reason," Laney said.

Jen gave a bitter laugh. "Do you remember how you described her after you spoke with her? Cold, hard. You really think someone like that had a broken heart over her lost child?"

Laney had to admit she couldn't picture Vanessa in a maternal role. Cuddling a child, hugging her—she simply couldn't picture it. "I don't actually know her," she said. "She could be different. Maybe there really is a reason why she left."

Jen looked up. "And maybe it was me."

"No. You were a child."

Jen stood and wiped the tears from her eyes. "She *left* me, Laney. She doesn't deserve any of my time, any of my thoughts. I'm glad to know where she is. But that's as far as it goes. She's in my past, just like I'm in hers."

Laney knew Jen wanted to believe the words she spoke, but she also knew that she didn't, not completely. Jen's mom was a question Jen had never been able to get past. She wanted to know what had happened to her.

"What do you want to do?" Laney asked softly.

Jen shook her head. "Nothing. I already have a mother."

Chapter Twenty

MALAMA ISLAND, HAWAII

AALIYAH WAS HURRYING down the path when her friend Bastet approached from the opposite direction.

Bastet stopped in front of her. "Aaliyah, is everything all right?"

Aaliyah fumbled for something to say.

Bastet stepped closer. "We're all upset about Kai. I just can't understand why he would be exiled. I know he helped Hanake, but reuniting them seemed the right thing to do. I can't imagine how upset you are."

Aaliyah nodded. She didn't have to fake the tremor in her voice. "It is difficult."

Bastet embraced her, whispering in her ear, "Anything you need, let me know."

Aaliyah gave herself a moment to enjoy the comfort of an old friend before pulling away. "Thank you. I think—I think I just need to be alone."

"I understand. But I'm here if you need me."

"Thank you," Aaliyah said, then continued home. It was getting close to time. She hustled up the path and quickly made her way to her bedroom. She counted out seven boards from the window, pried up the seventh, and from behind it she grabbed her cell phone. It was already lit up, indicating a call.

"Hello?"

"There you are," Kai said. "I was beginning to worry you had forgotten me."

With a smile, Aaliyah sank to the floor. "Never."

Kai laughed. "Good."

"How are you? *Where* are you?"

"I'm good."

"Did you find a place to stay? Do you have enough money?"

Kai had called Aaliyah when he had been dropped in Argentina, and although he had tried to sound all right then, she knew how unsettled he was.

"Yes and yes," Kai said. "It's actually a beautiful country, although the poverty…" He trailed off.

"I hate that you're out there."

"It's not so bad. But it would be nicer with some company."

"Oasu misses you. I want to tell him that I have a way to communicate with you—"

"Don't. It will only endanger him. It's bad enough that you're taking the risk. We can't endanger anyone else."

"I know. And I will look out for him."

"I know you will." He paused. "How are things going there?"

Aaliyah hesitated, not sure what to say. She didn't want to worry Kai. After all, there was nothing he could do. But at the same time, she needed someone to talk to. "They've started to move people. And I overheard something today—I just don't understand it. Maybe it's nothing."

"Tell me."

"Two of the Guard were talking. They mentioned something called Project Jerusalem."

"Project Jerusalem? What is that?"

"I don't know. We don't have any holdings in Jerusalem. No exiles have been relocated there. We have no dealings with the city at all."

"Could it be code for something else?"

"If so, I don't know what." Aaliyah had researched the ancient city after she had heard the men talking.

"What did the guards say about it?"

"Just that preparations were being made. I'm going to keep digging. See if I can find anything."

"Is that a good idea? The priestess already suspects you. Surely you're being watched."

"But what am I supposed to do? She's up to something—we know that. And we can't be caught unaware."

Kai sighed. "Please be careful. If anything were to happen to you—"

"I'll be fine. But take care of yourself. Have you contacted Delaney McPhearson, by the way?"

Kai laughed. "Well, seeing as the Chandler Group doesn't own a fishing fleet, I don't think they'll have a job opening for me."

"I'd feel better if you were around someone that could help you, Kai. Just promise me that if you run into any problems, you'll contact her. She'll help."

"She doesn't even know me."

"No, but I know her. She'll help you if you need it."

"All right. If the situation arises, I'll contact her."

"Thank you. Well, I should go. Noriko will be home any minute."

"Tomorrow, same time?"

Aaliyah clasped the phone, wishing she could speak with him longer. But it was too great a risk. "Same time," she said softly.

"Good night."

"Good night."

Aaliyah disconnected the call and sat there for a moment, staring off into space, imagining Kai's face. She missed him so much it hurt. With a sigh, she placed the phone back in its hiding place.

The front door burst open, and Aaliyah quickly put the board back into place and vaulted to her feet. She ran into the kitchen just as Vanessa came storming down the hallway, four members of the Guard on her heels.

"What is the meaning of this?" Aaliyah demanded.

"Aaliyah, you are suspected of conspiring against the priestess."

"I have never—"

"Search it," Vanessa ordered. The guards spread out through the house.

Aaliyah stepped forward, her heart racing as one of the guards disappeared into her bedroom. "You have no right. I am a member of the High Council."

Vanessa narrowed her eyes. "As was Kai before he was banished. Apparently being a member does not negate the possibility of violating the rules. In fact, your close relationship with an exile means you may have already been influenced."

"Prefect." A guard stepped out of her bedroom, two objects in his hands. Aaliyah's phone and laptop.

Aaliyah's stomach fell. She must not have placed the board back correctly.

Vanessa smiled as she took the phone. "Well, let's see what these tell us."

Chapter Twenty-One

BALTIMORE, MARYLAND

LANEY SAT in Henry's office at the Chandler Estate. She had wanted to see if she could find anything else on Jen's mother, and she didn't want Jen knowing what she was doing. Not that she wouldn't tell Jen later; she just wanted to have all the information at her fingertips when she did.

But her search had revealed little. Vanessa Rutledge had lived in San Francisco for six years before she had disappeared. During that time, she'd had no job, but she did have a large bank account that money was regularly deposited in —and that money came from Honu Keiki. She knew from their previous research into Honu Keiki that exiles were given a financial package when they left, one that would allow them to set up anywhere in the world. Vanessa Rutledge's financial situation fit that bill.

But besides that, there was very little information on the woman. Her social security number had been issued the same year she moved to San Francisco. When DCF had looked into her, they'd found no relatives or friends. Even neighbors said they barely knew her. The only place she was known to go to regularly was a gym in the neighborhood.

Laney pulled up Vanessa Rutledge's driver's license. The picture did look shockingly like Honu Keiki's Vanessa. Laney knew Jen had always wondered what had happened to her mother, but Laney didn't want *this* to be the answer. From what Laney could tell, there was no warmth in this woman.

But maybe I'm wrong. Maybe she's cold now because she lost her daughter.

Laney frowned. If this was Vanessa Rutledge, how exactly did she end up back at Honu Keiki? And why didn't she take Jen with her?

"Laney?"

"Hm?" She looked up. Tiffany Youler, the head of Public Relations for the Chandler Group, stood in the doorway.

Tiffany nodded to the laptop. "Sorry, I know you still have a lot to do, but I've had reports of our people fielding some unusual phone calls."

"Phone calls? From who?"

"Mike Wallace's research team."

Mike Wallace was the host of the top Sunday night news program. The show was insanely popular and highlighted issues of the day. But why on earth would he be calling Chandler Group employees?

"What does he want to know?" Laney asked. "Is this about the school?"

Tiffany shook her head. "No. He wanted to know about you."

"Me specifically?"

"Yes."

"Did he say why?"

"No. The people who called just said they were doing some advance work for a possible show."

It must be about the bridge accident. That had received a lot of press, particularly the Cleo angle, but so far Laney had been left out of it, beyond the fact that she was Cleo's owner. "Did they ask about Cleo?"

"No. Not at all."

"Did anyone tell them anything?"

Tiffany smiled. "No one would even admit they knew you."

Laney gave a small laugh. "Thanks, Tiffany. I'll take care of it."

Tiffany disappeared from the doorway, and Laney sat back. What was that all about? Even if it was related to the bridge incident, that certainly wasn't national news. So why on earth would Mike Wallace be interested?

Maybe he's doing something on Cleo or the school. But why ask about me?

She reached for the desk phone and dialed. Henry answered after one ring.

"Hey, Lanes. What's going on?"

"I think we might have a problem."

Chapter Twenty-Two

MALAMA ISLAND, HAWAII

THE PRIESTESS STORMED down to Vanessa's office. When her attendant opened the door, it was a struggle for the priestess not to bowl the man over. She glared at him to let him know her displeasure with his slowness.

Vanessa got to her feet, and the other three guards immediately snapped to attention. The priestess barely spared them a glance. "Leave us."

The guards filed out, closing the door behind them.

"Well?" the priestess demanded.

"She contacted the ring bearer anonymously four months back. That is how the attempt on Brian Hansen was thwarted in North Carolina."

When the attempt to take out Hansen had been interrupted, the priestess had wondered if someone had tipped the ring bearer off. But no one in Malama was supposed to have the means to communicate with anyone off the island, so when the ring bearer showed up, the priestess had thought it was just happenstance.

Now I know it was one of my people. Traitor.

"What else?"

Vanessa held up a phone. "I believe she has been in contact with Kai since his exile. She receives a call from the same cell every night at the same time. I had one of our people trace it. The cell towers for the call are in Argentina."

The priestess narrowed her eyes. "How did this happen? How did they even have this equipment?"

"I assume Kai smuggled it in. The logs indicate it's been in Aaliyah's possession for over two years."

"Is there anything in her computer history about Project Jerusalem?"

"No, but she was researching Jerusalem within the last few hours."

How does she even know about the project? "Has she contacted the ring bearer about it?"

"No—not by phone or email."

Well that was a small blessing. She could have blown everything.

"I will have her brought before the community in the morning and banished," Vanessa said.

The priestess nodded—and then frowned. "No. Let's not be hasty."

"But priestess, she has grossly violated your dictates."

"True. But the community is disturbed about the recent banishments, and the move is causing some... discomfort. Besides, Aaliyah is very well-liked."

"But you are the priestess. You are loved."

The priestess smiled at Vanessa. Vanessa believed duty came above all else. She had never understood the role emotions played in other people's lives and actions. It made her an excellent soldier; she received her commands and she carried them out. But it made her a lousy strategist.

"It is important to keep the community's faith," the priestess explained. "And Aaliyah's popularity can help us with that."

Vanessa frowned. "How?"

"By making her our ally. She has created some problems for us. Now it's time she cleaned them up."

Chapter Twenty-Three

BALTIMORE, MARYLAND

HENRY PUT down the phone and stared out the window. He'd just finished speaking with Mike Witt, Jen's brother. He had also received a phone call from Mike Wallace's advance team. They had moved on from the people on the periphery of Laney's life to those in her inner circle: him, Jake, Patrick, Jen, Jordan, Yoni, Matt, and Mike. They'd all been contacted.

There was a knock on his door, and Jake entered.

Henry took one look at his face and knew it wasn't good news. "How many?" he asked.

"At least another dozen have received phone calls."

"Has any one said anything?"

"No. But you know someone will."

"I don't get it. Why the sudden interest in Laney?"

Jake shrugged. "It must be the bridge thing. The second video was much more focused on Laney."

"Yeah, but she didn't do anything. She was just standing there."

"And giving orders, including controlling Cleo."

"We need to find out exactly what the Wallace team is up to."

"Henry, I think we know what they're up to," Jake said quietly.

Henry felt a weight press down on his shoulders. "Yes. They want to expose Laney."

Chapter Twenty-Four

AFTER LANEY HAD SPOKEN with Henry, he'd assured her he'd look into everything and would take care of it, and Laney had gone to the school to try and get some work done. But she hadn't been able to focus. She had the sinking feeling there were more holes in the dam than they could plug. So finally, she'd driven back to the estate and jogged up the three floors to his office.

Henry had been frowning but smiled when he caught sight of her. "I'm surprised you managed to stay away as long as you did."

"What do you know?"

Henry stood up and walked around his desk, gesturing to the couch. Laney took a seat and Henry sat next to her.

His purple eyes looked serious. "Okay, would you like the good news or the bad news first?"

"Good, please."

"Well, no one affiliated with the Chandler Group has agreed to speak with Mike Wallace's research team."

"Okayyy," Laney drew out the word; Henry did not

seem as happy as he should be about that outcome. "What's the bad news?"

"A few other people have."

Oh, crap. "Who?"

"A few of the men from the camp in Montana, a US diplomat in Ecuador, one of Rocky's superiors, a US source in China, and one of Grayston's followers."

Laney sat back, stunned. Most, if not all, of those people were associated with the Fallen and her work as the ring bearer. Which meant...

"They know I'm the ring bearer."

Henry took her hand. "No. I had Danny hack into their computer system. They don't seem to know about the ring bearer. But they *are* compiling a list of Laney's greatest adventures."

"Wait—Danny? Henry, we said we were keeping them out of—"

Henry cut her off. "And this was an emergency. We need to know what they know so we can prepare. Danny got in, got the info, and got out. He's not part of this."

"Okay, good, that's good. But why are they focused on me?"

"I don't know. It wasn't in any of the files Danny went through. But the segment on you is scheduled to appear tomorrow. I guess we'll find out then."

Chapter Twenty-Five

THE HOURS until Sunday evening were excruciating. Each minute felt like an hour. Every time Laney left the estate, she felt like she had eyes on her. She knew it was only in her mind, but she couldn't help it. She tried to fill her time with projects, just to keep herself from thinking about what was coming. Because she knew that whatever it was, was going to be bad. Really bad.

To pass the time, Jake had prepared dinner for her, Henry, Jake, Patrick, and Jen. They had kept the conversation flowing, cracking jokes, trying to make it seem like any other evening. But Laney couldn't help but watch the clock.

It would have been easier if they'd had some idea what the focus of the piece was going to be. Almost everyone Laney knew had received a phone call within the last week from Wallace's research team. Some of those people had told Laney about this directly; she wasn't worried about them. It was the people who hadn't contacted her that she was concerned about.

At least Jen seems to be doing better, Laney thought. Not that

Laney was surprised. Jen had pushed her concern for herself aside and was now determined to help Laney however she could. It was her way. So Laney had held off on telling her what she'd found out about Vanessa. She wondered if she ever would. After all, if Jen really wanted the information, she would do the same search herself. *I'll just have to play it by ear.*

Finally, show time rolled around, and they all crowded into Laney's small living room to watch *The Sunday Report*. Laney sat in the middle of the couch with Jake on one side and Patrick on the other. Henry and Jen sat on the loveseat. Laney's nerves were stretched thin. She had never enjoyed being the center of attention. She loved spending time with people, but she'd rather the focus was on someone else. Even birthday parties made her uncomfortable, at least birthday parties for her. So the idea of the entire nation—or at least Mike Wallace's viewing audience—watching her was enough to make her feel sick.

Her uncle took her hand. "It'll be all right. Whatever happens, it'll be all right."

Laney squeezed his hand. She was grateful he was there.

"It's starting." Henry turned up the volume as the opening credits for *The Sunday Report* began to play. Laney let out a breath. Jake placed his hand on her thigh, and Laney wrapped her free hand in his.

"Good evening." Mike Wallace, age fifty-eight, strolled across the set of *The Sunday Report*. Newspaper headlines from the week were splashed along the wall behind him. "Tonight, our first story is a little unusual. Normally, we focus on stories that you've heard about and bring them into more detail. But tonight, we're going to introduce you to a story that has been hidden from view. The story of a woman named Delaney McPhearson."

Laney cringed as an image of her appeared on the wall next to Mike.

"You may not know the name, but by the end of this segment, you will never forget her."

The image next to Mike shifted, and Laney gasped. It was the house she had lived in with her parents. "Delaney grew up in a middle class neighborhood with two loving parents. From all reports, they were a happy family—one that was torn part by tragedy."

An image of her parents' car after the accident appeared.

Laney felt lightheaded. Mike continued a quick recitation of her upbringing under the care of a Roman Catholic priest. The first twenty years of her life were summed up in two minutes.

"But while Delaney's upbringing may have been unusual, it was nothing compared to what was to come."

An African-American man appeared on the screen, and Laney recognized him. He was one of the men from Montana. "Oh, sure," he said. "I remember her. How could I forget her? She's the reason I'm alive." The man then launched into the tale of how Laney helped the captives escape the enclosure.

That story then segued into an interview with the US diplomat to Ecuador, who recounted Laney's role in helping the Shuar people. He concluded by saying, "I have no doubt that without Delaney McPhearson's involvement, the Shuar people would have suffered even greater losses. She is a hero."

A short commercial break was followed by interview after interview, each of them celebrating Laney's heroic deeds.

Laney stared at the screen in mute horror, but Mike

Wallace just smiled. "And that brings us to her latest heroic deed—on the Francis Scott Key Bridge in Baltimore, Maryland."

A video of the accident played. The recording was apparently taken by someone standing on the bridge, but on the other side from where the accident took place.

"Did you see someone taping?" Jake asked.

"No." Laney watched as she vaulted out of her car toward the bus. The scene replayed exactly as she remembered it and as the news chopper had shown. But the news chopper had focused primarily on the school bus; this camera operator never strayed from Laney.

Who took this?

By keeping Laney in the shot at all times, this video showed two things very clearly: that the bus fell off the bridge just as she dropped her hands; and that when the tanker blew, her movements coordinated perfectly with the movement of the flames and shrapnel off the bridge.

Oh no.

The TV cut back to Mike Wallace in the studio, a frame of the video frozen on the wall next to him. It showed Laney kneeling on the bridge with Cleo at her side. "So, just who is Delaney McPhearson? One thing is obvious: she is a hero. But I think she is also so much more than that."

A new still filled the screen: Laney in the cats' enclosure, standing at the top of the hill, the cats lined up on either side of her as if posed. Mike Wallace's voice accompanied the picture. "Delaney McPhearson has saved hundreds, maybe a thousand lives. And she has done so without drawing any attention to herself. But who exactly is she? And what incredible gifts does she have? I think it's time for America—no, the world to find out."

No one said a word as Henry shut off the TV. Laney

just stared at it, feeling completely exposed. Her life had just been laid bare for everyone to see.

"Laney?" Jen asked quietly.

Laney pulled her gaze from the dark TV screen to Jen's concerned face. "I—I—" She went silent. She couldn't form a thought.

"How did they get all that?" Jake asked. "Somebody had to have led them through each incident, telling them what to look for."

"I'll get everyone on it," Henry said. "We'll find out who's behind this."

Inside, Laney knew it didn't matter who was behind it. The world now knew she was different.

Her life was never going to be the same again.

Chapter Twenty-Six

THE PRESS SHOWED up at the estate almost as soon as the show had ended. Henry had ordered that no one from the press be allowed in, and no one was to say anything but a polite yet firm "no comment."

Laney was unaware of the press encampment until she woke the next morning and found a text from Henry warning her to keep her head down. She groaned. *Great. Now I'm a prisoner.* There was also a note from Jake on the nightstand, explaining that he was off to oversee security for both the estate and the school.

She leaned back against the headboard trying to figure out what that left for her to do. This situation couldn't last too long, could it? Another story would come along and push her out of the spotlight. She just had to wait it out. It would be annoying, but they'd lose interest soon, especially if they got nothing from her.

After a quick shower and change of clothes, Laney headed down to the kitchen, where she spied her laptop on the counter. She eyed it as she waited for her coffee. It was as if it was calling to her: *Come on, Laney, come see what everyone's saying.*

She sighed. *Fine. I'll just see how big a ruckus all this has caused and then get on with my day.* She pulled out a chair at the counter, opened the laptop to a search engine, and typed in "Delaney McPhearson."

She got five million hits.

With a shaky hand, she clicked on the news stories. Her jaw dropped as she read the first few headlines.

> *Miracle on the Francis Key Bridge*
> *Wonder Woman Discovered*
> *Delaney McPhearson, the World's First REAL Superhero*

And those were from the mainstream news wires. On the more out-there news wires, the headlines got even crazier:

> *Delaney McPhearson: The Alien Connection*
> *The Second Coming?*
> *The Rise of a Superwoman*
> *The Gods Walk Among Us*

Of course there were a couple of cool heads among the crowd, but they were paid very little attention when compared with their more excited counterparts.

Laney shook her head in disbelief. Barring those few outliers, all the articles seemed to be arguing the same thing: that she was some sort of mythical heroine with the powers of the gods. There were debates as to the origins of her abilities, from the New Age hypothesis that meditation was responsible, to the truly comic book-inspired theory that she was the victim of a chemical plant spill.

Laney sat at the counter going through page after page. Her image had been altered in some to depict her in a leotard and cape. In others she had a golden halo around her head. One site was set up basically as a fan club; they called themselves the McPhearsonites, and apparently had thousands of members.

There were also tons of news clips and YouTube videos where people excitedly reported having personally seen her perform miracles. One woman claimed Laney had flown into her burning house and saved her granddaughter. Another man claimed she had singlehandedly stopped his car from going over a cliff. Another claimed he had seen Laney and then, just a few minutes later, won thousands of dollars in a scratch-off game. Laney's disbelief grew as all these people she'd never seen before attributed their good fortune to simply catching a glimpse of her.

By the end of two hours, Laney's temples throbbed. Had the world gone nuts? Did people actually believe this stuff, or were they just trying to get their own fifteen minutes?

Laney wasn't sure if she should laugh or cry. Her world was being dissected. Pictures of her were being pored over by complete strangers looking for signs of her saintliness or alien-ness. Viewing totals for the TV broadcast weren't available yet, but an online version of "the McPhearson segment" had gone viral. It was already at fifty million views and climbing.

Laney wrapped her sweater tighter around herself, feeling exposed. This was insane. Her anonymity was now a thing of the past. She wasn't ready to face all of this. It was too much.

And with that thought, she realized exactly who she wanted to talk to about it.

Chapter Twenty-Seven

LANEY WALKED down the long hall at the SIA facility. Hanz ran his card over the scanner at the door. "He's in the courtyard."

"Thanks," Laney said as she stepped inside. She crossed the room and went through the open door at the back into a small, walled-in courtyard. Green grass and a small plastic patio set were all that offered color. It was an unusual spot for the world's only immortal.

Cain stood up from the table, his black eyes glittering. He smiled and held out his hands. "I didn't know you were coming."

Placing the takeout bag on the table, Laney placed her hands in his, surprised yet again at the direction their relationship had taken. He was Cain, the world's first murderer. When Laney had first learned of him, she was chasing him down to prevent him from harming her mother.

And now? Now, he was like her own personal guru, her sounding board. But she didn't question it; she just went with it. Because more than anyone on this planet, he had helped her truly understand what it meant to be the ring bearer—and what the cost might be.

She squeezed his hands before pointing at the bag. "I brought coffee and Danish."

Cain gestured for her to take a seat, then pulled out a coffee. He took a sip and let out a heartfelt sigh. "Oh, that is good. You're spoiling me."

Laney looked around his prison. "I don't know about that."

"This?" He shook his head. "Do you know, these last months that I've been in here, I have been me, really *me*, for the first time in a millennium? Do you know how freeing that is? I don't have to hide who I am. I don't have to look over my shoulder or worry. I'm at peace."

Laney studied him, but she got no sense that he was lying. He did seem at peace. There was a healthy glow to his Mediterranean complexion, his dark hair was neat and tidy, and he seemed serene.

"But I sense you're not as peaceful," he said. "I saw the broadcast."

Laney groaned. "I think everyone saw the broadcast."

"Has it been bad?"

"You could say that. The media has been camped outside the estate. I only managed to get here because I took the chopper."

"I'm honored."

Laney pulled an apple Danish from the bag and took a bite. She placed another one on a napkin in front of Cain, who nodded his thanks. They ate in companionable silence.

Finally, Cain wiped the side of his mouth and spoke. "So, who pointed Mike Wallace toward you?"

Jake's comment from last night repeated in Laney's

mind. *Somebody had to have led them through each incident, telling them what to look for.* "I don't know. And I don't know why."

Cain frowned. "It wasn't one of your people?"

"I don't see how. The people who know about those events—they're the people I trust the most in the world. Henry, Jake, Jen, my uncle, the Witt brothers. No one else knows all the details."

"Surely someone must—"

"No. Not at Chandler. We make sure that the people working on each Fallen incident haven't worked on previous ones. We don't want anyone to have the full picture. I suppose someone *could* piece everything together, but it would require a lot of work."

Cain studied her for a long moment. "And this happened shortly after Samyaza reappeared."

Laney looked at him in surprise. "Samyaza? Why would you think it's her? I mean, as much as I hated the piece, at least it was positive. I can't see why she'd want to start a fan club for me. Do you know I have a fan club by the way? They're called the McPhearsonites."

A smile lurked at the edges of Cain's mouth. "Well, that's a horrible name, but I'll have to see if I can join."

"Ha, ha—very funny. But seriously, why would Samyaza want any of this?"

Cain shrugged, but Laney caught the worry on his face. "Perhaps I'm wrong, but the timing is suspect. And I don't believe in coincidences."

Laney didn't believe in coincidences either. But Samyaza? "I just can't see what she would have to gain by all of this. It doesn't benefit her."

"Ah, but that is the problem with Samyaza." Cain took another sip of his coffee. "You don't see her angle until it is too late."

Chapter Twenty-Eight

BACK AT THE ESTATE, Laney felt restless. She couldn't go anywhere, couldn't even visit the cats, not with a small media circus outside the gate. She was in Henry's office looking for something to occupy her, but she couldn't find the papers she thought she'd left here. *Did I take them back to my cottage?*

Her phone rang, and she grabbed it. Luckily—and almost miraculously—no one in the press had gotten hold of her private number. If they ever did, she'd have to get rid of her phone. She felt isolated enough as it was.

"Delaney?" It was Jerry from the front gate.

"Hi, Jerry. What's going on?"

"There's someone at the front gate who wants to speak with you."

Laney imagined it was someone from the media. "Who is it?"

"His name is Kai Dawson. He says he's a friend of someone named Aaliyah. He said she doesn't have a last name."

That came as a surprise. "Have you searched him?"

"Yes. No weapons. And he doesn't look like one of the media types."

"Okay. Can you escort him to the main house? I'll meet you at the back veranda."

"Will do. Be there in five."

Laney made her way down the stairs, wondering at this unexpected arrival. Aaliyah had never mentioned a Kai, but that didn't necessarily mean anything. Was he a member of Honu Keiki? Had Aaliyah sent him? Was she in trouble?

She went out to the back patio. The security cart was already crossing the yard toward her, and in the passenger seat was a man with dark hair, dark eyes, and a definite Polynesian look. He looked back at her intently but she got no other readings from him. He wasn't a Fallen or a nephilim—just a regular human.

The cart stopped, and Jerry nodded at her. "You want me to wait?"

Laney shook her head as Kai got out. "No, we'll be okay."

Jerry turned the cart and headed back to the main gate.

Kai climbed the stairs to the veranda, and Laney held out her hand. "Kai? I'm Delaney McPhearson." She could see the exhaustion on his face. And the fear.

Laney shook her head. "Aaliyah has told me about you. She respects you a great deal."

"And I her. Is she all right?"

"I'm not sure."

Laney gestured to the table behind her. "Perhaps you can tell me what's going on."

Laney took a seat, and Kai sat across from her. "I am—*was* a member of Honu Keiki."

"You were exiled?"

Kai's face was tight. He gave her an abrupt nod. "Yes."

"How long ago was that?"

"It's been just over a week. But every night I spoke with Aaliyah. Until four nights ago. I haven't been able to reach her since."

"Perhaps the switchboard—"

"I did not call her through the switchboard. I got cell phones for Aaliyah and me two years ago—just in case."

"Just in case of what?"

Kai met her gaze. "Honu Keiki is not what it once was."

"You mean the priestess."

Kai nodded. "I think she knows Aaliyah is not loyal. I think Aaliyah's in trouble. In our last phone call, she mentioned a project: Project Jerusalem. She didn't know what it was about, but she was going to look into it. And I haven't heard from her since. Something's happened. The priestess got to her somehow. I know it."

Laney studied the tall man before her. She could tell he was truly worried for Aaliyah. And Laney had to admit, she was already concerned about not being able to reach Aaliyah herself. And then there was the priestess. Although Aaliyah had never said anything directly, Laney had gotten the impression she did not fully trust the woman.

"What do you think of the priestess?" Laney asked.

Kai looked away. "A priestess has always guided our people. It is our way. We believe in the great Mother. The priestess is our representative of her on earth to guide our people on the path."

Laney was familiar with the Great Mother. She was part of a religion that predated Christianity and rivaled Judaism in its ancient roots. And she was usually pictured with two large cats seated next to her throne, one of whom was a leopard.

As if on cue, Cleo walked up the veranda steps. Jake had snuck her onto the estate while Laney was visiting Cain.

Kai's eyes grew large.

"It's all right," Laney said, "She's not a threat." *You scared him.*

Not a danger, Cleo responded, before coming to sit on Laney's right.

Laney placed a hand on her back. *Still, you should have waited until I called you.*

Kai looked between the two of them, his expression changing from fear to awe. "She—are you talking to her?"

Laney nodded. "We understand each other."

"I had heard the ring bearer could, but to see it, it's—" Kai shook his head. "It's incredible. Ever since Aaliyah told me you were the ring bearer, I wondered about which of the tales were true. Can you control the weather?"

"Control it? No. But I can ask it to do what I wish."

"What about demons? Can you control them?"

"Yes."

"Can you fly?"

Laney smiled. "Not in my bag of tricks—although that would be fun."

"I'm sorry. I'm asking too many questions."

"No, it's fine. It's actually nice when I meet someone who understands."

Kai shook his head. "We have some people at Honu with some abilities."

Laney had heard about that. "I worry sometimes that people will fear what I can do."

"But you're the ring bearer. You're a force of good."

Laney laughed. "Well, you're officially hired as my PR man should I ever need one." *Although right now, I'd like less of a PR presence.*

Kai smiled, but then she saw his anxiety return, like a cloud moving across his face.

"How can I help you?" she asked softly.

"You can help me to help Aaliyah. I think this Project Jerusalem is important. I was hoping you could learn about it and find out if Aaliyah is safe."

"I'll call Honu. See if I can reach Aaliyah. But I've tried before. She's never gotten back to me." Not that that would stop Laney now. She wanted to know what Project Jerusalem was, and she wanted to know once and for all what the Companion Killers had to do with Honu Keiki. "There's something that's been bothering me ever since everything happened with the Companion Killers."

"That was a dark time."

Laney nodded. "I know and I don't think I've ever really understood the motivation behind it. It all seemed to revolve around the ritual of the end and the beginning. Do you know anything about it?"

"It's an ancient ritual from our earliest days. When the world began to break apart, our ancestors called on the Great Mother, but she did not answer. We thought we had angered her. So we set out to make things right—to take down the ones who were causing harm. It was a dark time in our world."

"How often has the ritual been used?"

"Too often. It became incorporated into other cultures, and they shifted it from the ones doing harm, to simply sacrifices to avoid harm. The ritual is the origin of human sacrifices—an attempt to appease the gods. But it was never intended that way."

"What was the intention?"

"To remind us of our duty—to this world and one

another. I believe the Companion Killers were trying to return the ritual to its first incarnation."

Laney pictured Sheila in the cave, her blood spread across the floor. "By targeting people without abilities?"

Kai nodded. "They viewed them as enablers. Without them, the evil ones could not move their plans forward. The thinking…" He shook his head. "It was desperate."

"And they honestly believed that with the ritual they would be able to prevent the end of days?"

Kai looked taken aback. "No. Through the completed ritual, they meant to bring it about."

Laney went still. "Bring it about?"

"Yes. To the Companion Killers, the end of days was just an end to this period of human existence."

Laney had to ask. "Kai, in the ritual, blood must be shed, right?"

"That's right."

"Does who the sacrifice is matter?"

"No, just the deaths."

Laney felt lightheaded.

"What is it?"

"We stopped the Companion Killers from killing their intended sacrifices. But they all died in the process."

Kai paled. "The ritual was completed."

"But it's just an ancient tale," Laney said. "I mean, you can't bring about the end of an era through a few deaths."

Kai swallowed. "Are you sure? After all, *you* were just a legend to us as well until a few months ago."

"Maybe. But there must be more to it. No one even knows about these deaths."

Kai looked up, his eyes worried. "The priestess does. And there's one other thing."

"What?"

"Aaliyah's daughter Noriko, she has the gift of sight. She had a vision the other night." Kai recounted what Noriko had seen.

"Is it possible it was a dream?" Laney asked.

"Possible, yes. Likely? No."

Laney had a vision of the world burning. She shuddered. *I need to learn what's going on with Honu Keiki.*

Chapter Twenty-Nine

MALAMA ISLAND, HAWAII

THE PRIESTESS WATCHED as the five Council members filed out of the room. The guards by the doors followed, closing the doors behind them.

These Council meetings were beginning to annoy the priestess. She knew she needed to keep up the pretense of the Naacal playing a role in the running of Honu Keiki, but honestly, it was getting tedious. When they reached Perth, the first thing she was going to do was disband the Naacal.

I just have to hold on a little bit longer, she thought before turning to Vanessa.

Vanessa had stepped into the room halfway through the meeting, and the priestess had immediately known something was wrong. "What is it?" the priestess asked.

"There have been some rumblings."

"What *type* of rumblings?"

"People are expressing doubts about the move. Wondering why it's being done in the way it is."

The priestess had expected this. About half the people had been moved so far; families had been separated. "I will speak with the community this afternoon and quiet any fears."

Vanessa bowed her head. "Thank you, priestess."

"Is there something more?"

"It's... the Aaliyah matter."

The priestess curled her lip. *Aaliyah*. She should have killed her when she had the chance. "What specifically is the problem?"

"The Council is wondering where she is, since she has not been at the last three meetings."

The priestess shrugged. She was still angry at Aaliyah's betrayal, but the woman was now fully under her control. "Tell them she's been ill. That's all they need to know." Her people would do as they were told, and none would be the wiser until it was too late to do anything.

"The other problem is Delaney McPhearson."

The priestess narrowed her eyes. That one would not be as easily led. "She's still trying to reach Aaliyah?"

"Yes."

The priestess drummed her fingers on the side of her chair. What to do? Delaney would not simply forget about Aaliyah. It was not in her nature. She'd need to be convinced that there were no problems.

She smiled. "I think Aaliyah should make a phone call."

Chapter Thirty

BALTIMORE, MARYLAND

LANEY GOT Kai settled into one of the guest houses. He was exhausted. And terrified.

But Laney wasn't sure what to make of his story. Maybe Aaliyah had just decided it would be easier to stop communicating with him. Long distance relationships were tough at the best of times, never mind with the inability to ever see one another again. But even if that was true, Noriko's vision was troubling to say the least. And Laney wasn't about to just write it off.

There was a benefit to Kai being here, too: it might actually help her get to the bottom of the Vanessa mystery. As a member of the Naacal, Kai must know a great deal about the people. Perhaps he could answer some questions. Laney sighed. *And then I can figure out how to tell Jen what I've learned.*

Laney sat down at the conference table and dialed Honu Keiki; she had the number memorized by now. When Keon's familiar face appeared, she said, "Hi, Keon. It's Delaney McPhearson—again."

Keon's voice was apologetic. "Dr. McPhearson. It's nice to speak with you. I have relayed your messages to Aaliyah."

"Thank you. Could you relay one more? Tell her I need to speak with her. It's important this time. Please have her call me as soon as she can."

"I will."

"Thank you, Keon. Take care."

"You too."

Laney hung up. She wasn't sure why she'd thought this time would be different. She needed a new approach. But what?

She did some internet searches on Honu Keiki, Perth, and rituals. But almost an hour later, all she had to show for her efforts was the beginning of a headache. She ran her hands through her hair and stood up. She needed some fresh air.

But just then her computer beeped, and when she glanced over, she was surprised to see the area code for Malama Island. She almost knocked over her water in her haste to accept the call.

Aaliyah appeared on screen, unsmiling. "Delaney, I hear you've been trying to reach me."

Laney wondered at Aaliyah's tone and her appearance. The woman was very subdued. There were bags under her eyes, and she looked like she'd lost weight. Had she been ill? But Laney forced a smile to her face. "Aaliyah, it's good to see you."

"You too."

"Is everything all right?"

Aaliyah smiled back, but Laney thought it looked forced. "Of course. Honu Keiki is paradise, after all."

What? "Yes, so I've heard. Um, I just wanted to check in and make sure everything was fine."

"That is very kind of you. But yes, everything is wonderful. Thank you for your concern. Is there anything I can help you with?"

"No. Um, like I said, I just wanted to check in."

"Well, thank you for your concern. And the priestess wanted me to convey that if there is anything the ring bearer needs, we are at your disposal."

The screen went blank.

Laney sat back and stared at the screen in confusion. *Well, that was a little short.*

After a moment, Laney replayed the recording of the call. Aaliyah had been polite enough, but her usual warmth was absent. Something was off. And as she listened to the call again, watching Aaliyah, she thought the woman looked stiff, scared—but trying to pretend she wasn't.

Or am I just imagining things because of Kai?

Laney watched the video yet again. Aaliyah sat perfectly still, except for one finger that tapped nervously on the tabletop. *Is she...?* Laney focused on the tapping for a moment. *Oh my God, she is.*

It wasn't random tapping. There was a pattern to it. Three short taps, three longer taps, and then three shorter again. The pattern repeated over and over again.

Laney's elation at recognizing there was a message was overwhelmed by her concern at what the message was:

Morse code for *SOS*.

Chapter Thirty-One

MALAMA ISLAND, HAWAII

AALIYAH STEPPED BACK from the screen, her whole body feeling shaky. She vacillated between hoping Laney had bought her lies and praying she hadn't.

"Well done," Vanessa said.

Aaliyah looked up, feeling her anger rise. "Well done? Do you even realize what you're doing? The type of person you're becoming?"

Before the call, Vanessa had pulled Aaliyah from her cell and ordered her to shower and change clothes. Aaliyah had refused at first—until Vanessa softly whispered all the accidents that could befall a young woman on the island.

"I am following the dictates of our leader," Vanessa replied, "as any good member of Honu would do."

"By threatening the life of my daughter?" Aaliyah narrowed her eyes and dropped her voice. "*Your* daughter?"

Vanessa's nostrils flared. "She is *not* my daughter. Giving birth to her does not make her mine. I have no allegiance to her. My allegiance is only to the priestess."

She grabbed Aaliyah roughly by the arm, pulled her

into the hallway, and pushed her toward the two guards waiting there. "Take her back to her cell."

Aaliyah twisted in the guards' grip so she could look at Vanessa. "This isn't right, Vanessa. You know that."

Vanessa's tone was cold and unflinching. "The priestess determines what is right. Not you."

Chapter Thirty-Two

BALTIMORE, MARYLAND

LANEY'S WORRIES for Aaliyah had stayed at the forefront of her mind all night. She had played and replayed the tape, and she definitely wasn't imagining it: Aaliyah was sending an SOS. But Laney couldn't figure out a way to help.

By the next morning, she was bleary-eyed from lack of sleep. But when Matt called with an update, she woke right up.

"Laney, it looks like the Fallen *are* still being targeted."

"What? I thought that had stopped."

"No. They just started getting more clever about it. They're making it look like accidents."

"How?"

"In one instance, a car tore through a fence, and the driver just happened to get impaled by a stop sign in the heart."

"That's horrible."

"No—that's impossible. The stop sign was ten feet from

where the car went into the fence. Someone pulled it out and impaled the driver."

"But that means—"

Matt's voice was heavy. "Yes. I think it may be a Fallen who's committing these murders. I've gone back and looked at some other cases that we had written off as accidents. I believe we're looking at a pattern."

"So they're... turning on one another?" Laney wasn't sure how she felt about that. If the bad Fallen were taking each other out, that was great. But if the bad were turning against the good...

"Who's dying?" she asked. "The good guys or the bad guys?"

"I don't know. Some of them we've never even heard of. We only realized they were Fallen after their deaths."

"Which means they're probably the good ones staying out of the spotlight."

"Yes."

Laney closed her eyes. When the Companion Killers had been rounded up, Laney had believed they had also found the people targeting the Fallen. But apparently someone else was involved.

"It has to be Samyaza," she said.

"Probably," Matt replied. "Although I can't see why."

"Maybe she wanted them to join her and they refused." But Laney knew she was grasping. They were completely in the dark. "Have any of the Fallen shown up in any new videos?"

"No. That whole 'look at me' campaign seems to have died down."

Laney still couldn't figure out why they had done that. It was as if they had all wanted people to know that individuals with their skills existed.

Just like someone wants people to know your skills exist.

She went still at the thought. The Mike Wallace broadcast had come out of nowhere. And then there was the tape, the one in which Laney had clearly been the camera's focus—not the bus falling off the bridge, not the burning propane truck. Someone was deliberately trying to out her, the same way the Fallen had recently seemed to be trying to out themselves.

Was that possible? Was there a connection?

"Laney?" Matt asked.

"Sorry. I—um—just had a random thought. There's a lot going on right now."

"I saw the broadcast. Are you worried?"

"No. I mean, it's just odd seeing yourself laid out for the world to see."

"Are you going to do something about it?"

The media calls had finally quieted down, for the most part, as had the crowd outside the front gate. "No. Not right now. Hopefully, if I ignore it, it'll blow over. Besides, we have some other things to focus on."

"Care to share?"

"An unexpected visitor showed up at the estate last night." Laney told Matt about Kai's arrival and his concern for Aaliyah. She also told him about her own stilted conversation with Aaliyah and Aaliyah's tapped message. "But I can't figure out how to check on her," she finished. "The group has closed ranks. I can't just wander in. If I do, I'll be the one breaking the law."

"Well, no offense, but you *have* done that a few times before."

Laney laughed. "True. But not to just check on someone. And I'd like to point out that those previous cases were all life and death, and therefore, no laws were really broken."

"That's your answer then."

Laney frowned. "I'm not following."

"Use the law. Honu Keiki is a closed group. But even closed groups are subject to the law. Look at Scientology."

Laney tried to see where he was going with this. Scientology was classified as a religion, although many people regarded it as a cult. Its beliefs were developed by science fiction writer L. Ron Hubbard, who focused on the spiritual rather than the physical nature of an individual. While in theory, the principles sounded good, Scientology had been plagued by accusations of abuse, extortion, blackmail, brainwashing, embezzlement, and the list went on. The book *Going Clear* and the associated documentary exposed the unattractive underbelly of the group. But how any of that related to her being able to see Aaliyah she wasn't getting.

"I still don't—" She went still. "Are you referring to Miscavige's wife?"

"Exactly."

Following the death of Hubbard in 1986, a member named David Miscavige took over. In 2005, David Miscavige's wife went missing, and in 2013, actress Leah Remini filed a missing persons report. The LAPD managed to track her down. The cult had to produce her."

"Will that work? If Kai files a missing persons report?"

"He'll have to do it in Hawaii, but I'm sure you can persuade the officers to allow you to investigate it."

Laney smiled. "You're brilliant, Matt."

"I do have my moments. So, when are you leaving?"

"As soon as I can get a plane up and running."

Chapter Thirty-Three

ARRANGING everything she needed took a few hours. Laney wanted to make sure there were police she could trust; the last time she'd received the help of police officers, the officers had been in Honu Keiki's pocket. But she'd gotten some recommendations from people Matt trusted, so hopefully she'd have better luck this time. She'd also spoken with Kai. He'd been thrilled with the plan and at the idea of going back to Malama.

Now Laney just had to have one more conversation before she left.

She rolled down her window at the gate to the school.

"Hi, Nate."

"Hey, Laney. How's it going?"

"Good. Have you seen Jen?"

Nate pointed to the right of the school, where Laney could just make out a crowd.

"What's happening?"

"Soccer game."

"Great. Thanks."

She parked and made her way over to the field. Jen stood along the near sideline, cheering on the kids, and Henry stood on the far side. Opposing team captains.

Rolly sprinted down the field, dribbling between defenders like they weren't even there. He passed to Zach, who dribbled only a few feet before passing it back. And then there was just Danny and the goalie standing between Rolly and a goal.

Laney swallowed. *Come on, Danny.*

But Danny stood still, just watching Rolly approach, his head tilted to the side like Rolly was an interesting specimen he was trying to figure out.

Move, Danny. Move.

Rolly was only ten feet away when Danny burst forward. He timed his move perfectly: just as the ball left Rolly's foot, Danny intercepted it and kicked it halfway down the field to Lou.

Rolly stared at Danny in disbelief. "How—But—I—"

Danny just grinned.

Yoni blew the whistle, and Jen's team leapt in the air. Laney laughed. It was just good old-fashioned fun, and watching the kids enjoy themselves was better than any drug.

"Okay everyone," Henry yelled, "there's pizza and dessert in the cafeteria!"

The teenagers broke off into groups and headed inside. Lou walked up to Rolly and Danny twirling the ball. Zach joined them, and the four made their way inside together.

Henry caught sight of Laney and jogged over. "Hey. We could have used you earlier."

Laney grinned. "I wish I had come earlier. Did you see Danny?"

Henry's grin was huge. "Yup. Even if he wasn't on my team, he was awesome."

Jen joined them. "Hey. I didn't know you were coming over."

"Well, I wanted to let you guys know I'm heading out of town."

Henry frowned. "Why?"

She explained Matt's idea about Aaliyah and the missing persons report.

"When are you leaving?" Henry asked after a glance at Jen.

"In an hour. It's just going to be me and Kai at this point." She turned to Jen. "I wasn't sure if you wanted to come too."

Laney had told her last night about the phone conversation with Aaliyah, and more importantly, what she'd found out on Vanessa Rutledge. Laney had asked her what she wanted to do, but all Jen had said was she needed some time.

Jen met Laney's gaze. "I don't know."

"You don't have to come. But I wanted to let you know, in case you wanted to speak with her."

Henry stepped closer to Jen. "It may be your only chance."

"She hasn't wanted anything to do with me for twenty years," Jen said quietly.

"No. But that doesn't mean you aren't owed answers," Henry said.

"I… I just don't know."

"Well, I don't mean to rush you," Laney said, "but we'll be taking off in an hour."

"Well…" Jen hesitated. "I'll think about it. But don't wait for me, okay?" She turned and headed inside.

Henry watched her go. "This is really hard for her."

"I know. She keeps everything bottled up. And she's strong. But this? " Laney shook her head. "I don't know how you wrap your head around something like this."

"I'll talk to her. I think she should go. She needs to close this door." He went after Jen.

Laney watched her strong brother head after the woman he loved. Life might have closed a door for Jen when her mother left, but it had certainly opened another incredible one when it gave her Henry.

Blowing out a breath, Laney headed back to her car. She needed to get moving. She had to pick up Kai and head out. And for once, it wasn't life and death. She was just heading for a tropical island to check on a friend.

What could possibly go wrong?

Chapter Thirty-Four

THE AIRPORT WAS quiet as Jake pulled to a stop next to the plane. Kai leaned forward from the back. "We're taking that?"

Ahead of them stood the Chandler Lear jet. Laney smiled, remembering her own reaction the first time she'd flown in a private jet. "Yup."

Kai grinned.

As they got out of the car, Laney said, "Why don't you go check it out? I'll be in in a minute."

Kai needed no further urging. He headed for the plane, a spring in his step.

Laney looked around but saw no sign of Jen.

"Are you going to wait?" Jake asked.

Laney shrugged. "I don't know. I know it's a big decision. And I know she also doesn't want to leave Lou right now. But I wish she'd come. I think she'll regret it if she doesn't."

"What are the chances that Jen's mom is in Honu Keiki?"

"Well, I certainly don't think it's a coincidence. We keep coming across more and more of these 'coincidences,' and the more we do, the more I think there's a plan underneath it all."

Jake looked out over the horizon before turning back to Laney. "So, you're off to a Hawaiian island without me. I'm going to be petty and hope it rains."

Laney laughed. "Don't worry—I promise to have no fun whatsoever."

Jake pulled her in for a hug. Laney hugged him back. There was no passion in it like before, but there was the comfort of a good friend, and the change made her feel a pang of loss. As she pulled away, a thin line of electricity ran over her skin.

She turned to see Henry and Jen pulling up. Jen stepped out of the car, and Laney walked over and hugged her. "I'm glad you're coming."

"Me too. I think."

"You ready for this?" Laney asked.

Jen nodded. "Let's go."

Chapter Thirty-Five

WHEN THEY WERE SETTLED in the cabin, Laney contacted the pilot and let them know they were ready to go. Then she turned to Kai. "Kai, this is Jen Witt, a good friend and a Chandler operative."

Jen raised an eyebrow at the last part of Laney's description. But Laney just shrugged. Explaining that Jen was a nephilim who helped Laney in the fight against the Fallen just seemed a little too much for a casual introduction.

Kai extended his hand. "It's a pleasure to meet you."

"Kai here lived on Malama until recently," Laney explained.

"Really?" Jen asked.

Kai nodded. "Malama Island is without a doubt the most beautiful spot in the world." There was a wistfulness in his tone that was impossible to miss.

Laney kept her face expressionless. "When we arrive, we'll most likely have to deal with Vanessa, her being the head of security. What can you tell us about her?"

Jen tensed and leaned forward.

"She is..." Kai paused. "A hard woman. She's strong, focused, devoted to the priestess."

"Is there any chance she would willingly share information on Aaliyah?" Laney asked.

Kai shook his head. "Not without an order from the priestess."

"What's she like? Outside her position?" Jen asked.

"I don't know that I've ever seen her outside of her position. They are one and the same. She is always the head of the Guard."

"Does she have any family? Husband, children?" Laney asked.

"No. She's had two children, but in accordance with our customs, she does not raise them."

Jen paled. "Two?"

Kai didn't appear to notice Jen's reaction. "Yes." He frowned. "She actually did leave the island for a few years. I'm not sure why. When she returned, her child was not with her."

Laney wanted to reach out for Jen, but she also wanted to keep Kai talking, and she worried he'd be more careful with his answers if he knew why Jen was interested. Not that she thought he was trying to keep anything from Jen, but from what Laney could tell, he was a kind man. He would want to spare Jen the pain.

"And the other child? She doesn't raise her?" Jen asked.

Kai shook his head. "No. And I think the child is better off for it. She is a remarkable young lady."

"You know her?" Laney knew about the Honu Keiki tradition of having the children raised by someone other than the biological parents, but for some reason, she had thought it was done in secret—that no one knew what child went with what family. But now that she thought about it, she supposed that would be impossible with such a small community.

Kai smiled. "Oh, yes. Noriko is wonderful. Aaliyah has raised her."

Laney sat back, stunned. Noriko—the young woman who had saved Lou. The woman who Lou thought could speak with Cleo.

Jen must have been thinking much the same thing, because her mouth hung open as she stared at Kai.

He looked between the two of them. "Is something wrong?"

"No, no," Laney said quickly. "Noriko—we've heard of her is all."

"Aaliyah is very proud of her. I'm not surprised she's spoken of her."

Laney let him think that was how they knew of her, but her mind was spinning. Vanessa had two daughters. So Jen wasn't just going to meet her biological mother. She was going to meet her sister as well.

Chapter Thirty-Six

THE FLIGHT to Hawaii was long but uneventful. They all fell asleep, and before Laney knew it they were in Maui, speaking with the chief of police. Kai swore out his missing persons report, and two hours after they landed they were in a police chopper heading for Malama Island.

Laney enjoyed the incredible landscape as they passed. The ten square miles of Makanalua Peninsula sat beneath the world's highest sea cliffs. The peninsula had once been the site of a leprosy colony that was created in the mid nineteenth century. The last victims had survived until the 1940s, when a treatment was discovered, removing the contagious nature of the disease.

As Laney stared at the barren land, she imagined how isolated the people here must have felt. Leprosy was in essence a bacterial infection that resulted in open sores and nerve damage in the legs and arms. The earliest records of the disease went back to 600 BC, and cases were seen across the globe. The afflicted were ostracized from friends and family due to the high contagion rate. But by the year 2000, leprosy touched less than one in ten thousand people and was easily controlled.

Soon they were once again flying out over the beautiful blue ocean.

"There," Kai said, looking out the window. Ahead, a large island stood alone. Dark black volcanic rock could be seen at the edge near the sea, but beyond that it was a lush picture of green: palm trees, tall grasses, colorful flowers.

"It's beautiful," Jen said.

Kai nodded, pride and longing on his face. "Yes. It is."

The chopper flew closer, and Laney leaned over to Jen. "Do you realize we're actually landing in the chopper? That's new for us."

Jen gave a soft laugh. "Well if you want, we can leap from it when we're about fifty feet up."

"Tempting. But I suppose we should play it conservative."

"You're no fun."

As they approached, the pilot looked back at Laney. "You want to hail them?"

"Will do." Laney reached for the radio. "Attention Honu Keiki, this is Agent Delaney McPhearson with the SIA. We request landing to search for a missing person."

A reply was returned only a moment later. "Negative, Agent. Permission is not granted."

"Well, the 'request' was really me being polite. We *will* be landing, and we will be conducting a search. McPhearson out." She put the radio back.

"So, we're not trying to make friends, I see," Jen said dryly.

"What? I was being nice. They're the ones not interested in friends." She turned to Kai. "What kind of response will we receive when we land?"

"I'm not sure. No one has ever arrived without permission before."

Laney sighed. "Oh, goody, we're breaking new ground. Well, when we arrive, let Jen and I handle it. You stay in the chopper until we signal you. All right?"

Kai nodded.

"Here we go," the pilot announced.

Kai had already explained that there was an open field to the west of the residential areas. That's where they planned on landing. Laney said a small prayer as they headed in.

The chopper flew above homes and what looked like a step pyramid that would not have been out of place in Egypt. People looked up in surprise, but Laney saw no alarm in their faces, only curiosity. Yet as they set down in the field, a dozen individuals in dark uniforms burst from the trees, guns aimed at the chopper.

"Laney," Jen said.

"I see them." She turned to Kai. "Stay here." To the pilot she said, "If this gets dicey, get yourself and Kai out of here. If they don't shoot us, we'll see you in three hours."

The pilot nodded at the unfriendly group approaching the landing area. "Are you sure?"

"Yeah, but keep your radio on."

"Let's go." Jen pushed open the door. Laney was out right behind her.

Vanessa strode across the field, her dark eyes flashing. "You have violated the grounds of Honu Keiki—"

Laney cut her off. "We're here on official government business. If you don't step back, you'll all be under arrest."

Vanessa smirked. "And how do you plan on arresting us all?"

Laney kept her gaze on Vanessa as lightning bolts struck the ground on either side of the group. "I have my ways."

Vanessa stared her down before waving at her guards. "Put your weapons away. The *agents* are allowed here."

Slowly, and looking awfully confused, the guards lowered their weapons.

Laney smiled. "Gee, thanks Vanessa. How kind of you." To Jen she whispered, "What do you think?"

Jen's eyes were fixed on the guards. "I think I can take anyone who twitches toward their weapon."

"Kai," Laney called, keeping her back to the chopper. Kai stepped out and walked around. His appearance caused another stir among the guards.

Vanessa's face turned red. "This man has been exiled from our land for violations against the community! How dare you bring him here?"

Laney ignored her. "You all right?" she asked Kai.

He nodded, but his eyes were glued to one of the guards, who stared back with wide eyes.

"Kai? Who is that?" Laney asked softly.

"That's my son. Oasu."

I wasn't expecting that.

Laney walked straight up to Kai's son. "You. I think it would be best if a guard accompanied us. You've been drafted."

"Um, I—" Oasu's gaze shifted between Vanessa and his father.

"Absolutely not," Vanessa said.

Laney ignored her. "Which way to the temple?"

Vanessa spluttered, but Laney didn't give a damn that the woman was looking powerless in front of her squad.

"Uh, this way," Oasu said.

"Kai, why don't you lead up front with Oasu? After all, you two know this place better than we do."

Kai quickly stepped up next to his son, and they began to walk. Laney and Jen fell in step behind them. Vanessa stayed where she was, and Laney could feel the holes being burned into her back.

Jen leaned in toward Laney. "Guarding their backs in case Vanessa attempts to attack?"

"Something like that." Laney looked over her shoulder, but Vanessa remained where she was. Although if looks could kill...

"Are you okay?" Laney asked.

"I don't know. When I saw her, I recognized her. But when she began to speak..." Jen shrugged. "I guess I'm beginning to see how lucky I really am."

Chapter Thirty-Seven

THEY HEADED to Aaliyah's home first. Aaliyah wasn't there, but Noriko was. She had a confused look on her face until she spied Kai.

"Kai!" She dashed past Laney and Jen and lunged at him.

Kai twirled her around with a laugh. "It's only been a week."

"It feels much longer," Noriko said. She regained her feet and grinned up at him.

"Noriko, I'd like you to meet Delaney McPhearson and—"

Noriko's eyes went wide at the mention of Laney's name. "The ring bearer! It's an honor."

Laney was afraid she might try to curtsy. She quickly took Noriko's hands. "Thank you for helping Lou and Cleo," she said.

Jen stood quietly next to her watching Noriko, her little sister. They did look a great deal alike, although Jen was much taller and had darker eyes. But personality wise, they appeared to be complete opposites. It seemed as if every emotion Noriko had crossed her face—unlike Jen, who was a closed book even to those closest to her.

Laney placed a hand on Jen's arm. "And this is my good friend Jen Witt."

Noriko turned her light eyes to Jen and smiled. "It's a pleasure to meet you. Oh—Lou. She said your name on the island. She thought I was you for a minute."

Jen nodded. "Yes, and thank you. You did a great thing helping them."

Noriko blushed. "I was only part of the group. Oasu was there too."

Laney nodded her thanks to him.

"Noriko, where is Aaliyah?" Kai asked.

Noriko's mood dimmed. "I—I don't know. I asked Vanessa, and she assured me she was fine. But I haven't seen her in days. And so much has been happening."

Kai frowned. "What's been happening?"

Noriko looked warily at Laney and Jen.

"It's okay to speak in front of them," Kai said.

"Aaliyah's not the only one who's gone. Other people have disappeared."

"What? Who?"

"Families. I've asked, but no one knows where they've gone, just that it's part of the priestess's plan. I'm supposed to leave, too. This afternoon."

Laney felt shock course through her. The priestess had started to move them. Had Aaliyah been moved too? Or was she trapped somewhere here?

She turned to Oasu. "Do you know where Aaliyah is?"

Oasu shook his head. "I didn't even know she was missing. I've been on duty on the far side of the island. I just got back a short while ago."

"Could she be held in the temple? Can you get us in?" Jen asked.

"I can. But shouldn't we ask Vanessa first?"

Laney studied the young man. He was a member of the Guard, and she knew he was worried about going against the priestess. "Oasu, I have the permission of the United States government to find Aaliyah. The sooner I can do that, the better things will be for Honu Keiki. Now—is there anywhere on the island Aaliyah could be kept where she wouldn't be seen?"

"There are cells under the temple," Oasu said quickly.

"Cells?" Kai said.

Oasu nodded. "The priestess had them created a few years back. We were sworn to secrecy. But Aaliyah can't be there. Only the priestess could send someone there, and the priestess would never do that. Not to Aaliyah."

"I think we need to see the cells," Laney said.

"I'll take you," Oasu said.

Laney knew the man was about to have his illusions of the priestess shattered. In fact, all the members of Honu Keiki were. But it needed to happen.

Laney saw Noriko wrap her arm around Kai's. Her happiness at his reappearance was plain to see, although at the same time she had dark circles under her eyes, no doubt from worrying about Aaliyah.

I just hope we're not too late.

Chapter Thirty-Eight

THE PRIESTESS PACED her living room. She'd seen the helicopter and had heard the stir that it had caused. She'd dispatched her guards to see what was going on, but they hadn't returned yet. It was possible that it had just been a tourist chopper—they occasionally flew over the island, and once or twice one tried to land—but she didn't think that was the case here.

The doors to the room flew open and the priestess whirled around. Vanessa strode in, a few hairs out of place and sweat covering her. She must have run the whole way here.

"What is it?" the priestess asked.

"The ring bearer is here. With an associate."

The priestess was stunned. She had never imagined the ring bearer would dare show up *here*. After all, Aaliyah had spoken with the woman, assured her she was fine. "What does she want?"

"Aaliyah." Vanessa spat the name.

The priestess turned away, her mind running through

the possibilities, a thin bead of sweat rolling down her back. Taking Aaliyah... she'd miscalculated. But at least Vanessa had warned her of the ring bearer's arrival. *If she hadn't...*

The priestess shuddered at the thought.

The ring bearer would find Aaliyah. There was no changing that. But it wouldn't matter. Not in the grand scheme of things. In fact, the sooner they found Aaliyah, the better. Because the sooner they found her, the sooner the ring bearer would leave.

And the sooner the priestess could get back to work.

Because I am so very close.

"Let them find her."

Vanessa frowned. "Priestess?"

"Have the chopper ready."

Vanessa's mouth fell open. The priestess had bought the chopper last year, but had never had cause to use it. Only a select few on the island even knew it existed. It was only to be used in emergencies.

"Surely the ring bearer doesn't count as an emergency."

"Have it readied!" the priestess yelled, her fear clawing up her throat. "And make sure the ring bearer gets nowhere near me."

Chapter Thirty-Nine

LANEY AND JEN made their way to the temple, accompanied by Kai, Noriko, and Oasu. Along the way, Kai, Noriko, and Oasu asked everyone they passed if they had seen Aaliyah. No one had. But they all gave Laney and Jen incredulous looks—especially Laney. With her pale skin and red hair, she really stood out.

And if they knew who I really was, I bet they'd stare even more.

The one good thing about Honu Keiki, Laney thought, was that the people didn't have TVs. According to Kai, there was one in the temple, but the viewing of it was highly regulated. Which meant no one had seen the Mike Wallace show.

The temple dominated this part of the island. It towered over one hundred feet above them, and it really did look like it had been created thousands of years ago.

"It's magnificent," Jen said.

"It was created by our ancestors when they first arrived," Kai said. "The blocks are basalt and fit without the benefit of mortar."

Jen nodded to some writing along the edges of one of the doorways they passed. "What does that say?"

"It's hard to translate, but roughly it means the children will always have a home. And that home will never be abused," Kai said.

Not sure the priestess has read that, Laney thought.

Two members of the Guard stood at the main entrance, but they stepped back and opened the doors as soon as the group reached the top step. Laney raised an eyebrow but said nothing as they walked through.

"Which way to the cells?" Jen asked.

"This way." Oasu headed down the hall, ducking through a doorway that led to stairs leading down. The others followed.

Laney frowned as they crept lower. It was like a dungeon in an old castle. "Why do you have cells?" she asked. "Did your ancestors create these as well?"

Oasu shook his head. "This area was used for the storage of food. The colder temperatures acted as a type of refrigerator. They were only converted to cells a few years ago."

A guard was posted at the bottom of the stairs. He frowned as he looked over the group. "Guard Oasu, what is the meaning of this?"

Oasu stepped forward. "We are looking for Aaliyah. These people are from the mainland and have legal authority to conduct a search."

"Why are you looking here?" The guard's confusion was obvious.

"We believe she is in one of these cells," Laney said.

The guard shook his head. "There's no one down here."

"Then why are you here?" Jen asked.

The Belial Guard

The guard hesitated. "I was sent here this morning. I go where I'm ordered."

Laney stepped past him and began opening doors. Jen did the same. The first six cells were empty, and Laney began to lose hope. But when they got to the seventh door, they found it was locked.

She looked back at the guard. "Do you have a key for this?"

"No."

"Oasu?" Jen asked.

He shook his head. "I'm sorry. Maybe we can break it down?"

Laney leaned toward the wooden door. "Whoever is behind the door needs to get to the far wall. We're going to open it." Then she moved aside. "Jen?"

Jen stepped forward.

Oasu and the guard walked up behind them. "Um, no offense," the guard said, "but I don't think she'll be able to open it without us."

A small grin appeared on Jen's face, and then she kicked the door open. It crashed into the opposite wall with a resounding boom.

Oasu stared at her. "How did you—"

"She does a lot of kickboxing," Laney explained as she stepped into the room.

A small figure lay curled up in the corner, and the room smelled of urine. With a cry, Kai pushed past Laney and leaned down, stroking his hand along Aaliyah's face.

Aaliyah's eyelids flickered, and she laid a hand on Kai's cheek. "I must be dead," she said, "because you are here."

Chapter Forty

KAI CARRIED Aaliyah from the cell and up the stairs. He cradled her gently, but Laney could read the anger on his face. Oasu's face was just as readable, but his expression was one of shock and disbelief. He kept glancing at Aaliyah as if to assure himself that they had really found her huddled in a cell in the basement of the pyramid. The other guard had looked just as surprised as Oasu; clearly neither of them had had any idea Aaliyah was down here.

Noriko walked beside Kai, keeping one trembling hand on Aaliyah, as if she didn't want to break the connection. Laney felt only disgust at the priestess as she followed them out of the temple.

At the bottom of the steps, Kai turned to her. "I'm going to take her home."

Laney nodded, although she was pretty sure Aaliyah was going to need a hospital. "We'll be there shortly."

As Aaliyah, Kai, and Noriko walked toward Aaliyah's home. Oasu watched, clearly wanting to go with them, but he stayed with Jen and Laney. *Even now he follows his orders*, Laney thought.

Jen looked at Laney. "We need to find the priestess."

"Agreed." She turned to Oasu. "Where will the priestess be?"

"Her home." He nodded toward a large building that overlooked the whole island, then pointed at a path that went around behind the temple. "This path leads directly there. There are no other homes along the way."

Jen tapped him on the shoulder. "You should be with your family. Go take care of Aaliyah. We've got this."

"Thank you. Thank you both." With a grateful look, he ran after the others.

Laney and Jen started down the path.

"You doing okay?" Laney asked.

"Yeah. It's—" Jen shook her head. "I don't know. It's weird. I mean, I know it's her. The minute I saw her, I knew it. But I don't *feel* like it's her. I don't feel *anything* for her."

"Well, that's because you know who your actual mom is, and she lives back in California—" A familiar tingle rolled over Laney's skin and her head jerked up in disbelief. She scanned the area.

Jen went on alert as well. "Laney?"

"There's a Fallen here."

Laney spotted movement in the trees. She sprinted forward, Jen at her side. As they broke through the tree line, they came upon a woman and two guards, apparently trying to escape.

"Stop what you're doing!" Laney yelled.

The woman went still. When she turned her head, anger burned in dark eyes done up as if to make her resemble Cleopatra.

Oh my God.

The priestess was a Fallen.

Chapter Forty-One

THE PRIESTESS WAS unable to move forward. She had heard about this power of the ring bearer, but she hadn't believed it. She had thought it was exaggerated, at best.

"Defend me!" the priestess yelled.

Her two guards immediately engaged the ring bearer and her friend.

The priestess recognized the friend as Vanessa's first daughter. They'd kept track of her over the years, making sure she didn't work against the humans. So she was pleased to see Jen stop the guard with a simple kick to the chest.

The ring bearer took a little more time. As the guard swung a staff at her head, she twirled toward him until her back was against his chest. Then, latching on to the staff, she continued the momentum of his swing. With a yell, his feet flew out from underneath him and went airborne. The ring bearer hung on to the staff and landed a hit to the back of the guard's head as he hit the ground, knocking him out cold.

Not even breathing hard, the ring bearer turned to the priestess. "You're a Fallen."

The priestess shrugged. "So?"

There was a rustle in the trees, and Vanessa and another six guards appeared, along with a dozen members of Honu Keiki. No doubt they had all heard the priestess's yell.

The priestess dropped the confidence from her face and her voice. "My people! This woman has attacked my guards and me. Help me."

They hesitated for only a second before surging forward.

Chapter Forty-Two

LANEY WATCHED the onslaught of people with disgust. But her disgust was not aimed at them, but at the priestess.

"Don't hurt them," she called to Jen as one reached her.

"Maybe you should suggest *they* don't hurt *us*," Jen replied as a man grabbed for her arm. She stepped to the side, grabbed the man's shoulders, and shoved him into another attacker.

A third man lunged at Laney. She sidestepped easily as he tried to grab her arm. She captured his wrist, turned it ninety degrees, and twisted him to the ground. The man cried out as he collapsed.

The other ordinary members of Honu Keiki backed off, but not the guards—which was fine with Laney, as she was less concerned about hurting them. She parried the first attack, stepped to the side, kicked the back of her attacker's legs and just managed to stop herself from snapping his neck. But she did yank him backward. As he crashed to the ground, she landed a solid kick to his jaw.

Another guard ran at her. This time Laney simply

stepped to the side and kicked him in the groin, followed by a round kick to the knee and an elbow to the face.

Jen had already taken out three other guards and was about to deal with the last one. That left Vanessa, who moved toward Laney with a smile, her staff twirling.

Laney jumped back as Vanessa lunged. She barely missed getting slammed in the ribs. She snatched the staff away and redirected it to Vanessa's knee. It made contact with a sickening crack. Laney swung it through and then brought it back again, catching Vanessa on the back of the thigh. One more swing through, this time knocking Vanessa flying backward. She landed hard.

Laney pushed the tip of the staff into Vanessa's neck. "Stop."

Vanessa glared up at her. "You're not a hero. You're a disgrace."

Laney shrugged. "Can't say your opinion of me carries all that much weight."

Laney looked up at the priestess—and her heart stopped.

The priestess was gone.

How? Laney had ordered her to stop what she was doing. *Which was walking*, Laney realized. *She could have started running. Damn it. I need to get more specific with my commands.*

Jen came and stood beside her. She looked down at Vanessa—her mother.

Vanessa narrowed her eyes. "You engage the help of abominations," she said, jutting her chin toward Jen. "You are not the true ring bearer."

Jen went still. "You know what I am?"

Vanessa looked at Jen directly for the first time. Her voice was cold. "Why do you think I left?

Chapter Forty-Three

LANEY PULLED her badge off her belt and held it up to the guards who remained conscious. "Okay, guys, before you get any more ideas, we're federal officers. You've already gotten yourselves into a boatload of trouble by assaulting us. Don't compound it by doing anything else."

The guards looked to Vanessa for guidance.

Laney glared down at her. "Don't make *them* pay for the priestess's mistakes."

Vanessa held her gaze for a long moment. "Stand down," she said.

Laney handed the staff to Jen. "Keep things calm here and call the mainland to tell them we need some reinforcements. I'm going after the priestess."

Jen nodded and eyed Vanessa. "I've got it under control."

Laney hesitated, trying to gauge if Jen's answer was accurate.

Jen met her gaze. Her voice was firm. "I'm good. Go."

Laney took off through the trees. But almost immediately she heard the sound of an engine. *No.* She looked up; a small chopper flew overhead. *Damn it.*

She considered using her powers to take it down—but she'd never tried a safe landing with an object that big, and she knew there had to be some innocents on board.

So instead she grabbed her phone and dialed.

Jake answered. "Hey. How's Hawaii?"

"Not great. The priestess just took off on a chopper. I'm guessing she's heading to the same place the rest of the members have disappeared to, but she'll have to switch to a larger plane. I'm going to ask around here and see if someone can tell us where. Can you get in touch with the local airports? And can you get someone to look into their computers remotely? See what they can find?"

"Will do. Did you find Aaliyah?"

"Yes. They had her imprisoned, but she's safe now. There's no inherent danger—I think. We just need to get the priestess."

"Can we let someone else do that?"

"Maybe the SIA."

"Why not regular law enforcement?"

"Oh—she's a Fallen."

Jake let out a low whistle. "That's cold. Taking out your own people."

Laney went still. She hadn't made that connection. If the priestess was behind the Companion Killers and the Fallen murders, she *had* taken out her own people.

"Why'd she do it?" Jake asked.

"I don't know," Laney said. "But I'm hoping somebody here can tell us."

Chapter Forty-Four

LANEY WENT BACK TO JEN. The guards were all conscious now, sitting on the ground, hands on their heads. Vanessa sat with them.

"All good?" Laney asked.

"Yeah. You?"

"No. She got away."

"I called Maui. They're sending some officers. Should be here in about thirty minutes."

Laney nudged her chin toward the group. "What shall we do with them in the meantime?"

"I suppose we can use the dungeons she locked Aaliyah in."

Laney looked over the captives. Vanessa was angry, but the rest just looked confused.

"Let's hold them here for now," she said. "Marching them through the middle of the island without reinforcements might cause some problems. When the police arrive, we'll secure them in a room and figure out where to go from there."

It only took the Maui police twenty minutes to arrive. Laney gave them the rundown. The officers secured the guards and took them to the temple, which Laney had decided was the best location for questioning them. Laney accompanied them.

As they walked, Laney observed the people of Honu Keiki. Something about them was bothering her, but she couldn't quite put her finger on it. Then she realized what it was.

She leaned toward Jen. "Do you notice anything odd about the people here?"

"What?" Jen looked like she'd been lost in thought.

"The people of Honu Keiki—look at them. Do you notice anything?"

Jen looked at a young man passing them with a cane, and an older couple who'd stepped out on their porch to watch them walk by. "They're all either older or injured."

Laney nodded. "Yeah."

Laney pulled one of the guards to the side of the path. He was young, no more than eighteen, and looked a little more scared than the rest. She waited with him until the rest of the guards were out of earshot, then said, "What's your name?"

He shuffled his feet. "Uh, Loe."

Laney waved her hand at the older couple and the young man. "Okay, Loe, where is the rest of Honu Keiki? So far, besides the Guard and Noriko, everyone we've seen has been either old or infirmed."

"The rest have already been moved," Loe said. "These people will be in the last group to go."

Laney frowned. "Go where? I thought you guys never left here."

"We don't. But the priestess—" He closed his mouth.

"But the priestess what?"

His eyes begged her not to press. "You're an outsider."

"I am. But I'm also a lot more than that. Do you know Aaliyah?"

Loe nodded. "She was my teacher."

"I came here to help her. She was being held in a cell underneath the temple by the priestess."

Loe's mouth fell open. Then he shook his head. "No, that can't be true. Aaliyah, she would never do anything wrong. And the priestess..." His eyes looked troubled.

Laney eyed the young man carefully. She could see he was sincere. He might be willing to help, but only if he believed. Finally, she said, "Come with me."

She led him to Aaliyah's house and knocked on the door. Oasu answered. He looked frazzled, which Laney thought was probably unusual for the man.

"Laney, we're—" Oasu caught sight of the guard. "Loe."

Loe bowed. "Guard Oasu."

"How is she?" Laney asked.

"Severely dehydrated, exhausted, hungry. She caught a chill. She's going to need a doctor."

Laney nodded toward Loe. "He needs to see Aaliyah."

Oasu hesitated.

"Now, Oasu," Laney said gently.

Reluctantly, he stepped aside. "She's in the living room."

Laney headed inside. Loe followed her, and Oasu brought up the rear.

When they entered the living room, Laney struggled not to gasp. Aaliyah lay on the couch, a light blanket on her. And she looked so pale. Her cheeks were sunken in. Her hair was damp with sweat. Noriko hovered beside her, and Kai stood to the side, looking completely destroyed.

Aaliyah gave Laney a weak smile. "I feel better than I look."

"Well I would hope so," Laney said softly. "Can you answer some questions?"

Aaliyah nodded. Kai helped her sit up, and she smiled her thanks at him. He stayed right beside her, looking content to be her leaning post.

Aaliyah looked back at Laney, and she caught sight of Loe for the first time. Surprise flashed across her face before she smiled. "Loe. How nice to see you."

Loe stumbled forward, his eyes wide, his mouth open. "What happened, Aaliyah?"

Aaliyah looked to Laney, who nodded. "He didn't believe me," Laney said. "And I need information from him. I thought perhaps you could tell him."

Noriko looked worried. "She really should be resting…"

"I'm all right," Aaliyah said reassuringly. "Just a little dizzy. Perhaps you could bring me some water?"

Noriko sprang into action, heading for the kitchen. When she returned, Aaliyah took a few small sips and handed the glass back to Noriko. "Much better."

Noriko didn't look convinced, but she accepted the water and stood protectively behind the couch.

Aaliyah turned her gaze to Loe. "I'm afraid the priestess is not who we thought she was." She told him about her abduction and the threat to Oasu and Noriko.

Loe shook his head. "It's not possible."

"Are you saying Aaliyah is lying?" Laney asked.

"No," Loe burst out. "No—of course not. She would never."

"It's true, Loe," Kai said.

"Now we need to know what is happening," Laney said.

"We need your help, Loe. Where are the other members of Honu Keiki?"

Loe looked at the floor. "They've all gone ahead to the new promised land."

Jerusalem—the promised land. That's what the project had referred to. It had nothing to do with Israel.

"But why?" Laney asked. "Your people have been here for centuries. Why move?"

"The priestess said there's a storm coming," Loe explained. "And that we would be the only ones who would survive. That we were chosen to survive. That she had been shown the way."

"Did she say what the storm was going to be?"

Loe looked up. "The end of days."

Chapter Forty-Five

THE PRIESTESS STARED down from the chopper as the ocean swept past her. She was headed for a small airport in Southern California. She was scheduled to board a commercial flight there—under a different name, of course—in two hours. It was the earliest flight she could get.

She seethed. They would be landing soon and Vanessa had still not called. Which meant she had been detained by the ring bearer. Vanessa was a loss. She had been with the priestess since she was Xia, and she had always been loyal. She believed wholeheartedly in the priestess—would die for her without question.

The priestess sighed. *Such a pity. Oh well. Life goes on.*

She looked at the two members of her Guard who had accompanied her. One was frowning.

"Is there a problem, Ephraim?"

Ephraim shook his head. "No, of course not."

"Good. Vanessa has been detained. She may not be able to join us. You will have to lead the Guard. Are you ready?"

The priestess saw confusion and curiosity cross his face,

but he merely nodded. "Of course, priestess. Whatever you need."

She looked back out the window and went back to her thoughts. McPhearson had chased her from her home—but in the grand scheme of things, it did not truly matter. She had planned on leaving anyway. She just had to accelerate her timeline—which meant her future could be realized sooner.

She pulled out her cell phone and typed a message.

Let it begin.

Then she sat back and smiled, imagining the world she was about to create.

Chapter Forty-Six

THE END OF DAYS. Laney looked at the members of Honu Keiki, all of whom looked as shocked as she felt. Apparently the priestess had been selective about who she shared information with.

The end of days—allegedly the time when the world would be devoured by plagues of violence. In some telling's, small pockets of humanity would survive, only to have to carve out a life in a bitter, destitute world. In other versions, it was the end of all humanity, or perhaps even all life on the planet.

Most of the common understandings and beliefs about an "end of days" scenario came from Christianity—in fact, Christianity had a whole study of God's actions at the end of days, known as eschatology—but it was a common topic of discussion in religions across the globe. For the big three —Judaism, Christianity, and Islam—the end of days often came through violence and in the form of judgment. Jehovah's Witnesses believed that only 144,000 people would survive. Laney preferred the view of the Eastern religions;

they had little to say about the end of times, and instead said you should worry about the here and now.

And of course, there were the end of days cults, which always seemed to pop up. In fact, the end of the millennium had brought out dozens of such groups. For instance, there was the group known as "Aum Shinrikyo," which was responsible for the 1995 sarin gas attack on the Tokyo subway. Their leader believed the world was going to end in 1999 as the result of a nuclear war, and that a spiritual awakening was the only way to create enough holy energy to avert the coming crisis—although Laney wasn't sure how trying to kill a subway full of people was supposed to bring the holy spirit into people.

Was that what was happening with Honu Keiki? Was the priestess just convinced the end of days were upon them and hunkering down in what she thought was a safe place? Was that what Project Jerusalem was? Simply a movement to a new, safe place protected from the destruction of the world? But why would she think destruction was at hand? And what, if anything, did Noriko's vision have to do with it?

Laney looked back at Aaliyah; the poor woman was having trouble keeping her eyes open. She needed to get to a hospital. "I think that's all we need for now," Laney said. "Why don't you take a little nap?"

"Maybe just a few minutes," Aaliyah said, and she lay back down on the couch.

Laney waved Kai down the hall with her. Noriko took his place on the couch, gently stroking Aaliyah's hair.

Laney stopped at the end of the hall. She spoke quietly. "I think we need to get Aaliyah to a hospital."

Kai nodded. "I know she would rather stay here, but I think you're right."

"I'll take care of it."

"Thank you." He headed back to Aaliyah.

Laney dialed the Maui police to see if they had a med chopper they could borrow. When she had made arrangements, she headed back to the living room. Oasu stood in the doorway.

She pulled him aside and nodded toward Loe. "Is it all right if he stays?" she whispered. "I think he wants to help."

Oasu nodded. "Yes. He's a good person. Most of the Guard are."

"Even Vanessa?"

Oasu looked away. "No. But if anyone was to know what the priestess was up to, it would be her."

Laney sighed, dreading the coming confrontation. "I know."

Chapter Forty-Seven

LANEY FOUND Jen inside the temple, speaking with a Maui police officer in the hallway. When Jen saw her, she excused herself and walked over.

"Any luck?" Laney asked.

"Afraid not. We've spoken with most of them. They don't have any details. Although they did say that the priestess's main guards have already left the island."

"So these guys are the ones out of the loop."

"So it seems."

Laney tried to get a read on Jen. She seemed to have her emotions buttoned down, but Laney knew this must be tough for her. And it was only going to get tougher. "Has anyone spoken with Vanessa?"

"Some of the other officers tried, but I don't think it went well."

"I'm not surprised. I'm going to speak with her. Do you want to join me?"

Jen didn't hesitate. "Yes."

Jen led Laney down the hallway to the room where

Vanessa and the guards were being held. Two officers guarded the door.

"We need to speak with one of them," Laney said.

"You want some backup?" one officer asked.

"Already got it." Laney indicated Jen. "But thanks."

The officer opened the door, and Laney and Jen stepped inside.

Vanessa was seated on the opposite side of the room. "I need to speak with you," Laney said.

Vanessa crossed her arms over her chest. "I've got nothing to say."

"Well, we'll see about that. Let's go."

Vanessa didn't move.

Laney sighed. "I will drag you out of here in front of your men if you make me. You really don't want to test me on that."

Vanessa glared. "Fine," she said through gritted teeth.

Laney headed out first, but Jen stepped aside to let Vanessa pass. "After you."

Vanessa didn't respond as she followed Laney out the door.

Jen directed Laney to an office at the end of the hall. It held a desk and three chairs.

Laney looked at the setup. "I don't think I want her on the other side of an obstruction."

With one hand, Jen pushed the desk against the wall. Vanessa's eyes grew wide.

"Sit," Laney said.

Vanessa crossed her arms and remained standing. "I think I'd rather—"

In one movement, Laney kicked out the back of Vanessa's knees and pulled a chair behind her, pushing her into it.

"I get it—you don't want to talk to us," she said. "But you're going to, so you might as well get comfy."

Jen went to stand near the door.

"Where has the priestess gone?" Laney asked.

Vanessa just stared back.

"Did she go to your properties in Australia?"

Vanessa's eyes widened for just a moment at the mention of Australia. *And score one for the good guys.*

"Why is she moving your people there? What does she think is coming?"

Vanessa smirked.

"Does it have anything to do with Project Jerusalem?" Once again, there was the slightest flicker in her eyes.

Laney continued to question her for ten minutes, but got no verbal responses. "Fine," she said at last. "We'll get the answers we need with or without you. We always do."

"But not in time," Vanessa growled. It was the first thing she'd said during the entire interview.

"What does that mean?"

Vanessa smiled. "You just told me you'll find out without me. So I think I'll just let you. Anything else?"

Laney shook her head. "No, I'm done for now."

Jen stepped forward. "But I'm not."

Chapter Forty-Eight

VANESSA LOOKED at Jen without an ounce of compassion or curiosity on her face. "I have nothing to talk to you about."

Laney had to clasp her hands tightly behind her back to keep from striking the woman.

"You're my mother," Jen said.

"I gave birth to you."

Laney felt her jaw drop. *Are you kidding?*

"Why did you leave?" Jen asked.

Vanessa sighed. "I really don't see the point in dredging up the past."

Jen crossed her arms over her chest. "Well it's my past too, and I'd like to hear it."

Vanessa studied her daughter for a long moment before speaking. "Fine. When I found out I was pregnant with you, I was quite content. I decided to keep you. It was all right at first. But then, when you were ten months old, one of our seers had a vision." She curled her lip. "She knew what you would become. You were banished, and I was banished along with you."

"And if you had been given a choice?"

Vanessa met her gaze without flinching. "You would have left, and I would have stayed."

Laney wanted nothing more than to punch this woman in her cold, unfeeling face. But Jen remained calm.

"And then when you left me?" Jen asked.

"I received word that I would be allowed to return, so I did."

Jen said nothing.

Laney moved to her side. "And Jen?" she asked. "What was your plan for her?"

Vanessa shrugged. "She was in America. I knew Child Services would be called eventually, and she would be put into the system."

"Do you *know* what happens to kids in the system?" Laney asked.

Vanessa looked at her nails. "I don't see how that's a concern of mine."

Laney clamped down on Jen's arm, afraid she was going to lunge at this woman—or maybe to keep herself from doing so. "Do you know what happened to Jen in foster care?"

"We had people keeping tabs on her should her abilities manifest negatively. I received regular reports."

"You knew I was being abused?" Jen said.

"I was aware there were some difficulties. But nothing life-threatening."

Jen's mouth fell open. "They threw me out of a *tree*. Without my abilities, I would have died."

Vanessa narrowed her eyes. "But you didn't die, did you?"

"You said people were keeping an eye on Jen in case her abilities 'negatively manifested,'" Laney said. "What would have happened if they had been deemed 'negative'?"

"She would have been taken care of. Now, I have duties—"

Jen cut her off. "Thank you."

Vanessa paused, confused. "For what?"

"For leaving me. It was the best thing you ever did for me." Jen turned and walked out of the room, her frame tight.

Laney's heart broke at the sight. Jen was trying to hold it together, but it couldn't have been easy.

Vanessa stood. "Right. Well—"

"Sit down," Laney ordered, her anger boiling over.

"I will not—"

Wind gusted through the room and slammed the door shut. Laney gritted her teeth. "I said *sit down*."

Vanessa sat.

Laney paced, trying to control her anger. Vanessa had left Jen. She had *known* Jen was being abused, and yet she had done nothing to stop it. Never in Laney's life had she wanted to hurt someone more.

But she reined in her temper and sat down across from Vanessa. "You are going to tell me everything you know about Project Jerusalem."

Chapter Forty-Nine

LANEY INTERROGATED Vanessa for the better part of an hour—but got nothing. Finally, she threw open the door and summoned one of the police officers. "Get her out of here."

The officer grabbed Vanessa by the arm and led her down the hall. Laney watched her go, trying to understand how someone could be so cold to their own child and so loyal to the priestess.

Laney asked one of the other officers if he'd seen Jen, and he pointed toward the main doors. Before she headed out, she called Jake for an update.

He told her he had some analysts remotely investigating the Honu computer system, but so far they'd had no luck finding out anything about either Project Jerusalem or the priestess's location. Laney was tempted to ask him to have Danny take a crack at it, but she had promised herself the kids wouldn't get involved.

She remembered the kids playing soccer before she left. *That's* what they should be concerned about: games, homework, college applications. Life and death should not be a regular part of their lives. So she bit her tongue and told Jake to let her know as soon as they found anything.

She shoved her phone into her back pocket and stepped out of the temple. She had to admit that, from here atop the temple steps, the island was stunning. Colors dotted the lush landscape and the homes all melded well with it, not disturbing the natural beauty of the place.

She looked around for Jen, but saw only a few members of Honu Keiki wandering by. She knew they all had to be burning with curiosity. So many foreigners on the island must have been a shocking event.

"Laney," a voice called.

She turned and saw Oasu coming from around the back of the temple, with a smaller man walking behind him.

Laney jogged down the steps to meet them. "Oasu. What's going on?"

Oasu took the small man by the arms and pulled him forward. The man was in his late thirties, his dark hair balding in the middle. "This is Ipo," Oasu said. "He used to work for the priestess as her personal assistant."

"I would see to all her needs," Ipo added. "Anticipate her needs as well."

"But you are no longer her assistant?" Laney asked.

Ipo's face flamed red and he looked away. "I did not wake the priestess when she had received a phone call. She had me replaced."

"How long did you work for her?"

"Twelve years."

"And she had you replaced for *one* mistake?" Laney asked.

He nodded.

Oasu nudged him. "Tell her what you know about the move."

"We were supposed to go there, to Australia. The facility there was designed as a modern day Noah's Ark."

"Does this have to do with the ritual of the end and the beginning?" Laney asked.

Ipo frowned. "The ritual? How do you know about the ritual?"

Laney realized Ipo did not know that the Companion Killers had been attempting to recreate the ritual, which meant it wasn't common knowledge. So had the Companion Killers' attempt spooked the priestess?

"The people left on the island. When were they scheduled to follow?" Laney asked.

Ipo shook his head. "Most of the people left—we are to be left behind."

Oasu's jaw clenched.

"What?" Laney asked.

"The plan was to only bring the able-bodied. Those left behind would be a drag in the new world."

"What about the Guard?"

"They were supposed to be on the next plane, with a few select others."

"Did they know that people were being left behind?"

Ipo glanced at Oasu before shaking his head. "No. Most didn't even know why the people were being sent away."

"What about you?" Oasu asked.

Ipo looked at his feet. "I have disappointed her. I was not going either."

"So that's what Project Jerusalem is. Saving the able-bodied," Oasu said quietly.

Ipo looked up, his brow furrowed. "That has nothing to do with Project Jerusalem."

"But I thought—" Laney began. "You know what, never mind what I thought. What is Project Jerusalem?"

"I only overheard some things. I do not know the whole plan."

"Just tell me what you do know."

"It's about the end of days."

"You mean preparing for it," Oasu said.

Ipo shook his head. "No. Bringing it about."

Laney stared in disbelief. "She's going to try to *bring about* the end of days?"

"Yes."

"How?"

"I don't know."

"Why is it called Project Jerusalem?"

"It's set in Jerusalem. Whatever the priestess is planning, it will happen there."

Chapter Fifty

LANEY HANDED Ipo off to a police officer, then she called Jake and instructed him to rustle up whoever he could find and get them on a plane to Jerusalem. In particular, she insisted he call Yoni; Yoni had spent the first twelve years of his life in Israel and would definitely want to be in on this.

Laney then called Matt to see what resources he could muster up. There were SIA agents in Europe, the Middle East, and Asia. They would all converge on Israel.

The end of days. Laney shuddered. Whatever the priestess had planned, the fact that it was in Israel didn't bode well.

Modern Israel was established in 1948 following the end of the British mandate. Technically the Balfour Declaration of 1917 paved the way for the creation of Israel by addressing the creation of a Jewish homeland in Palestine, but it wasn't until 1948 that Israel was officially recognized as its own country. But even then, things weren't nearly that simple. By the time Israel was created, Arabs had been living in Palestine for hundreds of years—and they pushed back.

In fact, the Arabs and Israelis in the region had been pushing at one another ever since the early days. And small incidents spiraled into extended periods of violence. The first intifada was triggered by an Israeli truck crashing into a group of Palestinians waiting to return home at a border crossing. Four were killed, and the area erupted. Small attacks prior to the incident, as well as years of oppression, provided fuel for the fire, but a simple car accident—interpreted by the Palestinians as a direct attack—was the last straw.

The heart of the issue was Israel's move to claim East Jerusalem during the Six-Day War of 1967, when they seized Arab land and moved settlers in. At first, the Palestinians demanded that the Israelis move back to the original demarcation line. But after decades of fighting and tensions, Arab groups began calling for the complete removal of Israel.

Israel was colorful and vibrant, but also dangerous. And now the priestess was attempting to do something in the middle of that simmering pot. Something that would cause the world to spiral out of control.

And without more to go on, Laney had no idea how she was going to prevent that from happening.

While Laney pondered all the possibilities, she had been walking the island, looking for Jen. Finally, she caught sight of her standing on a dock, and walked up to her.

"Jen?"

Jen didn't turn. She just stared out over the water. "It's really beautiful here. I can see why she wanted to come back."

Laney stepped up beside her. "It is beautiful."

Jen's face was absent any expression, but Laney could

feel the emotions swirling inside of her. "What if I'm like her?" she asked quietly.

"You are *nothing* like her," Laney said firmly. "Your family, your friends—you would do anything for them. We all know that. That woman is nothing like you."

"She gave me away, Laney. My own mother gave me away. She knew I was being abused, and she didn't even think to help me. I was just a kid." A tear tracked down her cheek.

"That says a world about her and nothing about you. Her decision has nothing to do with you. It's no reflection on you and who you are."

Jen turned to her, her eyes filled with pain. "My own mother didn't want me. How can that not say something about me?"

Laney took Jen by the shoulders. "Because you're amazing. You're everything she is not. She is not your mother. Your real mother is back in the States. With your brothers and your father."

"I know you're right. In my head, I know you're right. But it hurts, Laney. It just really hurts."

Jen's shoulders started to shake. Laney pulled her into her arms and held her as she sobbed, cursing Vanessa and the priestess for making their lives that much harder.

Chapter Fifty-One

HENRY'S HEART broke for Jen. From Laney's description, her mother was a complete piece of work. He'd tried to reach Jen, if only to talk, but she wasn't answering. And Henry had known she wouldn't. Jen closed up when she was hurt. And this—this had to cut deep.

But somehow, even Jen's heartache paled in comparison to Laney's other news: the end of days.

Was it even possible? He walked to the window that overlooked the courtyard of the school. A few teenagers lounged around, taking advantage of the unusually warm weather. He'd come to the school after Laney and Jen had left; he'd wanted to be nearby if the kids needed him. Besides, Danny had wanted to visit with his friends. One of the security detail had taken them over to the cats' preserve.

But as he looked out at the teenagers, his mind spiraled down a dangerous path. Multiple religions and groups talked about the end of days: the time for the ultimate battle between good and evil. Henry himself had almost been waiting for the notification that it was about to begin. After all, he, Laney, and Jake made up the triad—the three who would arise to fight the Fallen when the world had reached a critical point.

Part of him had hoped that with his mother's sacrifice, they had avoided the coming battle. But in his heart, he had known that wasn't the case. He knew this day would come.

He clenched his fist. *I just wish we had more time.*

"Henry?"

He turned. Danny hovered in the doorway.

And here's one of the reasons I want more time.

Henry had helped Danny escape an abusive home at the age of ten. Danny was an off-the-charts genius, and when Henry brought him into the Chandler Group fold, he had originally planned on having the boy work with him. At first, he'd hired nannies to look after him, but soon, he and Danny had fallen into the role of father and son. And like any father, Henry wanted Danny to experience life and be free from danger. And if the world was going to go to hell, he wanted Danny to be older when that happened.

Henry forced a smile to his face. "Hey. When did you guys get back?"

"Just now."

"Good. How are the cats?"

Danny grinned. "Awesome. Snow is absolutely attached to Lou. She was kind of hoping maybe Snow *and* Tiger could come stay at the school for a little bit. I told her I'd ask."

"Tiger?"

"The other cub—the yellow one. He's really sweet."

"Well, when Laney gets back, we'll see what she thinks of Tiger's control, okay?"

"Gets back? Where is she?"

"Uh, she just went for a, um, research trip."

Danny frowned. "What's wrong?"

"Nothing, nothing." Henry smiled again. "Hey, you want to order Chinese for dinner? Have your friends join us."

Danny shook his head. "Don't change the subject. What's going on? You're acting weird."

Henry sighed. "It's nothing. Laney and Jen are just working on a case."

"And I guess it's not going well."

Henry laughed. "They're always complicated."

"Can I help?"

"Absolutely not. None of you are helping in any more cases. After the last time— no, absolutely not."

Danny raised his hands apologetically. As he did so, his shirt sleeves fell down to his elbows, bringing his strong forearms now in view. And with a pang, Henry realized how much Danny had grown. He had muscle now, something he'd never really had before. *He's growing up.* And the thought of it brought him both pride and sadness.

"Look," Danny said, "I know we screwed up. We should have let you guys know what we were planning. But if Laney needs our help, or my help, shouldn't I help? I mean, is it serious?" Danny smiled. "Because if it's end-of-the-world serious…"

Henry tried to maintain a neutral expression, but he must have failed, because Danny's smile dimmed.

"Wait. It's end-of-the-world serious?"

"Maybe, I don't know. But you—"

"Is there some computer angle I can help with?"

Henry hesitated.

"There is! Henry, you need to let me help."

Henry shook his head. "No. We—"

"Have someone better with a computer than me?"

Danny stepped forward. "You know that if I wanted I could just hack into our computer system and learn what's going on. But I'm not going to do that. I want your permission to help."

"I just hate the idea of getting you involved in this."

"Well, if it is the end of the world, I'm *going* to be involved. And personally, I'd like my involvement to be trying to stop it rather than just trying to survive it."

Henry remembered the shy little boy he'd met so long ago. Danny had grown a lot in the intervening years, but especially in the last three. And Henry had to admit, all those experiences had made him stronger in many different ways. He stood up for himself, he socialized, he was turning into an incredible man. And Danny was right: if it was end of the world, he should have the opportunity to help.

"Okay," he said. "I need you to look through some computer files."

Chapter Fifty-Two

LANEY POCKETED her phone and called everyone she could think of. The ball was rolling; now she just needed to get herself to Israel.

She watched Jen and Noriko, who were helping get Aaliyah in the med chopper. Noriko and Kai were going to accompany the injured woman to Maui. She'd get checked out at the hospital there, and then Laney was having them flown to Baltimore—partly because she wanted them safe while the priestess was on the loose, but also because she thought they all needed some time away from Malama to figure out their next steps. She'd been surprised when they'd agreed.

Jen stepped back as the chopper started to lift off. When the chopper was out of sight, Laney approached her. "Your little sister seems pretty amazing."

Jen met Laney's gaze, and Laney saw the tears she was trying to hold back. "Yeah."

"You haven't told her."

Jen shook her head. "No. Besides the fact that it's absolutely not the right time, it wouldn't do anything to make her life better. She has Aaliyah, Kai, Oasu. If I told her, I'd have to tell her Vanessa was her biological mother, and I think she's better off not knowing that. I'm thinking *I* would have been better off not knowing that."

"I don't believe that."

"What part?"

"Any of it. You needed to know, and now you do. You can close that chapter of your life and focus on everyone you *do* have. And that's the other thing you could offer Noriko: you. Because you are *my* sister in every way, and I can tell you from experience, she shouldn't have to miss out on that."

Jen's chin trembled and she blew out a breath, trying to keep her tears at bay. "I don't do this—cry, talk about my emotions. I just—"

"Do what needs to be done. And you show your emotions in different ways. You put it all on the line for complete strangers. Even after everything you went through when you were younger, you didn't close off your heart. Lou's proof of that, and so is Henry. So yeah, maybe you don't 'do' this emotion thing, but right now, you're kind of getting batted around by them."

Jen nodded and wiped her eyes. "But now's not the time for that. Let's go stop the priestess and whatever plan she's got brewing—"

"No."

Jen looked surprised. "No? We're not going to stop her?"

Laney hugged Jen. "*I'm* going to stop her. *You're* going home."

Jen pulled back. "What? Laney, you need my help."

"I will always want your help. But whether you realize it

or not, you're not ready for this fight. Vanessa—" Laney saw Jen wince at the mention of her mother. "She hurt you. And that's playing around in your head right now. And I can't risk you getting hurt, or worse. Not even to save the world."

"Laney, I need—"

"To go home. To hug your family. To remember why you're important. Why you matter. You don't have anything to prove to me or Vanessa. And you should be there when Noriko and the rest arrive. They need you too. I've got this."

Doubt clouded Jen's face. "Laney…"

Laney took Jen's arm. "I have SIA agents swarming in from everywhere. Jake's about to get in the air with as many Chandler operatives as he can gather. We'll have the numbers. We'll be good."

"You're trying to protect me."

"Just like you're always trying to protect me. And I'm asking you to *let* me protect you this time, okay?"

Jen looked at her for a long time, and Laney worried she'd have to have Jen sedated to keep her from coming. And if it came to that, Laney would do it. Whether Jen knew it or not, she was in no shape for the coming fight. She needed to regroup and take a minute. Laney had already arranged for Jordan to meet Jen in California and fly home to Baltimore with her. Because more than anything, Jen needed to be with her family right now, not off trying to take down whatever the priestess had going on.

Jen's expression indicated that she had come to the same conclusion. "Just this time though," she said.

"You got it," Laney said lightly. She linked her arm through Jen's, and they walked back to where the police were gathering the Guard to take them in for processing.

Laney felt the loss of not having Jen with her on this one, but like she'd said, she was the ring bearer, and it was her job. She needed Jen to live her life.

She swallowed. *And if I don't succeed, it's going to be an awfully short one.*

Chapter Fifty-Three

LANEY WAS in the air on the way to Tel Aviv. She was in a Cessna Citation, one of the fastest planes in the world, able to travel at up to 700 miles per hour. Henry had called in a favor from a businessman in Dubai who'd had the plane stored in Hawaii. *My brother*, Laney thought. *The man who takes care of everyone.*

Besides the pilot, only Oasu was with her. He wanted to help, and he thought he might be able to identify members of Honu Keiki. The rest of the Guard were being interviewed by the Maui police. Vanessa was going to be charged, but Laney had talked the police into not charging the others as long as they cooperated.

Jen was on her way back to Baltimore, and Kai, Noriko, and Aaliyah should be following her within a few hours. Aaliyah was severely dehydrated and malnourished, but there were no emergency medical issues. Henry had promised to have his personal doctor stay with her when she arrived at Baltimore.

The priestess, Laney was pretty sure, was on her way to

Australia—although they had no confirmation of that. All they knew for sure was that the priestess had arranged for something to happen in Jerusalem; they still didn't know what it was, or even when it was supposed to happen. Laney just had to hope that whatever it was, she would be able to stop it in time. Because creating a bomb shelter on the other side of the world was a pretty radical step to take.

Laney wondered again why the priestess chose Australia. Of all the places in the world, why did she think she would be safest there?

Her head jerked up. *No, that can't be right.*

"Laney?" Oasu asked.

"I just—I think I might know why she chose Australia. But I'm hoping I'm wrong."

In college, she had taken a political science course, and one of the topics they had discussed was nuclear war. One of the facts that had come up was that Australia, if it wasn't directly involved in the conflict, would be one of the safest locations when the rest of the world started bombing one another. It was so geographically isolated that it would be able to survive better than most of the world.

And within Australia, Perth would be ideal. The country's strategic targets were on the opposite side of the island, and with the trade winds, very little fallout would ever roll over Perth.

Laney felt numb. It had to be a coincidence that the priestess just happened to choose a location that would protect her from a nuclear fallout—right?

Even she couldn't be crazy enough to aim for that.

At the same time, she knew the possibility of nuclear war was all too real. There had been several incidents in the twentieth century that could have led to it. The most famous, of course, was the 1962 Cuban missile crisis. But it was far from the only one.

For instance, in the same year as the Cuban missile crisis, a U-2 spy plane wandered into Soviet territory. Soviet MIG fighters were scrambled to intercept, and the US sent two nuclear tipped warheads aboard two 102 fighters in response. Luckily, the U-2 pilot managed to glide his ship, which was out of fuel, out of USSR territory before either set of fighters could reach him.

And believe it or not, on the exact same day as the U-2 incident, a second incident evolved underwater. As a warning, depth charges were dropped near a Soviet submarine blockading Cuba. The sub captain, interpreting these as the beginning of World War III, ordered that a nuclear weapon be prepared to be fired. Luckily, cooler heads prevailed, and the sub surfaced before firing and requested instructions from Moscow—who told them *not* to fire.

Two other near-misses involved technological glitches. In 1979, NORAD's computer system indicated that the Soviets had launched missiles at the United States. The US was prepared to respond in kind before the glitches were detected. Similarly, in 1983, a lone lieutenant colonel in the Soviet Army received a warning that missiles had been launched by the US. Luckily, the lieutenant colonel realized the warning was false and so did not raise an alarm.

And then there was the time the Soviet Union misinterpreted a US war game as being the real thing. In their defense, all the moves the US took—moving troops into place, changing their alert status, et cetera—were moves that would occur in the event of an actual strike. The USSR raised their own level to high alert, but fortunately the game ended without incident.

Laney mulled over these previous incidents. They all

were part of the Cold War battle for control—and they all occurred within a cloud of old fears, grudges, and suspicions.

The Middle East had those in spades, especially when it came to Israel.

In fact, Edgar Cayce had said that the strife in the Middle East would lead to worldwide turmoil. Specifically, he'd suggested that Iraq would attack Israel with nuclear weapons, resulting in US intervention and the advent of World War III.

But that hadn't happened. Saddam Hussein had attempted to draw Israel into the 1992 Iraq War, but the US had managed to avoid that. Did that mean that the prophecies were not guaranteed? That they could be avoided?

That was the ray of hope in all this.

Laney's phone rang, and she glanced at the screen before answering. "Hey, Henry."

"We know what Project Jerusalem is," Henry said without preamble.

Laney tensed, although part of her was relieved. At least they'd have something to focus on. "Okay. What is it?"

"Members of Honu Keiki are going to set off a bomb at the Temple Mount."

"*The* Temple Mount?"

Henry's voice was heavy. "Yes."

Laney's jaw dropped. *Well, that will do it.*

Chapter Fifty-Four

THE TEMPLE MOUNT was the thirty-five-acre rectangular plot of land at the center of the strife between Palestine and Israel. Technically, the Temple Mount was in Eastern Jerusalem, and had been under Israeli control since 1967. But while Israel held political sovereignty, *religious* sovereignty was held by the Waqf, an Islamic council that had controlled the Mount since 1967.

But the Temple Mount was much more than a small piece of land. It was a site of critical importance for three major religions: Judaism, Islam, and Christianity.

For Judaism, the rock on the Temple Mount was where Abraham was instructed to sacrifice his only son, Isaac, before being stopped by God. The Temple Mount also abutted the Western Wall, the last remaining remnant of the second Temple of Solomon, built after King Nebuchadnezzar destroyed the first in 587 BCE. The second temple was destroyed by the Romans in AD 70, along with most of Jerusalem, and now only this bit of wall remained. According to the Roman Jewish historian Josephus, during the eleven-year-long construction of the second temple, it never once rained during the day, so as not to interfere with the work. And within that temple was the holy of holies: the room that housed the Ark of the Covenant and the Ten Commandments.

For Islam, the Temple Mount was the site of Mohammad's ascension to heaven. The Dome of the Rock was created to protect that rock, and the Al-Aqsa Mosque was the third holiest site in Islam.

For Christians, the temple on the Mount was the site of Jesus's famous speech against the temples. He was also believed to have played on the steps and the land surrounding it as a child.

Because of this, the Temple Mount had become a sacred symbol of religious identity—a religious identity that had grown increasingly violent on both sides since the early 1980s.

In more practical terms, the Temple Mount was also a very, very crowded place. It drew pilgrims of all three religions, as well as tourists from around the world. A bomb at the site would kill hundreds, if not thousands, with victims from multiple religions and nationalities. And the effects would be felt well beyond Jerusalem. They would ripple out to all corners of the world as the devoted of three major religions felt the hurt and the anger.

"Henry, we cannot let this happen," Laney said. "We cannot let anyone even *think* this is going to happen." She knew all too well how small issues could flare up into geopolitical nightmares in that part of the world.

"I know," Henry said. "Everyone's going to point fingers at everyone else."

"I wouldn't be surprised if the Islamic states immediately declared war on Israel."

"And Israel's allies will rush to Israel's defense."

"It *will* be the beginning of World War III."

Laney knew her words weren't an exaggeration. Israel had been an unwelcome addition to the Middle East from the moment it was created. Tensions often ran hot with its neighbors. And in times of strife, it was not unusual for countries to exploit that strife. For instance, after the invasion of Kuwait by Saddam Hussein, when the United States led an international coalition of countries to push back the Iraqi forces, Iraq turned around and began to bomb Israel. The Iraqis wanted the coalition to be perceived as infidels defending Israel against a Muslim country.

The US realized that the coalition would be doomed if that's how it was perceived. And the US military knew that if Israel got involved, that would be the end of the coalition —the situation would transform from an international coalition allied against one rogue country to a chaotic conflict of countries against countries. So, even though the US didn't have time, they made the time to search out the missile sites, because Israel was threatening to send its own missiles into Iraq.

And if Israel was a land of strife, Jerusalem might be the most contested city in the world. The history of the land was a tale of multiple handovers of control. Now both Muslim and Jewish groups maintained that they were the true people of the land, and both had claims that involved hundreds of years of settlement. Were the Muslims' claims any less valid because they settled the land after the Jews? Were the Jews' claim any less valid because they predated the Muslims? The fact was both had centuries of settlement to back up their claims. It was a Solomon-like riddle that politicians had tried to sort through for a hundred years.

And now she wants to throw a bomb in the middle of it. Laney

The Belial Guard

shook her head. *Good God.* She didn't even want to imagine the world response.

She couldn't let that happen. "We'll stop them before we get to that point."

"But Laney, even if you stop them, if word even gets out about the attempt, that may be enough. Remember what started the second intifada?"

Laney groaned. "Ariel Sharon's visit to the Temple Mount. It was the death knell for the Oslo accords."

Back in 2000, the Prime Minister of Israel, Ariel Sharon, visited the Temple Mount surrounded by about a thousand guards. His visit was interpreted by the radical Islamic terrorists as a claim to the Temple Mount. Rioting began almost immediately after his departure, completely derailing the peace talks.

By the afternoon, Yasser Arafat had called for retaliation, stating that Sharon's visit was a defilement of the mosque. An Israeli security patrol was the first official target —a Palestinian officer who was a member of the patrol opened fire on his Israeli counterparts. Later that day, Israeli forces opened fire on Palestinian protestors who were throwing rocks at the Western Wall. Four were killed.

And the second intifada was born.

The intifada was a deadly war between Palestine and Israel. Over a thousand Israelis and fifty-five hundred Palestinians were killed in the violent clash. But perhaps most damaging to the world, the second intifada introduced suicide bombing as an effective method of subverting a stronger opponent.

And Laney knew the second intifada was not merely the result of an unfortunate choice of touring spots. From the time of the 1993 Oslo agreements to the year 2000, the Palestinians had seen Israel expanding its housing settlements into the disputed lands. They had seen their own poverty levels increase while their control over the Western Bank decreased. Sharon's visit to the Temple Mount was just the spark; the kindling had been laid for years. This part of the world was a tinderbox.

"Every move made by one side is interpreted through a lens of suspicion by the other," Henry said. "Some of it is legitimate, and some is paranoia."

Laney closed her eyes. "And now, we're what—going to walk into the middle of that quagmire? I mean, on a good day, we'd be let nowhere near the Temple Mount. How are we going to get anywhere near the Dome? How are the priestess's people going to get there?"

"I'm guessing she's had people in place already, maybe even for years." Henry paused. "The second intifada was triggered by a mere *visit* by the wrong person. Can you imagine what would happen if they make it look like a *bombing attempt* was being done by an Israeli citizen? Or someone from Palestine? The response will be swift and brutal. Cooler heads will not prevail."

Did the priestess really mean to set this all off? Did she realize how far the effects of their actions would reach? How many people would die?

"I can still get there," Henry said.

Laney shook her head. "No. We've got the SIA, Jake, Yoni—we'll be good. And if all of us can't get it done…"

"Then it can't be done," Henry finished softly.

Chapter Fifty-Five

VENICE, ITALY

ELISABETA FINISHED her dessert and delicately wiped the edges of her mouth with her linen napkin. She pushed away from the table with a contented sigh. It was an incredible feeling when one's hard work paid off.

She wandered out to the balcony and watched as a gondola floated past, sans passengers. The gondolier, in his black and white striped shirt, black cap, and red scarf, moved lazily down the canal.

The sun shone brightly overhead. Elisabeta turned her face to it and smiled. *Ah, life is good.*

The opening of the door to her office signaled the entrance of Hakeem. She had been expecting him, but she was still annoyed that he was intruding on her moment. With a sigh, she turned. "Yes, Hakeem, what is it?"

"You wanted to be informed when Delaney McPhearson left for Israel."

"Yes." She paused. "And?"

"And she's left for Israel."

God grant me patience. "You should have led with that. Who is with her?"

"Henry Chandler is still in Baltimore, and Jen Witt is returning there. But the SIA is mustering their agents."

Elisabeta frowned. She had counted on Laney bringing her usual team. That could be a problem. But no matter. They were only going against humans. It would be fine.

"How long until she reaches Tel Aviv?"

"Six hours."

Elisabeta drummed her fingers on the railing. Six hours. It would be enough time. "Tell the pilot to be ready to go in two. And have my team head to Tel Aviv immediately."

"Yes, Samyaza. Anything else?"

She looked down at her fingernails. "Yes, send in Hilda. My nails are a mess."

Hakeem bowed and backed out of the room.

Elisabeta turned back to the canal. *Time for the next act, Delaney. Let's hope you're ready.*

Chapter Fifty-Six

HENRY STOOD beside the golf cart, watching the Chandler helicopter approach. He hated that Jen had gone through all that emotional upheaval without him. He'd spoken with Jordan during the long flight, but Jen had been quiet, barely speaking. Jen always kept a lot to herself, but this... this she couldn't keep to herself. She needed to let it out.

Laney's description of Jen's reaction to Vanessa broke Henry's heart. Even now, his heart ached for her. He wanted nothing more than to tell Vanessa what he thought of her. But he knew that would do little good. The woman simply didn't care.

The chopper hovered overhead and then landed. Jordan hopped out and held out his hand for Jen, who looked more fragile than Henry had ever seen her. Jordan placed his arm around her shoulders, helped her into the cart, then walked around to Henry.

"I'm going to jog back to the main house. I need to stretch my legs."

Henry read the anger in Jordan's face and knew he needed to get rid of some of it. He'd undeniably been holding it in since he'd met up with Jen in California.

"I've got her," Henry said.

Jordan gave him a nod and took off at a jog.

Henry sat next to Jen and took her hand. She squeezed it back, but said nothing. They drove silently back to the main house, where Henry turned toward the back.

Jen looked over at him. "Where are we going?"

"I arranged a little something on the back veranda."

"Henry, I'm really not—"

He squeezed her hand. "It's just a reminder of who you are."

Ahead on the veranda was a woman with blond hair just starting to turn gray, a gray-haired man by her side. Behind them stood Lou, Rolly, Danny, and Jordan's twin, Mike. Henry stopped the cart and nodded at them.

"That's your family. Those are the people who know you, who love you. Vanessa—she doesn't deserve any emotions but your pity. Because she lost out on getting to know you. And I pity anyone who doesn't have you in their life."

Jen turned to him, her eyes shining with tears. "I love you, Henry."

He kissed her softly. "Not as much as I love you."

Jen placed her hand on his cheek, then stepped out of the cart and jogged toward Martha and John Witt. They engulfed her in a hug. And Henry knew that Jen was on her way to healing.

Chapter Fifty-Seven

TEL AVIV, ISRAEL

LANEY LOOKED out the window as the plane began its descent. Israel had always held a fascination for her. So many of the Biblical stories she'd been told had taken place here. Flying over it felt like flying over history.

This was her second trip to Israel. She'd been to Israel years ago and had been amazed by the beauty of the place. The Jerusalem Market had been her favorite. Narrow alleys cut down rows and rows of colorful stalls selling all sorts of exotic merchandise: jewelry, fabrics, spices, scarves, candles, and artifacts of dubious authenticity. And it wasn't unusual for a merchant to invite you in to sit and talk—very different from an American store, where salespeople sometimes seemed like they were doing you a favor by being there at all.

And the food! It was everywhere. The smells reached out at you as you walked, enticing you to stop for baked goods, shakshooka, jachnun, kibbe, fruits, cheeses, Bedouin tea, and more.

Plus, you could literally see the history of the place. Apartments were built from buildings hundreds of years old. Excavations took place right next to main walkways. In any direction you walked, you were guaranteed to see a piece of history. This was the land of Herod, David, the Ottoman Empire, Saladin, the crusades, the Romans—all the periods of history layered one on top of the next. It was incredible.

When she was last here, with Drew and Jen, they had spent days wandering from one incredible site to another. But sightseeing was not part of the trip this time, and she was pretty sure she wouldn't be stopping by the market for any souvenirs.

Well maybe if nothing blows up I can, she thought glumly.

The plane touched down at Ben Gurion International Airport, and they taxied around to a hangar where Jake was already waiting. After thanking the pilot, Laney headed for Jake, with Oasu right behind her.

Laney made the introductions. "Jake, this is Oasu, Kai's son. He's hoping he can help."

Jake shook his hand. "Good to meet you. We can use all the help we can get. And actually, we have some pictures back at the safe house we're hoping you can go through. We think they may be Honu Keiki members."

"Anything I can do to help," Oasu said.

"Where is everybody?" Laney asked.

"At the safe house. The SIA agents are slowly trickling in—we have about a dozen so far. Matt and Mustafa will be arriving within the hour. And Yoni is off meeting with some members of his old unit to see what he can find out."

"Did he see his mother?"

Jake nodded. "He convinced her to go stay with his cousins for a little while."

"Good."

Jake waved over one of the Chandler operatives. "Sean, can you take Oasu back to the safe house? Explain everything we know so far and get him started on those IDs?"

"Will do." Sean extended his hand to Oasu. "Good to meet you. If you'll follow me." They walked off together to one of the SUVs.

Laney watched Oasu as they left, hoping the young man was up for what was ahead. He'd been on Malama all his life, and the next few days were going to be a crash course for him in how the rest of the world worked.

"How's Jen?" Jake asked quietly.

Laney shook her head. "Devastated. I couldn't ask her to help with this, Jake. It's too much. Her head wasn't in it, and if she got hurt—"

"Hey, you don't need to explain it to me. We've got this." Jake looked like he wanted to hug her, but he just stuffed his hands into his pockets. "You okay?"

"Besides being slightly terrified, yes."

"Only slightly? Well, you're doing better than me then."

Laney gave a small laugh, and she and Jake shared a genuine smile. But then she became serious again. "Okay. Anyone have any ideas how they're going to smuggle a bomb into the Temple Mount?"

"Well, as you know, only Muslims are allowed into the Temple Mount sites."

Laney nodded. In 2000, the sites on the Temple Mount were closed to all but Muslim visitors. Christians and Jews were still allowed on the Temple Mount—in small groups, due to the increase in clashes between Jewish and Muslim activists—but while on the Temple Mount they were not allowed to pray, and they could not visit the Dome of the Rock or the Al-Aqsa Mosque.

fence had been controversial, to say the least—it had cut off Palestinian farmers from the land, destroying crops and livelihood—but it had also finally brought an end to the suicide bombs that had become commonplace.

Out of the corner of her eye, Laney saw Jake also surveying the landscape. Jake was so solid. His feet were always firmly planted on the ground. Religion didn't play much of a role in his life, and according to Victoria, it was his pragmatism and common sense that made him an integral part of the triad.

"Jake?"

He turned to her.

"Who do you think is right in this battle for control? The Israelis or the Arabs?"

"Honestly? After all these centuries, and the amount of time that each side has settled here, I'm not sure it's possible to declare one side as more deserving of the land."

"Who controlled it longer?"

Jake shrugged. "Even that's a bit hard to say. David conquered it in 3000 BC and declared it a Jewish Kingdom. That lasted until the first century AD, when Rome conquered it. Then there were the Persians in 600, followed by the Christians. Muslims controlled it from at least 1099 to the twentieth century, when the British took control in 1917."

"And then they created the state of Israel in 1948."

"Yep."

"So, if you had to choose: Who would you say has the stronger claim to the land?"

"Neither, both." Jake shook his head. "I suppose it depends. The Jews had it earlier on, but then the Muslims controlled it for over a thousand years into the modern era.

They both have a claim. I'm just not sure which one is more valid."

"Well, the 1948 doctrine didn't really help." In 1948, the city of Jerusalem was split between Israel and Jordan. But then in 1967, Israel went to war and reclaimed most of Jerusalem. They'd been fighting off attempts to go back to that 1948 line ever since.

Jake sighed. "I guess as someone who's not very religious, I don't understand why this particular piece of land is so critical. There were previous attempts to provide a homeland for the Jewish community. Uganda was one. There was even an attempt to create one in upstate New York at Grand Island."

"Really? I've never heard that." Jake was a history buff, and was always coming up with these little nuggets of information.

"It was back in the late nineteenth century. Major Mordecai Manuel Noah came up with the plan. He was the editor of a newspaper and had a bit of political influence. He convinced a friend to buy Grand Island on the Niagara River. He was intending to call the town Ararat. He came out for the naming ceremony, was unable to get to the island, and that pretty much ended the attempt.

"At least that would have been a voluntary settlement. Later, the Third Reich had a not-at-all voluntary plan to evacuate Jews to the island of Madagascar. It was actually the first Final Solution to what the third Reich termed the 'Jewish problem.' While it's cringe-worthy, in retrospect it would have been preferable to Hitler's eventual 'solution.'"

Laney thought about the terrible atrocities forced upon the Jewish population by the Nazi Party. And the Nazis were far from the first people in history to target the Jews. She couldn't blame the Jewish people for wanting a home of their own.

She looked over at the West Bank. Reports varied on the level of poverty there, but she had seen estimates as high as 67%. On the Israeli side, settlements were well laid out; on the other side of the fence, small homes were built close together. In some areas, homes were little more than hovels.

But who was right? Who was wrong? It wasn't a question she was equipped to solve, and neither was anyone else. In fact, she had a feeling time and demographics would solve that problem for them. According to the Palestinian Census Bureau, by 2020 there would be more Arabs in Israel than Jews. Some argued it wouldn't occur until 2035 or 2048, but no one argued that it would happen. Arab birth rates simply dwarfed the birth rates of Israeli Jews, because the Arab family size was larger than that of their Jewish counterparts. And that meant that in a few short decades, the demographic composition of Israel was going to shift dramatically.

Perhaps that would bring peace at last. Or maybe it would only create more violence as a majority shifted into the minority.

Laney turned from the wall and spied the Har Hazaitim cemetery. It was said to be at least three thousand years old and contained in excess of seventy thousand tombs—tombs dating back to the time of the first temple. But it was more than just a popular place to be buried. The Mount of Olives provided holy land to spend your time while awaiting the next life. And the resurrection of the dead was said to begin with the second coming of Christ at that very spot.

There was so much history in such a relatively small area, both ancient and new—and all more than a little tragic. And now Laney needed to not only keep that history from being destroyed, but to do so without letting anyone outside her group from learning about the danger. Because in this case, the threat alone could create just as many global repercussions as an attack itself.

"What are you thinking?" Jake asked.

Laney looked at him, and for a moment she let all her doubts crowd in. "I'm thinking this might be impossible."

Chapter Fifty-Eight

AS JAKE DROVE SLOWLY through the streets of Jerusalem, Laney remembered spending every night with Drew and Jen at a restaurant on the beach, watching people set hookahs up right in the sand. It had been an eye-opening and life-changing trip—and one that brought only good memories. Jerusalem was a beautiful place.

But when you looked for them, you could see plenty of signs that Israel was not like most other countries. Bags were inspected at all businesses that could afford the guards. Occasionally you'd pass someone, usually a male, with an automatic weapon slung casually over his shoulder. And this wasn't like Texas—this wasn't about swagger. This was a true act of defense. Every able-bodied individual in Israel was required to serve time in the military, and all were allowed to open carry.

While they slowed for traffic, Laney watched a car pull up at the gate of a non-descript concrete building surrounded by a fence. A concrete divider separated the car from the street, and metal plates rose from the ground both behind and in front of the car, trapping it in place. Two guards walked over to the car; one kept a weapon trained on the car's occupants, while the other walked around the car slowly. He had a mirror attached to a long pole, and he placed it under the car, searching for incendiary devices.

Laney swallowed. Even without the priestess's new threat, Israel was a dangerous place.

Jake drove along Ha-Yarkon Street, the boulevard that ran along the Tel Aviv beach for nine miles. They passed the spot where the Dolphinarium had once stood. The Dolphinarium was a teen nightclub that was attacked by a suicide bomber on June 1, 2001. The man was intercepted before entering, so he set off his bomb right there at the doors. Twenty-five people died, almost all of them under the age of eighteen.

Laney pictured the teenagers lined up outside the club as the bomber blew himself up. She understood the academic reasons for suicide terrorism, but she struggled to understand how someone could look at innocent teenagers and see the need for their deaths.

Jake's phone rang, and he answered it. "Jake here." Then, after a short pause: "What? When?"

Laney looked over. Jake's face was serious.

"We're on our way." He disconnected the call.

"What's going on?" Laney asked, dread filling her.

"Mustafa's been attacked."

Chapter Fifty-Nine

JAKE DROVE AS FAST as he could through the crowded streets. By the time he pulled into a spot three houses down from the safe house, Laney was practically climbing the walls of the car. As she ran toward the house, the SIA agents saw her coming and opened the door. She hurried inside, with Jake right behind her.

Matt appeared at the end of the long hallway. He waved them down. "Back here."

As Laney hustled down the hallway, she glanced in the doorways she passed. They were clearly intended to be bedrooms, but from the weaponry on display, they had another use right now.

Laney stepped into the kitchen and took in the figure sitting at the table. His right eye was swollen, and he had cuts on his cheek and hands. "Oh, Mustafa."

Mustafa gave her a small smile. "It's not as bad as it looks."

Laney whirled on Matt. "What happened?"

"It's not Matt's fault," Mustafa said. "It was mine. I

went to get a gift for my sister. I thought I could go to the market quickly and be back. And I did. Unfortunately, I was jumped as soon as I left the market."

"Was it a Fallen?"

"From the way they moved?" Mustafa said. "Yes."

Laney sank into a chair across from him. "How are you alive?"

"They didn't want to kill me."

Jake frowned. "So what did they want?"

Mustafa pulled a phone from his pocket. "To give Laney this."

Laney stared at the phone like it was a snake.

"Laney?" Mustafa prompted.

She looked at Jake, who nodded at her. She took the phone from Mustafa's outstretched hand. "Any instructions?"

"I was told you'd be receiving a call at 4:45." Mustafa looked at his watch. "That's in fifteen minutes."

Laney looked down at the phone. It was a burner. And she had a feeling it was encrypted to make it impossible to trace the caller. She sighed. "Well then, I guess we wait."

Chapter Sixty

THE FIFTEEN MINUTES DRAGGED BY, even though Laney was actually quite busy. They reviewed the security setup at the Temple Mount, which was impressive—she didn't see how someone could possibly smuggle a bomb in.

But Jerusalem was also known for its underground structures. Ancient tunnels were constantly being unearthed—like Hezekiah's Tunnel, a water tunnel that dated to the eighth century BCE and ran from Gihon Spring to the Pool of Siloam, outside the walls of the Old City. And there was much more under Old Jerusalem: Roman sewers, medieval chambers. The idea of someone finding some ancient entry to the Temple Mount was not completely out of the question.

On the other hand, maybe the priestess's people didn't even have to get into the Temple Mount itself. If they even got close with a large explosive, they could do a lot of damage, especially seeing as there were faults running all throughout the area.

And the priestess's people were definitely here. Thanks

to Oasu, they had been able to identify eight former Honu Keiki members in the area. Unfortunately, all of them had disappeared prior to Laney's team's arrival. Which meant they needed to somehow search the Temple Mount—a virtual impossibility due to the religious restrictions.

Matt explained that he had two dozen agents, ten of whom were either Fallen or nephilim, in the city. Another six would arrive within the hour. With the dozen Chandler operatives they now had, they had close to forty people.

Was that anywhere near enough?

As they wrapped up their review of the situation, everyone went silent and watched the clock count down to 4:45.

At 4:45 on the dot, the phone rang. Taking a deep breath, Laney put it on speaker. "Hello?"

"Delaney, lovely to speak with you. This is Elisabeta Roccorio."

Laney's mouth fell open. "Elisabeta?"

"You sound surprised to hear from me. You shouldn't be. There's quite a lot happening. A talk between us seems well overdue."

Laney had no idea why Elisabeta would be calling her. "Well, I'm a little busy right now, so—"

"That's why I am calling. It seems you and I share a purpose."

Laney couldn't keep the surprise out of her voice. "We share a purpose? Do tell."

"The priestess, as you call her, is planning to set off a bomb in Jerusalem."

Laney frowned. "How do *you* know that?"

Elisabeta laughed. "I'm Samyaza. There is very little I do not know. Nonetheless, the priestess—pretentious name by the way—needs to be stopped."

"Why would you want to stop one of your Fallen?"

Elisabeta's voice was ice cold. "Because she is not following *my* dictates, but her own." She paused, and when she spoke again, the emotion had disappeared from her voice. "And her plans do not coincide with mine."

"And what *are* your plans?"

Elisabeta gave a throaty laugh. "Oh, I won't reveal my secrets quite that easily. But I will tell you the priestess's plan."

"Okay then. What's her plan?"

"Why, she's going to start World War III."

Laney said nothing.

"I see you already know," Elisabeta said. "That's good. You know, this has always been a tempestuous part of the world. It's changed hands many times. And each hand has clung to it long after it has been removed. This place inspires loyalty, reverence, and hate like almost no other place on earth. And very little is needed to spur the whole area into violence. But of course, you know that as well."

"So far you're not telling me anything helpful."

Elisabeta continued as if Laney hadn't spoken. "Israel is the unwelcome neighbor in this part of the world. And if they turn against their Islamic neighbors? Well, those Islamic neighbors will respond. Iran will retaliate, and Russia will side with Iran. The other Islamic states will demand that Israel be brought to justice. And the US? Where will they be? Seeing as the greatest amount of the US's foreign aid goes to Israel, they will be viewed as Israel's allies. And we already know how willing the world has been in recent years to turn against the US."

Laney shook her head. "But that's insane. Even with the skirmishes lately, it's never come to a full-blown world war." She wasn't sure who she was trying to convince.

"Yes, but then no one has bombed the Temple Mount before."

Laney saw the stunned looks on the faces of her friends. They had already known that was the plan, but apparently all of them, like Laney, had hoped they were wrong.

"Even you know that a move like that would be disastrous," Elisabeta continued.

"Why are you telling me this?"

"Why, to help, of course."

"And why would you want to help?"

"Because it's the right thing to do."

Laney laughed. "Yeah. Try again. Are you looking for her?"

"I am. And I am offering you the help I can."

"Yes, but *why*?"

A little frost returned to Elisabeta's tone. "Because *she* does not get to determine what *my* world looks like. And I have no intention of sitting back while she turns it into a nuclear wasteland."

"So, how are you going to help? We already know the target."

"Ah, but you see, I know where the bombers are right now."

Chapter Sixty-One

ELISABETA HAD GIVEN them an address where she claimed the bombers were, but no one was about to take her at her word. A team had been sent out to check it out—discreetly—and Matt was on the phone with his contacts in the Israeli police. Jake was also on the phone, speaking with Henry.

Laney slumped into the kitchen chair and looked over at Mustafa. "What do you think?"

"I think if a bomb goes off anywhere near the Temple Mount, there will be a lot of finger-pointing and very little listening."

Laney agreed. "What about her assessment of the world taking sides?"

"A few years ago I would have said she was wrong. But now?" Mustafa considered. "The violence in Syria has changed the world, hasn't it? Russia has openly sided with Syria. Iran has been more involved in world affairs. ISIL is stirring up more and more problems. And if the Israelis are viewed as targeting Muslims at one of their most holy sites?

Or if Israel blames another country for initiating an attack?" He shuddered. "The ramifications would be world-changing."

"Yeah, but the Temple Mount is revered by Israel. They would no more destroy it than they would destroy themselves."

"But what if someone were to target the Western Wall? What do you think Israel's response would be?"

Laney groaned. "But how are we supposed to do this? We can't empty the Temple Mount. The Waqf would view any such attempt as a provocation."

"So we have to neutralize the threat before it can become an international incident."

"And in a place that receives millions of visitors per year, we need to do it in a way that draws absolutely no attention to us."

Mustafa smiled. "See? We have a plan."

Laney laughed at Mustafa's wildly unrealistic optimism. "Now I'm hoping Elisabeta really is giving us accurate intel. And I'm not sure what's scarier: her helping us, or her *not* helping us."

Yoni walked into the kitchen and took a seat.

"You up to date on recent events?" Laney asked.

He nodded. "Yeah. Although I'm not sure how much stock we should put in Elisabeta's word."

"Did you find anything from your Israeli contacts?" Mustafa asked. "Did they mention anything about the Temple Mount?"

"Well, there's been a lot of anger about the idea of putting cameras on the Temple Mount," Yoni said.

"That was Jordan's idea right?" Laney asked.

"Yes. And I can't blame them."

Laney agreed. After all, when King Abdullah of Jordan

had visited the mosque in 1951, he had been assassinated. The Israelis believed the cameras would offer a chance to protect all the visitors to the area, but the Palestinians feared they would be used to target Palestinians who spoke out against Israel.

"So what's the status of the cameras right now?" Mustafa asked.

Yoni shrugged. "On hold."

Laney blew out a breath. "Well, that sucks." While she understood the concerns about the cameras, they would be awfully useful.

Jake stepped into the kitchen and gave them a grim smile. "Elisabeta's info checks out," he said. "We've got them."

Chapter Sixty-Two

LANEY SAT in the van with Jake, Yoni, and four members of the Israel counterterrorism team. Laney had decided to leave Oasu behind—he wasn't ready for this. *She* was barely ready for this. Another van was just down the street from them, carrying more security operatives, and there was yet another group of operatives waiting at the back of the house.

The house where the terrorists were meeting was two houses down. When they arrived, they had done thermal imaging and identified four people inside. Since then, three more had entered, and none had left. Laney hadn't sensed any Fallen or nephilim nearby, so they at least had that going for them.

Arie, the leader of the counterterrorism unit and a surprisingly small man, was in charge of the op. He was just waiting for confirmation that the backup team was in place before moving in. When the call finally came in on his radio, he looked around the van, making eye contact with everyone, before answering. "We're a go."

Jake pushed open the back door of the van, and he and Arie sprinted for the front door. Down the street, the occupants of the second van did the same. Laney was running across the street as well when she noticed a man on the opposite side of the street step out of an alley and go still. He locked eyes with Laney—and then sprinted away.

Laney yelled into her mike. "There's a runner! I'm going after him."

She raced after the man, her long strides shortening the distance between them. Soon she was only twenty feet away. The man misjudged a curb, tripped, and rolled into the street. As he stumbled to his feet, Laney launched herself at him, tackling him around the back of the knees. With a grunt, he slammed back into the ground.

Before he could react, she had yanked one arm behind his back and placed him in a wrist lock. He let out a yell. Laney got to her feet, keeping his wrist at ninety degrees. An Israeli officer ran up behind her.

"You have cuffs?" she asked.

The officer snapped a pair of handcuffs around the man's wrists.

Laney then turned the man around so she was facing him. Blood dripped from his nose down to his chin, and there were scratches on one cheek.

"Where is the bomb?" Laney asked.

The man's eyes widened. "What are you talking about? I was out for a walk."

Laney grabbed his sleeve and yanked it up, revealing his tattoo: a lotus flower with three lines behind it. "No, you're a member of Honu Keiki, and you're here under orders from the priestess."

The man shook his head. "No. I'm—"

A gunshot shattered the air. The officer yanked Laney to

the ground, and the shackled man dove for the ground as well.

As Laney lay on the ground eye to eye with him, she realized her mistake. The shackled man hadn't dived to the ground at all. The perfect hole in the middle of his forehead told her that someone else had dictated that action for him.

Chapter Sixty-Three

THE OFFICER STAYED with the body while Laney rejoined the rest of the group. They had called in support to try and find the shooter, but he could have been in one of a hundred apartments in the area. It was obviously Honu Keiki that had taken him out—which meant there was another member at large. Someone they didn't know about.

Laney jogged up to the house just as Yoni stepped outside. "What have you got?" she asked.

"Nothing," Yoni said.

"What do you mean?"

"I mean, they're all dead. Seven members, dead."

Laney looked at him in disbelief. "Did we kill them?"

"No. They've been dead for at least thirty minutes."

"But—they've been under surveillance."

"Well, apparently somebody missed something."

"Anything on their plans?"

Yoni nodded. "Yes. They were planning on bombing Solomon's Stables."

Solomon's Stables was an underground space with

vaulted ceilings that sat under the southeast corner of the Temple Mount. The Knights Templar used the space to house their horses during the crusades. Some said it dated back to the time of Solomon, although no one was really sure of the actual date. In 1996 it was converted into a prayer hall, to accommodate some of the overflow from the Al-Aqsa Mosque.

Laney imagined how much damage a bomb in the stables would have done. An underground blast might even have set off earthquakes, devastating the entire city. "Who killed them? Was it suicide?" she asked.

"Not unless one of them went around breaking the others' necks—and then broke his own."

A chill crawled up Laney's spine. "Their necks?"

Yoni nodded.

"What the hell?"

Chapter Sixty-Four

IT WAS AN HOUR LATER, and Laney was sitting in the surveillance van with Yoni. Yoni had managed to talk one of the officers into letting them see the surveillance tapes of the house. The Israeli police had already looked at them and seen nothing of value, but planned to have them analyzed by experts later.

"Where do you want me to start?" Yoni asked.

"We've verified that the three people we saw entering the building were among the dead, so obviously the killings must have occurred after that. Let's start with their arrival. And if we don't see anything, we'll go back further."

Yoni queued up the tape to the time of the last members' arrival, then slowly fast-forwarded from there. They watched the three members of Honu Keiki, a woman and two men, enter the building. Then there was nothing more to see until their group stormed the front door.

Yoni switched over to the surveillance tape from the back of the house, and they repeated the process. Ten minutes later, Laney was forcing her eyes to stay open. "Is there anything less exciting than watching—"

She stopped, squinting at the screen. "Wait. Can you back up a little bit, and play it at normal speed?"

"Yeah, what did you see?"

She leaned forward. "I'm not sure."

The back of the house remained quiet, and a line of static flickered on the screen.

"Piece of crap machine," Yoni muttered, reaching for the controls.

"Wait," Laney said. "Let's just watch."

About a minute later, the static flickered once again.

"Back up to the static and then pause," Laney said.

Yoni did.

Laney sat back, her hand to her mouth. On screen, in the static, the figure of a man could just barely be made out.

Yoni stuttered. "Is that—that can't be."

Laney nodded. "It was a Fallen."

Chapter Sixty-Five

LANEY CALLED JAKE, Matt, and Mustafa to join her and Yoni. Quickly they explained what they had discovered on the tape.

"A Fallen?" Jake asked. He turned to Matt. "Was this one of your guys?"

"No. All my guys have been accounted for since they arrived."

"So who is that?" Yoni asked.

"I'll have the image cleaned up," Mustafa said. "Maybe we'll be able to identify him."

"No need, I already sent it to your people," Laney said. "They're going to rush it back to us." Just then her phone beeped, and she read the text message before clicking on the attached image. "Well, they rushed it all right—here it is. They say they'll aim for an even cleaner picture in a few hours." Laney turned the phone around to show the others. "Anybody know this guy?"

On screen, they could make out a tall, muscular man.

His face was still undefined, though they could see that he had a large nose.

"He's not one of my men," Matt said.

"I don't recognize him either," said Mustafa.

Laney tried to figure who could have sent the man. Had he come on his own somehow? Had Elisabeta sent him? She looked at Jake. "Anything inside that can help us?"

"With this guy? No. But we did find one thing interesting: a body."

"Another one?"

"Yep. But this one was in the basement in a freezer. And he was not a member of Honu Keiki."

Laney frowned. "So who is he?"

"He's an Iranian dissident," Matt said.

"Iranian?" Yoni asked.

Laney understood the implication immediately. "Holy crap."

Jake nodded. "We think he was going to be the fall guy for the bomb. He was being kept on ice in the basement."

"To slow down the body's deterioration," Mustafa said. "It would throw off the time of death in an autopsy."

All Laney could think about was what would have happened had they succeeded. Iran had a history of making inflammatory comments about Israel. In 2001, the Ayatollah Ali Khamenei had said, "It is the mission of the Islamic Republic of Iran to erase Israel from the map of the region"—and that was one of the least repugnant statements. Over the years, Iran had denied that the Holocaust had ever happened, explaining away all evidence of its occurrence and claiming that tales of gas chambers were simply propaganda to gain sympathy. In recent years, the Iranians' tone had changed a little—publicly, anyway—but

Laney knew these sentiments still held sway in much of the country.

"If Iran was blamed..." Laney started.

Jake nodded. "Israel would retaliate."

"Against a Muslim nation, which, as Samyaza explained, would result in a domino effect of other countries picking sides," Matt said quietly.

Laney frowned. "And now, handily, that's all been avoided."

Jake looked at her in surprise. "What's the matter? This is a win."

Laney shook her head. "Yeah, I know. But it just doesn't feel right. We didn't do anything. Someone else did."

"It was probably Samyaza," Jake said. "She found out where they were and took them out."

"If that was her plan, then why tell us where they were? Why not just take them out? Why involve us at all?"

Jake shrugged. "I don't know. I mean, it *is* Samyaza. I'm sure she has her reasons."

"Yeah. That's what worries me," Laney muttered.

Chapter Sixty-Six

LANEY SAT on the porch of the SIA safe house watching the street. There wasn't much to see—only an occasional car or someone walking by. But that was all right; Laney's mind was busily turning things over.

The door behind her opened, and she turned as Mustafa and Yoni stepped out. They were the only ones to have returned to the safe house with her; the others had stayed to help out at the crime scene.

"Hey," Laney said.

"Hey yourself," Yoni said, taking a seat next to her. Mustafa sat on her other side.

"What's wrong?" Mustafa asked.

"Nothing," Laney replied with a shrug.

"Laney..." Yoni gave her a look.

She sighed. "I don't know. I just feel like it's not quite over. It's like everything that happened with the Companion Killers. We got the bad guys, and yet something was off."

"We got all of the members of Honu Keiki, right?" Yoni asked.

"Yeah, as far as we can tell, all the Honu members in the area have been accounted for. And all the bomb components were also accounted for."

"But you're not convinced," Mustafa said.

Laney shook her head. "I don't know. Maybe it's that Elisabeta helped us that makes it feel wrong. But something isn't right. I mean, who took that shot? And why?"

Yoni looked out over the quiet street. "I spent my childhood here. I came back and did my military service. Israel is in my blood. I have a lot of family still here." He looked back at Laney. "I need to know that I did everything I could to protect them."

"We still have contacts on the Mount and the surveillance van," Mustafa said.

Laney looked between the two of them: one Israeli Jew and one Egyptian Muslim working together. "How about if we just go watch for a while?"

Chapter Sixty-Seven

LANEY ROLLED HER SHOULDERS, trying to work out the kink that had developed in them. She'd been sitting in the surveillance van by herself, outside the public entrance to the Western Wall, for the last thirty minutes. Before that, she had walked the Western Wall and surrounding area but had seen nothing out of place. Yoni had gone to speak with the security at the Western Wall, and Mustafa was speaking with the security at the Temple Mount. Their SIA badges had gotten them full cooperation.

Laney sighed, wishing not for the first time that there were surveillance cameras on the Mount. Right now, all she had were shots of the entrances and the Western Wall. Danny had linked in a satellite feed of the Mount, but it was too far out to get much detail—although it did show the hundreds of people, if not thousands, milling about.

As she sat, she couldn't help but think about all the history of this place—and most especially, the one historical event most personal to her: the reign of Solomon. It was here that the ring of Solomon gained prominence. Solomon had used the ring to control demons to build his temple—and in doing so, had in essence publicly outed himself as the ring bearer. It would be like wandering into the middle of New York and raining lightning bolts down; there would be no way anyone could look at that accomplishment and not know that something was special about the person who had done it.

Laney recoiled from the idea. Especially after the bridge incident and the Mike Wallace segment and the media inquiries, she wanted no part of that. It was tough enough doing what she had to do without having Joe Public breathing down her neck.

But I suppose, for Solomon, it was different. He was already a king. The world bowed and scraped before him. If he had been a nobody, had come out of obscurity, their reaction wouldn't have been as kind.

Now Solomon's temple was long gone, as was the second temple built to replace it.

That only leaves the third, a voice whispered in the back of Laney's mind.

There was a prophecy regarding the building of a third temple. It was said that it would be built on the same site as the two previous temples—but that when it was erected, the Antichrist would desecrate the temple and declare himself to be God.

The Antichrist—the individual who was believed to bring about the end of days. At first he would be viewed as a hero, a saint among men, his true face hidden from view. But soon his true nature would be revealed. And he would lead to the downfall of the human race.

Laney stared at the Temple Mount on the satellite feed. How on earth would anyone be able to erect a new temple there? No one would ever agree to construction of a new temple, and it wasn't as if someone could just wander in with all the building materials and get to work. Everyone who went in was searched.

Laney examined the satellite feed and frowned. A water tent had been set up outside the Al-Aqsa Mosque. Due to the high temperatures, that seemed normal enough—but it was also the only new addition to the Temple Mount.

She drummed her hands on the table, her unease growing. She grabbed her radio. "Mustafa?"

"Yes, Laney."

"I need you to go check out the water tent. But do it quietly, okay?"

"On my way."

Laney stepped out of the van and looked toward the Western Wall. There were thousands of tourists and devotees here, and up on the Temple Mount would be just as many.

We stopped it. Whatever was going to happen, we stopped it. She repeated the words, but somehow she couldn't make herself believe them.

"Laney." It was Mustafa's voice, and he sounded panicked.

Laney's heart jumped. "What is it?"

"There's a bomb. It's in the tent, wrapped in the tent fabric."

Laney was already running for the entrance to the Western Wall. "Is there a timer?"

"Yes. Twenty-one minutes."

Laney stared at the enormous crowds. *That's not enough time.*

Chapter Sixty-Eight

THE SECURITY FORCES at the Temple Mount were incredibly efficient. People were being herded away from the location mere minutes after Mustafa spoke with Laney. But they were still moving too slowly. At this rate, hundreds would be killed. Laney was tempted to ask one of the officers to shoot a weapon in the air, but she was worried that would cause a stampede, and potentially create precisely the political incident she wanted to prevent.

Laney looked around in frustration. *Damned if we do, damned if we don't.* It seemed no matter what she did at this moment, people were going to be hurt or killed.

She grabbed her radio. "Mustafa, report."

"They're moving them out, but it's taking time."

"What about the bomb squad?"

"They were called away to another location. They'll be here in ten minutes."

That's cutting it close.

"Where are you?" Laney asked.

"Still on the Mount."

"Get out of there."

"Not until everyone else is out."

"Mustafa," Laney warned.

"Would you save yourself?" Mustafa asked quietly.

Laney closed her eyes. "Just get everyone out as fast as you can."

"What are you going to do?"

"I'll help the security forces with the evacuation on this side."

"Good luck."

"You too." *And be careful.*

She pushed her way into the crowd, driving against the tide and hoping to save as many as she could.

Chapter Sixty-Nine

IT TOOK TIME, but the security forces did manage to get people moving faster, and Laney finally made it through the crowd to the Western Wall. A few devotees still stood at the Wall, their eyes downcast, ignoring the Israeli police who were trying to get them to leave.

Yoni came running up.

"Update?" Laney asked.

Yoni's eyes darted to the people at the Wall, and she could feel his frustration. "We're having trouble getting a few people to leave. And we need to empty out the women's prayer area, but there are no female security officers here right now."

Laney gritted her teeth. The Western Wall was separated into two parts, one for men only, and one for women only. And while she understood the religious reasons behind the separation, bombs really should outweigh those considerations. "I'll take care of the women. You take care of the men."

Yoni was already heading for the Wall. "I'll throw them over my shoulders if they don't move."

Laney knew Yoni would do exactly that.

She spent the next few minutes getting the women to leave. Luckily, they all understood the urgency and packed up quickly. When they were gone, she looked up at the Temple Mount and grabbed her radio. "Mustafa, report."

"We have about three hundred people left."

Laney closed her eyes. *Damn it.* "Where's the bomb squad?"

"I don't know. They should have been here by now. Hold on." Her radio went silent. A few seconds later, Mustafa was back. "There's been a problem."

Laney stopped walking. "What?"

"The bomb squad has been ambushed. They're not going to make it in time."

Laney felt her stomach bottom out. "Get out, Mustafa. Get out now."

"Not until everyone else is out." He paused. "It has been my greatest honor to serve with you."

"Mustafa—"

But he didn't respond. And Laney knew he wouldn't. He would stay until the very last second and try to save as many as he could.

And he would die in the effort.

Laney stared up at the Mount. *If only I was up there.* But she'd never be able to get through the crowds to reach the Mount. Not to mention she'd have to talk her way through security.

There had to be something she could do. She couldn't just stand here and watch this happen. The priestess couldn't do this. The ramifications were going to be worldwide. And Laney needed to stop it from happening, no matter the cost.

An idea formed in her mind. She knew it was crazy. She knew it was reckless. But it was also the only thing she could think of.

She looked for Yoni, and spotted his familiar bald head amid the crowd. He had a man thrown over his shoulder, squirming as Yoni carted him to safety.

Laney ran up to him, and Yoni handed the man to an Israeli officer. "The bomb squad's not coming," she said.

Yoni's face was set. "I heard."

"I need you to speak with the police here and have Mustafa speak with the ones on the other side."

"What should I tell them?"

Laney started running for the Wall. "Tell them not to shoot me."

Chapter Seventy

LANEY STOPPED thirty feet from the Western Wall. Back when the wall was under Muslim control, there had been only a twelve-foot-wide alley to accommodate pilgrims coming to visit it. But when Israel took control of the Wall after the Six-Day War, they demolished the neighborhood around it to allow for more access. Now thousands of pilgrims could visit the site.

Laney gazed upon the centuries of history contained in the wall: the rocks laid at the time of Herod, followed by the stones from the Umayyad era, and then finally the Ottoman era. And in between those stones were all the little pieces of paper with the prayers of thousands of people.

Laney hoped that maybe, just maybe, all those prayers might send a little positive energy her way. *Because God knows I'm going to need it.*

She grabbed her radio. "Mustafa?"

"Yes?"

"I need you to cordon off the tent. And did you get Yoni's message about making sure no one shoots me?"

"Yes. But why would they shoot you?"

"I'm coming to you."

"You won't make it. The people have packed the exits. You'll never get through."

"I don't plan on using the regular entrances. Be there in a minute."

Laney shut off her radio and dropped it on the ground. The less weight, the better.

Taking a deep breath, she pictured a funnel in her mind and called forth the wind. She'd used a platform of wind before to lower herself to the ground; now she'd see if one could raise her up.

And sure enough, she slowly began to rise. And then she picked up speed.

She could feel the eyes of the people on the ground behind her. Some screamed and ran. Others froze in place, knelt, or made the sign of the cross. And when she reached the Mount, her appearance was greeted similarly. People stared in disbelief. They ran from her path, some stumbling and falling. She felt bad about the chaos she was causing, but it was better than the chaos a bomb would cause.

Up ahead, she could see the dome and the mosque, and they were beautiful. But her focus was on the tent, and on the group of armed guards surrounding it. *Please don't shoot me*, she begged silently.

One of the guards let out a yell and took aim. But Mustafa sprinted over and pushed the barrel of the man's gun down.

A few seconds later, Laney dropped to the ground in front of them.

Mustafa stared at her, his mouth hanging open. "You just flew."

"Sort of. It was more of a glide, really. How much time have we got?"

"Just under five minutes."

"Where is it?"

"Here."

Mustafa pulled her into the tent. The bomb was only a few bricks of C-4—not nearly enough to destroy the entirety of the Temple Mount, but even a small explosion at this site would be catastrophic, because of the inevitable response from the rest of the world. The bomb was encased in plastic, with the detonator clearly visible.

"How much does that weigh?" Laney asked.

"Maybe twenty pounds."

She knew C-4 was relatively stable, which meant they could move it without it blowing up. *Theoretically.* "I need a backpack."

One of the guards stepped forward and shrugged the pack off his back. He dumped the contents on the ground and handed it to her.

"Thanks." Laney held the bag open toward Mustafa. "Put it in," she said.

Gently, he lifted the bomb and placed it inside the bag.

Taking a breath, Laney strapped the pack to her back and stepped back out of the tent.

Mustafa grabbed her arm, his eyes wide. "Laney, what are you doing?"

"What needs to be done."

And without another word, she took off into the sky.

Chapter Seventy-One

THE MEDITERRANEAN SEA was to the west of the Temple Mount, and Laney could see its blue waters in the distance. As she flew closer, she could see the restaurants along the beaches of Tel Aviv. People were out sunbathing and enjoying themselves, completely oblivious to the bomb flying above their heads.

Laney ignored the tremors in her arms and legs and the sweat that covered her. "Flying" like this required intense effort and concentration, and she was reaching the point of exhaustion. She just prayed that she'd have the bomb clear of people before she finally hit the wall.

Unfortunately, as she passed over the beach she realized the entire area was dotted with boats. There was no clear place to set down. *Damn it.* In her head, she was counting down the seconds. *Forty, thirty-nine...*

The ache in her shoulders increased, and for a moment the funnel of wind that held her aloft weakened. She dropped like a stone. But with her heart in her throat, she regained her concentration and her control. As quickly as she could, she turned to the east—where finally she found a stretch of open water.

She slipped the backpack from her shoulders and let it drop into the water.

She'd done it.

But as she started to head back to shore, her control failed her again, and she dropped toward the water. She managed to summon enough wind to keep her from a free fall, but she was going down. And the whole time she counted.

Six, five, four, three, two, one.

A blast erupted under the surface. A plume of water jetted up into the sky, followed by a wave of energy that coursed through the air. It was fortunate that Laney was so close to the water when it reached her, because it hit her with the force of a truck, and sent her flying head over heels, crashing into the ocean.

Chapter Seventy-Two

CLUTCHING THE BLANKET AROUND HER, Laney stepped off the boat and onto the dock. She turned back to the family who had dragged her out of the water. "Thank you."

The two children, a boy and a girl around six or seven years old, grinned at her, but the parents still wore the same stunned expression they'd had ever since they'd fished her out.

Laney started to hand the blanket back, but the mother shook her head. "No. Keep it."

"Thank you," Laney said again.

Heavy footsteps sounded on the dock, and Laney turned to see five Israeli police officers storming toward her. With a sigh, she gave the family a weary smile and headed for the officers. Holding the blanket with one hand, she held out her badge with the other. "United States Intelligence Officer."

The police were unmoved. Their weapons out, they stopped six feet from Laney. "Get down! Get down!"

Laney lowered herself to the dock with a groan. Her back had not enjoyed the slap of the water, and she was so tired from her exertions that it was a struggle to keep her eyes open. She wondered if she'd even be able to stand back up again without assistance.

Just as Laney's knees hit the dock, a voice barked out across one of the officer's radios, and the officers lowered their weapons. One of them stepped forward. "Agent McPhearson? "

Laney nodded wearily. "That's me."

He extended his hand to help her up. "We are to escort you to Hamateh HeArtzi."

Hamateh HeArtzi—the national headquarters of the Israeli police. It was on the western side of Mount Scopus and was home to a bunch of other government buildings, including the Ministry of Public Security.

"Okay. Escort away," Laney said, getting to her feet.

Chapter Seventy-Three

DESPITE THE SIRENS and the speed of the driver, Laney fell asleep on the ride over. Then, after being woken up, she got to spend the next hour being grilled by an Israeli police officer in a tiny interrogation room. So she was relieved when a knock at the door sounded and the Israeli officer was called out into the hallway.

Laney could hear raised voices, and a moment later, a woman in her early sixties stepped into the room. A dark blue suit with a pale blue blouse brought out the blueness in her eyes, and her white hair was cut in a chic, no-nonsense blunt cut.

Laney couldn't hold back her surprise. It was Nancy Hannigan, the United States Secretary of State.

Laney stood. "Secretary."

Nancy smiled and waved her back down. "Dr. McPhearson. It seems you've had a busy day."

"You could say that," Laney said, settling back into her chair, not sure what else to say.

"The officers tell me you keep saying you need to leave."

Laney tried to gauge where the career diplomat fell in all this. She knew the secretary had been in Saudi Arabia, so she must have hopped on the first plane over here. But what was her role? Was she here to help Laney and the SIA? Or to get in their way?

Laney nodded. "The individual behind the attack today is still at large. I'd like to get to her before she gets away."

Hannigan's blue eyes pierced Laney. "And you know where she is?"

"Australia."

"Is she like you?" Hannigan asked quietly.

Laney paused. "Not exactly. In some ways, she's more powerful."

"Can anyone else stop her?"

"No. Myself and the SIA are the best equipped to deal with her."

Hannigan sat back. "I've known Matt Clark for years. I remember when he first met you. His respect for you is immense. And Matt is not easy to impress."

Laney wasn't sure what to say to that, so she stayed silent.

"What you did today—it saved a lot of lives. And it averted a major diplomatic incident, although already there are arguments and accusations going back and forth."

Laney cringed. "We had hoped to do everything quietly."

Hannigan gave her an amused smile. "Floating over the city with a bomb strapped to your back is your idea of 'quietly'?"

Laney shook her head. "No. It was my version of 'there's no other way.'"

Hannigan eyed her appraisingly. "You realize that what you did today shined a spotlight on you. Who you are, what you're capable of. What you did... it has changed the world."

Laney felt the enormity of her actions. "I know," she said quietly. "And if there was an alternative to that, I would have seized it. But it was either this, or allow the bomb to explode..." Laney shook her head. "And then the world would have changed in a very different way."

"I wonder which way is better for the world? I suppose we have to hope it's this one." Hannigan stood. "I have arranged for you and your team to be released. I assume you'll be going after the priestess?"

Laney stood. "Yes."

"Well, you have the full backing of the United States government, as well as the cooperation of Israel, Saudi Arabia, Great Britain, and about a dozen other countries."

Laney felt her jaw drop. "What?"

"Like I said, Dr. McPhearson, you changed the world. And your role in it as well. Good luck."

Chapter Seventy-Four

SOMEWHERE OVER THE MIDDLE EAST

DRUMMING her fingers on the side of the leather chair, Elisabeta waited for the report. The bomb had been set to explode an hour ago. Why was she still waiting? She stood and paced the bedroom on her plane, trying to tamp down her anger. She really needed to replace Hakeem.

A knock sounded on the door. *Finally.* She sat behind her desk. "Enter."

Hakeem ducked into the room.

"Well?"

"The bomb exploded in the Mediterranean."

Elisabeta frowned. "How did that happen?"

"Um, McPhearson. She took the bomb there."

Elisabeta waited for him to continue—but apparently he thought that was an adequate explanation. She entertained the notion of tossing him out the plane door, but pushed it aside. "Is there anything else?"

"Um, yes. There's video." He handed her a tablet.

She flicked it on and saw that a news report was queued up. She started it and waved Hakeem away.

"Ma'am." He bowed and let himself out.

On the screen, a male news reporter was speaking excitedly about the events that had just occurred on the Temple Mount. "Jerusalem is a city of miracles. And today, the world has just seen another one."

The video cut away from the reporter to a shot of the sky above Jerusalem. Elisabeta frowned. *What does this—*

She halted in mid-thought. An object in the sky was growing larger. People around the camera operator began to murmur, and fingers pointed. The image in the sky became clearer as it moved closer. And then Elisabeta's jaw dropped.

It was Delaney McPhearson.

She watched in shock as McPhearson flew over the beach and out over the sea. The camera operator kept his focus on her, zooming in as she grew smaller. She dropped something, and then turned and headed back. A moment later, a plume of water shot into the air behind her, and McPhearson tumbled into the ocean.

The reporter came back on. "I can report that the woman is alive and was taken to Israeli Police Headquarters immediately after returning to shore. We still do not know her identity—"

Elisabeta paused the recording, her mind reeling. McPhearson had flown—*flown*—over Jerusalem.

A giggle trickled from Elisabeta's mouth, followed by a chuckle. Soon she was laughing hysterically. Her stomach ached, and she had to hold on to the desk to keep herself upright.

After a few minutes, she wiped at the tears on her cheeks and smiled. *Oh, ring bearer. You are simply making this way too easy.*

Chapter Seventy-Five

YOU CHANGED THE WORLD. *And your role in it.* The Secretary of State's words replayed in Laney's mind as she made her way to the airport courtesy of the Israeli police. She knew Hannigan was right: there was no chance her little flight wasn't caught on someone's camera. But she couldn't regret what she had done. She had changed the world; she just had to hope that she had changed it for the better.

Just a few short hours ago, she had been wondering at how Solomon could have so readily revealed his abilities on the Mount. And then she went ahead and did the same thing, in the same location.

The gates to the airport were pulled back to reveal the Chandler jet. Laney thanked the officer for the ride and boarded the plane. Matt, Mustafa, and the other SIA agents were already on board.

Matt grinned at her. "Oh, I thought you were going to fly on your own."

"Not funny, Matt," Laney growled as she walked past him.

Matt reached out and took her arm. She stopped and looked down at him. His eyes were serious. "You did what you had to do, Laney. And you saved a lot of people today. No one will forget that."

Laney sighed. "Is it wrong that I kind of wish they would?"

He smiled. "No, not wrong. But also not possible."

She nodded and headed toward Jake at the back of the plane. She had barely taken her seat before the plane was moving.

"Any word from Australia?" Laney asked as she buckled herself in.

"There's been movement at the facility, but the place was buttoned up tight when the police arrived."

"Do we have permission to go in?"

"Laney, the priestess was behind a plan to set off World War III. There's not a government in the world that doesn't recognize our authority to go in."

"Are they going to wait for us?"

"It's your show. They're going to follow your lead."

Laney frowned. "What does that mean?"

"It means, I have been contacted by at least a dozen different countries to offer their help. You've basically created a global coalition to go after the priestess."

Laney shook her head; the idea seemed insane. "Me?"

"You."

"Do they know what I can do? What the priestess can do?"

"The priestess—no. But after your little flying adventure, they're getting a clearer picture of what *you* can do. And they're glad you're on our side."

Laney looked out the window. A sense of foreboding came over her as the plane sped down the runway and into the air. *I wonder what happens if they think I'm not on their side?*

Chapter Seventy-Six

LANEY all but passed out after her chat with Jake. She didn't wake up until ten hours into the eighteen-hour flight.

Jake looked over at her as she stirred. "I thought you were going to sleep the whole way through."

Laney stretched. "I think that would have been preferable. Why does everything have to be so global? Couldn't these guys at least stay on the same continent?"

Jake laughed. "Well, next time we run into a criminal mastermind, I'll be sure to lodge your complaint."

"Not sure I'm happy about how you just assume there *will* be another criminal mastermind," Laney grumbled.

"When it comes to the Fallen, there's always another one."

"You're not wrong. Speaking of which, any word on Samyaza?"

Jake shook his head. "No. No one's seen hide nor hair of her. Even her office seemed unsure as to her location."

Laney frowned. She still couldn't figure out what Elisabeta's angle was back in Jerusalem. Was she being honest when she said she just wanted to avoid world catastrophe? Laney did suppose a nuclear winter would mess up Elisabeta's access to the finer things in life, but somehow that felt wrong. *Like I'm missing something—again.* For the life of her, she couldn't see what else Elisabeta had to gain from her actions.

When Laney and Jake grabbed a bite to eat, Mustafa and Matt joined them.

"You guys get any sleep?" Laney asked.

"Yes," Matt said.

"These seats are so comfortable," Mustafa said. "I don't think I can go back to flying coach."

Laney laughed. "That's a rich person's problem, Mustafa. But the jet is yours whenever you need it."

He grinned. "I will take you up on that."

Laney rubbed her eyes. "Okay, so what do we know about the Honu Keiki facility?"

"A lot more than we did, and still not much," Jake said. "We got our hands on the blueprints at least."

"How'd we manage that?" Laney asked.

"The Australian government was more than happy to hand them over when they learned of the group's involvement in the Israel plot. They even chased down some of the individuals who helped build the facility."

"And we have confirmation that the priestess is in the bunker," Jake added.

"How?"

"The Australian police attempted to intercept."

Laney groaned. "Oh no. What happened?"

"Apparently three of the men on the detail were killed, and the fourth said he doesn't know what happened. One minute he had the priestess in his rifle sights, and the next she was gone. And then he was flying through the air and slammed into a pole."

Poor guys. They had no idea what they were up against. "Why did they go after her? Didn't we tell everyone to wait?"

"They thought they had a clear shot and they went for it. They didn't know what she could do."

Well, they do now, Laney thought. "All right, well, at least we know where she is. We just have to get to her. What did we learn from the blueprints?"

"About what you'd expect from a bomb shelter," Matt said. "A large structure underground, with pipes for plumbing, air, et cetera. The thing is, there's a lot more vents than should be needed for a facility of the size indicated on the plans, which leads us to think…"

"That the facility is larger than what's on the blueprints," Laney finished.

"Exactly."

"Well, that's just great. Any idea how we get in?" Laney asked.

"Picture Dom's bomb shelter," Jake said. "How would you get into that?"

"You said there are vents. Can we use them?" Laney asked.

Mustafa nodded. "There are some vents, but they would be a tight fit, not to mention difficult to climb down. The vents run at least three hundred feet deep and are only four feet wide."

Laney felt claustrophobic just thinking about it. "But it can be done?"

"Yes," Jake said. "And once inside, that person should be able to open some of the other doors to let the rest of the team in."

Laney sighed. "Well, I guess we're going to rappel down an air vent. How fun."

It took a while to work out the specifics, but by the time the plane was approaching Australia, the team had a plan mapped out. They would use the Australian law enforcement units to cover the exits in case anyone got out. Laney, Mustafa, and two of the smaller SIA agents would then go through the vents. The two agents would be responsible for opening the doors to allow the rest of the force in, while Laney and Mustafa tracked down the priestess.

Matt's phone rang, and he stepped away to answer it while the others finalized the details. When he returned, it was only because Laney knew the agent so well that she recognized the concern on his face.

"What happened?" she asked.

"Samyaza's been seen."

"Where?" Jake asked.

"Perth. She just arrived at the airport we're heading to."

Chapter Seventy-Seven

THE PRIESTESS GROWLED as she stormed into the facility. Her new attendant, Aido, ran up to her, his eyes large. "Priestess, are you all right?" he asked, taking in her bloodstained clothes.

The priestess waved him off. "Run me a bath. I'll be right there."

"Yes, of course." He gave her appearance one last look before scurrying down the hall to do her bidding.

The priestess seethed. The ring bearer had destroyed all her well-laid plans. She had underestimated the woman. She'd heard the stories of the ring bearer—it was part of the lore of Lemuria—but it was just so *unbelievable*. A single mortal woman who was given powers by a ring? And not even powers like the priestess had—not the strength or the speed. How could she possibly be a big threat?

But she had been, and now, undeniably, she was on her way here. The police that had tried to intercept them were proof of that. They had tied her to the Jerusalem event. The botched Jerusalem event.

Now what do I do?

The priestess became aware of the heavy silence around her, and she could feel the stares of her guards. She cursed McPhearson again before calming her face and turning.

Six of her guards stood before her. Four had been with her in the car and had seen her use her abilities. *Another wrinkle.* The priestess nodded at the other two. "You two are dismissed."

They headed down the hall. When they were out of earshot, the priestess addressed the remaining four. "I'm sure you have questions. My abilities are a gift from our ancestors. A way to keep us safe. I have never shared them before, because there was no need. Today, protecting you became my goal. And I would do it again—without hesitation."

The guards' faces were unreadable, and for the first time she wasn't sure of her control over them. *If they are disloyal, they are dead*, she reminded herself.

"What is important now is protecting our people. And I fear that a greater threat is coming." She paused, and let the silence hang in the air.

"What?" asked Ephraim, her second-in-command.

"Her name is Delaney McPhearson. She believes herself to be the ring bearer, but she is not. She is the devil in disguise. If she enters our home, it will be the end of us all. We will not let that happen, will we?"

Her guards stood straighter and answered as one. "No, priestess."

She nodded. "Good. Stay vigilant."

She headed down the hall toward her suite of rooms. She knew the ring bearer would be able to defeat her men; with her powers, she would tear through them, and there was no way to stop that. But she had no intention of making it *easy* for the woman.

She smiled as an idea formed in her mind. *Let's see exactly how committed to taking me down you are.*

Chapter Seventy-Eight

LANEY STARED at Mustafa in disbelief. "Samyaza's in Australia? What the hell?"

"Where is she now?" Jake asked.

"She's off the airport grounds and heading in the direction of the Honu Keiki facility," Matt replied.

"Just make sure no one gets in her way," Laney said. "I don't want anyone else getting killed."

"Already done," Matt said.

"What the hell is she doing?" Jake asked.

"Damned if I know," Laney growled. "I mean, she didn't appear to have any personal interest in the priestess, so I can't figure out why she's here." Samyaza involving herself in the Temple Mount incident made a certain amount of sense. But why follow the priestess here? Revenge? Anger that one of her former lieutenants was playing by their own script?

"Are we sure she's not working *with* the priestess?" Jake asked.

Laney groaned. "No, I guess we're not. But I can't see

why she would help us defeat the priestess if she was in cahoots with her. Matt, is there any connection between them?"

"We never found one. But if they both remember their past lives, it's possible."

Laney ran a hand through her hair, and had to stop herself from yanking some of it out. "It's bad enough we need to find a connection in *this* life. How the hell are we supposed to figure out a past life connection?" She looked at Matt. "Do you remember your past life?"

Matt shook his head. "No. Occasionally I have glimpses of things: feudal Japan, the Roman coliseum—but there's no identity attached. I don't know who I was in the past or what those scenes mean to me."

"Do any Fallen know?"

"Only Gerard and Samyaza. And Gerard only learned because of your mother. I've never heard of anyone knowing any more than I know."

"So if the priestess doesn't know who she used to be," Jake said, "what does Samyaza want with her?"

"Could she want to help us take her down?" Mustafa asked. "Like in Israel?"

Laney scoffed. "So what—she's now Team Chandler? One of the good guys? I can accept Cain not being who we thought, and Gerard, even, heading toward the light—but Samyaza? I just can't buy that."

"She has done a lot of good in the world lately," Mustafa said quietly.

Laney felt like she'd fallen down the rabbit hole. Were they honestly thinking Samyaza was turning over a new leaf? "No. Whatever reason Samyaza has for being here, it's not to help the world, out of the goodness of her heart. There's some other angle here, and we're just not seeing it."

"She is Samyaza," Jake said. "Which means she's seeing things from an angle or angles we're not privy to. It's like learning chess one week and going against a grandmaster the next."

Laney wanted to be insulted by the comparison, but she knew it was probably accurate.

"We do have eyes on her," Matt said. He typed something on his computer, and a satellite feed appeared.

Laney leaned forward. "Where is she?"

Matt pointed to three SUVs driving through traffic. "There."

"How long will it take them to reach the bunker?"

"I'd guess about an hour."

And we land in fifteen minutes, Laney thought. "Okay, let's make sure there are some choppers waiting for us when we land. Whatever's going on with her, we need to make sure we beat her to the priestess."

Mustafa stood. "I'll see that it's done."

Laney met Jake's concerned gaze and turned away. A sinking feeling was forming in the pit of her stomach. Samyaza was up to something, and yet again they had no idea what.

Jake placed his hand on Laney's shoulder. "We'll stop her."

She nodded, but she knew that for both of them, the sentiment was only a hope—not a promise.

Chapter Seventy-Nine

LANEY HAD NEVER VISITED AUSTRALIA, though it had always been a place she had dreamed of getting to one day. She'd seen the incredible images, like everyone else—the opera house in Sydney, the Great Barrier Reef, the Blue Mountains, Ayers Rock. And then there was Perth, the capital of Western Australia, sitting along the Indian Ocean. It was known for a lot of things, including its incredible beaches, but Laney had always wanted to go to Nambung National Park and see the Pinnacles, rock spires that seemed to push out of the desert floor right along the coast.

As they flew over the land around Perth—in choppers loaned to them by the Australian police force—she felt she could appreciate the appeal of the rugged landscape. She could see what drew people to it. And the fact that Hugh Jackman was from here didn't hurt, either. Australia was only slightly smaller than the mainland United States, but with less than a tenth of its population, it was regarded as a place full of tough, adventurous people.

Laney remembered an article she had read on all the animal species in Australia that could kill you. There was the box jellyfish, which had millions of nearly invisible stingers that dealt lethal doses of venom; the Easter brown snake, which was responsible for most snake deaths in Australia; the poisonous but gorgeous blue-ringed octopus; the saltwater crocodile, which had the strongest bite of any living reptile; and the bull shark, which liked to swim in shallow waters. They even had giant stinging trees whose painful effects could be felt for months after the initial encounter. And then there was the flying fox. It was basically a bat the size of a fox, and was known to hang from people's porch roofs. Laney imagined opening your door one morning and having *that* greet you. Not the way to start the day.

But of all the horrifying creatures that might live in Australia, none was as dangerous as Samyaza. She had arrived just ahead of them and should still be en route to the priestess.

They had no new reports on the priestess—everything was quiet out at the shelter—but she must know by now that her plan had failed. The woman had tried to start World War III. Who does that? What was she vying for, most evil Bond villain?

But you stopped her, a voice whispered at the back of Laney's mind. And she wouldn't change that, but if she could have changed the *how*....

Laney cringed at what the world response to her actions was going to be. She had intentionally not checked any news reports; she didn't need that crowding into her mind when she needed to focus. But she knew it was going to be bad. The response to the bridge had been bad enough. She should probably go hide out for a while until everything died down.

Maybe I'll go stay at the SIA facility in West Virginia. I could help out the SIA, visit with Cain, and stay out of the spotlight. Wait—was she actually thinking of voluntarily placing herself in a government facility? *Oh, yeah, my life is on the right course.*

"Five minutes," the pilot said in her headphones.

Right, head in the game.

Laney looked ahead for Samyaza's caravan. If their estimates were correct, they should be arriving at the Honu Keiki's underground facility at almost the same time Elisabeta did. Matt's best guess was that each of the three SUVs held four Fallen—whereas even with the SIA agents, Laney had only six Fallen on her side. She hoped she could turn some of Elisabeta's men, to help even out those numbers. Plus, they had an additional four guns, including Jake and Mustafa.

Still, she did not have a good feeling about this. Talking Samyaza out of something seemed highly unlikely, which meant it was going to get bloody.

"Up ahead," Jake said.

Laney could just make out the caravan now. They were at least a half mile from the nearest bomb entrance.

"Let's get in front of them," Laney ordered.

The chopper put on a burst of speed, and tingles ran over Laney's skin, letting her know that Fallen were below. She threw open the chopper door and focused on the cars, willing a wall of wind to slam against them. The SUVs immediately slowed, their back wheels coming up as they tried to continue forward.

A flash from one of the other choppers indicated a rocket had been launched. Jake launched another from theirs.

The Fallen leapt from their cars, narrowly avoiding destruction. One SUV was engulfed in flames, and the other slammed to a stop and just missed being destroyed as well.

Laney stepped from the chopper.

"Laney!" Jake yelled.

But Laney was already heading down, using the wind to soften her landing. Matt jumped out of the other chopper, hit the ground with a roll, and raced toward her. He assumed a protective position in front of her, and she placed a hand on his shoulder.

Matt began firing at the Fallen, while Laney ordered the two Fallen within shouting distance to remain still and not fight back. More SIA agents leapt from the choppers and engaged the Fallen or sprinted after the ones that were trying to run.

Chaos and gunfire surrounded Laney, but she ignored it all, looking only for Samyaza. But she was nowhere to be seen.

Surprisingly, the fight was over in seconds. All the Fallen were incapacitated, and none of the SIA agents were harmed.

Laney looked around. "What the hell?"

Matt met her look. "That was way too easy."

"There!" Mustafa yelled, pointing at a lone figure running in the distance.

Matt took off at a sprint.

"Matt, no!" Laney yelled. "Damn it!" She jumped into one of the SUVs, which the Fallen had left running. Slamming the car into gear, she took off after Matt, really wishing super speed was part of her bag of tricks.

Chapter Eighty

BY THE TIME Laney had caught up with Matt, he had tackled Elisabeta to the ground. The two were trading blows that would have pulverized a mere human.

Laney bolted from the car. "Stop!"

Elisabeta paused in mid-swing, and a look of disbelief crossed her face. Matt stopped as well.

Approaching them, Laney said, "Matt, you're released."

Matt shook out his shoulders. "Well, that's an awkward feeling." He looked over at Elisabeta. Her hair was disheveled and the sleeve of her blouse was torn. But what really stood out was the look in her eyes—there was murder in them. "You got her?" Matt asked.

"I got her," Laney said, meeting Elisabeta's gaze. She smiled. "It's over, Elisabeta."

Elisabeta raised an eyebrow. "Oh, you think so?"

"Why are you even here?" Matt asked. "Why do you care what the priestess does?"

Elisabeta's eyes narrowed. Her voice was cold. "She disobeyed. That must be punished."

"You know, there are greater things at risk here than your ego being tarnished," Laney said.

Two more SIA agents ran up, looking between Matt, Laney, and Elisabeta. Matt nodded at them, and Laney didn't miss the glower Elisabeta sent the agent. "Laney," Matt said, "if you've got this, I'm going to button up the rest of her team and get the transport going. These agents will stay with you."

Laney waved him away. "No problem."

Matt blurred and disappeared from view.

"It's not, you know," Elisabeta said softly.

"Not what?" Laney asked.

Samyaza's face showed no sign of defeat. No concern for her predicament. "It's not over."

A feeling of dread crawled over Laney. "What do you mean?"

Elisabeta laughed. "You really don't know who I am, do you? You think *this* was my final move? I've already made it."

Laney stepped forward. "What are you talking about? What move?"

The struggle to stay silent played across Elisabeta's face. Her lips became a tight line. But she couldn't fight the compulsion. "Three days ago, I set bombs around the shelter. They will detonate within the hour."

Laney's mouth fell open. "There are innocent people in there."

Elisabeta shrugged. "Not really my concern."

Oh my God. Laney turned to the SIA agents. "You stay with her." To Elisabeta she added, "You will stay with these agents. You will not attempt to escape them or harm them in any way."

Elisabeta glared, but Laney paid it no mind. She was already running for the SUV and pulling out her radio. "Jake, there are bombs around the bunker! We need to get everybody out!"

Chapter Eighty-One

LANEY RACED toward the facility in the SUV. There were four entrances into the facility, which they theorized extended underground for a minimum of two acres. *How are we going to cover all of that in time?*

She pulled to a sharp stop at one of the entrances, dust rising around the car. Jake and Mustafa pulled to a stop behind her in the second SUV. They joined her while two agents hopped out and began pulling climbing gear from the back of the vehicle.

"Jake?" Laney said.

Jake scanned the facility. There were no guards, no sign of life. "I'm going on a bomb search. The other SIA agents and the Australians are already searching, and the bomb squad has been mobilized from Perth. One of our guys already found one of the bombs—it's set to go off in forty-five minutes."

One of the agents handed Laney a harness, and she started to climb into it. "What about Honu Keiki? Has anyone tried to reach them?"

Mustafa nodded. "I've tried. I have someone continually trying. Oasu is with them. Hopefully he can convince them. But so far, no one has answered."

"We're not even sure that the phones are working yet," Jake said. "Laney, are you sure about going in?"

"There's no choice. We'll open the doors as soon as we get down there."

The agents, a man and a woman, were already harnessed, a rope slung over their shoulders.

"Laney, these are Agents Parks and Felix," Mustafa said, nodding to the woman and man respectively. Laney got a reading off Parks, which told her she was a nephilim. Felix wasn't, but the way he held himself told her he was former military.

"There are two vents near the closest entrance," Parks said.

"Set up the anchor," Laney said. "Mustafa and I will take one vent, you two head down the other. We're going as soon as you're set."

The two agents jogged to a spot about two hundred yards away.

Mustafa looked at Laney. "We need to hurry."

"I know. I'll be right there."

He jogged over to join the agents.

Laney turned to Jake. "Well, this feels familiar."

"You stepping into danger while I stand back and watch?" he asked lightly.

"Jake."

He shook his head. "I don't mean it like that. I know this is your job. The same way I have mine. But I won't ever stop worrying about you."

"Right back at you."

Jake pulled her close and kissed her forehead. He held

her for a moment longer than necessary, and Laney's breath went quiet. With a pang, she realized this was not just a going-into-danger goodbye. It was much bigger than that. Jake was saying goodbye to *them*. To them as a couple. She could feel it. It was time.

Jake pulled back. "I'll be at the door waiting for you. If it's getting close, get yourself out of there. And please be careful." He paused. "I love you, Laney. I always will."

She felt tears press at the back of her eyes. "I love you too, Jake."

He got into the SUV and pulled away.

Laney felt his loss, but she knew it was the right thing, even if the timing was beyond horrible. She had to live this life, just like he did. And he couldn't handle being her partner in her destiny *and* in love. He wanted her to choose one.

And I guess I have.

She took a deep breath to clear her head, knowing she had no time to dwell on it. Then she turned and headed toward Mustafa.

Besides, if Jake doesn't find those bombs, I won't have much time to be heartbroken anyway.

Chapter Eighty-Two

THE FIVE-MINUTE CLIMB down the vent was nerve-wracking. It was pitch black, and the vent was only about three feet by four feet. Laney had a small light attached to the band around her head, but it did nothing to illuminate what was below her. To add to the claustrophobia, she kept imagining a bomb going off and burying her alive. And for some reason, she also couldn't help but imagine rats scurrying around and dropping on her head from vents above her. Not that she had passed any vents, or had any reason to believe they contained rats, but her imagination was in overdrive right now. She could not reach the bottom soon enough.

"Laney, how are you doing?" Mustafa asked through her earpiece.

"Um, good. I think I'm reaching the end."

A few seconds later, her feet touched something solid. "I'm here," she whispered. "Hold on." She disconnected the rope from her harness. "I'm disconnected. Start making your descent."

"On my way," Mustafa said.

Laney crouched down, feeling along the wall. Just below the bottom of the shaft she found the horizontal vent that would lead them inside. She shimmied inside, then crawled on hands and knees. It was only about ten feet before she reached the grate.

"At the grate," she said. She peered through it; on the other side was some sort of storage room, and there was no one inside. "I'm going in."

Saying a quick prayer, she pushed on the grate. It didn't budge. *Damn it.* With some difficulty, she managed to turn herself around so her feet were next to the grate. She kicked hard, and the grate popped open and crashed to the floor. She grimaced at the noise and lowered herself into the room.

"I'm in."

"I'm almost there."

A few minutes later, Mustafa was lowering himself down next to her. "Anything?" he asked.

Laney shook her head. "No. It's quiet out there. You ready?"

"Let's go."

Laney eased the door open. The hallway was empty. *So far so good.* She stepped out, with Mustafa right behind her, and they crept silently down the hall.

Mustafa tapped Laney on the shoulder. "Do you think we should—"

"Halt!" A guard had stepped around the corner ahead of them, flanked by three others. Laney whirled around and saw another four guards appear in the hallway behind them.

She put up her hands slowly. *Oh, crap.*

Chapter Eighty-Three

SAMYAZA STUDIED the men Laney had left to guard her. *Such a silly girl. She really is going to have to get a little more seasoned if she ever intends to beat me.*

She recognized one of the agents, the man. His name was Turel, and he had at one point been one of *her* men. He had jumped every time she said jump. He had even made the ultimate sacrifice to demonstrate his loyalty. And now he guarded her as if he was more powerful than her.

The other agent, the woman, was only a nephilim. Samyaza thought she might be the child of Gadriel, but she couldn't be sure. As generations passed, it became harder and harder to recognize the offspring.

Neither paid her much attention, and Elisabeta bristled at the lack of respect, but at the same time she knew it was exactly what she needed. Laney had disappeared fifteen minutes ago. Off to save a bunch of people she had never met, who would never even know all she had sacrificed for them. What a waste. When you did something, you should lay it at the world's feet to have them praise you. *Apparently the ring bearer hasn't learned that little lesson either.*

Ah, so many lessons this one needed. Too bad she didn't have much time left.

Speaking of which. Samyaza rolled her wrists. It had been a while since she had done her own fighting. She was a little excited at the prospect.

She waited.

When the nephilim turned toward the bunker, no doubt wishing to be part of the action, Elisabeta sprang forward. With one move she broke the neck of the Fallen first, and then, when the nephilim spun back around, Elisabeta kicked her in the ribs, grabbed her by the hair, and plunged her hand into her chest. Ribs cracked as she reached inside and ripped out the woman's heart.

She dropped it to the ground with distaste. Fighting was always so messy.

She wiped her hands on the woman's jacket and took the knife from the sheath on the agent's leg. She turned as Turel began to stir.

"Eh, eh, eh." Elisabeta plunged the knife into his heart over and over again. His eyes flew open, and he grabbed at her. "You really should have stayed loyal."

The light dimmed from his eyes, and he went still.

Elisabeta dropped the knife and once again wiped off her hands. Carefully, she reached into her ear, pulled out her earplug, and then reached into the other ear for the second one. She dropped them on Turel's chest. *Like lambs to the slaughter.*

Chapter Eighty-Four

LANEY STOOD NEXT TO MUSTAFA, shaking her head. They had been trying to convince the Guard of the danger they were in, but with no success. And Laney was painfully aware of the time slipping by. "We're not here to hurt you or expose you. You're in *danger*."

The guards glared down at her. "The priestess told us about you. You're one of the reasons we had to leave our home. She said *you* are the danger."

Laney frowned. "What are you talking about?"

"She is the ring bearer," Mustafa said quietly.

The guard scoffed. "Sure, and you're Superman."

"I am," Laney said. She held up her ring.

One of the older guards stepped forward. "A ring means nothing. The ring bearer—"

A gust of wind blew down the hall, knocking one of the guards down.

"You were saying?"

The older guard shook his head, his face pale. "It's not possible."

Slowly, Laney reached for her radio. "I have someone who can help you understand. Okay?"

His eyes narrowed, but he nodded.

Laney clicked on the radio. "Oasu, are you there?"

"I'm here."

"I need you to speak with someone." She held the radio out to the guard.

"Who is this?" the guard demanded.

"Guard Oasu."

"Oasu?"

"Is that you, Sigil?"

Sigil kept his eyes on Laney. "Yes."

"You can trust her. You can trust Laney. She *is* the ring bearer. She's here to help. You're all in danger. There are bombs outside the facility. You need to get everyone out."

The guards exchanged looks, shifting from foot to foot.

"It's true. An enemy of Honu Keiki set bombs around the perimeter. She's after the priestess, but she'll take out the rest of you to get to her. We have to get everyone out of here."

"Our duty is to the priestess," Sigil said, but Laney read the uncertainty in his face.

Laney knew she was on shaky ground here, and she didn't want to attack their loyalty to the priestess. "You also act in the best interest of the people in Honu Keiki," she said. "And it is in their best interest to leave here, for now. If we are wrong, everyone can come right back in. But something about this must feel wrong. Moving from your homeland, leaving people behind—that is not the Honu Keiki way."

Sigil frowned. "Leaving people behind? What are you talking about?"

Mustafa and Laney exchanged a look. Then Laney

spoke. "Not everyone from Honu Keiki is here. The older members and the less able-bodied were left behind."

A guard stepped up from the back. "The priestess said they were coming later. My brother, he—he's not here yet."

Laney looked at the young guard, and knew immediately who his brother was. "Ipo?"

The guard's eyes went wide, and he nodded.

"He displeased the priestess, and she forbade him from coming. He is still at Malama, along with Aaliyah, Andre, and dozens of others."

"But they—It's not—"

Laney shook her head. "I know this is difficult, but trust Oasu. Have you ever known him to be anything but loyal to Honu Keiki? You are in danger. Please help us get everyone out."

A new guard came striding down the hall. Laney could tell from his walk that he was in charge. "Why is she still here?"

Sigil spoke. "Guard Ephraim," he said, and then began explaining what Delaney had said.

Ephraim narrowed his eyes as he listened. When Sigil was done, he turned to Laney. "What proof do you have of this?"

"Bombs have been found around your facility," Laney said. "Guard Oasu can verify that. The priestess is not who you think she is." Something shifted in Ephraim's eyes, and Laney understood. "You *know*," she said quietly. "You know what she's capable of. You've seen her abilities."

Ephraim said nothing. The only indication anything was wrong was the slightest tightening of his jaw.

"The point is, you're in danger. We need to get you all out."

Doubt flashed in his eyes but his tone betrayed none of it.. "Not until we speak with the priestess."

Laney realized she wasn't going to get them to go anywhere if they couldn't speak to their priestess first. *Damn.*

"Okay," she said. "Let's talk to the priestess."

Chapter Eighty-Five

EPHRAIM LED them to a security room at the end of the hall. There were monitors displaying the common areas along the back wall, as well as a console with three computers. He explained that the priestess had placed herself in seclusion, but she could be reached by videophone.

Why is she in seclusion? Laney wondered. But she didn't have time to ponder that before Ephraim had the priestess on the screen.

"What is it, Ephraim?" the priestess demanded.

"We have had a security breach. A woman claiming to be the ring bearer has—"

"Remove her immediately. You are responsible for defending me, to the death if necessary."

The guards looked uneasily at one another.

Laney stepped in front of the camera. "Yeah, that's not going happen. This facility is in danger. You need to evacuate. Now."

The priestess was practically spitting. "You *lie*. And they are *my* soldiers. They will follow orders."

"Don't do this. Don't put them at risk."

"Your words have no power over me."

"You're going to get everyone here killed."

"I am doing no such—"

"Samyaza was out there. *She* set bombs around your facility."

The smallest flash of fear crossed the priestess's face, but she quickly covered it. "Samyaza is not concerned with my activities."

"She was in Israel. She was the one who helped stop you. You disobeyed her, tried to change the world based on *your* desires, not hers. How supportive of that do you really think she would be?"

The priestess narrowed her eyes. "If Samyaza is really out there, it makes no difference whether I stay in here or go out there. I'll be dead either way. Might as well go with some company."

The screen went black.

Laney turned to the guards. "Did you hear her? She's going to take you all with her. You need to go. You need to save your people. You have survived for thousands of years. Don't let her destroy all that."

Ephraim still looked uncertain.

Laney pushed on. "You have my word that if anyone wishes to return once the danger has passed, they can. But you have children here. Don't place them in danger. Please."

Ephraim considered for a moment, then gestured for her radio. Laney handed it over.

"Oasu?" he said.

"Yes?"

"Can we trust this woman?"

"Yes." Oasu's voice came out in a rush. "Yes. Please, Ephraim, you are all in danger."

The man stared into Laney's eyes. His duty to the priestess was wrestling with his need to protect his people. Finally, he nodded. "We will get everyone outside, just in case. And then we will determine the truth."

Relief washed over Laney. "Thank you. Now please, open the doors—all of them. How long will it take to get everyone out?"

"Maybe fifteen minutes."

Laney paled. "That's too long. We need to go faster." She turned to the other guards. "You need to get everyone you can and *run*, not walk them, to the nearest exit."

The men looked to Ephraim, and he nodded. "Do as she says."

The guards took off at a run.

"I will go with them," Mustafa said, and ran after them.

Ephraim stepped up to the keyboard and input a series of numbers. A siren sounded, and the room was bathed in red light. In the distance, she could hear the blast doors opening.

"How many people are in the facility right now?"

"Three hundred seventy five."

Oh god.

"But most are located in areas near exits. The siren should get people moving."

"There's not much time. The bombs are set to explode in, she glanced at her watch, twenty-five minutes. Can you announce an evacuation?"

Ephraim stepped up to the intercom. "Attention. There is an emergency. Everyone must quickly make their way to the nearest exit. This is not a drill. I repeat, evacuate immediately." He turned to Laney. "The Guard will make sure everyone gets out."

"My people will be standing by at the exits."

For the next fifteen minutes they evacuated the members of Honu Keiki, with Laney keeping track of the time. She kept looking for the priestess but didn't see her in any of the rooms. Mustafa ran by her with another group, and Laney grabbed his arm. "Have you seen Parks and Felix?"

"They're here, helping with the evacuation."

"Get them and yourself out of here."

"What are you going to do?"

"I'll look for stragglers and the priestess," Laney said. "I order you out of here, Mustafa. You've done what you can now go."

Mustafa looked like he wanted to argue, but he nodded. "I'll grab everyone I can on the way out."

"Be careful," Laney said.

She headed down the hall, deeper into the facility, checking every doorway for anyone left behind. Along the way, she continued to pass people who were exiting. Laney prayed they would all be able to get out in time.

She keyed her radio. "Does anyone have eyes on the priestess?"

The groups at each exit reported a negative.

"Laney, just get out," Jake said. "If she's there, she's signing her own death warrant. You don't need to sign yours."

Laney knew he was right. "Do we have numbers on all those out yet?"

"We're still getting them, but I'm sure we're getting close. You just need to get out."

"How's the search for the bombs coming?"

"We've found eleven and disarmed four. We won't be

able to get them all disarmed in time. You need to leave now."

He was right. This was suicide. Laney turned back for the entrance. "I'm heading out."

"Laney!" Oasu's voice came through her earpiece.

"What's going on?"

"One of the guards reported in. The priestess is still inside. She's barricaded herself in the community room."

"Well, she's about to get buried."

"She's not alone."

"Who's with her?"

"The children. She barricaded herself in with the children."

Chapter Eighty-Six

LANEY SPRINTED down the hallways of the compound, following Oasu's directions. Ahead, she saw three members of the Guard standing before a heavy door. From beyond it, she could hear loud music.

"What's going on?" Laney asked.

"We can't get in," one of them said.

Running footsteps sounded behind Laney, and Mustafa and Ephraim came sprinting down the hall. Ephraim nodded to the door. "That's the community room. The cameras showed her inside with at least three dozen children."

"What's with the music?" Mustafa asked.

"To make sure she can't hear me," Laney said.

Ephraim addressed the guards "Can you get the door open?"

They shook their heads. "She's jammed the controls. And we can't cut through it."

Ephraim's hand trembled, and in that moment Laney

knew two things: one, he had a child in that room, and two, his loyalty to the priestess had been severed.

"There has to be a way in." Laney looked around. *Come on, think.* Eyeing the lights in the hallway, she remembered a theory Dom had shared with her once.

She looked at the men around her. "Okay. I'm going to try something."

Chapter Eighty-Seven

FOR THEIR OWN SAFETY, Laney had sent Ephraim, Mustafa, and the three guards to hide in a closet down the hall from the community room. If her plan worked, and she got the door open, their job was to get the kids out.

They were to leave the priestess to Laney.

Laney clenched her fists. *Okay. Let's see if this idea works.*

She couldn't control the lightning from the sky down through the building. There were too many places where that could go wrong. And the hallway wasn't long enough for a good wind. But Dom had suggested something a few weeks back that might be able to help them. He said that maybe it wasn't just lightning she could control, but *electricity*. This ability wouldn't be mentioned in the history of the ring bearer, because, well, until recently there was no electricity available besides what lightning produced.

Laney closed her eyes and tried to tap into the electricity in the facility the same way she did the lightning.

Nothing happened.

Focus, Laney ordered herself. She took a few deep breaths, trying to calm her racing heart.

Keeping her eyes closed, she tuned out all the sounds around her: the people scurrying for exits, the heavy bass music, even the sound of her own breathing. She focused only on the electrical energy.

And she found that she could *feel* it. Tingles of electricity ran through the walls. She concentrated on it, drew it toward her, just as she did with the lightning. Her hair began to stand out from her head as she let it build inside her, taking it in until she could control no more.

And then, in one torrent, she unleashed it.

She directed the energy through the light closest to the community room and into the door. In a blinding flash, the door tore away from the frame and fell to the floor, taking part of the wall with it. The kids scampered back with a scream that could barely be heard over the loud music.

Laney's knees weakened at the exertion. Mustafa and the guards stormed past her into the room. On shaky limbs, Laney followed. *Thanks, Dom.*

The children ranged in age from three to fourteen. Most had tears streaming down their cheeks and their hands covering their ears. The guards started to usher those closest to the door out into the hallway, but Ephraim rushed straight to a little girl with dark pigtails and scooped her into his arms. He hugged her tight before grabbing two other children and herding a group of older ones to the door.

For a moment the priestess was taken by surprise, but she quickly regained her composure. She grabbed a young boy and girl and pulled them to the back of the room, holding them like shields in front of them.

Laney strode toward the priestess. The music was painfully loud, but she ignored the pain, knowing the kids, with their more attuned hearing, were hurting even more than she was.

"Give it up!" Laney yelled, but her words were lost in the music.

The priestess grinned, then picked up one of the children—a girl who couldn't have been more than three years old—and held her to her chest.

Laney went still. She knew the priestess could kill the child as easily as she breathed. The girl's big eyes looked at Laney, and tears traced down her cheeks.

Mustafa and Ephraim came to join Laney. *The guards must be escorting the rest of the children out of here*, she thought. *Please hurry.*

Ephraim began to move toward the priestess's other captive, the young boy, but the priestess placed her hand on the child's neck, and he stopped.

Laney didn't know what to do. She wasn't nearly as fast as the priestess; the priestess could crush the child's neck before she got anywhere near her.

But then she spotted something—a sprinkler head directly above the priestess. *It's worth a try.* Without taking her eyes from the priestess, she focused on the electricity again, feeling for it, drawing it from the walls. *Come on.*

A surge of electricity leapt from the nearest light, just missing the sprinkler and setting the ceiling on fire. The priestess jumped back, startled, and Laney took advantage of the distraction to lunge forward, yank the girl from her grasp, and kick the priestess back against the wall.

"Get them out!" Laney yelled, even though she knew neither Mustafa nor Ephraim could hear her. But they got the message. Mustafa grabbed the girl, and Ephraim the boy, and they took off, leaving Laney alone with the priestess.

Laney held her ground, staring down the priestess, blocking her exit. Above them, the sprinklers came to life as the fire from the ceiling spread. Laney struggled not to groan. She had intended to set off the sprinklers to distract the priestess, but now they weren't much help.

Or maybe they could be.

She could make it rain and draw lightning from the sky. It seemed possible she could draw water from sprinklers. *After all the electricity worked.* She focused on increasing the water pressure to the sprinklers. With a pop, several sprinkler heads broke off the ceiling and water came gushing into the room from the open pipes.

The priestess let out a yell and dove for Laney, but Laney sidestepped, slamming her palm into the priestess's face. But Laney knew it was a lucky hit. The priestess turned and, with lightning quick moves, picked Laney up and tossed her across the room. Laney landed on a table with a bone-jarring thud, rolled off the other side, and hit the floor with a splash. The room was now covered in about two inches of water.

Laney scrambled to her feet, called on the wind, and aimed it at the water. With the power of a fire hose, water blasted the priestess's face, throwing her backward and lifting her off the ground. She landed with a splash. When she got to her knees, Laney directed the water at her again, not letting up as she sprinted for the priestess.

The priestess struggled against the onslaught. She couldn't escape the water, and it blinded her to Laney's actions. Laney ran around behind her, then released the wind and water at the same time as she slipped her hands around the priestess's chin.

She twisted.

The priestess's eyes went wide, and then she slumped into the water below.

Chapter Eighty-Eight

THE MUSIC SHUT OFF, and the silence was almost painful in comparison. Her ears ringing, Laney grabbed the priestess's arm and keyed her mike. "How much time, Jake?" she yelled.

"Three minutes."

Damn it. Laney grabbed the priestess's arm and dragged her across the room. The woman wasn't dead, and Laney couldn't leave her here to be blown up. Well, she could—but she kind of liked being considered one of the good guys, and good guys didn't leave people to get blown up.

Besides, if Laney left her behind, there was also the possibility she would wake up and escape the blast on her own. And then Laney would have to track her down all over again.

Another set of arms reached down to grab the priestess, and Laney looked up into Mustafa's face.

"Let me help," he said.

"I thought I ordered you out."

Mustafa smiled. "You did? I must not have heard that."

Together, they hoisted the priestess to her feet between them, each taking one of her arms across their shoulders. Then they raced as fast as they could down the hall.

"What's the closest exit?" Laney asked.

"The southeast exit. Just stick with me."

Laney keyed her mike. "Jake, we're coming out the southeast exit."

Jake's voice was urgent. "Laney, there's a bomb not too far from there. You need to move."

"Shit."

They tore down the hallway. More than once Laney thought of ditching the priestess, but she didn't. They turned right and then another right. Laney saw daylight ahead.

The sight urged her on. And just as she and Mustafa burst through the exit, the priestess between them, a Jeep pulled to a stop in front of them.

Behind the wheel, Jake yelled, "Get in!"

Laney and Mustafa tossed the priestess roughly in the back and then leapt in after her. Laney barely caught hold of the roll bar before Jake took off.

They were no more than fifty feet away when she heard the first rumble. Then six explosions sent dirt into the air. A cloud of dirt descended on the Jeep, and Jake screeched to a stop while Laney and Mustafa covered their heads.

Chunks of dirt and rocks pelted them. Laney held her breath, squeezing her eyes tight. Finally, the cloud of dirt passed, and Laney raised her head.

Next to her, the priestess stirred. Laney reached over, placed one hand on either side of her head, and snapped her neck again. "Oh, no you don't."

Chapter Eighty-Nine

JAKE DROVE them to where most of the Honu Keiki members had been gathered. Mustafa jumped from the Jeep. "I will get a sedative for her."

Jake looked back at Laney. "You good?"

"I am." She coughed and wiped away the mud that was dripping from her wet hair into her face. "Well, sort of."

Jake smiled. "You really need to stop these last-minute rescues."

"It's part of my charm," she said, wiping more mud from her arms.

He laughed. "That it is. I'll go see what needs to be done."

He walked away, and Mustafa jogged back over with an SIA agent in tow, a black briefcase in hand. Laney hopped from the Jeep and let them take custody of the priestess. They'd sedate her with amobarbital and transport her to the West Virginia facility. Laney knew the woman would be locked up for the rest of her life, but she felt no sympathy—not after what the priestess had been planning.

Laney keyed her radio. "Did everyone get out?"

"It looks like we got everybody," Matt replied.

"Any injuries?"

"Some, but none are life-threatening. Good job."

"Your guys, too. Tell them for me, would you?"

"Will do."

Laney pocketed the radio and stared at the crowd of people. They all looked lost. Spotting a familiar face, she walked up to Oasu.

She tapped him on the arm. "Hey."

He looked down at her, and his eyes went wide. "What happened?"

Laney reached up a hand to the back of her neck and came back with mud. She flicked it to the ground, then wiped her hand on her pants, trying not to picture how much mud was probably coating the back of her. "It was a little tricky getting out. Everyone all right?"

"I think so. I don't know."

A rumble tore through the ground, feeling like an earthquake. Oasu reached out to steady Laney as part of the underground facility collapsed, sending up another plume of dirt. Laney put her hand to her mouth, imagining what would have happened had they not gotten everyone out in time. *Oh my God.*

"I don't know what we do from here," Oasu said softly.

Laney spied a line of ambulances and emergency vehicles already making their way toward them. She squeezed Oasu's arm. "We'll get you all back to Malama. But right now, we need to take care of your people's medical needs. Some may be hurt, some in shock. Can you gather your people together and pull out the ones who are going to need medical attention?"

Oasu nodded, but his gaze drifted to the columns of smoke rising into the sky.

"Oasu," Laney said gently, not entirely sure *he* wasn't going into shock. But when he looked back at her, his eyes were clear.

"The priestess?" he asked.

Laney met his gaze without flinching. "She's contained."

He nodded. "Then I'll get to work."

He moved off into the crowd, stopping to talk with people here and there. And Laney's heart broke for him—for all of them. This situation would be tough for anyone to understand, but for a group that had been cut off from the world, it was going to be that much more difficult.

Laney's radio came to life. It was Matt, and his voice was urgent. "Laney."

She hit the call button with a sigh. It would be nice if sometime she could hear her name come over the radio in a way that didn't suggest serious trouble. "What's up?"

"It's Samyaza. She's gone."

Chapter Ninety

AS LANEY DROVE to the spot where she had left Samyaza, she saw Matt standing over two bodies. Her heart dropped. She pulled to a stop and stumbled from the car. "Matt?"

He turned, his face drawn. Laney's gaze immediately dropped to the two agents. A red stain had spread across both their shirts. The woman's chest was slightly caved in, reminding Laney of the Companion Killers' victims.

"Samyaza?" Laney asked.

"Gone."

"How? We had all her people."

Matt knelt down by the male agent and picked something up. He held it out for Laney to see.

It was an earplug. The truth of what happened slammed into Laney, and she took an involuntary step back. Her gaze flew to Matt's face. "She was never under my control. She was faking it."

Matt's eyes stayed on the two downed agents. "Yes."

Laney's words came out as a whisper. "Why would she pretend to be under my control?"

Matt didn't say anything.

She must have been reading our lips. Laney stared at the two dead agents. *This is my fault. These two people are dead because of me. I'm so sorry.* She closed her eyes and pictured the smug look on Elisabeta's face. *Why did I think I could beat her? Why did I think it could be that easy?*

She brimmed with the humiliation of it, but also with the anger. *Damn it. I need to be better than this.*

Her gaze shifted back to the people of Honu Keiki. All these people... Samyaza would have killed them all to get to the priestess.

Laney looked back at the two agents, and then back to the members of Honu Keiki.

"What is it?" Matt asked.

"Why did she tell us about the bombs?"

"To get you to leave, so she could escape."

Laney shook her head. "No. She let us capture her—*that* much I'm sure of. She wanted us to know there was a bomb. She *wanted* us to go in."

"But why? Why would she care if all these people died?"

"She wouldn't. She must have had some other reason."

"But what?"

Laney felt completely lost. "I have no idea."

Chapter Ninety-One

THEY SPENT another three days in Australia helping the people of Honu Keiki get transferred back to Malama Island. In that time, they had found no trace of Elisabeta. They knew her plane had taken off from Perth Airport, and so they'd had SIA agents waiting when it landed in Italy—but she wasn't on board. No one had seen her since Laney had left her with the two SIA agents.

Laney was not so lucky—*everybody* seemed to be able to find her.

Representatives from the Israeli government arrived in Perth to get a fuller accounting of the incident in Jerusalem. British officials arrived to get a fuller accounting of the incident in Australia, as did Australian officials. And an American official showed up to hear about both.

Laney spoke with each group individually, and then all of them collectively. She took them through everything, omitting only the information about her abilities and the Fallen's.

But they weren't letting her get away with those omissions. They wanted to know how she had flown over Jerusalem. And Laney was at a loss as to what to stay. "I'm the ring bearer destined to fight the Fallen" sounded a little melodramatic and unbelievable, even if it *was* true. So she simply said she didn't know.

It was a weak answer. But honestly, she was so wrecked by everything that she couldn't come up with anything better. And she wasn't yet up for telling them that the world they lived in was a lot more complicated than they realized.

Surprisingly, they hadn't pushed it too much—but Laney knew that she was only being given a short reprieve. Soon, the world was going to demand answers.

For now, the officials were mostly interested in the specific events of the priestess's making. They had been astounded at the potential scope of the damage. A single individual from a small island had almost set off World War III. And by Laney's tenth time telling the same story, she'd lost all emotion in the re-telling, which probably wasn't helping the believability of it. But she didn't care. She was exhausted, emotionally, physically, and generally.

And every time she let her mind wander, she saw the little girl that the priestess had held, and she imagined what would have happened if she had made a wrong move. Or she imagined all that could have gone wrong in Israel. Then she'd wonder where Samyaza was and what she had been up to—and why she had gotten involved.

All she really wanted was to go home.

Finally, the governments were satisfied—for the moment—and Laney was allowed to board a plane back to the States. Jake had headed back a day earlier, so it was just Laney and Oasu for the long ride home. Oasu had decided to go to the States to see Kai, Aaliyah, and Noriko before heading back to Malama Island.

Laney slept for the entire trip. The wheels lowering woke her.

She sat up and stretched, rubbing her eyes. Then she looked over at her phone. She'd missed a ton of calls. Some were from Henry, Patrick, Jake, and a few others she recognized, but there were also at least a dozen calls from numbers she didn't recognize.

She shoved the phone back in her bag. She'd land in a few minutes, and she'd speak with them then.

Oasu smiled at her from across the aisle. "I was afraid I was going to have to wake you."

She grimaced. "Sorry. I wasn't very good company on this flight."

"That's all right. You needed to sleep. I slept a little as well, and watched TV for most of it."

Laney raised an eyebrow. "You watched TV?" Access to TV would have been a first for him. "What did you watch?"

"A lot. Have you heard of the *Real Housewives of New Jersey*?"

Laney tried not to smile. "What did you think?"

"Are all women like that?"

Laney laughed. "No—just reality TV women."

Oasu gave her a small smile but a furrow appeared in his brow. And she realized what a big step this was. Besides Australia, he'd never really been off Malama. And he certainly hadn't had the freedom he was going to have now. "So, are you ready?" she asked quietly.

The smile on Oasu's face dimmed. "I don't know."

Laney knew this was a big step. "Well, where Kai, Aaliyah, and Noriko are is very quiet. In fact, the Chandler Estate is usually very quiet. It's not a city, or very near one. It'll help you ease your way in. In fact, the airport we're going to is one of the smaller ones. There's usually no one there when we arrive, besides whoever's picking me up."

Oasu smiled. "Quiet sounds perfect."

When the plane landed, they gathered their things and headed to the door. The flight attendant pushed open the door and lowered the stairs.

"You'll see," Laney said. "It's nice and—"

She went still as the sound of a thousand voices reached her ears. She peered out the doorway, and her eyes grew wide.

Barricades had been erected around the terminal, and behind them were dozens of reporters and hundreds of other people. Police patrolled the barricades, making sure everyone stayed back. Some people held up handmade signs reading, "God Bless You Laney," "Welcome Home to our New American Hero," and a half dozen similar sentiments.

And when they saw Laney, the crowd let out a roar.

Laney stared, her jaw hanging open.

Oasu leaned down and spoke in her ear, "Does quiet mean the same thing here as on Malama?"

Chapter Ninety-Two

JORDAN AND JAKE pushed through the crowd toward the plane. Laney watched them with a sense of disbelief. She knew that her stunt in Jerusalem would have an impact, but she hadn't thought it would start as soon as she arrived home. And she hadn't looked at any press while in Australia —there had been too many other things to focus on.

"Come on, Lanes," Jake said, grabbing her arm as he reached her side.

"Hey, Laney," Jordan said with a grin as he took her other arm.

Oasu fell in step behind them.

The crowds surged against the barricades as Laney passed. Two police officers held the door to the terminal open, and Laney hurried inside.

"What the hell is going on?" she asked as the doors shut behind them.

Jordan raised an eyebrow. "I guess you haven't watched the news since Jerusalem?"

"I slept on the flight. And I was too busy meeting with

every official under the sun when I was in Australia. What *is* this?" She gestured back to the doors.

"Believe it or not," Jordan said, "when you fly over one of the best known cities in the world with a bomb strapped to your back, people notice."

Laney groaned. "Oh, God."

"Well, they *are* making you out to be a hero—again," Jake said.

"This is nuts."

She turned to Oasu, who was looking back out the doors with a frown on his face. "Jordan, this is Oasu, Kai's son. Can you get him to Aaliyah and Kai? No need for him to go through any more of this ridiculousness."

Jordan held out his hand. "Nice to meet you, Oasu. Noriko's told me a lot about you. I have a car ready to take us."

Oasu looked down at Laney. "Will you be all right?"

"Yeah. They're an annoyance, not a danger. Go on. Get out of here while you can."

With a salute to Laney, Jordan led Oasu away.

Laney then turned to Jake. "So, how are *we* getting out of here?"

Jake just grinned.

"Jake?"

Just then a man and woman approached them. The woman was Laney's height, and her hair was styled the same way as well. And the man looked an awful lot like Jake.

Jake turned to Laney. "Give her your jacket."

Laney did.

The woman smiled. "Thanks. I'll get it back to you."

The man took the woman's arm, and the two headed for the front door. They paused for just a moment before heading outside. Shouts and yells reached Laney as the couple, their heads down, ran to a waiting SUV. As they hopped in the back, the journalists sprinted after them. Some even continued to run after the SUV as it drove away, while others ran to their cars, no doubt intending to pursue.

"Did that really just happen?" Laney asked.

Jake put an arm around her shoulder. "Welcome to the life of a celebrity."

Laney groaned. "Oh, I *so* don't want to be a celebrity. And I'm really hoping that wasn't our only way home."

"No." Jake took her hand and led her toward the lounge. "I thought maybe we could have a little bite to eat before we left. That'll give everyone a chance to leave before we make our escape."

Laney really wanted to go straight home, but Jake was right. No point setting off another frenzy. "Okay. Let me call Henry and let him know—"

Jake opened the door to the lounge, and Laney went quiet. The lounge was empty except for one table, where Henry, Patrick, and Jen all waited. An iPad set up on the table showed Dom, who waved at her. And Cleo was there as well. She padded up to Laney and rubbed her head against Laney's chest.

Wrapping an arm over Cleo's neck, Laney laughed, then kissed Jake on the cheek. "Thank you."

"Any time," he said.

Laney hugged each one of her friends in turn, but her thoughts were never far from the media horde outside.

What have I done?

Chapter Ninety-Three

THE MEDIA ASSAULT on Laney was all-encompassing. Her face was plastered everywhere, all across the country and in all forms of media. Newscasts recounted the events of both Israel and Australia, accompanied by footage from not only Jerusalem but the bridge incident as well. Physicists and geneticists discussed the possibility of human flight.

Laney's grade school teachers were given their fifteen minutes of fame. Talk shows and academics discussed what factors led to strong women role models. Entertainment shows discussed the possibility of her life being made into a movie. Book deals were floated. And Laney received dozens of offers for interviews and a few offers from Hollywood, including one to be the next *Bachelorette*.

The PR team for the Chandler Group turned down all offers, at Laney's request. She knew that people wanted an explanation for her flight, but she wasn't ready to discuss who she was with the world. She needed a little more time. What she really wanted was to slip back into anonymity—

but it became increasingly clear that she would never be anonymous again.

Finally, after two weeks of what felt like non-stop coverage, the attention began to wane. There were still reporters parked outside the estate, but it was nothing compared to what there had been at the peak. And each day, as the crowd of reporters gradually thinned, she felt like she could breathe a little easier.

A few days after that, she even took the chance of going over the fence to visit the cats. Cleo was waiting for her at the gate of the preserve, and Laney jumped from the car and threw her arms around the big cat. "Oh, I missed you."

Cleo bumped her hard in the chest.

"Yes, yes, I know it's been too long. How is everybody?"

A picture of each member of the pride flashed in Laney's mind. Her smile spread when pictures of Rolly, Danny, and Lou appeared with them as well. Apparently those three kids were now considered members of the tribe.

Noriko and Lou stepped out of the trees. Noriko let out a squeal and ran for Laney, flinging her arms around her. "You're here!"

Laney laughed. She couldn't help but think of the difference between Jen and Noriko. Noriko was going to be good for Jen.

Lou just rolled her eyes good-naturedly at Noriko's exuberance.

"How are you two doing?" Laney asked.

"Good," Lou replied, after hugging Laney herself. "Noriko can actually talk to these guys, like you."

"But that's nothing compared to what Lou can do," Noriko said. "Have you seen how fast she is?"

Laney smiled as the two of them talked about which one had the better ability. Lou looked almost like her old self again, and Laney credited a lot of that to Noriko. Having a female her age around really seemed to be helping Lou. Oasu had flown back home after about a week, but Kai, Aaliyah—who was very much on the mend—and Noriko were still here, and Laney had told them to stay as long as they wished. Watching Lou smile, she couldn't help but wish they had a really extended visit.

The sound of a car announced Yoni's arrival at the gate, and Lou and Noriko ran for the fence. Laney watched them go, then turned to Cleo. "Want to go for a run?"

Cleo grinned and dashed into the trees.

"Cheater!" Laney yelled, giving chase.

As Laney sprinted through the trees, she felt freer than she had in days. Soon the rest of the pride joined them, and the cats' footfalls echoed through the woods.

Now this is my normal.

Chapter Ninety-Four

BY THE TIME Laney had been home for three weeks, the crowd outside the gate had almost completely disappeared. Laney was able to come and go without a horde of media attention, although an occasional reporter did follow her when she left the estate. She was still big news, but the lack of oxygen being fed to that fire had caused much of it to wind down. All in all, things were much better, and her life had mostly slipped back into its normal pattern.

Laney returned to her work back at the school, and brought Snow, Tiger, and Cleo over for visits as much as she could. All the kids at the school were fascinated by the cubs, and Laney could see that Lou liked the fact that the cubs—while happy to say hello to everyone—would always return to Lou's side. Laney considered allowing them to stay over a few nights with Lou alone. They really were incredibly gentle.

It was late afternoon as Laney pulled up in front of her cottage. A familiar figure sat on the wicker bench on her front porch. She smiled as she stepped out. "Hey. This is a nice surprise."

Henry stood up, his laptop in his hand. "Hey. I wish it *was* just a visit."

Laney sighed as she stepped onto the porch. "Henry, I'm having a good day. Don't ruin it."

"Sorry. But I think we might have a problem."

"Just *a* problem? Well, that's a nice change."

Henry grinned. "Sorry, I misspoke. Another problem."

"Ah, that makes more sense. Well, come on in."

Laney walked into her living room and flopped down on the couch. It really was just *her* living room now, and her couch, as Jake had moved into a cottage down the street. She felt weird having the place to herself; it felt empty. But she knew it was the right call. And she was beginning to appreciate the quiet.

Henry took a seat on the couch next to her.

She eyed his laptop warily. "Okay. What's going on now? Is it Elisabeta?"

"No. We still haven't heard anything about her."

The SIA had been searching diligently for Samyaza with no success. Laney hoped maybe she'd disappear for a nice long stretch like she did before. "Okay. So what is it?"

"Danny has been looking into the Jerusalem incident."

"Wait, Danny?"

Henry put up his hands. "Nothing big. But honestly, it's kind of impossible to keep him out. It's not like I can lock up his computers."

Computers—plural. Laney sighed. "Okay. So what's he found?"

"You know the SIA has been monitoring the internet chatter on the incident, right?"

Laney nodded.

"Well, some disturbing trends are popping up."

Laney felt a sense of dread—a feeling she was becoming all too familiar with. But she told herself to hold off worrying. "Go on."

Henry opened the computer and turned it so Laney could see. On screen was a blog post with the header: "Who is Delaney McPhearson?"

Laney scanned the text of the post. It was a pretty scathing indictment, saying she wasn't the saint the media had made her out to be. A picture of her was attached. Her eyes were narrowed, her mouth open, and she was looking down, which gave her a nice double chin. *Well, that's not my best shot.*

Laney shrugged and sat back. "I mean, I'm not a saint, so it's a reasonable opinion. And internet trolls need something to focus on."

"Laney, that's the *least* disturbing post I've seen."

"The internet is full of people who say nasty things while hiding behind their computer screens," Laney said. "It's a sad fact of the modern world. This is just my turn to be their focus. It'll die down."

Henry paused, then typed. "I debated with Matt whether or not to show you this, but I think you need to see it. I'm sorry." He turned the screen back around.

This one was a Twitter feed—and the venom aimed at Laney was alarming. Death threats, rape threats... the vitriol was so thick it practically leapt off the screen.

Laney's hand went to her throat. "That's—what's *wrong* with these people?"

"That's not the worst part. Look at the hashtag."

As Laney scanned them, her disbelief grew. *#LaneyistheAntichrist.*

"They think I'm the Antichrist?" Laney laughed. "Okay,

that's nuts. Come on. Everybody that's unpopular is labeled the Antichrist. Every president, pope, public figure that has been around since Twitter was invented has been labeled the Antichrist." But when she looked up at Henry, she saw the wrinkle in his brow and the concern in his eyes. "Henry, it's no big deal. There *is* no Antichrist. And if there ever was, he's been dead since the Romans controlled Jerusalem. Why is this worrying you so much?"

"Because it's worrying Matt. A handful of websites have popped up with the same argument—that you are the Antichrist."

Laney gave a nervous laugh. "Okay, so people have time on their hands. That doesn't—"

"The websites have appeared across the globe *and* in different languages. The people at the SIA think that one single person or group is behind all of the sites. It's not being done spontaneously. It's a campaign."

"A campaign? To nominate me for Antichrist? But that's—" Laney wanted to say *ridiculous*, but she knew that a lot of people did believe in the Antichrist, or a figure like him. The known characteristics of the Antichrist went through her head, and she realized that, with a little tweaking, she might actually fit them. *Uh-oh.* "Show me one of the sites."

Henry shook his head. "I don't think that's a good idea."

"Henry, it's the internet. Show me a site, or I'll just go grab a computer and find it myself."

"Fine." Henry punched a few keys, and then turned the computer back around.

"The Antichrist has arrived!" was in large font across the top of the screen, the letters adorned with flames that Laney could only assume were meant to reflect the fires of hell. And the same unflattering picture of her was positioned just under it, although in this one her eyes were red and someone had given her horns and a pitchfork. *Lovely.*

Despite the inflammatory opening, the blog itself was actually relatively academic in its approach.

The Antichrist has been a feature of the Bible and common culture. In both Revelations and the gospel of Mark, the Antichrist is discussed as the opposite of Christ and the bringer of the end of days.
But what are the actual signs of the Antichrist? How will we recognize him? Or, as is becoming more apparent, her? Below are the characteristics of the Antichrist and the alarming way in which Delaney McPhearson meets each and every one of these requirements.

* The Antichrist will display miraculous powers.
Delaney McPhearson has demonstrated what can only be classified as miraculous abilities. We all watched in awe as she saved that bus of children. But what caused that crash? We have learned that the tire was shot out. No one knows who did it. But isn't it a coincidence that Delaney McPhearson happened to be there to save them, and that someone else was there to capture the whole thing on film? And then of course, there was her flight over Jerusalem, the holiest of cities. Who can forget that incredible image? Can there be any doubt that she has abilities that are beyond what a normal human is capable of?

* The Antichrist will be worshipped.
Following the events in Baltimore and the more recent events in Jerusalem, the cult of Delaney McPhearson has popped up across the internet. People have proclaimed her virtues and claimed she has saved them from death. She has made herself a god amongst people.

* The Antichrist will blaspheme God.
This one is rather simple. Delaney McPhearson has cursed God's name over and over again.

Laney clicked on the associated link, and heard a compilation of her saying "God damn it" repeatedly. She smiled at Henry. "Wow, I really do say that a lot."

Henry frowned. "Laney, you need to take this seriously."

She put up a hand and turned back to the screen. "I am, I am."

<u>The Antichrist will recover from a mortal wound.</u>
Three years ago, Delaney was hospitalized with a wound that most people would have died from. As a child, she walked away from a crash that left both her parents dead. Is she just lucky, or is there more at work here?

<u>The Antichrist will desecrate God's temple.</u>
Three years ago, Laney brought a gun battle to the church of St. Hugh of Lincoln. The parking lot was bathed in blood by the time she was done. But that is merely one desecration. She has even spilled blood at the site of the first temple—the Temple of Solomon on the Temple Mount. What greater desecration could there be?

Laney turned to Henry. "There was no blood shed at the Temple Mount. In fact, it was just the opposite."

"Yeah, well, I don't think those facts suited their narrative. Keep reading."

<u>The Antichrist will be a scarlet covered beast.</u>
A small point, I know, but is the fact that Delaney McPhearson is also a redhead not also a sign that we should be concerned?

And these are just some of the facts we know of that fulfill the requirements of the Antichrist. But moreover, consider that Delaney McPhearson has led a life of violence and has left a slew of bodies in her wake. Who is Delaney McPhearson? For me, she is not the saint she is portrayed to be. I fear she may be the exact opposite. Who will stand up and see her for who she truly is?

Laney sat back, feeling sick. They had brought up the death of her parents. She'd only been eight during that horrible car crash. And somehow the fact that she hadn't died then had been held against her. "That's—that's—I mean, everything is out of context. It's being twisted to fit his argument." She looked up at Henry. "You can't think anyone would buy into this. It's insane."

"I agree. But *someone* is making this"—he pointed to the screen—"into a campaign. Websites like this are popping up all over. I'm worried that soon the idea will move away from the fringes and into the mainstream."

"No one would believe this, Henry. It's crazy."

Henry hesitated, and when he spoke, his eyes were deadly serious. "Yes—it's crazy. But we live in crazy times, don't we? And the world saw what you could do in Jerusalem. The total media frenzy may have died down for now, but the world has not forgotten. And if you're not going to give them answers, they're going to look for answers somewhere else."

Laney wanted to argue with him and tell him that no, it wouldn't come to that. But she knew the interest in her hadn't really died down, even if the journalists at the gate had disappeared. "What am I supposed to do about this? Assure everyone I'm not the Antichrist? Somehow I don't think that's going to work."

Henry took her hand. "You could tell them who you *actually* are."

Laney shook her head. She hadn't stayed silent simply because she didn't want the attention. She also knew that any answer she gave would lead to more questions—and most likely, more problems. She could live with people thinking whatever they wanted about her. But if the world found out that there were Fallen among them...

That would cause chaos.

"If I tell them I'm the ring bearer," she began—and then stopped, imagining the response. "That won't solve anything. It's just going to open a whole new can of worms. Because I can't explain that I'm the ring bearer without also explaining what that means—which means telling the world about the Fallen, nephilim, Samyaza. That won't put fears to rest."

"So what do you want to do?" Henry asked quietly.

Laney wrapped her hand around the ring on the chain at her neck. For some reason she pictured Cleo, and she imagined what people would think if they knew about her ability to communicate with animals. Her gaze flicked back to the picture of her as the devil. "I don't know," she said. "But you're right, we do live in crazy times."

Henry's eyes were serious when he squeezed her hand. "Yeah. But now the question is: Exactly how crazy are things going to get?"

Chapter Ninety-Five

ONLY A FEW DAYS LATER, Laney had her answer—or at least the beginning of one. Protesters had appeared outside both the Chandler Estate and the Chandler School. They seemed to fall into two camps: one, people who thought she was the Antichrist and wanted her burned at the stake; and two, people who thought she was the Antichrist and wanted her to know they were on her side.

Apparently, no one showed up to say they thought it was all a big bunch of BS.

The mainstream media picked up the protests and online chatter, and some began to remark—mostly tongue in cheek—about her being the Antichrist. And then they got word that Mike Wallace was going to do another special report on her. From the rumblings they heard, this one was not going to be as positive as the last one.

"Penny for your thoughts," her Uncle Patrick said from across the breakfast table.

Laney gave him a small smile. "Sorry, just thinking."

"About the broadcast tonight?"

Laney nodded. "That, but mainly all this Antichrist nonsense. I mean, I thought the Antichrist was just symbolic of the Roman takeover of Jerusalem." She knew that at different points in history, others had already been identified as the Antichrist: Paul of Tarsus, Emperor Nero, and frankly, almost every powerful religious or political leader. Numerologists had found it easy to "prove" that almost anyone was the Antichrist, from Adolf Hitler to Henry Kissinger to even Bill Gates. "I've always thought of him as merely a bogeyman that was used to keep Catholics in line."

Her uncle smiled. "Well, there are some who believe that, and some who believe he heralds something much more dire."

"What do you think?"

"I think it's complicated."

"Of course you do."

Patrick smiled. "The term 'Antichrist' was only used seven times in the Bible, and a distinction was made between antichrists and *the* Antichrist."

"Antichrists? As in more than one?"

Patrick nodded. "The word 'antichrist' just means the opposite of Christ. So anyone who did not believe in Christ, or who engaged in behaviors in conflict with Christ's message, was considered an antichrist. Which meant there were quite a few at the time the gospel of John was written. But the term has since morphed quite a bit.

"Most people now refer to '*the* Antichrist'—with a capital A. That Antichrist is the individual who arises at the end of days, when the world is about to go through judgment. The Antichrist will be a source of evil, opposed to truth, and will lead people to abandon the good in their lives. Some believe the Antichrist is not necessarily a singular person, but a group or organization of people.

Others argue that the Antichrist has already come and gone, during Roman times, and that the Biblical discussion of the Antichrist is a warning for us not to be fooled again by false words.

"But I'm not so sure that Antichrist ever existed—or ever will."

"Why?"

"The idea for *the* Antichrist comes from Revelations and the book of Daniel. Both books address the end of days and the final battle between good and evil. The problem is—the word 'antichrist' doesn't appear even once in either of those writings. Readers have taken the descriptions used in those books and just *assumed* they must be talking about the Antichrist. But they don't. Instead, they speak about 'the beast' or 'the dragon.'"

"So there is no end-of-days Antichrist?"

Patrick shrugged. "I obviously can't know for sure, although I do believe *someone* would have to be in charge of the fighters for evil. But it doesn't matter what is true, but what people believe. Many believe that the Antichrist will come, that he will signal the beginning of a time of trial and tribulation for mankind, and that he will try to win people over to his side. People's beliefs can be a powerful thing."

Laney nodded, knowing that was true.

"But there is good news. In the end, according to Daniel and Revelations, all those who follow Satan will be thrown in a lake of fire and destroyed. So those on the wrong side… well, they don't have a wonderful ending."

Laney remembered the picture of herself with horns and a pitchfork. "Yeah, but for a growing portion of the population, the person on the wrong side is *me*."

Chapter Ninety-Six

WITH HER UNCLE'S thoughts still running through her mind, Laney now sat in Henry's living room to watch Mike Wallace on *The Sunday Report*. She was surrounded by the same friends as last time, with one exception—Mustafa had flown in to join them as well. He had said he was "just in the area," but Laney knew he was worried and wanted to be here in case she needed a little extra security. She was touched by his concern.

Matt would have liked to have come as well, but he was bogged down after Australia—and he was undeniably preparing for whatever the outcome of this broadcast was going to be.

But despite having the same group of friends together as they'd had for the last *Sunday Report*, the lead-up to this show felt very different. Last time, they'd had a nice dinner, chatting about their week. This time, everyone was quiet, subdued. There was no easygoing chatter, no small talk. Everyone was waiting for the bomb they all knew was about to drop.

Time crawled, but finally, eight o'clock rolled around, and they gathered in front of the TV. Patrick took Laney's hand and gave it a squeeze as the show started.

Mike Wallace once again appeared on screen. He smiled as he strode onto the set, but as soon as he began to speak his face became much more serious.

"It was only a few weeks ago when we first brought Delaney McPhearson to your attention—and for most of you, that broadcast was the first time you had ever heard of Delaney McPhearson. But since then, she seems to have taken it upon herself to make sure the entire *world* knows who she is."

Mike walked once again through the set, with newspaper headlines appearing behind him. But this time, Laney noticed it wasn't only newspapers that were being displayed; there were also screen shots from websites. Websites she was all too familiar with.

Oh, no.

"No one is unfamiliar with the incident in Israel last month, when an attempt was made to destroy the Temple Mount, one of the holiest sites in the world." Mike paused at a still shot of Laney hovering above the Temple Mount. Laney cringed, wishing, not for the first time, that there had been some other way she could have handled that situation. "Delaney McPhearson was in the thick of that incident—and she has been hailed by many as a hero."

Mike paused again, turning to look straight into the camera. "But is she really? We all watched in awe as she rose into the sky in the land of miracles, replicating the actions of those viewed as the holiest in our world's history. Was that McPhearson's plan? To have the world view her through the same lens?"

Laney's jaw dropped. Was he kidding? She had been forced into a corner. Either fly, or let the bomb go off.

"Apparently he's not worried about providing two sides to a story," Jen muttered.

Mike continued. "She looks otherworldly as she flies above the landscape. And maybe she is. But which world?"

"What the hell does that even mean?" Jen grumbled.

"Rumors have begun to circulate on the internet, claiming that McPhearson is not who she appears to be." Mike stopped in front of a wall splashed with the headline of a blog: "The Antichrist is Alive." "These rumors paint a very disturbing picture of Delaney McPhearson's activities in Australia and Israel—and indeed her very role in this world."

Mike then went in depth into the internet campaign to paint Laney as the Antichrist. He discussed the different websites and their rationales. He even brought some academics in to discuss the descriptions of the Antichrist found in religious texts. Each expert stopped short of calling Laney the Antichrist, but Mike acted like they had emphatically labeled her as the bringer of doom.

Laney gaped. How could they do this? Just slander her this way?

"Is this even legal?" Jake demanded.

Henry shrugged. "He's not saying she's the Antichrist. He's just reporting on what all these websites are saying."

The show went to a commercial break, and Henry muted the set. Everyone sat silently. Laney looked at the faces around the room, and they all reflected her own fear.

"It'll be all right," Patrick said, using an upbeat tone that Laney had last heard in the doctor's office when she was a kid and he was assuring her the shot wouldn't hurt. It was no more convincing now. "Whatever happens, we're in this together."

"All of us," Henry said.

Everyone in the room nodded in agreement.

Laney clasped her uncle's hand, trying to tap into some of his strength, but she felt hollow. All these accusations were being hurled at her, and she couldn't defend herself. How did you prove a negative? How did you prove what you weren't?

"No one is going to believe this," Jake said. "Most people don't believe in the Antichrist."

But Laney knew that wasn't true. Poll numbers indicated that at least forty percent of Americans believed that Armageddon would occur, and that it would be a fight between Christ and the Antichrist. Then again, four percent of people believed that lizard people controlled society, so people really believed all sorts of things that were crazy.

"Laney, it's going to be okay," Jen said. "It's just a bunch of nut jobs on the internet. Everyone knows you can't trust the internet."

Laney hoped Jen was right, and that there was nothing to worry about.

"It's back," Henry said, unmuting the set.

Mike Wallace now sat in a club chair facing the camera. Laney knew that chair—it was where he sat when he interviewed people. But who was he interviewing?

"Most of you know our next guest. She has been a figure on the global circuit for years, renowned for her philanthropic endeavors."

Gasps and muttered curses were heard all around Henry's living room. The screen panned over to a woman in her fifties, with small eyes, a Mediterranean complexion, and dark hair pulled back.

Laney felt her stomach drop. *Oh my God. Samyaza.*

The camera panned back to Mike Wallace, whose chin was tilted down, his eyebrows drawn together. "For those of you who don't know Elisabeta Roccorio, let me give you a little background. Elisabeta was born into a very wealthy family, but from an early age, she recognized the need to give back. In a world where wealthy socialites have stood out for their rampant selfishness, Elisabeta has stood out for her charitable works. Just this last year she has completed the building of three schools in poverty-stricken nations to aid underserved populations. She is on the board of over a dozen charitable organizations with global reach. Thank you for joining us tonight, Elisabeta."

Laney stared at the screen in disbelief. *I'm the Antichrist, and she's Mother Teresa. The world has officially gone insane.*

Elisabeta spoke quietly. "Thank you for having me."

"Now, I know this is a difficult topic for you," Mike said, "and that you have come here to speak even though you believe it places your life in danger."

Elisabeta took a shaky breath, her chin trembling just a bit. "Yes. But I believe that the truth must come out. And that even if I am hurt or killed as a result of speaking out, the world must know who Delaney McPhearson is."

Laney sucked in a breath. Patrick squeezed her hand.

"Can you explain what you mean by that?" Mike asked.

Elisabeta took another trembling breath. "I'm sorry. This is very difficult."

"Take your time."

If Laney didn't know Elisabeta, she would have been concerned for the woman. Instead she steeled herself for what was to come.

Elisabeta raised her head and stared straight at the

camera. "It was not Honu Keiki who was behind the attack on the Temple Mount. It was Delaney McPhearson."

Chapter Ninety-Seven

AS SOON AS the words left Elisabeta's mouth, Henry was on his phone calling his legal team and ordering them to the estate immediately, and Jake was on the phone with his security team, doubling the patrols on both the estate and the school. But Laney just sat there numbly, staring at the screen. *It was not Honu Keiki who was behind the attack on the Temple Mount. It was Delaney McPhearson.*

How could she say that?

Jen took the seat Jake had vacated and took Laney's hand. Mustafa moved his chair closer to them. But even with Patrick, Jen, and Mustafa surrounding her, Laney was adrift. *This can't be happening.*

Onscreen, Mike Wallace's face was supposed to be full of concern, but Laney could make out a glimmer of happiness in his eyes. He knew what a huge coup this was. "That's a strong statement," he said. "Do you have anything to back it up?"

Elisabeta nodded. "I have video recordings and documentation that show she purchased the explosives that the bombers attempted to use. I have made it available to whoever wants to read it or see it." She rattled off a web address, and *The Sunday Report* helpfully displayed the address across the bottom of the screen.

Mike then looked straight at the camera. "I should tell the viewing audience that I have reviewed the video and paper documentation and I find it very compelling." He turned back to Elisabeta. "Now, Elisabeta, why are you only coming forward now?"

Elisabeta took a breath. "I was scared."

"Of McPhearson?"

Elisabeta nodded. "She's not who the media has portrayed her to be. The world knows she's powerful, but they don't know that she's cruel. She's dangerous."

"That is not the picture we, the world, have of her."

"I know," Elisabeta said. "That's why I waited. I wasn't sure anyone would believe me."

Mike reached over and took her hand. "Well, I believe you. And I did some research. I came up with some concerning incidents."

He turned to the camera. "Last year in Washington, DC, there was an attack at the Capitol Building. It was thwarted. But what the world didn't know was that Delaney McPhearson was involved. We have some videotape."

Laney remembered the suicide bomber and his partner. She had killed one before he could set off his bomb vest, and she had disabled the other. What could they possibly say she did wrong there?

The video played. It showed people running down a hallway. A police officer was stabbed and fell to the ground. Then Laney appeared in a doorway, which Laney knew led to the stairwell. She stopped a few feet from Rico Fuenes, the bomber who had on a suicide vest with enough explosives to take out the whole building and parts of the buildings on either side. The video stopped right after she broke Fuenes's neck.

"That is Delaney McPhearson," Mike said. "But let's back up a little." He rewound the tape to when she first appeared, stopped it when she was a few feet from the bomber, and zoomed in.

On screen, Laney was smiling.

"Why is she smiling?" he asked. "What kind of person would be *smiling* at the sight of a downed officer of the law and a bomber? And just seconds later, she snapped his neck as casually as someone would kill a fly."

"He wasn't a Fallen," Laney mumbled. "I was smiling because he was just a human and would be easier to disarm. I saved hundreds of people that day." She knew her words were true, but they sounded defensive even to her own ears.

"Coincidentally, McPhearson's involvement with a shadowy government organization was under scrutiny at that time. She, along with her colleagues, were in DC, being grilled by Senate committees about their actions. But *after* the bombing attempt, those committees went away, their investigations tabled until a still undetermined future date. Quite a coincidence, isn't it?"

Mike paused to let his words sink in.

"And that's just one incident. There are more. Many more. When she was in Ecuador, hundreds of the Shuar tribe lost their lives. In Montana, over three hundred men were killed in an enclosure where Laney just happened to show up. Wherever Delaney McPhearson goes, death follows."

"That's insane," Jen said. "The men in Montana were already dead, and you saved the Shuar. So did I!"

"Even the event which brought her notoriety has now

come under scrutiny. It has been determined that the bus on the bridge had a tire shot out. *That's* what caused it to careen uncontrollably toward the railing. But who would do such a thing? And right at the very spot where someone was taping? At the very spot, and the very moment, where someone would see Delaney McPhearson and her amazing abilities?"

Laney felt her mouth fall open. "They think I caused the bus accident too?"

Mike Wallace turned back to Elisabeta. "And that's not all, is it?"

Elisabeta shook her head, her eyes downcast. "No." Her voice was barely above a whisper.

"I know this is difficult, but can you tell us the last time you saw Delaney McPhearson take a life?"

Elisabeta nodded. "It was in Australia. McPhearson—she was obsessed with tracking down the head of Honu Keiki—the priestess."

"The woman who many, at the urging of McPhearson, said was responsible for the attempt at the Temple Mount."

Elisabeta trembled, clutching the handkerchief in her hand tightly. "Yes. I saw McPhearson chase this poor woman down. McPhearson—she's an incredible fighter. This woman didn't stand a chance. She was terrified. And McPhearson calmly and with no emotion snapped her neck—in a room full of children."

Mike let the silence play out for several agonizing seconds. "Snapping her neck. She does seem to like that method, doesn't she?"

"Yes." Elisabeta's response was barely audible.

"How did you happen to see this?"

"I had my people tap into the security feeds at the Australian facility of Honu Keiki. I had them record

McPhearson's moves inside. I knew if I didn't, the evidence would be lost. McPhearson would make *sure* it was lost."

"And was it?"

"The facility was destroyed. The recordings survived only because I had them copied in real time."

"They were destroyed because *you* blew up the facility!" Jen yelled at the screen.

"And now you're worried for your own safety, aren't you?" Mike asked.

Tears crested in Elisabeta's eyes. "I've seen what she can do. She has no compunction about killing. And now I'm speaking out against her. I have no doubt I will now be on her list."

"Thank you for your bravery today." Mike turned to the camera. "So who is Delaney McPhearson? The hero we all thought her to be after the Baltimore bridge incident? The miraculous savior we thought her to be in Jerusalem and Australia? Or a serial killer leaving a trail of bodies in her wake?"

A portion of another blog post appeared behind him, with the word Antichrist highlighted. "Or is she possibly something much more sinister? It's up to you to decide." The background shifted to the image of Laney, her eyes wide, her face focused, and her hands on Rico Fuenes's neck. "But in this case, I think actions speak much louder than words."

Chapter Ninety-Eight

LANEY WAS STUNNED. She didn't feel angry. She didn't feel scared. She didn't feel at all. She was too shocked for any emotions.

Henry was arguing with someone on the phone in his kitchen. Jake was talking to a group of security people who had shown up at the house in the front hall. They would now be Laney's shadows twenty-four seven. Her uncle was on the phone with the church hierarchy, who were no doubt demanding an explanation. Jen was calling the school to make sure Yoni knew what had been reported, and instructing him to tell the staff so they could deal with the student response. Mustafa was somewhere on his own phone, talking with the legal team at the SIA.

And Laney just sat there—not moving, not talking. For the last three years she had spent nearly every moment as the ring bearer, the defender of the innocent, combating the Fallen every time they popped up. Her life had been completely taken over by her destiny. She had lost people she loved. She had lost her relationship with Jake. She had given up on any sort of normal future. And she had come to terms with that. She had accepted that this was her life, and it was a life she would constantly be risking for the good of others. She didn't expect thanks. She didn't expect notoriety.

But she sure hadn't expected this.

Antichrist. Serial killer. She flinched as the words rolled through her mind. Samyaza had made her a pariah.

"No!" Henry yelled into the phone. "Without a warrant, they are not getting in. You tell them that."

Laney looked up as Henry stormed into the room, jabbing at his phone. "Henry?"

He took her hand, trying to force a calm expression on his face and failing horribly. "It's nothing. The FBI called and want to do a sit-down with you. But without a warrant you aren't speaking with anyone, and no one's coming here."

"They'll get a warrant," Laney said.

"And we'll fight it." Henry's phone rang, and he glanced at the caller ID. "It's the legal team. I have to take this."

Laney nodded, but Henry didn't see; he was already answering the call and bounding across the room.

Laney watched the activity around her. Everyone was busy doing something to help her, and yet she felt strangely detached from it all, as if she had no part in it.

She stood and quietly made her way out of the room and out the back door. She pulled out her phone and hesitated for only a minute before dialing.

"Laney? Are you all right?" Matt asked.

"Yeah. I'm just—I don't know. Shocked, I guess." She paused. "What's going to happen now?"

Matt sighed. "A bunch of law enforcement agencies will get involved. They'll all want to speak with you."

"Have you looked at the proof Elisabeta put online?"

"Yes. I'm not going to lie—it looks damning. But I have my people tearing it apart. They'll find the forgeries."

Laney leaned against the porch railing and closed her eyes. "God, how did I get here?"

"I'm sorry, Laney. But we *are* in your corner." He paused. "The priestess is here. Elisabeta made it seem like she was killed, but we know that's not true. We could show her to the world."

Laney considered that. "Not yet. I don't know how this is all going to play out, but the priestess is just part of a litany of acts I'm being demonized for. And besides, if we show her to the world, we need to tell the world how she survived. We need to tell them the Fallen exist."

"Maybe we should," Matt said quietly.

"Maybe. But I don't think this is the right time. If this turns out the way I think it will, people won't be in the right mindset. Revealing that the Fallen exist will create panic. Neighbor will turn against neighbor. We can't do that. If and when we reveal their existence, it needs to be in a way the world can handle."

Matt sighed. "You're right. But Laney, I'm worried."

"Me too."

"Well, whatever you need, you have the SIA at your disposal."

"Thanks. In fact, I'm calling because I *do* need something."

"What's that?"

Laney took a deep breath. "I need to speak with Cain."

Chapter Ninety-Nine

IT WAS ONLY a few minutes later when Laney's phone rang. With a quick glance at the caller ID, she answered. "Hello?"

"Ring bearer, are you all right?" Cain asked.

Laney felt tears prick the backs of her eyes. Even Cain was worried about her. "No. I'm not."

"What can I do?"

"This was Samyaza's plan all along—to build me up so she could see me fall."

Laney quickly laid out every detail of Samyaza's plan—which had all clicked into place for Laney when the broadcast ended. Samyaza had been the one who had set up the accident on the bridge, being sure to catch Laney at her most heroic. She had started the online campaign to make sure the world knew about her. She had led her to Israel. She'd taken out the Honu Keiki members at the house in Israel, leaving Laney with only one thing to do—reveal herself in order to save lives at the Temple Mount. And then in Australia, she had told Laney about the bombs, knowing Laney would run to help and confront the priestess.

"How could I have been so stupid?" Laney asked.

"You weren't stupid. You were protecting people. It's what you are. *Who* you are. Samyaza used that against you. She's always been good at the long game. I'm sorry. I should have seen this coming."

"It's not your fault."

"It is. I've failed you. I am sorry."

Laney looked up at the night sky, content for a moment to just breathe with the immortal on the other end of the phone. Finally she spoke. "Has she ever done this before?"

"No. She's raked reputations through the coals, but not like this. In fact, you, in one of your previous lives, are one of her most successful cases."

"What do you mean?"

"Helen. Samyaza had you recast as a home-wrecking woman of loose morals. The real Helen… well, she was a force of nature. Much like you are now."

Laney laughed, because if she didn't she was going to cry. "Right now if I'm a force of nature, it's a misty drizzle."

"You're more than that, Laney."

Laney shoved her self-pity away. "I wasn't trolling for compliments." She paused. "Okay, not *just* for compliments. I was also wondering about the end of days. If Samyaza is behind all this and trying to get me painted as the Antichrist, it has to be linked to the end of days, don't you think?"

"Yes, I would say you're right."

"So I was wondering. Seeing as you've been around forever, there must have been other times in our history when we reached the end of days. That's when the ring bearer is supposed to be called."

Cain was quiet for a moment. "That's true. We *have* reached this point before—many times in fact. You know of some of those times, the Trojan War being the most recent, but there are earlier times, too, when whole societies were destroyed."

Laney felt a chill. "Is that Samyaza's end game? To destroy the world?"

"I don't think her end game is ever destruction—at least not from her perspective. She views it as molding the world to her view. But if anything gets in her way..." He didn't need to finish the thought.

"And now, Samyaza is trying to get me pushed aside," Laney said. "To clear the way for whatever plan she's set in motion."

"I think you underestimate her."

"What do you mean?"

"If she merely wanted you 'pushed aside,' there are myriad ways she could accomplish that. Instead, she's made you the target of multiple nations and organizations. She wants more than to get you out of the way." He paused. "I believe she wants you dead."

Chapter One Hundred

I BELIEVE *she wants you dead.* After she hung up with Cain, Laney couldn't stop those words from replaying in her head. She stared up at the sky, wondering how things had come to this.

Jake burst through the back door onto the porch. His eyes were wild until he caught sight of her. "Laney! I didn't know where you were."

"I'm sorry. I just needed a little air."

He pulled her in for a hug. Laney didn't need it—she was too numb for comfort—but she could tell Jake needed it. So she wrapped her arms around his waist and leaned her head against his strong chest.

"This was all Elisabeta's plan from the start," she said. "She built me up, thrust me into the spotlight, and then made me the Antichrist."

"Why?"

"To discredit me. To make it impossible for me to do what I need to do: fight her."

"But you can still—"

Laney shook her head and stepped out of his arms. "Jake, I'm probably only hours away from being arrested. And you know Samyaza will have someone in the system 'take care of me.' That's been her plan all along."

"But why? What does she want?"

"To take over the world? I don't know. But once I'm gone, whatever her plan is, it will be a lot easier." A thought hit her then, and she could have smacked herself for not realizing it sooner. "She's the one behind the Fallen killings, too! She's been taking out anyone who would have sided with us, whittling away our supporters. She's set this whole thing up so that when she makes her move, she's in a position of strength."

"But what *is* her move?"

"I don't know. But as soon as I'm dead, I'm sure she'll make it."

"That's not going to happen."

Laney sighed. Jake would be loyal to her to the end, but right now she needed some of Jake's pragmatism, not his optimism. Because she knew he was wrong: Samyaza was going to make sure she was killed. Thus far, Laney had danced along perfectly to Samyaza's tune. And there was no reason to think Laney was going to stumble over her feet now. Samyaza had boxed her into a corner.

Laney looked away from Jake's concerned eyes and stared up at the sky once again, this time to try and keep her tears at bay.

How on earth am I going to get out of this?

Chapter One Hundred One

ON THE PORCH with Jake last night—that had been her last peaceful moment. Ever since then, she had been in constant motion. Henry had sat her down with his legal team, who assured her they would be with her every step of the way. Jake had taken her through the extra security protocols. Patrick elected to stay at her cottage that night, sleeping on the couch while Jake took the guest room. Laney knew they were both positioning themselves to stand in front of whatever danger was coming at her.

It was a long, dark night. She didn't sleep much. She finally stumbled from bed at five a.m. As she made her way down the stairs, she tried to be quiet so as not to wake the others, but she needn't have bothered. Patrick was already sitting at the kitchen table with a pot of coffee brewed. He stood and wrapped her in a hug. "I was hoping you'd sleep a little longer."

"I was hoping the same for you," she said.

He gently pushed her into a chair and poured her a cup of coffee. "Jake?"

"Sleeping. I don't think he fell asleep until an hour ago." She had heard him pacing through the night, occasionally showing up in her doorway to peer in and make sure she was all right. She had kept her eyes closed, faking sleep, hoping if he thought she was sleeping, he might get some of his own.

She took a sip of coffee, and they both sat silently for a while.

Finally, Laney broke the silence. "What did the church say?"

"Nothing. It's all right."

"Uncle Patrick."

He sighed. "They want me to appear before the bishop for an accounting of all of my dealings with you."

"When are you leaving?"

"I'm not. They can wait. I *know* the truth, and if they can't see what I see, well—"

Laney took his hand. "No. Don't say it. You love being a priest. You should speak with them."

"I will. But you're the priority right now, not appeasing their curiosity."

Jake stepped into the kitchen, and Laney gave him a tight smile. "Sorry. Did we wake you?"

Jake shook his head and kissed the top of her head. "No. I wasn't really sleeping. I heard you get up. Henry will be here in a second. He just texted me."

Laney closed her eyes. *Henry at five a.m. That doesn't bode well.*

There was a light rap at the back door. "Come in," Jake called.

Henry stepped in, dark circles under his eyes. *And yet one more who needs some more sleep*, Laney thought. But he smiled when he saw her. "Hey."

"Hey yourself." She held up a mug. "Coffee?"

"Please," Henry said, taking a seat.

Patrick poured him a cup and put another pot on.

"Where's Jen?" Jake asked.

"At the school," Henry said. "She wanted to stay with the kids, help them through. But if you need her…"

Laney shook her head. "No. She's got her priorities straight. The kids need her. Besides, there's not much she can do here. But can you have extra security put on the cats' preserve? I don't want anyone trying to get in there."

"Already done. And I've got a crew who's going to erect metal plates around it, to keep out any lenses."

Laney knew that was a good idea, but she hated the idea of preventing the cats from being able to see out. It felt like she was imprisoning them.

"So," Henry said. "It's been a busy night."

"What's happened?" Jake asked.

"I've been in touch with sources all over the world. The impact of *The Sunday Report* has been… wide-ranging." His gaze flicked to Laney.

"Tell me," she said. "All of it."

"I—" Henry paused. "I don't even know how to say half of this."

"Just say it," Laney said softly.

He sighed. "Okay. Six different jihadist terrorist organizations have put out a fatwa calling for your—" He stopped.

"Death," she whispered.

Henry nodded. "My Israeli contacts tell me a special Mossad group has been called up to investigate you. The Australian Defense Force has done the same, as have the FBI and the CIA."

Laney put her hand to her mouth.

"The media has been having a field day. They're

scrounging up every possible piece of footage they can find on you. Almost all Chandler Group employees have reported that they've received calls from the media. I don't think anyone has spoken with them, but I can't guarantee their silence will continue."

"What about the SIA?" Jake asked.

"I spoke with Matt an hour ago. A special Senate committee has been convened to investigate your connection with the SIA. But as of right now, their activities have been suspended and their budget frozen."

Laney closed her eyes. *This can't be happening.*

"Any good news?" Jake asked.

Henry gave a small smile. "The people Laney has helped have been calling to pledge their support. They've offered to speak with the media on your behalf, or testify if it comes to that. I told them to hold off until we have a plan in place."

Laney felt a hysterical giggle building up inside her. "A plan? I have, what, a minimum of three nations' security and intelligence forces looking into me, a half dozen terrorist groups who want my head, everyone who has ever known me under siege by the media, and every aspect of my life under the microscope. What plan could we possibly come up with to combat that?"

"Laney, we will get through this. We always do," Jake said.

Laney looked at the men around the table. They all loved her. They would all walk through hell for her. And they would all now be targets *because* of her. "I can't—"

"No," Jake said before she could finish. "None of this was your choice. There's a way out. We just haven't figured it out yet."

Henry's phone beeped. "Hold on." He stepped away

from the table to answer it. "Hello?" He paused. "No. Make sure they stay at least ten feet from the front gate. And double the patrols around the perimeter." He hung up, looking none too pleased.

"What happened?" Patrick asked.

"The media is at the front gate, and one reporter tried to sneak in. Security caught him."

"We're under siege," Laney said. She looked around the table. "I think I need some air."

Without waiting for a reply, she headed to the back yard. She stepped out onto the porch and took a deep breath. *Well, Samyaza, you succeeded. I'm sidelined, and so is the SIA.* The Fallen could now run around unchecked. Human law enforcement agencies weren't equipped to deal with them.

But was Samyaza really doing all this just to get to Laney? Sure, Samyaza had everyone focused on her—but to what end? Just to give herself more freedom? Or was there more at stake? Laney didn't think Samyaza would go to all this trouble unless she had something big planned. And whatever it was, it was not going to benefit mankind.

The back door opened, and Henry stepped out. When he opened his arms, Laney stepped gratefully into them.

"You okay?" Henry asked.

Laney nodded against his chest. "Yeah, just trying to see a way out of this."

Henry moved her back so he could see her face. His eyes were the same color as Victoria's. "You're not alone, Laney."

"I know." She thought of all those they had lost: Drew, the Shuar, King Julian, Rocky, detectives Frank Miller and Marcos Sanchez, and all the dozens of others she hadn't been able to protect. Now the guns were aimed directly at her. And everyone she loved was in the crosshairs too. For the first time, she was glad that Kati, Maddox, and Max were gone. At least *they* would be spared this.

Henry mistook the fear on her face for a fear for her own safety. "Laney, don't worry: anyone comes for you, they have to go through us."

"I don't think that's a comfort."

Henry hugged her once more. "But it's exactly what you would do for us: protect us at all costs."

Laney's heart broke as she realized what must be done.

Yes, I will *protect you at all costs.*

Chapter One Hundred Two

"DR. MCPHEARSON, we still don't understand why you think Ms. Roccorio would make such a statement if there was no truth behind it."

Laney tried to hide her frustration. Her legal team had encouraged her to speak with the FBI agents in a conference room at Chandler's HQ, but an hour into the interview, she was pretty sure there was nothing she could possibly say to convince them to see things her way.

Apparently her legal team had finally come to the same conclusion. Brett Hanover stood, and the other six members of the team followed his lead. Hanover was the head of the team, with thirty years' experience in the law. "I think that will be all for today," he said. "If you have any further questions you can reach me at my office."

Agent Mary Radford shook her head. "We still have—"

"I'm sure you do. But Dr. McPhearson is done for the day." Hanover nodded to the two guards that stood at the back of the room. "Crow and Figel will see you to the gate."

Agent Radford stood slowly, her eyes on Laney. "This

would go easier if you would answer our questions now. Perhaps it will help us avoid any future unpleasantness."

Laney could barely contain her snort. *Right. Like anything I could say or do would make this go away.*

Hanover put a hand on Laney's shoulder—a warning to stay silent. But Laney didn't need the warning.

"Thank you and good day," Hanover said.

Agents Radford and Green gave a nod and headed out after Figel. Crow waited until they left, then followed.

Laney slumped down in her seat as soon as they were gone. "Well, that was horrible."

Hanover sat down next to her and patted her arm. "You did very well."

"I barely said a word."

Hanover grinned. "Like I said, you did very well."

Laney smiled in spite of her situation. She liked the lawyer. He had a sense of humor and wasn't as dour as some of his companions. "So now what?"

"Now we wait. But you need to prepare yourself: at some point you will most likely be brought in for a more formal interview."

"Will I be arrested?"

"I don't know. It's possible. I've also learned that Israel has petitioned The Hague to bring charges against you."

Laney couldn't have been more surprised. *The Hague?* That's where the international criminal court was. She ran through the charges she could possibly face, and stopped at one phrase: *crimes against humanity.* Oh, the company she would keep if that charge stuck: Muammar Qaddafi, a sea of African warlords responsible for genocide… *A bunch of tyrannical monsters and then me.*

"Do you think they'll succeed?"

"I think it's premature. But I thought you should know."

"Great. Thanks."

Hanover stood. "I'll contact you if anything else develops."

"Okay." Laney looked down the long line of lawyers. "Thank you all."

They nodded back at her before heading out. Hanover paused at the door. "Dr. McPhearson, we will do our best by you. And if it's any consolation, I don't believe any of that report."

Touched, Laney nodded. "Thank you."

Hanover smiled before disappearing out the door.

Laney sat in the silence of the conference room, wondering what she should do now. She should probably find Jake or Henry and let them know how the meeting had gone. But she couldn't seem to make herself move. She just stared out the window, watching birds soar in formation through the sky, and thinking of all that had happened and all that still might.

"There you are," Jake said from the doorway.

"Here I am."

He sat across from her. "How'd it go?"

Laney shrugged. "I don't really know. Hanover would have a better read. But I got the feeling they were hoping I would let something slip. Like, 'Yes, I am the mastermind behind it all.'"

Jake raised an eyebrow. "I'm hoping those words didn't actually come out of your mouth while the agents were here."

She smiled. "No. But from their questions and looks, you'd think they had. How's everything else going?"

"Good." Jake looked away.

"What?"

"It's nothing you need to worry about."

"Jake," Laney said with a warning tone.

He sighed. "A known terrorist was stopped at Logan's two hours ago."

"He was coming for me."

"That's what we think."

Laney closed her eyes.

"It's okay. He was detained. He's being deported."

"But there will be others."

"Yes, and we'll stop them too."

Laney looked into his brown eyes and knew he believed that. But she also knew there was a good chance someone would get hurt—if not killed—if they had to keep protecting her from every nut job out there.

"Henry's at his house," Jake said. "He wants to discuss next steps. You ready to go over everything?"

"Yeah. Um, actually, I just need a quick minute."

"Everything okay?"

"Yeah, fine." Laney forced her tone to be light. "I just want to call Kati's parents. They called earlier, and I haven't had a chance to speak with them. They're really worried about all the news coverage."

"I didn't realize you kept in touch with them."

Laney didn't meet his eyes. "Well, with Kati out of the picture, I told them to call if they needed anything. I speak with them about once a month."

"Full of surprises you are." He squeezed her hand. "Okay. I'll meet you downstairs."

She waited until he disappeared down the hallway. Then she closed the door and pulled out her phone. She stared at it for a long moment. Was she doing the right thing? Part of her was terrified of taking the next step, and the other part of her was terrified of *not* taking the next step.

How did things all get so out of control?

You went against the world's greatest strategist and lost, a voice reminded her. Not that she needed the reminder. All Samyaza had needed to do was act like she was willing to kill people, and Laney jumped right through her hoop.

Laney sighed. But what else could she have done? Was she supposed to have called her bluff? Because Laney knew as soon as she did that, Elisabeta would no longer bluff.

And that's the problem. Wherever I am, the people with me will be at risk. And I can't chance that.

She dialed before she could change her mind. Dom picked up on the first ring.

"Dom, I need your help."

Chapter One Hundred Three

"SO, we do know that The Hague has taken the petition, and they're considering it," Henry said.

Across the table from Laney, her uncle took a sip of tea. There was the slightest tremor in his hand. His face was drawn, and he looked like he'd aged overnight. In fact, Henry and Jake weren't exactly looking their best either.

Not that I'm a beauty queen right now. She knew she had the same bags and dark circles under her eyes, the same pale cast to her skin. But she also knew a good night's sleep was at some far-off point in all their futures.

"What about the American government?" Jake asked.

"Matt still has contacts inside the FBI," Henry said. "He says it's only a matter of time before they put out an arrest warrant."

"What will the charges be?" Patrick asked.

"He's not sure. It's complicated because everything happened on foreign soil. But he believes it will be some variation on treason, or even terrorism."

"So now I'm a terrorist?" Laney asked quietly.

Patrick's eyes went wide. "If she's labeled a terrorist, she won't be granted any of the protections of the Constitution."

"No, she won't," Henry said, his face serious.

"They could have her extradited to a country that allows torture."

Henry's voice was grim. "Yes."

Patrick shook his head, his eyes wild. "No. They are *not* allowed to do that. After everything you've done, after everything you've lost and fought for—"

Henry put his hand on Patrick's. "Patrick, we won't let that happen."

Tears sprang to Patrick's eyes. "But they can't—"

"We'll run if we have to," Jake said.

Laney's head jerked up. "What?"

"Henry and I discussed it," Jake said. "If it gets to the point where we think you're going to be railroaded, we're going to disappear."

"No. Absolutely not," Laney said.

"Laney—" Jake began.

Laney stood up. "No. If we all disappear, Elisabeta wins. The triad is gone. The world is unprotected. She didn't do this just for spite. She has a plan. She needs me out of the way. You two can't volunteer to get out of the way as well."

"Then *I'll* go with you," Patrick said.

Laney wanted to cry, picturing her uncle standing between her and a United States government convinced she was enemy number one. She shook her head. "No. *No*— none of you are going anywhere. The best way you can help me is out in the open, not on the run." She stepped away from the table. "This is not up for discussion. We don't know that I'm going to be taken in anyway. We need to focus on my defense, proving to law enforcement that I wasn't behind everything. *That's* our play."

"We *are* working on that," Henry said. "We can already demonstrate that one of the tapes was tampered with, and we're getting statements from people involved in each of the incidents. Nana and Elena have even offered to fly up from Ecuador to testify."

Laney smiled—her first genuine smile of the day—at the image of the diminutive but mighty Nana facing off against a host of government lawyers from multiple nations. "Well then, we have nothing to worry about."

"Laney…" Jake said.

She shook her head. "No. It will be fine. We just need to give it time."

None of the men around the table looked convinced.

"Please?" she asked. "Let's try it my way, and then we can discuss it again if things start to look dire, okay?"

"Okay," Patrick said. "Whatever you want." But she heard the subtext beneath his words: *I am not letting anyone hurt you*. The same message was on Jake's and Henry's faces even as they nodded their agreement.

She felt tears burn the back of her eyes. "I love you. All of you."

Patrick started to stand to hug her, but Laney knew if he did that she would lose it, and she couldn't afford that right now. "No," she said quickly. "I'm all right. I'm just going to go for a walk. Clear my head."

"You want some company?" Jake asked.

"No. I, um, I need to be alone for a little bit."

Patrick kissed her cheek. "We'll see you later then."

Laney struggled to keep her face impassive as her throat tightened. "Yup. Later."

She turned and headed for the front door. But at the

end of the hall, she stopped and looked back at Henry, Jake, and Patrick—the three most important men in the world to her.

She took a shuddering breath. *Goodbye.*

Chapter One Hundred Four

BY THE TIME Laney reached Dom's place she had her emotions under control. She left her two shadows outside the shelter and made her way down through Dom's levels of protection. Five minutes after she stepped past the first blast door, she was striding into Dom's main living area.

She smiled at the pictures Dom had placed in frames around the room: Lou, Rolly, Danny, herself, Jake, Henry, Patrick, Cleo. When Laney had met Dom he was a reclusive agoraphobe, but now, as evidenced by these photos, he was coming out into the world more and more, at least socially. She was hopeful that one day he might even start taking more trips up to the surface—but she knew not to hold her breath on that one.

"Laney." Dom stepped out of the hallway leading to his office.

"Hey, Dom."

Dom was carrying a large backpack, which he set on the kitchen counter.

"Did you have any trouble?" Laney asked.

"No. Everything's ready."

"Were you able to wire the money to that other account?"

"Yup. And your IDs are in here as well." Dom unzipped the bottom pocket. "But this should see you through for a while."

Laney's eyes bulged as she stared at the rolls of hundreds. "Dom, that's got to be fifty thousand dollars."

"Seventy-five, actually."

Laney shook her head. "I can't take that. That's yours."

Dom shrugged. "What am I going to use it for? It's part of my rainy day money. I keep it down here, just in case."

"Dom—"

"Laney, take it. I'll feel better if I know you at least have some money."

Laney looked into Dom's brown eyes. Fear, sadness, and concern were all reflected back at her. The catch appeared at the back of her throat again. She looked away, blinking back tears. "Thank you. Oh, and here." She handed him five envelopes. "Give them to everybody when I'm gone, okay?"

Dom nodded.

"There's one for you, too."

Dom took a hasty step back, cleared his throat, and placed the envelopes on the counter. She could tell he was forcing his voice to sound normal, but there was still a tremor in it. "Come on. We should get you moving."

He led Laney toward the back of the shelter. "How'd you even know I had another exit?" he asked.

Laney smiled. "Dom, you are prepared for everything. It never made any sense to me that you would only have one way in and out."

Dom grinned, but Laney still saw the sheen of tears in

his eyes. "There's actually four. But the plans only show two."

Dom pushed open the door to the storage room and wound past rows of just about everything imaginable: food, paper goods, an inflatable raft, a dozen hazmat suits, oxygen canisters, and boxes and boxes of Cheerios. Laney smiled. *Note to self: in the event of an apocalypse, head to Dom's.*

When they reached the back wall, Laney scanned it, looking for a door, but she couldn't make one out. Dom reached up to a high shelf and pulled down a box marked "plastic forks." He wiped away a tear that slid down his cheek, and Laney had to look away for a moment to get control of her own emotions.

When she turned back, Dom held a remote in his hand. "Ready?"

Laney nodded.

Dom hit a button on the remote, and the wall behind him slid to the right, revealing a tunnel.

Laney gaped. "Wow, that's some serious Batcave stuff."

Dom handed her a flashlight from the racks, his eyes bright behind his glasses. "It was an old tunnel used by the Underground Railroad—one of the few sections that was literally underground. It goes two miles east of the estate. The car will be waiting for you to the east of the exit. It's a silver Toyota Camry."

Laney nodded. Toyotas were one of the most common cars on the road. She'd blend right in.

Dom handed her the pack, and Laney strapped it on her back.

"Your phone," Dom said.

"Oh, right." Laney pulled it out of her back pocket and placed it on one of the shelves. "Well, I guess this is it."

Dom nodded, staring at the floor. When he spoke, there

was a hitch in his voice. "I'll give you as much of a head start as I can. But once they get down here…"

"I understand. Just do what you can."

"Be careful, Laney."

"I will." A shudder ran through her, and she had to take some deep breaths before she could speak without crying. "Take care of them, okay? All of them."

Dom hugged her quickly and then stepped back, tears running down both cheeks. "You should go," he said, his gaze on the floor.

Laney wiped at the tears on her own cheeks. She placed a hand on his shoulder and gave it a squeeze before turning on the flashlight and stepping into the tunnel. "Bye, Dom."

"Bye, Laney."

The door to the tunnel closed behind her.

Chapter One Hundred Five

AS THE CLICK of the closing door echoed down the tunnel, Laney felt the finality of her actions. She was well and truly on her own. But she shoved those emotions aside. She promised herself that when she was far enough away and the rest of them were safe, she'd allow herself to cry for a week if she needed to.

She flashed her light around, revealing a dirt tunnel hollowed directly out of the earth, with no supporting beams that she could see. She hoped it hadn't collapsed anywhere along the line, or this was going to be the shortest escape ever. But as she moved forward, she saw that the tunnel had held up well, and she was actually able to jog. She made the two miles in just over twenty minutes.

At the end of the tunnel, an old iron gate was set in the ceiling, overgrown by bushes on the other side. Laney stopped to listen intently, but hearing nothing, she said a quick prayer, unbolted the gate, and pulled it open. It let out a giant screech that made her cringe, but no one came running.

She pulled herself up, pushed her way through the bushes—and the night sky twinkled down on her. She was in the middle of a field, the moon shining brightly overhead. Turning off her flashlight, she jogged east. The car was parked only a few hundred yards away. She removed the keys from the wheel well, unlocked it, and threw her bag in the back.

Thirty minutes later, she was leaving the state of Maryland.

Laney felt the tightness in her chest ease as she crossed the border into West Virginia. She stopped checking the rearview mirror quite as often—though her eyes did stray to the exit for the SIA facility as she passed it.

Even keeping to the speed limit, it wasn't long until she was in Ohio. She stopped for gas, picked up a phone, and hit a fast food place for coffee and food—being sure to keep her hat pulled low over her face, in case there were cameras—and then she was off again. She planned on driving as long as she could. She'd get a cheap motel and sleep a little bit when she grew too tired, and then she'd be back on the road.

The lanes continued on ahead of her, and as the night wore on, she passed fewer and fewer cars. She had only Bruce Springsteen on the radio to keep her company.

It's for the best, she told herself over and over. *If I'm gone, they're safe.*

She just hoped they understood.

Chapter One Hundred Six

PATRICK SAT at Henry's table as Jake and Henry discussed the possible directions they could take with Laney's legal and physical defense. Patrick tried to listen, but all he could see was Laney as an eight-year-old with her big green eyes staring up at him, her arm wrapped in an impossibly large cast. He'd failed to protect her then, and while he knew she was grown now—and that in many ways she was stronger than him—he couldn't get past his need to protect her this time like he had failed to do before.

"Patrick?" Henry asked.

"Sorry, what?"

"We were saying that the kids at the school are going to need a lot of help to get through this if Laney is arrested. Do you have any thoughts about what we should do there?"

Patrick nodded. "Yes. I've already put out calls to a number of people: counselors, rabbis, pastors, just friends of the school. They'll be available for whatever we need."

"Good," Jake said. "How are the kids doing?"

Patrick had visited them this morning. "There's no one answer for that. Shocked, angry, in disbelief. They don't want to believe it of Laney. She's had such an impact on all of them. But for some of them... I can see the news at least has them wondering."

And that was another thought that terrified him. All the students at the school were either nephilim or Fallen, and some believed their abilities meant they should be given special considerations. He worried that if they believed Laney had committed these acts, it would help them justify their own bad behavior. After all, if Laney doesn't play by the rules, why should they?

"Some of the parents have contacted my office," Henry said. "They're talking about pulling their kids from the school."

"What?" Jake exclaimed.

"But—" Patrick began.

Henry put up a hand. "I've talked them down for now. But we need to be prepared for that possibility."

This keeps getting worse and worse, Patrick thought. The school wasn't perfect, but it was a safe place for these kids to explore their abilities and the changes they were going through. Pulling them from that safety wasn't going to help anyone.

"I can have some experts in trauma flown in," Henry said.

Patrick nodded. "It may come to that." He looked up at the clock with a frown. It had been an hour and a half since Laney had gone for a walk. He stood. "I think I'll go see where Laney is. It's been a while."

Jake stood as well. "I'll go with you."

Henry promised to find them after he made a few calls.

Patrick and Jake fell in step together, neither of them really having a destination in mind.

"How are you doing?" Jake asked.

"I don't know," Patrick replied. "The idea that, by law, we're supposed to just sit back and let them put Laney in harm's way... I don't think I can do that. I can't sit back and let her be hurt. She's done nothing to deserve this."

"If it comes to that, we'll get her away. Keep her hidden until things cool down."

Patrick looked at the strong man walking next to him. He knew Jake and Laney had decided to take a break, but he also knew how much they loved each other—and that each would do whatever was necessary to protect the other.

They walked to the main building, but saw no sign of Laney. Jake called down to the front gate, but they hadn't seen her either. Finally, he called her security detail. He hung up his phone. "She's at Dom's."

They turned in that direction.

"How come you didn't call her detail first?" Patrick asked.

Jake gave him a small smile. "Laney hates having people watching her every move. I'm trying to not use them as spies."

A reluctant smile tugged at Patrick's lips. "You know my niece well."

"That I do. But I'm still learning—every day."

"Me too."

After checking in with Laney's two guards, they headed into Dom's shelter. But the second blast door wouldn't open for them.

Jake used the intercom next to the door. "Hey, Dom? Something's wrong with door number two."

Dom's face appeared on the screen next to the door. "Oh. Well, give me a minute. I'll get it fixed."

A minute turned into five, then ten.

Jake jammed the intercom again. "Dom? What's going on?"

"Sorry, sorry. Here you go."

The light above the door flashed green, and Jake and Patrick proceeded to the next blast door. But when Jake placed his hand over the hand scanner, it glowed back red.

"What the hell?"

He tried it again—with the same reaction.

He punched the intercom next to the door. "Goddamn it, Dom," he growled.

"Yes?" Dom asked.

"Door number three's acting up too."

"I'll get right on it," Dom said before disappearing from view.

Patrick frowned. Two doors down? That wasn't like Dom. And Dom not being nervous about it wasn't normal either.

The wait this time was only about five minutes. Finally they were inside, where Dom stood waiting for them, his smile overly bright.

"What's going on with your doors?" Jake asked.

"Not sure—a little bug. I'm pretty sure I've got it worked out," Dom said, looking anywhere but at Jake and Patrick.

Patrick stepped past Dom without a word and made his way to the living area, looking for Laney. But she wasn't there. His heart began to race.

"Patrick?" Jake asked.

Patrick whirled on Dom. "Where is she?"

"Um…"

Patrick stepped toward him. "Dom! Where. Is. She?"

Dom stared at the floor, and his voice was quiet. "She's gone."

"*Gone?* Gone where?" Patrick asked.

"Into hiding."

"What did you *do*?" Jake demanded.

Dom shook. "She—you know what the government's like. They would have locked her away, tortured her. We never would have seen her again. This was the only way."

Jake stepped menacingly toward Dom. "Tell me *everything* you did." Patrick had to grab his arm to stop him.

Dom backed up, shaking his head in defiance even as he trembled. "No. She asked for my help, and I gave it. She's my friend, Jake. And I won't tell you anything."

Jake's eyes narrowed. "If she gets hurt, it's on your head," he growled. Then he pulled out his phone and stormed out the door.

Dom looked shattered. Patrick took his arm and led him to the big leather sectional.

"If something happens to her," Patrick said, "it's not your fault. She asked you to help her, and you did. If you hadn't, she would have found another way to go. One thing about my niece—she's determined."

"She's my friend," Dom said. "And she asked me for help." He stared up at Patrick, his eyes begging the older man to understand.

And Patrick did. Dom had very few friends and no family. Laney, Henry, the teenagers—they were his whole world. And he would do anything to help them—even if it hurt him.

"You were a good friend to her," Patrick said, though he was terrified at the idea of Laney being out there on her own. "You gave her what she needed. And I know it was hard."

Dom sniffed. Then he looked up quickly. "I forgot." He dashed over to the kitchen island and came back carrying several envelopes. "This is for you. From Laney."

Patrick took it with a shaky hand.

"I'm going to go see if Jake wants his." Dom headed for the entrance.

Patrick turned his attention to the envelope. With a shaky hand, he opened it and removed the letter inside.

Hi, Uncle Patrick. Not sure how long after I left you're getting this. I hope it's a couple of hours. I needed to go. There's too much focus on me. And I know that you're all in danger the longer I stay. Even if one of the groups with a death warrant out on me doesn't get through, I will in all likelihood be arrested. I know that you, Henry, and Jake won't let that happen—which just means you'll all be arrested as well. Or worse. I can't let that happen. I love you too much for that. The same way you all love me.

I'm counting on you to keep them together, to keep the kids at the school together. I'm hoping you can talk Noriko into staying a little longer to help with the cats. She has a way with them. And they need the companionship, so please make sure Lou and Rolly visit as much as possible. And tell Cleo I'm sorry I had to leave.

Please don't look for me. Hopefully, you all can find some proof to get the heat off me. I'll come home when it's safe for you all to be around me. Until then, I'll stay hidden. Until that time, know that I love you and that I always have.

Laney

P.S. I don't know how long I'll be gone. But if it turns out to be a while, can you go visit Cain? He likes chess and cappuccinos.

Patrick stared at the words through a veil of tears. He had to laugh, because if he didn't, he would sob.

She's on the run for her life, and she's worried Cain will be lonely.

His eyes flicked back to the sentence in the letter that she should have known better than to write: *Please don't look for me.* He shook his head. *No, Laney, I can't promise that.* He stood up. *Because no matter what, I will find you.*

Chapter One Hundred Seven

VENICE, ITALY

ELISABETA STRETCHED AND SAT UP. White silks were wrapped around the four posts at the corners of her king bed. She reached for the remote on the side table and hit one of the buttons. The room-darkening shades began to slowly pull back, letting sunlight in.

Another beautiful day.

She rang the bell and then took her robe from the end of the bed, wrapping it around her as she walked to her balcony.

The door to her room opened a few moments later. Her servant appeared, pushing the breakfast cart. "Ma'am?"

"Out here," Elisabeta said.

The woman quickly laid out her breakfast of coffee, fruit, and croissants before disappearing.

Elisabeta sat down and took a bite from the croissant as she pulled over her tablet and pulled up the BBC. The lead headline: *Delaney McPhearson At Large; Manhunt Begins.* She quickly scanned the article. McPhearson was being charged with murder in the Capitol Building killing, as well as terrorism for her involvement in the incident in Israel. They were still debating the charges in Australia.

Delaney running was not unforeseen. She would do anything to protect the ones she loved, and removing herself from the equation was the best insurance. But the world's resources were moving against her, and it was only a matter of time before she was found.

Elisabeta smiled. *And then killed.*

And even before that glorious day, Elisabeta could put her plan in motion—finally. The ring bearer was sidelined. Her running would mean all those nearest and dearest to her would be completely focused on finding her. With one blow and no deaths, Elisabeta had effectively taken out the triad and all of the SIA, leaving no one to block her.

She took a sip of her coffee. *Yes, it is definitely going to be a lovely day.*

Chapter One Hundred Eight

JAKE WALKED up the stairs to the third floor of Chandler Headquarters. It had been a month since Laney had disappeared, and no one had found any trace of her—not the Chandler Group, not the government agencies, and based on the chatter they picked up, not the terrorist groups either.

When she had first gone missing, Jake had been out of his mind terrified. He knew it was only a matter of time before she was caught. There were so many people looking for her, how couldn't she be? But somehow she had eluded them all. And he couldn't help but feel a little proud of her for that.

He also knew that if anyone did find Laney, she would not go quietly. He pictured her raining thunderbolts down on anyone trying to get near her, maybe whipping up a tidal wave or a wall of wind.

But the manhunt for her was continuing. Her face had been splashed across newspapers and news shows, even more than it had been after Israel. Everyone in the country knew who she was and had an opinion of how she should be treated.

And yet, no one had sighted her. Jake didn't know what to make of that. Late at night he sometimes thought the worst. She'd been in a desolate area, broken an ankle, and had been unable to get to help. That was his fear—that she had already died and they didn't know. His stomach clenched at the thought.

She's fine. She's smart. She's doing what she needs to do.

Now he walked into Henry's office, although Henry no longer used it. The whole place had been transformed into Laney Central. The legal team had part of the room, and the analysts who were scouring the internet and video feeds across the nation were set up in another portion. Henry wanted everyone in one place, in case anyone needed to consult. The conference rooms down the hall were also being used when people needed to have quieter discussions or work spaces.

Jake walked over to Danny, who was overseeing the video analysis. The kid had refused to be kept out of the search. Henry had resisted for about a week, but finally relented after learning that Danny was searching on his own anyway.

"Anything?" Jake asked.

Danny shook his head. "No. A few false IDs in Kansas, but turned out it was just a nurse in Kansas City with the same height and build."

"So what have you got?"

Danny looked around, then gestured for Jake to follow him to a quiet corner.

"I tapped the feds a couple of weeks ago," Danny whispered.

Jake shrugged. "I kind of figured that. Have you gotten anything?"

"There was a sighting in Nevada two weeks ago. They just figured it out last night. Dark hair, darker skin, cheekbones were more pronounced, and she was taller. But I think it was Laney."

Jake grinned. "She changed her appearance."

"That's what I think. Anyway they're focusing their efforts in the west. And that lead went cold. I just thought you should know."

Jake clapped him on the shoulder. "Thanks, Danny."

"I'll keep looking."

"I know you will."

Danny headed back to his workstation.

Jake looked around the room. On the whiteboard was a picture of Laney. He walked over to it, studying her face and trying to imagine what she looked like now.

Wherever you are, Laney, just keep your head down.

Chapter One Hundred Nine
CORTEZ, COLORADO

AFTER PULLING into the back of the parking lot next to a three-foot snowdrift, Laney turned off the engine and watched the store. There were a few other cars around, most from the restaurant next door. She was in a little shopping area outside Cortez, Colorado, population eight thousand.

Dark had fallen a few hours ago. It had snowed another six inches last night, on top of the eighteen inches that were already on the ground, an unusual occurrence for this part of the country. And for Laney, a convenient one. The snow, plus the cold snap that had moved in, should keep the place quiet.

Laney put on her new glasses with the non-prescription lenses, pulled on her navy blue hat over her dark brown hair, and looked at herself in the rearview mirror. She had brown contacts to hide her green eyes, and she'd even used a self-tanner to change her skin tone. She pulled cotton wool from her bag and pushed it into each cheek. She was amazed how even that small amount changed the shape of her face.

To cover her fingerprints, she pulled on leather gloves, and last, she tugged the sides of her hat lower to make sure it was covering her ears. She knew law enforcement agencies used ear shape to help identify people now. Ear shape stayed practically the same from birth, and the image ray transform algorithm boasted a 99.6% accuracy rate. All they needed was a profile shot.

Which is why she chose this particular grocery store—they didn't have security cameras. But seeing as everyone had a cell phone with a camera these days, she knew she still needed to be cautious.

She waited until a couple from the grocery store got in their car and pulled away before exiting her car and entering the store. She ignored the clerk behind the counter, grabbed a basket, and made quick work of getting her supplies: milk, eggs, beef jerky, turkey, canned fruit, bread, and mayo. Only minutes after entering, she was at the checkout with everything she needed.

"How you doing tonight?" the cashier asked.

"Good. Thanks." Laney made sure to not make eye contact and to keep her voice small and her shoulders rounded as if she were very shy—a persona she had perfected over the last month.

"That'll be $27.38."

Laney handed over the money, got her change, and was out the door with only a few more words exchanged. As she stepped out into the cool air and took a deep breath, her heart was racing. Each time she went out in public, she had the same reaction—which was one reason why she tried to go out as little as possible.

In the last month, she'd only shown herself in small towns, and even then only late at night when cashiers were least likely to be paying attention. This particular town was a full one hundred miles from where she was staying. She'd been in this grocery store once before, a week ago, and today would be her last trip. She'd find another one next time so as not to leave much of a trail.

A light snow had started. Pulling the collar of her jacket up, she headed for her car.

The door to the restaurant next door flew open, and two figures stumbled out into the cold. Laney glanced at them out of the corner of her eye as she walked. They were two men, one tall, one short, both stocky. They walked around the side of the restaurant, then stopped and peered back around the corner at the door they'd just exited.

Laney frowned. It was twelve degrees—not exactly hanging out outside weather.

Not your problem. Keep going.

Laney walked to her car, opened the back door, and placed her groceries on the floor. As she turned, she saw the restaurant door open and a young woman step out. She was thin, with a pink barrel coat and blond hair twisted into two braids. She walked to her car and stopped, fumbling in her bag for her keys.

Laney shook her head. *Always have your keys ready, sweetheart.*

Laney had a sinking feeling in her stomach, but she got into her own car, started it up, and pulled out of her spot. And as she did, the two men started toward the woman.

It's not your fight, Laney. You need to stay out of it. They're probably just going to their car.

But she couldn't help herself. She watched in the

rearview mirror as the two men separated, one approaching the woman from the front, one from the back. Laney hesitated. All the reasons why she should just keep driving flashed through her mind.

Damn it.

She turned the wheel hard, did a U-turn, and headed back.

One of the men had reached the woman. He grabbed her shoulder. She spun around, then backed up until the back of her legs hit her car. The shorter man came around the other side so they boxed her in. The woman's head swiveled back and forth between them.

Laney angled her car so her headlights lit up the threesome. The men blinked in the light. The taller man shielded his eyes.

Leaving her car running, Laney stepped out. "Is there a problem here?"

"No problem," the shorter man said.

Laney stepped forward. "I'd like to hear her say that."

The woman just stared quietly at Laney, but a tear was making its way down her cheek. She couldn't be any older than twenty, and beneath her jacket Laney could see an apron. She must be a waitress at the restaurant.

"I think you guys should go now," Laney said, her voice cold.

The taller guy snorted. "Brett, take care of her."

Brett smiled, which did nothing to increase his appeal, and walked toward Laney. "Lady, I think you need to learn a lesson."

Laney sighed. *Why do all assholes think they're teachers?*

When Brett reached for her, Laney slid her hand down his arm to the elbow, grabbed his wrist with her other hand, and bent it. She then grabbed his wrist with both hands and stepped back, twirling him off his feet and onto the ground. He hit the icy parking lot with a scream. She was tempted to break his arm, but that would draw more attention, so she settled for a kick to the face, which knocked him out.

She straightened up and looked at Brett's friend. "Well, that was a fun lesson. Now *you* need to step away from her."

The tall guy was apparently not much smarter than his friend. He pushed the woman toward Laney, then charged right behind her. Laney sidestepped the woman and slammed her boot into the middle of the man's chest. She kicked out his knee and finished with a front kick to the groin that would have made a punter proud. The man squealed, his hands grasping his groin as he collapsed to the ground.

The woman was now leaning against another car, her eyes wide.

"Are you all right?" Laney asked.

The woman nodded. "How—You—"

Laney patted her arm. "It's all right. You're fine now."

"I—I need to call the police."

The door to the restaurant opened, and three people strolled out.

Laney faced away from them. "Okay. But I have to go."

The girl's big blue eyes turned to Laney. "But you saved me."

"Yup, but now I need to leave. Call the police from inside."

Laney quickly got back in her car as the three people from the restaurant caught sight of the men on the ground and hurried over. The woman burst into tears, gesturing from the men on the ground to Laney while Laney quickly reversed into the shadows so they couldn't get a look at her license plate.

She drove as calmly as she could down the street, her eyes flicking to the rearview mirror, but no one was following her.

She pictured the young woman's face. She was glad she had helped her. She didn't regret that.

But she really hoped it didn't come back to bite her.

Chapter One Hundred Ten

PATRICK SAT in Henry's office, where he'd been organizing an event for the school. Henry had some contacts in Hollywood who had agreed to screen a movie for the kids—one that was not yet out in theaters. Patrick thought it would be a nice surprise. He'd already arranged for the catering and had spoken with the film studio representative, who promised the film would be delivered promptly at six tomorrow.

Now there really was nothing else for him to do—and yet he couldn't get himself to leave. He was the only one in the office for a change, which was nice—calming.

He strode over to the wall of windows that overlooked the rolling hills of the estate. It really was beautiful, with the moon shining down on the blanket of snow that had been falling on and off over the last month.

The month that Laney was gone.

Patrick clenched his fists as the familiar stab of fear pierced him. He knew she was capable and could handle herself. Even before she had received her abilities, she had been more capable than her peers. He just hated that she thought she had to do this on her own, to protect her friends and family. It killed him that it was yet another sacrifice she had to make.

And the cries for her capture only seemed to be growing louder. An international incident had barely been avoided when a Mossad group had been found operating on American soil. The US government had demanded an apology from Israel, Israel had refused, and it had all led to a very tense week. Relations had now calmed down a bit, but things were still delicate—like they were in a permanent holding pattern.

And that's exactly how Patrick felt—like his life was on hold until he knew Laney was safe.

The door opened behind him, and he turned to see Jake. Despite the change in Jake's relationship with Laney, the man remained absolutely dedicated to her. He had been looking for her nonstop since she'd disappeared.

"Oh, hey, Patrick. I didn't realize you were here. I was looking for Henry."

"He and Jen are having dinner at his place. He should be back shortly."

"Okay. I'll try them there." He turned to go.

"Jake?"

Jake turned back.

"Is there anything new?"

Jake hesitated.

Patrick felt his heart lift. "Jake?"

"It could be nothing."

Patrick hurried across the room. "What is it?"

"There was an attempted sexual assault in a small town in Colorado."

Patrick's hand flew to his chest. "Laney?"

Jake reached out his hand. "No, no. And the attackers, they were stopped. Neither the victim nor the attackers could describe the woman who had intervened. But they all agreed that she was a damn good fighter."

"You think it's Laney?"

"I don't know. Local police think she may have shopped at the grocer next to the restaurant where the attack occurred. But there were no cameras, and it was late. The cashier couldn't remember what she looked like. The cops who took his statement thought he might have been stoned."

"Do the feds know about it?"

"I don't know. I don't think so. I think they have so many tips they're probably being run ragged."

Well, maybe that will help keep Laney hidden. "Where did this happen?"

"Colorado. A little town called Cortez."

A memory stirred just out of reach. "Where in Colorado is that?"

"It's in the southwest corner."

Patrick headed for a computer at the conference table.

"Patrick?"

"I just want to check something."

Patrick pulled up a map of Colorado, sent it to the large projection screen above the conference table, then walked over to it. He pointed to a small dot in the corner of the map. "This it?"

Jake nodded. "Yeah. What are you thinking?"

"I don't know."

Patrick scanned the map, looking for something. Colorado. Something about Colorado. His eyes fell on a town about a hundred miles from Cortez, and he felt his heart skip a beat. *Could it be?*

He pointed to the small town. "Here. Pagosa Springs. Drew's grandfather had a cabin there. He left it to Drew when he passed, but it went into probate because Drew didn't have a will. It's been sitting empty since then, tied up in the courts."

"Did Laney know this?"

"Yes. She spoke with Drew's mom a few months back. She's the one who told me."

Jake grinned. "Which means—"

Patrick's heart lifted. "Which means I think we might have found her."

Chapter One Hundred Eleven

PAGOSA SPRINGS, COLORADO

THE SNOW DRIFTED SLOWLY past the window of Drew's grandfather's cabin. It was a true log cabin, the logs having been taken from the trees that had formerly stood on this very spot. Drew's great-grandfather had built it by hand, and each successive generation had added their own stamp —adding indoor plumbing, electricity, et cetera. Drew's contribution had been cable and internet access. But despite the modern amenities, the place still retained its timeless look. Its old couch had a frame made out of tree limbs, the stone fireplace had a hewn log for a mantel, and a pair of Grandpa Masters's ancient snowshoes hung by the front door.

Laney curled up under the thick lamb's-wool blanket Drew's mom had made for him the year before he died. She felt closer to Drew here. Before he died, they had spoken every day; after he died, there'd barely been time to mourn. But here, she could remember the good times.

Laney had now been here for four weeks, having driven almost straight here from Baltimore. For the first few days, she'd jumped at every sound, fearing the police or worse were going to knock down her door at any minute. But no one had come, and she had allowed herself to fall into a sense of safety.

The incident outside the grocery store had shattered that. She was back to jumping at every sound. She knew she should hit the road. The problem was, she wasn't sure where to go. Everything was electronic these days, and most places had cameras. Avoiding those was key, but it was hard to do that when she didn't know where they were.

But she'd started researching her next destination. Dom had put a laptop in her bag, along with a note stating that it was encrypted and that no one should be able to trace it. Even so, she had been nervous about using it. She'd seen the magic Danny could do with a computer, and she knew the forces arrayed against her included people with similar abilities. But at this point, she had no choice. She had to move on.

And she finally thought she might know where to go: Alaska. She had identified a little cabin that was sitting in the middle of nowhere, miles outside Juneau. She wasn't thrilled about banishing herself to a winter wasteland, but as she looked out at the blanket of white outside, she realized, she had already kind of done that anyway.

She stood up and stretched, rolling her neck. She'd fallen asleep on the couch last night. The couch might look wonderful, but sleeping on it reminded you it was an antique, and not exactly the most comfortable piece of furniture ever created. *No offense, Grandpa Masters.*

She headed for the coffee maker and brewed herself a cup, debating when to make her move. She'd have to cut through Canada, which would be tricky. But if she went through at night, she should be all right at one of the smaller border crossings. Truth was, these days the border patrol agents were more concerned with terrorists coming across the border from Canada into the United States, not the opposite. At least, she hoped that was the case.

She poured her coffee, added some sugar and milk, and took a long drink. Something about a good cup of coffee made everything seem more manageable.

When she finished her cup, she went and got changed. She pulled on her boots, grabbed her jacket and hat from the counter, and pulled on her gloves. She glanced out the window. With the new snow, she was going to have to clear off her—

She went still. Her eyes went wide at the unmistakable sight of six heavily armed police officers in riot gear hunched low as they approached the house. Their dark clothes were practically a neon sign against the white background.

Laney's mind whirled. She didn't want to hurt them, but she couldn't let them get her.

What the hell am I going to do?

The officers stopped their advance, lining up twenty feet away, their weapons aimed at the cabin.

Chapter One Hundred Twelve

PATRICK SAT in the back seat with Henry, behind Jen in the passenger seat, as Jake drove them down the dirt road—*mud* road was probably more accurate—steering between three-foot-high walls of snow on either side. Patrick had to hold on as Jake took a turn too sharply and the back wheels skidded out.

No one said anything. In fact, no one had said anything since they had touched down and learned that law enforcement was converging on Drew's family's cabin. Each and every one of them was focused entirely on getting to Laney.

"Shit," Jake mumbled.

Up ahead, a line of cop cars was blocking the road. Three officers stood beside them.

"Plan?" Jake asked, his voice calm.

"I'll take care of them," Henry said.

"No," Jen said. "Let me handle it. You guys are all in the news. Let me do the talking."

One of the officers waved Jake to a stop. Jake slowed,

then rolled down the window and held out his badge. "Officer, we need to get through."

Jen leaned over across Jake. Her voice was brisk. "Officer, Agent Park." She flashed her badge. "They're expecting us."

"Ma'am, I'll need to—"

"You need to move your cars before I call your superior and let him know you're detaining us from reaching the scene. Do you know who they have up there?"

"Yes, ma'am. Sorry, ma'am."

"What radio channel are they on?"

"Um, twelve." The officer continued to stand next to the door.

Jen glared at him. "The car, officer?"

He practically jumped. "Right, sorry, ma'am. Right away." He hurried over to the patrol cars.

Jake grinned at Jen. "Remind me never to get on your bad side."

Jen smiled sweetly at him. "I thought you already knew that."

Jake gunned the engine as soon as the police car was out of the way, and Jen turned the radio they had brought with them to channel twelve.

In another half mile, they came to a second roadblock. This time there were dozens of cars, including vehicles from the FBI Special Response Team and SWAT. Jake pulled to a stop.

"Visual of suspect acquired," a voice announced over the radio. "Suspect is confirmed inside. Repeat, suspect is confirmed inside."

Jake leapt from the car. Jen handed Patrick the radio, then she and Henry followed. Patrick was left alone in the car.

A second voice came over the radio. "Lethal force is authorized."

Patrick's eyes flew to the small cabin, barely visible at this distance. He started to shake so hard he had to grab the seat in front of him.

And then the air filled with the sound of round after round being fired at the cabin. Patrick's mouth opened, but no sound could come out, and no breath could get in. Up ahead, Jake fell to his knees, and Henry had to wrap his arms around Jen to hold her back as she screamed.

Tears streamed down Patrick's cheeks and spots danced before his eyes. He barely got the door open before he lost all the contents of his stomach. Then he stumbled outside and fell, too numb, too weak to even push himself back to his knees.

Laney, no.

Chapter One Hundred Thirteen

HENRY HELD Jen back as she fought him to get to Laney. At the sound of the first shot, he had known they were too late. Even with their abilities, they were too far away. And each successive shot hammered home the loss.

Laney. They were shooting at Laney.

No. They were *killing* her.

Jen stopped fighting him when the sounds of the guns died away. She collapsed in his arms, sobbing. Henry's own knees gave out, and he sank to the ground, his arms wrapped around Jen as if somehow holding each other would make this better.

Nothing was going to make this better.

He barely registered Jake, who stared in mute horror at the cabin ahead.

The three of them stayed there for what felt like forever. Henry watched the men in tactical gear move forward into the cabin. It all felt unreal. Like it was a movie. In his mind's eye, he could see Laney in the cabin, lying in a pool of blood. He closed his eyes, but the image remained.

Then a commotion could be heard from the cabin.

Jake's head jerked up. "Something's wrong." He got to his feet and started running.

Henry kept his eyes glued to the little cabin. For a moment, there was nothing. Then a body in tactical gear came flying through one of the destroyed windows.

Henry felt weak, and he wanted to yell and cry at the same time. He grabbed Jen, turning her to face the cabin. "She's alive, Jen. She's alive."

Chapter One Hundred Fourteen

AN ELECTRIC TINGLE rolled over Laney as the first shot rang out. She dove to the ground, but knew she would have collapsed anyway due to the intensity of the electrical signal. The back door burst open as the windows shattered from the spray of bullets, and a body flew across the room, landing on her and holding her tight.

"No!" Laney screamed.

The man holding her sighed. "Ring bearer, could you please be quiet? My ear is awfully close to your mouth."

Laney went still as disbelief flooded her. "Drake?"

Above them, glass shattered and wood splintered from the hail of bullets striking the cabin. Drake wrapped one arm around Laney's waist and the other around her head, covering her entirely and pulling her tightly into his body. He jerked a half dozen times, and each time she knew he'd been hit.

And had kept *her* from being hit.

When the barrage finally ended, Laney's ears rang from the gunfire. "Drake?" she said. Her voice was shaky.

He groaned. "Give me a second. It's been a while since I've been hurt like this." He pushed himself up and onto his side, allowing Laney to scramble into a sitting position.

"How—? Why—?"

Drake put up his hand. "Hold those thoughts for a minute." He grabbed her by the waist and tossed her roughly across the room. She landed on the bed, bounced off it, and rolled onto the floor on the other side just as the front door burst open and officers poured into the room. The agents circled Drake, looking confused.

"Who—?"

The first agent didn't even get to finish his sentence. Drake moved through them like a whirlwind. One hit the ceiling, another flew out the window, and the rest were thrown to the floor.

Then Drake sprinted across the room and grabbed Laney. "Time to go." Without waiting for her reply, he pulled her into his arms and blurred out the back door.

Chapter One Hundred Fifteen

"THE SUSPECT IS GONE. Repeat, the suspect is gone." The call came over the radio. It took a moment for the words to register with Patrick.

"Say again?" came an incredulous voice.

"The suspect is gone."

Patrick gripped the radio like it was a lifeline.

"You had a visual."

"Yes, sir. But the subject is gone and the breach team is down." The voice paused. "The backup team is also down."

"What the hell happened?"

"Not sure yet, sir."

"Well find out, Goddammit!"

"Roger."

Patrick struggled to his feet. He searched for Henry, Jake, or Jen. He didn't see them, but he heard raised voices coming from behind the SWAT van and recognized one of them as Jake's.

"You are not part of this operation!" a man yelled.

Patrick walked around the end of the van and saw Jake toe to toe with a giant of a man.

"And I told you I'm not leaving until I know what happened!" Jake barked. Patrick could tell he was two seconds from ripping the man's throat out.

Patrick rushed forward. "Jake—she's not in the cabin."

Jake turned toward Patrick, and Patrick read the hope and the fear.

He placed his hand on Jake's arm. "She wasn't there." He turned to the SWAT officer. "I can take it from here."

With a glare, the man stormed off. Henry and Jen appeared from the woods, their cheeks red from the cold, snow covering their pants from the knees down.

"Where were you two?" Jake asked.

"Checking the cabin," Jen said. "Someone took out the agents stationed at the back. There was a trail leading into the woods. We followed it. They must have had a car waiting. They were gone before we got there."

"Did you sense anyone?"

"No. Which means they were either human or full-fledged Fallen. And I don't see how a human could have done that. We were at the cabin seconds after the team went in. We should have caught up with any human who was trying to escape."

"So it was a Fallen," Jake said.

"But who? Matt?" Patrick asked.

Henry shook his head. "No. Matt was still back east this morning."

"Gerard?" Jen offered.

"I can't see him helping," Henry said. "In fact, I can't think of any full-fledged Fallen on our side besides Matt, or maybe some other SIA agent."

"Matt would have told us if he was sending someone," Patrick said.

Jake cut in. "Either way, she's alive, right?"

Henry nodded. "Yes. There was a little blood in the cabin but not much. She's alive."

Patrick smiled. "Now we just need to find her again."

Chapter One Hundred Sixteen

LANEY SAT in the passenger seat of a tan 1990 Ford Bronco next to Drake. The seats were ripped, and the car reeked of secondhand smoke. Fast food wrappers and cups were strewn everywhere. "Is this yours?"

"Nope, I borrowed it." Drake grinned, and Laney knew "borrowed" meant "stole."

She looked behind them, but no one was giving chase. Some of the tension left her shoulders, and she slumped lower in the seat.

Drake nodded toward the glove compartment. "If you're hungry, there's some food in there."

"I'm good," Laney said. "How are you here? Why are you here?"

Drake glanced over at her. "Was there a 'thank you' in there somewhere?"

Laney smiled. "Thank you. Now why are you here?"

Drake shrugged. "I had some vacation time coming and I thought a ski vacation was just the thing. By the way, I really like the new hair. It suits you."

Laney ignored the remark. "So you had some vacation time and you thought a quick pit stop through a police raid sounded like a good idea."

"Well, you know how much I like a good fight."

"Seriously, Drake. How did you even know I was there?"

"I have my ways. Archangel, remember?"

Laney could only shake her head. "So what's the plan?"

"Well, I figure we'll drop off this marvel of American craftsmanship in another hour or so, pick up another car, and head for the airport."

"By 'pick up another car,' you mean steal, right?"

"You know, for a woman wanted for trying to start World War III, you're awfully concerned about the law. If you really wanted to be a Girl Scout about it, you should have turned yourself in."

"Well, seeing as that would have meant signing my own death warrant, I elected for a different route."

Drake's voice was soft, and for a second the levity that was always on his face disappeared. "I heard. I know how hard it was for you to reveal yourself in Israel. I'm assuming you had no choice."

Laney was taken aback at the concern in his face. "Yes."

"Then everything is playing out the way it has to. And you'll overcome this."

"I don't know about that." She paused. "How did you find me anyway?"

The levity returned. "Oh, I have my ways."

Laney fingered a new hole in the arm of her jacket. She was thankful to the archangel; without him, she would no longer be breathing. But this incident just confirmed her need to stay away from those she cared about. "Well, let me out somewhere along the way and I'll be out of your hair."

Drake raised an eyebrow. "Did you miss the part of the conversation where I explained my plan?"

"No, I heard it. Now pull over."

"We need to keep going."

"No, *I* need to keep going. You need to leave."

Drake's eyes flicked toward her, but he pulled over to the side of the road.

"Thank you for saving me," Laney said. "But I need you to go. I'm not letting anyone else get hurt because of me. Not even you."

"I'm pretty hard to kill."

Laney nodded. "You are. But not impossible."

Drake sighed. "I'm sorry about this."

"There's nothing for you to be sorry about it. None of this is your fault. And you did just save my life."

"No, I don't mean for any of that."

Laney frowned. "Then what for?"

"This."

His fist moved so fast Laney didn't have time to react. Pain exploded across her temple, and then her world turned black.

Chapter One Hundred Seventeen

THE PATH behind the cabin led to a dirt road that, according to the map Jake had pulled up, dead-ended in one direction and emptied onto a highway in the other. Having no idea which way Laney might have gone, they had split up: Jake and Patrick had managed to borrow a car from the Colorado PD and were heading north on the highway. Henry and Jen were heading south. Henry also had a team of Chandler analysts keeping an eye on every single video feed they could identify, anywhere in the area. But the truth was, there weren't going to be many cameras out here; it was mostly open country.

Henry and Jen had now been driving for thirty minutes without seeing even a single car, and Henry was growing more tense with each passing mile. Who had taken Laney? Was it a friend or foe? Had Elisabeta sent someone in to finish the job?

Henry felt like he was going to crawl out of his skin. He loved Laney, but right now he could kill her for worrying them all like this. She should have stayed. They would have faced all this together.

But even as he thought it, he discarded the idea. If Laney had stayed, she'd have been incarcerated at best. She'd *had* to run. He just wished she'd let them run with her. Better together than Laney alone, and everyone else flailing about in complete ignorance.

Jen's phone rang, and she answered it. "Where?" she said after a moment. "We're on our way." She disconnected the call and turned to Henry. "Turn around. Patrick and Jake found the car she was in."

"How do they know that?"

"They're not sure. It was abandoned. But Jake spoke with the local police and cars abandoned along that strip tend to be moved pretty quick. And the engine was still warm when they reached it."

"Damn it!"

Henry turned the car around, but he knew it was futile. There was nothing to go on. Perhaps the analysts would spot something on a camera somewhere, but Laney had already evaded their search for a month—there was no reason to think that would change now.

What Henry couldn't figure out was *how* Laney had escaped. Because she was definitely in there. The spotter for the breach team insisted he saw her, and his description certainly sounded like her. And he saw her moving, so it wasn't a dummy or decoy. Besides, they would have found a dummy or decoy in the cabin if that had been the case.

No, someone had obviously been there. And someone had clearly been hurt—they had spilled a great deal of blood.

And now that person was gone.

Could Laney have escaped on her own? Those agents

had filled that cabin with holes, and Laney didn't have a healing ability or enough speed to get away. It didn't make sense.

Henry's phone beeped. Jen grabbed it and answered. "Hello?" She paused. "Great, send it."

"What is it?" Henry asked.

"Laney's been spotted. She was at the Perry Stokes Municipal Airport in Trinidad, Colorado. It's east of Pagosa. There's video."

Henry pulled over and Jen grabbed the iPad from the back seat. She pulled up an airport security feed, showing a black and white image. A twin prop plane stood in the background, and a light-colored car pulled up in the foreground. A man stepped from the driver's seat. Jen froze the film as the man turned toward the camera.

"Who is that?" Jen asked.

Henry frowned. "I think that's Drake."

"Drake? The archangel slash Vegas entertainer?"

"Yeah."

Jen restarted the video, and they watched Drake walk around to the passenger side. He opened the door and gathered a woman into his arms.

Henry's pulse picked up. *Laney*.

Drake turned and walked to the plane. It was a white twin prop with a dark stripe along the side. He opened the back of the plane and placed Laney inside. Then he stood there for a minute, his back to the camera.

"What's he doing?" Jen asked.

"I think he's buckling her in."

They kept watching. Drake got into the plane. A minute later, they taxied out of view.

Henry was on his phone immediately, and the information he wanted was relayed back to him only a few minutes later: the plane belonged to Drake. There was no flight plan. And Drake had taken an indefinite leave from his Vegas show.

Henry shut off his phone and stared out the windshield. But he didn't even see the snowy landscape in front of him; instead, he was watching Drake carry Laney to the plane.

Drake took her.

What the hell was he up to?

Chapter One Hundred Eighteen

AN INSISTENT BUZZING outside Laney's head competed with the loud pounding inside her head. She groaned.

"Oh, good, you're awake."

Laney squinted. "Drake?"

"Morning, sunshine."

Laney blinked, and the interior of the small plane came into view. She turned her head—too sharply—and groaned. *Okay, no quick movements.* She looked out the window, and saw only a barren landscape. "Where are we?"

"Right now, just over Northern California. There's some binoculars back there if you want to try your hand at spotting Bigfoot."

Laney gritted her teeth. "*Why* are we flying?"

Drake gave her a bewildered look. "Because walking would take *way* too much time."

She gritted her teeth again. She'd forgotten how difficult it was to get answers from the archangel. She narrowed her eyes as her last moments of consciousness came back to her. "You—you hit me."

Drake grinned. "In my defense, you were being unreasonable."

"Unreasonable? I was trying to protect you, you jackass."

"Tsk, tsk—such language."

"Drake, land the plane and let me out."

He sighed. "You know, for the ring bearer, you're a slow learner. The last time our conversation went down this path, you ended up unconscious. Besides, you need my help."

"I—what?"

"You have a mission to complete."

Laney stared at him in disbelief. She knew he was extravagant and not afraid to take a risk, but she'd never before gotten the impression that he was unhinged. "You do realize half the world's law enforcement is after me, right? Not to mention more than one death squad?"

"True," Drake said happily.

"So why would you want to get in the middle of any of that?"

"Well, now that Ralph is no longer with us, keeping you on mission falls to me."

"'On mission'? My 'mission' is over for the time being."

Drake shook his head. "No. You need to get ready."

"Get ready for what?"

The smile dropped from Drake's face, and for once Laney saw the warrior underneath. "The war."

She met his gaze, startled at the seriousness in it. "War? What war? Didn't I just help avoid a war? The priestess is contained. There is no war."

"That's not the war I'm talking about. I'm talking about the one against Samyaza."

Laney groaned. "Drake, I can't even poke my head out in public. And in case you missed it, I'm completely on my own. I mean, I know the military has that whole ad campaign about being an army of one, but against the Fallen, I think I'm going to need a few more soldiers."

"Oh, don't worry about that. You'll have the world helping you when you need it."

"The same world that's trying to kill me? And there is no war, Drake. Samyaza, horrible individual that she is, isn't starting a war."

"She already has. You just haven't seen it. So now you need to get ready so you can win it."

Laney laughed. "Drake, I'm not up for fighting any war. And I'm certainly in no position to win one."

"Oh, but you are. You've been in this position before. You just need to remember."

Laney tried to make sense of what he was saying. War? She knew that the world had gone to war in the past with the Fallen—but they were nowhere near that point, were they?

"It's coming, Laney," Drake said quietly.

Laney looked away from his probing eyes. Even if it was, how was *she* supposed to help? If she came out of hiding to fight the Fallen, she'd also have to fight the humans who thought she was responsible for everything that had happened in Israel and Australia. *Oh, and Washington, DC, and probably another half dozen incidents at this point.*

She shook her head. To say her image was in tatters would be an understatement. The situation was impossible.

"I can't. Not now, not with everything that's swirling around me. Samyaza's made it so I'm public enemy number one."

"True. But it's not the first time she's employed this particular approach. You just need to remember what you're capable of. How you overcame before."

"You said that already. Are you talking about one of the ring bearer's past lives?"

"You *are* the ring bearer, Laney. You have to accept that in your soul. Those past lives are *you*. You are the same now as you were then."

"Which incarnation are we talking about?"

Drake smiled. "Your most famous and most maligned."

Laney thought back. *Most famous? Who—*

Then she went still, remembering her conversation with Cain. "Helen."

Drake nodded. "It's time you learned the real story."

Laney shook her head. "Drake, I appreciate that you want to help, but you're not exactly inconspicuous. So just land somewhere safe and let me out."

Drake sighed. "You're always so stubborn."

"What do you mean?"

Drake pointed out the window. "Oh, look! Bigfoot."

"Drake."

"Seriously—you're going to miss him."

Laney turned. "What are you—?" She felt a pinch at the back of her neck. Her hand flew to the spot, and she whirled back around. Drake held a small needle in his hand. "What did you do?"

"You were being unreasonable—again. Now, close your eyes and take a nice little nap. When you wake up, I'm sure you'll see things more clearly."

The drug was already working. Exhaustion washed over her. "I hate you, Drake," she mumbled as her eyes closed, the darkness pulling at her again.

"But you haven't always," he whispered softly.

Next in The Belial Series

vinci-books.com/belialwarrior

Fugitive Delaney McPhearson must embrace her past as Helen of Troy to survive.

Turn the page for a free preview…

The Belial Guard: Chapter One

THE CHANDLER SCHOOL FOR CHILDREN, BALTIMORE, MARYLAND

Six months before the world turned against Delaney McPhearson

The sea of teenage faces looked up at Father Patrick Delaney as he stood in front of the classroom. Most were engaged, although more than a few glanced toward the clock, counting down the last few minutes of the class.

Patrick ignored the clock-checkers and focused on the engaged instead. "The city of Troy and the Trojan War were long believed to be a legend, until the 1870 discovery of Troy in Turkey by Heinrich Schliemann."

A girl with long, dark, wavy hair and bright eyes shot her hand into the air.

"Lou?" Patrick asked.

"But I was reading that Schliemann actually stole the site from a guy named Calvert."

Patrick smiled. Lou Thomas, age sixteen and a Fallen, had taken to history like a duck to water. She was always looking for more reading above and beyond what he assigned in class.

"That's true," he said. "Originally, Schliemann wasn't even interested in Troy. It wasn't until after touring the world that he met up with Frank Calvert and developed an interest in the ancient city. At the time, there were three potential spots in Turkey where Troy was believed to be located: Bunarbashi, Hisarlik, and Alexandria Troas. The third was believed by many to be a long shot. The first, Bunarbashi, was believed to be the most likely. But Frank Calvert, he was digging at Hisarlik. In fact, by the time Schliemann arrived, Calvert had been digging at Hisarlik for seven years. He had dug three trenches and found enough to convince him he was at the correct site."

"So how did Schliemann get the credit?" asked Rolly Escabi, who was sitting next to Lou.

"Well, Calvert told Schliemann all about his finds and beliefs. Within a year, Schliemann was digging at Hisarlik under Calvert's permit and with Calvert's men. When he struck pay dirt, he gave Calvert absolutely no recognition."

"Jerk," Lou muttered.

Patrick smiled. "Yes, I would have to agree."

A hand shot up in the back. Patrick called on Chris Santos.

"So," said Chris, "if they found Troy, does that mean everything that Homer said about the Trojan War was right? Gods, a ten-year war, and cheating Helen?"

A few students chuckled at Chris's last words, and Patrick tried not to cringe. Ever since he had learned that his niece, Delaney McPhearson, had been Helen of Troy in a previous life, he had been researching the historical figure to try and figure out the truth about who she was. And while it was proving a difficult endeavor, he could at least say that history seemed equally clueless when it came to the famous queen.

"Well, that's the question, isn't it?" Patrick said. "But you have to remember that the Spartans never wrote down their own history—the facts were handed down by oral tradition only. And Homer's tale was written five hundred years *after* the Trojan War, so it—like any tale handed down by oral tradition, or like any game of 'telephone'—undeniably changed in that time, no doubt making it more exciting, and less accurate."

Theresa Schneider, who usually sat quietly in the first row, spoke up, her voice shaky. "But the gods—they were *us*, weren't they?"

Now Patrick had the attention of everyone in the classroom. Every set of eyes looked at him, as everyone wanted an answer to that question. Because the Chandler School for Children was no ordinary school. All the students here were either Fallen, or they were nephilim—the child of a human and a Fallen angel. And all of them knew that this was not the first lifetime they had lived—although none could remember those past lives. Now like Patrick, they wondered which moments of history they had been a part of.

The idea of past lives wasn't an easy thing to accept—especially for Patrick, a Roman Catholic priest. But when he was preparing for this lecture, he knew this question was going to come up. He took a breath, sitting on the edge of his desk. "I think it's possible, yes. The gods had incredible abilities—speed, strength—but also some that were supernatural, like the ability to control the weather or move the sun across the sky. I think the stories of the gods, like the tale of the Trojan War, are based in fact but diluted by exaggeration."

The Belial Guard: Chapter One

The bell sounded, and everyone looked up. "Okay, read chapters seventeen through nineteen by Friday. There will be a quiz."

A groan sounded across the room, making Patrick smile. He gathered his papers and pushed them into his briefcase as the students filed out.

"Father Patrick?"

He looked up. "Lou. What can I do for you?"

"The Bronze Age, it was also called the Age of Heroes, right?"

Patrick nodded. "Yes."

"But there were no women. All the heroes—they were men. The women were all supporting players. Cassandra, Leda, Hecuba, even Helen—and the whole war's about her."

"That's how it's written, yes."

Lou shot a quick glance behind her, and Patrick had the impression she was checking to make sure everyone was gone before speaking. "Do you think that's true? That the women had nothing to do with the war besides Helen being the catalyst? That it was only the men that were the heroes? I mean, do you really think Helen of Troy was nothing more than the adulteress history has made her out to be?"

As Patrick looked into Lou's eyes, he knew this question was more than just an academic one. All the students knew Laney was the ring bearer, and they looked up to her; Laney was a superhero come to life. Lou felt the same way. But what Lou knew that the others didn't was that Laney had once been Helen of Troy.

"What I said in class was true," Patrick said. "*The Iliad* was written at least five hundred years after the Trojan War. And that was a time when women were viewed as little more than property; a strong woman in any capacity would have been viewed unkindly. And history was written by men. I think Helen is another case of history being particularly judgmental, if not downright inaccurate, about women."

"So you think she was more than an empty-headed woman controlled by her passions?"

Patrick smiled. "Helen is called Helen of Troy but remember, Helen was the Queen of Sparta. Spartan women were not easily fooled, nor did they suffer fools easily, which is what Paris appears to have been. She was known around the world well before *The Iliad* was written. For hundreds of years after her death, there were cults dedicated to her across the Mediterranean. So no, I don't think she was simply a pretty face who launched a thousand ships. I think history has been very unfair to her."

"What do you think the real story is?"

"I don't know. And I don't think we ever will."

Lou grinned. "But it's probably a good story."

Patrick pictured his niece. Time and time again she had faced every challenge presented her, at great cost to herself. And she had kept her morality and her priorities correct through it all—*protect as many as you can and do the right thing, no matter how hard it may be.*

"Yes," said Patrick. "I think whatever the true tale is, it's probably amazing."

Grab your copy...
vinci-books.com/belialwarrior

Afterword

FACT OR FICTION?

Thank you for reading *The Belial Guard*. I hope you enjoyed yourself and took a break from life for a little while to get lost between its pages. As with all the books in The Belial Series, *The Belial Guard* is a mixture of fact and fiction. I take some facts and try to weave them into the story line. So, here we go!

Honu Keiki. Honu Keiki is a fictional group, as is their island of Malama. The Children of the Law of One and Lemuria, however, were mentioned by Edgar Cayce, among others, in their discussion of the world during its early, early history.

Alternative Jewish Homelands. Other potential Jewish homelands besides Israel were suggested at one time or another. As mentioned in *The Belial Guard*, Grand Island, New York was one of those suggestions, although the settlement went nowhere. And Hitler did indeed consider moving Jews to Madagascar before moving on to his more horrific final solution.

Afterword

Lizard People. I was looking for information on the number of people who believe in the Antichrist when I came across an interesting finding. According to a conspiracy theory poll conducted by Public Policy polling, four percent of Americans believe that the government is being controlled by "lizard people." Yup, lizard people.

Leper Colony in Hawaii. There was a leper colony on Maui. The colony existed for a hundred years. During that time, over eight thousand people were forcibly removed from their homes and sent to the isolated peninsula. Since it was closed in the 1960s, the colony has been unused, although there is talk about opening it up to the public as a park.

Australian Aborigines. The Aborigines have one of the longest known histories of any people in the world. As described in *The Belial Guard*, their early history had no direct ties to Lemuria. However, the lifestyles were extremely similar.

World War III Close Calls. The World War III close calls were all real. The two U-2 spy plane incidents and the false missile reports all actually happened.

Education in Afghanistan. The facts on the state of education and childhood in Afghanistan are, sadly, true. Half of the schools don't even have a building, and child brides are all too common. And Afghanistan has one of the highest homicide rates for children in the world.

Scientology and Miscavige's Missing Wife. The information on Scientology is true, and while terrifying, it's also fascinating. If you're looking for a really good book on the cult, try *Going Clear* by Lawrence Wright. Miscavige's wife? That s true as

Afterword

well. The police say they spoke with her, but she has not been seen in public since 2005. When you read the book, you'll understand why her disappearance is so concerning.

End of Days. Christianity, Judaism, and Islam all discuss the end of days, as do a few other Western religions, and in these religions, the end of days is typically characterized as the ultimate battle between good and evil. The eastern religions tend to have little to no focus on the end of days. Instead, they encourage individuals to focus on their actions in the here and now.

Australia and Nuclear War. If a nuclear event broke out, Australia, due to its geographic location, would, theoretically, be a reasonably safe place to avoid radioactive fallout.

Temple Mount. The information on the Temple Mount is accurate, except for the role of Honu Keiki. Christianity, Judaism, and Islam all consider the Mount to be one of the most important sites in the world.

Antichrist. It's hard to say what is fact and what is fiction with regard to the Antichrist. Before I started writing this book, I thought it was a lot more cut and dried than it is. The Antichrist is only mentioned by name in the Bible four times, but many believe "the beast" and "the dragon" mentioned in Revelations and the book of Daniel are meant to refer to the Antichrist, even though they go by different names.

Waqf. The Waqf is the Islamic council that has religious sovereignty over the Temple Mount. Even though Israel technically controls Jerusalem, decades ago they extended religious sovereignty to the Waqf when they gained physical control of the Mount.

First and Second Intifada. The information on the first and second intifada is all accurate to the best of my ability, including the sparks that ignited each of the violent clashes. The second intifada was unfortunately the first widespread use of suicide bombing. From there, it began to spread to other violent clashes across the globe. And the fence, while controversial and extremely problematic, especially for the Palestinian people, did coincide with a reduction in suicide bombing.

Demographic Shift in Israel. The research indicating that within another one or two generations there will be more Arabs than Jews in Israel is real.

Mount of Olives. According to Zachariah 14:4, when the second coming arrives and the dead rise, the people buried on the Mount of Olives will be the first to rise. And the graves on the Mount date to over three thousand years ago.

Israeli Security. The description of Israeli security measures is accurate. Most businesses have security at the doors to check the bags of anyone entering. And the incident with the security checking the car was an incident I actually witnessed when I was in Israel. A car was stopped outside of a building with heavy concrete walls, with another concrete wall between the car and the street. Then two metal plates rose from the ground, trapping the car, and two individuals moved in to check the car for bombs. Needless to say, I picked up my pace and hurried on by.

Afterword

Dolphinarium. The bombing of the Dolphinarium was a real terrorist incident. As explained in the text, a suicide bomber was turned away at the door of a teen disco, exploded the bomb outside, and killed nearly two dozen teenagers waiting to get in. Although the event occurred back in 2000, the site remains as a reminder of the horror of terrorism.

Iranian Quotes. Unfortunately, those are real, as are the sentiments that involve the denial of the Holocaust in all its parts.

Ear Shape Identification. Ear shape identification is an actual tool used to identify people. As stated in the *The Belial Guard*, ear shape remains essentially the same almost from birth, and ear shape identification has a 99.6% accuracy rate.

About the Author

Author, Criminologist, Terrorism Expert, Jeet Kune Do Black Sash, Runner, Dog Lover.

Amazon best-selling author R.D. Brady writes supernatural and science fiction thrillers. Her thrillers include ancient mysteries, unusual facts, non-stop action, and fierce women with heart.

Prior to beginning her writing career, R.D. Brady was a criminologist who specialized in life-course criminology and international terrorism. She's lectured and written numerous academic articles on the genetic influence on criminal behavior, factors that influence terrorist ideology, and delinquent behavior formation.

After visiting counter-terrorism units in Israel, RD returned home with a sabbatical in front of her and decided to write that book she'd been thinking about. Four years later she left academia with the publication of her first book, *The Belial Stone*, and hasn't looked back.

Acknowledgments

First and foremost I have to thank the readers who have joined me on this incredible journey. The emails and notes some of you have been kind of nice to send always make my day. It's so rewarding to see that you are enjoying The Belial Series as much as I am. Stephen King when speaking about writing, says the stories are there, it's an authors job to just chip away at the rock and reveal them. And that's truly what I feel has been happening with the Belial series. So a giant thank you for helping me uncover Laney and her gang's story.

Thank you to what has become my production team! Thank you David Gatewood for all your editing expertise. I am very happy to have found you. And to Damonza, once again your book cover has captured the heart of the story.

To my family and friends, thank you for all your support and help. You've listened to me and given me feedback and understood why I've tucked myself away for weeks. Thank you for everything.

To my husband, I would not have been able to start this process without your unwavering support. Thank you for always being in my corner. And thanks to my little ones, who think it is so cool that Mom is a writer, even if that sometimes means when asked the names of the continents they mention Atlantis and Lemuria as well as the other seven.

And last but not least, thank you to my four faithful furry companions - Hobbes, Sadie, Rosie, and Gilly. Writing can be for many a lonely process. But thanks to the four of you, I am never alone in my process.